MW01519688

LOVE

IN THE SHADOWS

Final Book of the Passaic River Trilogy

STEVE BASSETT

Copyright © 2024 by Steve Bassett.

All rights reserved. No part of this publication may be reproduced, distributed, or transmitted in any form or by any means, including photocopying, recording, or other electronic or mechanical methods, without the prior written permission of the publisher, except in the case of brief quotations embodied in critical reviews and certain other noncommercial uses permitted by copyright law.

This book is dedicated to the women of all classes and ages who have shown the courage to let me interview them despite the ever-present threat of violent reprisal by their abusers. If they had not come forward, it would not have been possible for me to write and produce the Emmy-winning documentary, The Abused Woman, or author The Battered Rich, published by Ashley Books. Several women were in hiding with their children when interviewed at women resource centers financed by donations and operated by some of the most selfless individuals I have encountered during more than thirty years as a journalist. One counselor insisted that unless my book depicted the universal nature of physical, mental, verbal and emotional abuse, "Why in hell waste your time writing it." I accepted her dare.

ACKNOWLEDGEMENTS

I do not think there has ever been a work of fiction written in a vacuum. The Passaic River Trilogy, being a historical work of fiction, required a vast amount of research. My thanks to librarians in five New Jersey communities - Newark, Newton, Elizabeth, Toms River and Freehold; and English-speaking academics in France, Portugal and Italy were more than generous with their help. Paul Patwell, renowned for digitizing the entire Newark Library System, offered encouragement and advice from the very start of my work on the Trilogy. Pete Noyes, a Peabody Award winner, a multi-Emmy recipient, and author of The Original L.A. Confidential was selfless with his advice. Christine P. Cappuccino, my right hand for fourteen years, accomplished the near impossible task of understanding a legally blind author given to occasional impatience. My wife, Darlene Chandler Bassett, whose faith salvaged the Trilogy's first manuscript, has lovingly continued as my first reader and editor.

"I don't think there is anything particularly wrong with hitting a woman, though I don't recommend hitting her the same way you hit a man.

Sean Connery,
Academy Award Winner,
Playboy interview, November 1965

"Each time a woman stands up for herself, without knowing it, possibly without claiming it, she stands up for all women,"

Maya Angelou,
the late author and distinguished lecturer,
winner of the Presidential Medal of Freedom,
National Medal of Arts

"Domestic violence was a way of life in my home growing up; my brother and I watched helplessly numerous times as my mother was beaten and knocked unconscious while we dialed 911."

Troy Vincent,
2002 NFL Player of the Year,
Hall of Fame Nominee,
now NFL VP of Football Operations

"Threatening a current or former partner isn't passion, or love, or heartache. It's violence, it's abuse, and it's a crime."

Miya Yamanouchi,
Author of *Embrace Your Sexual Self*,
Counselor/Therapist Sydney University,
Australia

1

On the evening of Monday, August 18, 1947, everything became clear for Margie Bruning, she had to kill her husband before he killed her. His brutal assault that morning finalized her decision.

It had been months in the making. The progression was predictable. Shared frustration as days of fruitless job hunting grew into weeks, then months and Ned's drinking began. He had become a lush, and her once bottomless love for him evaporated as his verbal abuse gave way to violence.

"Do you think I haven't been looking?" Ned said as he was about to leave their apartment on another futile job search. He pulled up short, turned and grabbed Margie by the hair as slaps seared both her cheeks, "That's what you fucking think that I've been out there playing around?"

The force of the blows spun Margie over the kitchen sink, where she blindly reached for the faucet to keep her balance. Once again, there was the taste of blood on her tongue.

Margie's rage controlled every move she made. *No, god damn it! Not this time. He's not getting another cheap shot,* she muttered to herself and without thinking, she turned from the sink and in one fluid motion, drove her right fist into his left temple.

"Now get the hell out of here. Yeah, you can beat the piss out of me, but it won't be easy. Go on, scram!"

He turned and tenderly rubbed his swelling temple. *This can't happen. What the hell did she just do?*

He was poised to throw his six-foot-two, two-hundred-and-ten-pound frame at Margie, but stopped when confronted by the woman in classic boxer stance, legs shoulder-width apart, both fists at the ready.

"To hell with it. Don't think this is over yet cuz it ain't," Ned said, and shed of any dignity, slammed the door behind him as he left the kitchen. It was all over in fifteen seconds.

It took a few minutes for Margie to regain her equilibrium. She sat down at the kitchen table and with her right forearm, brushed aside the remains of Ned's breakfast. She poured a cup of coffee, Zippo'd a Camel, inhaled deeply and as the smoke flattened like a fog across the table thought, *How the hell did I let it get this goddamn far? Because I love him? And I believe he still loves me? That's bullshit, so let's face up to it. It's time for me to get going while I still have the guts.*

The man she had loved had fallen into an abyss of paranoia as he gradually discovered there was no longer any need for a former Marine Gunnery Sergeant with a

Bronze Star and a Good Conduct medal.

There was little demand for a high school dropout, and even his low-level job as a forklift operator at Harrison Foundry ended. The Foundry's owners had taken full advantage of Uncle Sam's endless wartime generosity, invested wisely, put their once frenetically active plant up for sale and fled to Rumson. They joined the country club, took up polo and bought a newly restored Chris Craft yacht. Abandoned were two hundred and fifty blue-collar workers who sweated around the clock to forge spare parts for Sherman tanks, howitzers, and gun carriages. It didn't take long for these men and women to realize they were trapped in a back-alley crap game with shaved dice.

This morning, she waited for the thud of Ned's heavy footsteps to abate, certain it wouldn't be long before he would be sharing cheap Muscatel with other Harrison Foundry lay-abouts. With the back of her right hand, she wiped the blood from her chin and felt with her tongue where the left lower incisor had ripped into her lip. A once unimaginable plan began to take shape.

Two weeks later, he took her by surprise in the kitchen with a right-hand blow to her left shoulder. She lost her balance, slammed into the refrigerator and slid to the floor. As Ned had warned, it wasn't over yet.

"That'll teach you to keep your goddamn trap shut. Keep your ass right where it is. You got one lucky shot in, better not try it again," Ned said.

In the beginning, she believed that for Ned, the enemy was the bosses who padlocked their shops, warehouses and factories. She was wrong. Now she realized it was insane jealousy spurred by her accomplishments that were torturing him.

The Sears Cold Spot refrigerator that he had just bounced her off was one of several glistening surprises Margie bought for his homecoming, along with a Whirlpool washing machine that fit neatly into the far end of their bathroom. She got rid of the old wall-mounted, pull-chain toilet and replaced it with a new porcelain, self-contained flush model.

"Where did the dough for all this come from?" Ned asked after she had led him by the hand on a tour she was certain would end with a kiss and a hug. Not so.

"I earned the money, every cent of it," she remembered answering. Her answer only increased his incredulity.

"You earned it? I knew you got a defense job at Todd Shipyards, but hell, this had to cost a lot."

"Got it all on sale and that's not all," she said, taking a small black book from her apron pocket. Her pride echoed from every word as she thrust a New Jersey Bank & Trust bankbook to Ned. "Here, take a look. Seven hundred fifty smackers."

"And I sacrificed to give you money every month," an agitated Ned said, leafing through several pages of the deposit book. The veins in his neck and temples were close to exploding. "Jesus, fucking Christ! How'd you think I'd feel about this?"

"Don't know if you realize it, buster, things have

changed," she said, at the same time pushing against him with her hip while rolling up the right sleeve of her blouse. "Here, feel this."

She tightened her shoulder and forearm, pumped three times and guided his left hand to her undoubtable biceps. "Thirty months as a hot-rivet catcher-holder. Then they had me wrestling with ten lift and throttle levers in the cab of an overhead crane. Got a little raise, and said I would have fun working the crane. What bullshit."

It was then that she got the first ominous hint as to where their marriage was going. She no longer recognized the man she had married, and she was now convinced that Ned could never accept the woman she had become.

Before Ned's three years of overseas service, she had been hauling food trays, pushing food and liquor carts, and rearranging chairs and tables at the Hahne's Department Store's upscale Pine Room. A lithe, smooth-muscled body emerged strong enough to convince the misanthropic foreman at Todd Shipyards she could handle any slop jobs they gave her.

And it didn't take long for Margie to convince dirty-minded creeps to get lost if they knew any better. That was proven at a Weehawken saloon not far from the shipyards.

2

The proof came just before the saloon closing when a drunk co-worker sidled up to her at the bar. "Nice tits, and a face that ain't too bad, even without makeup," the punk said. "Betcha, it's nice down there, too don't cha think?" he sneered, grabbing the crotch of Margie's bib dungarees.

Using the dexterity she had earned as a riveter and crane operator, Margie pushed back, knocking over her stool, threw her beer in the guy's face with her right hand, and landed a hard left-hand punch to his right temple. He lost his balance and landed on his ass.

Co-workers moved in, and it was all over in a few seconds. Margie picked up her stool, made her way down the bar and squeezed in between two welders who were still laughing after watching the mini-brawl. They made room, and the one on her right asked, "What'll you have Margie? I'm popping for it."

"In that case, it's a boiler," she said, then turned to the barkeeper who had set a coaster in front of her. "Make it a

Four Roses with a tall Ballantine chaser." She was the only one at the bar who realized it was more than a one punch slap-down. It was a matter of dignity, such as it was amid the camaraderie of wartime defense workers.

For the next fourteen months, Margie enjoyed the respect from her co-workers that the victory punch had given her. When she got her pink slip a month after VE Day, the new reality was like a fist to the gut. Shift boss Emil Sandowski, waiting at the timeclock, told the twenty-two women working for him to step aside for their male co-workers to pass through. When the last guy clocked-out, he motioned the women over, visibly pissed-off and embarrassed by what he had to do.

"I'm not gonna soft-pedal this," Sandowski said, taking the top envelope from the stack on a table next to him. "Perkins. Here you are, Dottie. All I can say is...." He paused, searching for the words to express his feelings. "It's one fucking shame, and the white-shirts in the office can shove it up their asses."

Sandowski was saying goodbye to a family of women he had nurtured, grudging skepticism giving way to the hardnosed reality that as their physical strength and mental toughness increased, his gals were doing men's work and in some cases doing it better.

He loved those posters of Rosie the Riveter warning Hitler, Tojo and Mussolini that they had bitten off more than they could chew. For three years, his admiration grew, and you didn't have to look any farther than diminutive Angela Massima and Flo Simmons to see why. They weighed in at no more than one hundred and ten pounds but had to be seen to be believed as they positioned heavy steel plates for the welders and riveters, never complaining as they worked their asses off.

"So, this is it," Margie said, removing her final paycheck from its envelope. "Whoa there, fifty-three bucks and eighty cents; I can't remember any OT last week." She turned to Sandowski with a wink and a smile, "You're a sly dog, boss."

Every family member reacted the same way, knowing that the extra gravy was the big Polack's way to say thanks. Many of them teared up and didn't care who saw them.

"Hey, none of that ladies. Now let's get over to Barneys' the drinks are on me."

The laughing, damp-cheeked contingent followed their boss to the saloon, knowing their close-knit camaraderie was of the once-in-a-lifetime variety. Pushed aside, at least for tonight, were any thoughts of the subservience that would soon be expected from them. Don't bet on it, pal.

It took months for Margie to reach the conclusion that it was all over for her and Ned. Thanks to the physical demands of her wartime work, she was muscular and agile, but she was no match for her husband, six inches taller, seventy pounds heavier, with long arms and fists as hard as rocks.

After making up the bed, she walked over to the smallest of three kitchen cupboards, pulled out the bottom drawer, and withdrew an object she hoped never to use. It was a gift from Eduardo Solano, a shipyard co-worker who worried for her safety after learning she lived alone at the corner of

Fulton and Rector.

"Not good for you to live by yourself in such a neighborhood," Eduardo said after they had hoisted a few cold bottles of Pabst Blue Ribbon at Barney's. A week later, same time, same place, he pulled from under his peacoat his weapon of choice, sharpened and with a leather sheath, its Marine insignia clearly visible. He refused to take no for an answer, and after four turndowns, Margie accepted his gift, but only after he unsheathed it and put the handle in her right hand. "I saw you welding and know this is where you're strongest."

He waited until she had hefted it to her satisfaction and awkwardly jabbed its needlepoint blade into the empty darkness of the alley before grabbing it from her. "No, no. This stiletto is serious business, not for punching holes in dummies," Eduardo admonished. "It's simple, here I'll show you. Push in all the way to the handle, and then you can twist up or down, side-to-side. All very easy," the wiry, smooth-muscled Puerto Rican advised with a smile that acknowledged he spoke from experience. The war made for strange bedfellows.

During her three and a half years at the shipyards, Margie became one of the top dart players at the Weehawken saloon. A healthy part of the seven hundred and fifty dollars in her savings account was dart game winnings. It was a natural transition from darts to a perfectly balanced, razor-sharp stiletto that, from a distance of twenty feet, could split a three-inch target. She hoped never to use it, but here it was in its leather sheath, the perfect weapon.

Margie rewrapped the stiletto and returned it to its hiding place. *God damn him down to hell if he forces me to do it. One more attack, and that's it. Never again, I mean it this time, never again will I suck my own blood,* she thought, as she washed her face, combed her hair and applied fresh makeup in the bathroom.

Satisfied with what she saw in the mirror, she went to the closet and removed her newest dress, a blue cotton shift, with three-quarter sleeves and white trim. The loose belted shift disguised her muscular stature and the sleeves, as intended, hid the bulge of her biceps. Sheer hose, white heels, a Bulova wristwatch, white gloves, a faux pearl two-strand necklace, and serving tongs earrings completed the ensemble.

She took a bus downtown, got off at Broad and Market, walked to Hahne's Department Store, and after only a half-hour interview, she was hired as the late afternoon and evening Pine Room hostess, a high-profile job that paid more than twice her waitress salary, including tips. They had called her; she hadn't called them. It had Rita Metcalf written all over it. Rita, a well-designed, still-closeted lesbian, had barely hidden her desire for Margie during her three years as a waitress. She and Margie shared a split of French Chablis in the Pine Room to celebrate, recounted what they had been doing for the past three years, then parted outside the store's entrance with a soft kiss on the cheek from Rita. After her crucible of fire at Todd, Margie was confident she could handle this. Punches and slaps to the face were something else again, but now she had a plan, and she and the stiletto were waiting.

3

It was nine o'clock in the morning when Reginald Rouge awoke to the incessant ring of his bedside phone, a vintage Western Electric Imperial. He knew what it was, the predictable annoyance after one of his special facial camouflage sessions.

"This is Reggie Rouge?" the practiced timbre of his voice rarely failed to be reassuring. He was "Reggie" to his clients, no one knew him as Reginald, a name he hated, and "Reggie" was so much easier to remember, a trademark that he hoped would put him among the make-up artists' Hall of Fame.

"Uh-uh, uh-uh. That's good," Reggie purred. "Exactly as I instructed. You have the kit with everything you need to get through this tragedy. Remember that the spirit gum and latex are meant to cover only the bruises on your cheek and neck, never on the cut. It's superficial and will heal quickly with only an antiseptic and band-aid. If you have any questions, Mrs. Paasche, I'll be here for you."

Still listening, Reggie stretched the phone cord to its fullest and retrieved the August 20, 1947 final editions of the *New York Daily Mirror* and the *Daily News* from under the apartment front door. He then glided his snow-white, perfectly pedicured feet back to bed.

"That's a wonderful idea, Mrs. Paasche. It makes no sense for you to stay at your New York City apartment when your family home is only a short drive away." A box-score fanatic and bookie's delight, Reggie was anxious to tackle the morning sports pages to see how the city's three major league baseball teams did. "Drive carefully and let me know when you arrive."

He waited for the click, puffed up two pillows against the headboard and scanned Tuesday's baseball results.

"I'll be a son of a bitch, there goes a quick Benjamin and a Grant," Reggie raged out loud. He was finally making pretty good dough, but a hundred and fifty bucks was nothing to sneeze at.

It was a ten-year climb that began when he answered an ad for an apprentice in the make-up department at Universal Studios. His first job was to gofer for Jack Pierce, the make-up wizard, like none other in Hollywood, the monster-maker. Frankenstein, Dracula, Wolfman, and the Mummy made Boris Karloff, Bela Lugosi, Lon Chaney and Lon Chaney, Jr., household names as the Halloween mask industry exploded.

It was Reggie's good fortune that his first uncertain steps were onto the soundstage of a comedy starring Vincent Price in his screen debut. He marveled at how Pierce transformed Price's image by simply attaching hair plugs on both sides of Price's distracting widow's peak, giving him a full head of hair.

After almost a year of ignoring Reggie's fawning pleas, Pierce finally gave in and allowed him to set aside his grunt work for half an hour every now and then to observe how he worked his magic. It took another year for Reggie to convince Pierce to give him a chance, a dab of rouge here, a beauty mark strategically placed there and, of course, lipstick, but only applied to extras with roles so small you better not blink or you'd miss them.

It was after one such practice session Pierce said, "Not bad, kid. What's it been now, almost two years as my personal pain in the ass? You've become a passable technician, not yet an artist. But good enough for a real job somewhere else, not here or any Hollywood studio where the ass-kissers have things sewed up."

"So, what the hell do I do?" Reggie implored. "It's all your fault. This is going to be my life! You can see that, can't you?"

"I've been thinking about it, kid. Ever think of New York and Broadway? I've got family, friends and contacts there. What do you say?" the Greek-born Pierce's native accent, carefully hidden most of the time, popped to the surface.

Reggie studied his mentor's face, not entirely sure he wasn't just being blown off. Desperate, he snapped his make-up kit closed and said, "When can I get going?"

When the studio lights dimmed for the day, Pierce laid it all out for Reggie during a sit-down in his cluttered office.

"Here's my brother and sister-in-law's address. Sophia and Damen Piccoula. I'll let them know you're on your way."

"Piccoula?" an amused Reggie said, even in Hollywood, a "Piccoula" turned "Pierce" is a stretch.

"Something funny about that?"

"No, no, nothing funny at all," Reggie responded quickly hoping he hadn't messed up his big chance. And when the session ended, he had a small bundle of file cards with the names of Broadway émigré, some big and important, other theater wannabes just like him. "Good luck," he said as he put on his wrinkled linen jacket, picked up his make-up kit and extended his right hand.

"Luck is a crutch for the weak," Pierce said. "I've got *Wolfman* and *Phantom of the Opera* already on the drawing board. Get going, kid."

Reggie searched for the lowest bus fares and settled on Trailways with its special excursion rate that beat the hell out of Greyhound. So, for five days from grimy coach windows, Reggie discovered small-town America and hated it. When he emerged at the main bus terminal in midtown Manhattan, he knew what Lady Liberty meant when she said, "Give me your tired, your poor, your huddled masses yearning to breathe free."

When he arrived at the door of the upper Broadway apartment, Damen Piccoula's greeting was hardly warm. Not that he expected a welcoming, but certainly more than, "So you're Janus' make-up marvel. Well, come on in. My brother says you're an okay guy, don't prove him wrong."

Damen gestured Reggie into the living room, and made no effort to relieve him of his scuffed, imitation leather suitcase purchased at a downtown Los Angeles pawn shop. A thin, well-proportioned woman of about forty-five emerged, her deep-set eyes atop high cheekbones were like two onyx-tipped gimlets that penetrated deep into Reggie.

A full-toothed smile softened her olive-skinned features, easing things up a bit, and Reggie appreciated the gesture. "Put your suitcase over there, you must be hungry, you can take care of it after you eat." The three of them sat at the kitchen table where Sophia put out a steaming earthen pot of *avgolemono*, a garlic-laced lemon, rice and chicken soup. Reggie slurped two bowls, then wolfed down half a dozen *dolmathakias*, a traditional Greek appetizer. The lubricant was ouzo, an anise-flavored liquor that went down easy, but for many first-timers like Reggie, erupted noisily over the toilet. Much to Damen's displeasure, Reggie abruptly called it quits.

4

His room was small but had a large window that looked out over Broadway with its never-ending human and vehicular traffic. It contained a small closet, more than ample for his meager wardrobe, a four-drawer bureau, a single bed, two cushioned chairs, and in one corner, a sink, toiletry shelf, small shaving mirror and a towel rack.

The next day, Reggie started working on the index cards Pierce had given him. The contacts were real, but he was kidding himself if he believed that dropping Pierce's name was an "open sesame." He was treated cordially, coming away with a perfunctory handshake and very little eye contact. For the next two years, he worked in the wings, accepting any job, burlesque in Jersey legit, off-Broadway and Summer Stock. But his big break came when he bedded down for two weeks in a storage room at the Paper Mill Playhouse just to see how Dorothy Kirsten, already a budding star at the Met, was made up for her role as Sonia in *The Merry Widow*.

"You there, come on over," Kirsten's rich soprano was barely muted when she insisted during a rehearsal break, "Yes, you. I won't bite."

Surprised that Kirsten was calling him over, Reggie put down his coffee cup, hitched his trousers with John Wayne aplomb and sauntered over to where Kirsten and her entourage, including make-up artist Gus "the Brush Man," sat in a tight circle. They had worked the theater dodge for years and recognized fake insouciance when they saw it. Since Reggie was not a threat, their greetings were warm.

"I watched you huffing and puffing with the scenery and props," Kirsten said, reaching out to take his hands in hers. "Let's take a look. I don't see any hammers, saws or callouses. What's your name?"

"Reginald Rouge, but all my friends and colleagues call me Reggie."

"Colleagues? Tell me, what's your line? Certainly not this. So, give, you have showbiz written all over you."

"Make-up. Earned my spurs sweating it out for Jack Pierce at Universal. He could be a bastard, but a real master at his craft. Couldn't have a better mentor."

"Pierce, the Monster Maker," the Brush Man said. "Not much call on Broadway for mummies, bloodsuckers, hoof-footed monsters with spike heads and wolfmen."

"Lay off, Gus," a young, very pretty brunette member of the entourage admonished. "You were there once yourself. Can't hurt if you push Reggie in the right direction." There were nods all around the circle.

Reggie and Gus never got close, but over the next year, there was a growing appreciation by the Brush Man that this Hollywood dropout would take his make-up kit anywhere there was a job, no matter how small. He willingly accepted pauper's pay from NBC for dabbing the faces of would-be television talent.

Oklahoma opened on Broadway in March 1943, an immediate box office success. Anyone working on the Rodgers and Hammerstein blockbuster could cash-in their stage credit at any bank in town. Reggie put the Brush Man's recommendation to work, getting one of the three openings for make-up technicians to work on minor cast members. One of them was Bambi Linn, a seventeen-year-old ingenue who snared the minor role of Aggie.

During rehearsal, they nurtured a show business camaraderie that allowed secrets to filter through the banter typically shared during downtime. During their first make-up session, Brooklyn-born Bambi self-consciously rolled up the right sleeve of her gingham dress, the stage costume for her brief scenes on stage, to expose a black and blue bruise. It took only a few minutes for it to disappear under Reggie's latex and make-up magic.

"How did you get this?" he asked, making eye contact as he gently touched the area around her bruise. "Does this hurt? If you want me to hide it, there'll be some pressure."

"Yeah, it does, but nothin' like my knee when I crashed my bike into a goddamn trash can," Bambi said, her Brooklyn street lingo surfacing. "This time, it was that stage backdrop, that one over there. Wasn't looking when they were moving it into place."

"Better start looking; it's hectic as hell backstage," Reggie said as he completed Bambi's shoulder camouflage.

"I'm just a kid learning the ropes," Bambi said.

"Been thinking about that, how a kid like you got a plum role in a big Broadway musical."

"Dumb luck. A nervous little agent named Abe Grosser spotted me and liked what he saw. My mom and dad signed on the dotted line, and he began peddling me to producers, directors and writers at all those boring cocktail parties. Abe made sure the word was out that I was perfect for the Aggie role.

"One night, I was nursing a Shirley Temples while high-borne ladies were guzzling the real stuff. Most of them were just rich hangers-on who got goosebumps rubbing shoulders with theater-types.

"That's when this rich, gorgeous lady came over, and out of the clear blue, started talking real low and confidential, 'If Abe's telling the truth, you're a lucky gal. So young with only bright lights ahead if you play it right. I wish I could say the same.'"

"Tell me everything," Reggie, a born gossip-monger, implored.

It took less than five minutes for Bambi to lay it all out, how Mrs. Paasche, who had been inhaling her drinks but not slurring her words, described how her brute of a husband, Johan, had made the transition from verbal to physical abuse. Bambi learned that Johan was not the only rich and famous brute who shared silk sheets with a wife he slapped around for exercise.

"Now, this is what really floored me," Bambi said, "She actually pulled aside her pearl necklace and showed me a bruise on her neck. That was two weeks before rehearsals began, but I was thinking about it all along, especially when she said three friends were being slapped around and afraid to go out sporting their bruises."

"That's crazy! Did Mrs. Paasche say why she and the others didn't up and leave? They're not tenement punching bags who show-up at the local police precinct with bruises and blackeyes," an agitated Reggie said. "They are real ladies trapped, stuck with misfits whose wages put clothes on the kids and food on the table."

Bambi saw that Reggie barely controlled the growing anger that coursed from head to toe, the balls of his feet rat-tap-tapping, his fingers tightly entwined and his face taking on the red shine of a Delicious apple.

"I hope you're not talking from experience?" Bambi said. "That would be horrible."

Bambi had her answer when Reggie silently turned away and peered into the dark theater and labored over what to say. Words would open family wounds he had left three thousand miles away and had no intention of reinflicting.

"Let's change the subject, shall we? We can start with a question. Are you the one who put Mrs. Paasche onto me?" Reggie said. "I wondered how she got my name."

"Yes, that was me. They all belong to the watercress

sandwich and tea for lunch bunch, where there are no dirty little secrets. Mrs. Paasche brought your name up, and it spread like a miracle headache remedy they had been waiting for. How'd you feel if one of them asked you to work your magic, as you did on my shoulder? I can give you one name and number right now. You can name your own price."

Reggie took a slip of paper with all the personal data from Bambi. It was the first of twenty such notes and phone calls he would receive, several from repeat customers, over the next four years. Each carried a sizeable price tag.

5

If the denizens of Manhattan were looking for a near-perfect summer day, they couldn't look much farther than Wednesday, August 20, 1947. Except for some wispy clouds lingering four miles above, the skies were clear and visibility to the north was unlimited. At nine-thirty that morning, the mercury on the terrace of Deborah's twelfth-floor Riverside Drive co-op read seventy-five degrees.

She closed and locked the second of two steamer wardrobe trunks stenciled *Deborah Hammerstein Paasche* and motioned to the two burly men waiting in the foyer to come and get them. Mayflower Van Lines would deliver the two trunks to the Hammerstein family mansion in Tuxedo Park thirty miles up the Hudson.

She had just gotten off the phone with Reggie. Yesterday was the third time he had performed his make-up magic. The first two times, her husband, Johan, had left her with only bruises, but this time his diamond-encrusted wedding band had sliced through the skin over her right cheekbone.

The two cuts were small and could be easily explained, one band-aid was sufficient. Now came the test as to how well she had followed Reggie's instructions.

Deborah made sure the trunks were secure, then turned to the two moving men, handed the trunk keys to the older one and signed the clipboard he extended for her signature. She searched his and his helper's faces for any signs that her disguise had failed. There were none. She had passed with flying colors.

Buoyed by her success, she doubled her intended tip from ten to twenty dollars. "Thanks a lot, Mrs. Paasche. We'll be quick and careful, the trunks will be waiting when you arrive home," the driver said.

The co-op, with its two treasured underground parking spaces, was in her name. It was free and clear, but Johan, ever a bottom-feeder, would sleaze his way into laying claim.

What the hell was wrong with me? What a sap. I was never one of Katherine Anne Porter's magazine ingénues who goes gaga over a smooth-talker. She never noticed that her white knight was riding a rented horse.

Thinking back, Deborah still marveled at how it had taken less than two hours of dancing, joking and the sharing of small confidences for the tall, handsome Johan to captivate her at a college tea dance in the spring of 1938. He was twenty-five, she was twenty-one and in her final year at Vassar, a comfortable forty-five-mile drive from the Hammerstein mansion in Tuxedo Park. They were married nine months later and honeymooned amid the castles of Bavaria.

It puzzled her that Johan, coming from a family with pacificist leanings, had chosen for their two weeks of bucolic lovemaking a region with warrior instincts and unbending support for Adolf Hitler. Within a few days, it became clear to her that he cared little for river cruises, historic castles or towering mountains.

She felt abandoned when he left her with a tour guide in the picturesque Danube River town of Regensburg after climbing aboard a speed boat with two dark men she didn't know. They were a matched pair, each about three inches shorter than her six-foot husband. White shirts, Windsor-knotted black ties outlined by the lapels of gray suit jackets poked from under smartly tailored black overcoats. Well-brushed, dark, snap-brimmed hats and expensive black wingtips completed the ensemble.

To Deborah, they came across as two thugs who worked hard to dress up their image. They failed. Under their cocked hats, their swarthy faces betrayed them. They nodded in her direction with the practiced, tight smiles that had made James Cagney, George Raft and Edward G. Robinson famous. Johan waved and threw her a perfunctory kiss as the boat sped away in the direction of Munich.

Two nights earlier, a courier had knocked heavily on the door of the Paasches' hotel suite. Debbie checked the bedside clock wondering who in hell would be pounding on the door at two o'clock in the morning. She thought it better not to disturb Johan and, in only a thin negligee and slippers, padded over to the door, released the lock, grabbed the ivory and gold-plated doorknob, pulled the door halfway open and confronted the pop-eyed courier who couldn't take his eyes off the plunging gown that partially exposed her dark nipples. "This better be good, buddy. Hand it over."

"I'm sorry, Madame, but I have orders that only, let's see now," he studied the name on the small manilla package, "that only Johan Paasche should receive this, that his signature is necessary."

By this time, a groggy and angry Johan came to the door and, in German said, "I'm Johan Paasche. Give me it." He was surprisingly rebuffed.

"Only after the signature," the uniformed young man said, removing the cap from his pen, along with a receipt pad. "Sign here and date it, please."

"Can you beat that," Debbie said as she followed her husband into the bedroom. "A kid pounds on our door, gets us out of bed, and then starts ordering you around."

Johan replied with a shrug, opened the package with a letter opener and scanned the first two pages. He turned and kissed both of her cheeks, "This is too important to put off. Go to sleep, and you'll have forgotten it all tomorrow."

The first thing that caught his eye was the letterhead on the top sheet of the three-page memo: *Hotel Nacional du Cuba, Calle 21 y O, Vedado, Plaza, La Habana, Postal Code: 10400, Cuba*.

Paasche's photographic memory was put to good use as he sped through the single-spaced pages. The last paragraph made it clear to him the identity of the writer.

Who else would have the precise details of an illegal international investment scheme that, to his knowledge, had never been attempted before. This was a very smart guy who took no chances.

"After digesting the foregoing information, I am confident you understand why it is not necessary to attach a name to this memo. In two days, at nine o'clock in the morning, two colleagues fresh from a trip that took them from Havana to Naples to Munich, will invite you into their boat at dockside outside your hotel. If you climb aboard, you will be entering a world of great consequences and great payoffs."

Johan returned the memo to its envelope before joining Debbie, who was only faking sleep in bed. He snuggled up, ran a moist tongue into her right ear, turned her chin slightly upward, and inserted his tongue for a long goodnight kiss. He said nothing about the memo, and during her tossing and turning, Debbie discovered that he had placed it not only under his pillow but inside the pillowcase. Upon arising, he dropped it into his attaché case and snapped it closed.

After watching the boat with Johan and the two thugs disappear into the haze that shrouded the Danube, Debbie began quiet sleuthing of her own. She learned the two men had arrived in Munich from Naples a few days earlier. Johan's sudden departure was for a pre-arranged meeting in Munich with top officials of the National Bank for Deutschland, a huge international money broker that owed much of its growth to his mother's family. Awaiting the trio was a Daimler-Benz limo, complete with chauffeur, two armed bodyguards in the front seat and two blonde female ornaments in the back. It took some mild pressure to convince her father, Lee Hammerstein, to contact brokerage and banking stalwarts in Munich to keep an eye out for Johan. It was a dangerous time in Europe, and Debbie was worried for his safety.

She had no way of knowing she needn't worry. Her husband was about to meet with officials of several large German companies who had jumped on the Hitler bandwagon and with his knowledge, were devouring all German corporations of less than $40,000, stripping them of their assets while they got fat on government contracts and low-interest loans.

In 1939, fueled by the blood of murdered rivals, America's Mafia Commission and the Nazis (Germany's Social Democrats) were in bed together. The Mafia, with Jewish financial wizard Meyer Lansky, pulling the strings and the Nazis, under the tutelage of Herman Göring and Walther Funk, were in pursuit of cash.

For two days, telegrams and phone calls from both sides poured into the Regina Palast Hotel around the clock. The mismatched negotiators arrived at a simple and logical formula.

Lansky was looking for safe and profitable ways to launder the endless supply of cash generated by the Mafia throughout America and the growing treasure chest in Cuba. He saw no better investment than Germany's rapidly expanding public works, armament, shipbuilding and chemical industries powered by inexhaustible slave labor. It was a cornucopia of plenty. The money would be funneled through the National Bank for Deutschland, where Deborah's mother-in-law, Ellen Witting Paasche, held sway, and her son Johan, with Swiss, U.S. and German citizenship and passports, would have little trouble being the transatlantic bagman.

Once in the hands of M.L. Kraus and Topf & Sons, the money powered their industrial expansion and a Swiss investment portfolio that brought greedy smiles to the faces of Lucky Luciano, Frank Costello and Vito Genovese, the former "Boss of Bosses," who had fled to Naples to escape his murder conviction in New York.

The money was split 50-50 between Switzerland and Germany, a country criminally controlled by an insatiable lunatic with a comic opera mustache who viewed the world as his.

On August 20, 1947, Deborah Hammerstein Paasche handed over two suitcases, a pair of hat boxes, the leather satchel with her make-up kit, and the Daimler-Benz keys to her co-op doorman. She knew there was no need to worry about getting rid of Johan.

She wanted no part of the apartment, and except for her personal belongings, he could have it all, including the parking spaces. It might be an impossible task to erase all the memories of Johan, but she'd give it a damn good try.

6

Johan's innumerable trips to Switzerland and Germany, and of all places, New Jersey, transformed their apartment into no more than a stopover. Only once did she accompany Johan on his clandestine trips, and it was not to Germany but to Newark. After the fleeting encounter on the Danube and her husband disappearing upriver to Munich, she could understand the trips to Germany, but New Jersey, this was a real eye-opener.

He prefaced this trip by pleasantly but firmly asking her to take all the mental notes she wanted but never to mention it. She agreed but had to bite her lip to do so because of how unbelievably bizarre the dinner in Newark was. This was a world she had seen in the movies, the only things out of sight were tommy guns and pistols.

"We're taking a little trip today, I'm certain you'll find it enjoyable and, yes, even thought-provoking," Johan said off-handedly as he dug a silver demitasse spoon into his soft-boiled egg, cooked perfectly at one hundred ninety degrees

Fahrenheit by their maid Tisha. "For both of us, it will be a journey of discovery."

"So glad you tuned me in, just where is this wonderful 'journey of discovery' taking us?" Deborah said sarcastically. "How long ago did you hatch this up without telling me?"

"It's only across the river to Newark. I know you've never been there, so this provides an excellent opportunity to see how the other half lives."

"Newark! What in hell is so damn important in Newark that necessitates a visit and dragging me along, no doubt for window dressing?"

"Debbie, you're not only the most beautiful creature I've ever known, but your intuition continues to astound me." Johan decided the best way to counter spousal sarcasm was a rakish rejoinder. He studied Debbie's face. Ah yes, it had worked again.

"Alright, you're beginning to win me over," she replied. "Is there anything else I must wrap my intuitive mind around?"

"Only one request, I want you to dress your sexiest," Johan said, his words little more than a soft, purring whisper. "Dig into your wardrobe and pull out the clingiest and most enticing dress. You know what I mean, refined upper-class sluttiness.

"When you meet the other ladies tonight, you'll see what I mean."

It was three-thirty in the afternoon of April 16, 1939, just two months after the Paasche wedding, when Johan took the keys to the Daimler-Benz from the parking attendant just as another co-op flunkie opened the front passenger door for Mrs. Paasche waited for her to be comfortably seated, then gently closed it. Mr. Paasche took the beautiful machine onto Riverside Drive, heading toward 39th Street and the recently completed Lincoln Tunnel.

"Well, here we are, about to enter the dark wilderness of New Jersey," Johan said. "Excited?"

"Curious is a better way to put it. New horizons are my steak and potatoes," Debbie said, then added playfully, "Yippy I Yo Kyai, I'm an old cowhand!"

Johan failed in his effort to keep a straight face, turned to Debbie and let loose a loud guffaw that kicked off a giggling spasm that she made no effort to control.

"Where have I heard that before, familiar, but I can't quite place it," he said.

"From the Old Crooner himself, Bing Crosby," Debbie said, her emerald green eyes sparkled mischievously atop perfect cheekbones that dominated her flawless face.

She shifted across the front passenger seat and brushed her hand along his right thigh before turning her attention to the gaping tunnel mouth.

Barely two years old since its ribbon-cutting, the tunnel was still shiny and new despite the noxious clouds of progress that spewed from the trucks, moving vans, buses, taxis, cars, and motorcycles passing westward through its entrails to God knows where. Debbie could sense her husband's impatience, even appreciate it, as he slowly guided a mechanical marvel built for speed bumper-to-bumper with a meat delivery truck in front and a semi-trailer trapping him from behind.

Midway through the tunnel, Debbie unfolded a sheet of instructions Johan had prepared, scanned it to her satisfaction and said, "Okay, this cowhand is ready. Let's get our chuckwagon moving."

She has no idea how important tonight's meeting is to our future, Johan thought, *and let's hope it stays this way.* A smiling Johan couldn't ask for more shared levity that masked the reason for their trip.

He steered around the meat truck and maneuvered through the jumbled traffic spilling from the tunnel and spreading voraciously like gypsy moths through the streets of Weehawken.

Debbie guided them through a series of depressing blue-collar towns, finally crossing the Passaic River into Newark. He pulled to the curb on Broadway, switched off the ignition, removed an inscribed platinum cigarette case from an inside jacket pocket, offered a Benson & Hedges to Debbie and took one for himself.

After a few deep drags, she turned to her husband and said, "So, here it is, wondrous Newark. It's about time, wouldn't you say, to let me in on what the hell is going on?"

"Remember those castles during our honeymoon in Bavaria? Well, you're about to dine at another one right here in Newark. It's called Vittorio's Castle. It's the first time for both of us."

"Oh brother, a castle in Newark. Are you serious? From what you suggested for my wardrobe tonight, I have a pretty good idea of the kind of ladies I'll be chit-chatting with. What about the men?"

"Remember the two fine chaps that I met at dockside in Regensburg? My guess is that we can expect more of the same tonight."

It was five o'clock when they arrived at the corner of Summer and Eighth Avenue, and sure enough, there it was, Vittorio's Castle, complete with four corner towers, topped with turrets that rose above the roofline of the three-story brick building.

They had barely pulled to a stop at the corner when a phantom valet materialized out of nowhere, and with an obsequious smile creasing, his dark, oily face bowed as he opened Debbie's door. "Mrs. Paasche, please let me help you," gently taking her right hand to guide her over the curb.

7

It took less than a minute after they were ushered into the Castle's dining room for Debbie's anxiety to escalate into fear, a feeling she rarely experienced.

Standing at a circular bar, drinks in hand, were the two swarthy men who had been waiting for Johan in Regensburg. They and four others formed an all-male, cookie-cutter tableau: dark suits, white shirts, black ties, pomaded hair, pinky rings, oversized wristwatches, and black shoes buffed to a professional shine.

Their women were sitting isolated at a long marble cocktail table prominently centered out of earshot of their men. Their appearance held no surprises for Debbie. Everything about them was what she expected, from their lacquered hair to deep *décolletage*, over-abundant jewelry and pampered red fingernails.

As if a silent cue had been given, once the men had finished their drink, the women arose from their table. Debbie and Johan watched with bated breath as the jewel-encrusted entourage advanced in lockstep to the dining table by their host, Ruggiero "Richie the Boot" Boiardo and his son, Tony Boy.

"Everyone's here, and I'm hungry," the senior Boiardo said. "Except for our special guests who'll be sitting next to me, there are no special places; grab a seat and get comfortable, that's what my castle is for: comfort, good food and…." He paused, crinkled a smile as he sized-up the uncertain faces around the table, then added, *Compagnia di amici di cui ti fidi,* and if a person can't be trusted, he shouldn't be breathing."

"And we don't have too much good air here in Newark to share it with punks," Tony Boy said as he slid into his seat at the far end of the table from his father. As if attached to a master puppeteer's strings, there were nods all around as ten chairs glided across the highly polished, white and black checkered tile. White damask napkins were unfolded, cigarette cases clicked open, fags were fired up, and deep drags created a gray nimbus that wafted across the table thick enough to mask the studied, furtive looks directed their way.

"Deborah, it's okay to call you Deborah? I'm not being pushy or anything like that am I?" entreated a lacquered, high-bonneted blonde two places to the left of Debbie. "I'm Roslyn, but everyone calls me Rosie."

"Oh, I think Deborah is a little too fancy. If you're Rosie, then I'm Debbie," she said, uncertain where to go next, but for Johan's sake, more than willing to give it a good try. *I have no idea how to talk to these women,* she thought. *What the hell!*

Easy now, time for a smile, not too many teeth but wide enough to look like I mean it, these gals can spot a phony a mile away.

Four waiters busied themselves pouring from bottles of robust Chianti, a lighter Toscana Sangiovese and a vintage Lambrusco, then placed the bottles on the tables within easy reaching distance of the guests. A patois took shape as Italian and English remarks were exchanged, the men keeping mainly to themselves, their unmistakable Sicilian dialect taking over whenever their features darkened and their tone became lugubrious.

The women were entrapped by their curiosity, crowding Debbie with one banal question after another, never giving ground until they got an answer. Isabella Bonini, "just call me Izzy," was fascinated with her tight-fitting, full-length, black Chanel silk gown.

"Your dress, Debbie, it's really beautiful. I think my shape is good enough for it," Izzy said. "Point me in the right direction, where can I pick one up?"

"Well, I ordered this one from Saks. They had it shipped to me for our six-month anniversary."

"Saks, I've heard the name, but I don't think there's one around here," Izzy said. "How about the fancy suburbs, maybe Upper Montclair or West Orange? We've got a Hahnes here in town, real fancy and expensive. Would it be anything like Saks?"

What the hell do I say to that, Debbie thought.

"I've heard of Hahnes, that it's a great store and women

love it, but I don't honestly know if they handle the same merchandise as Saks."

The banal chit-chat was interrupted at one point when Tony Boy snapped his fingers, and a liveried waiter produced two framed photos.

"Pop, do you want to do the honors, or do you want me to take over?" Tony Boy nodded toward the far end of the table where Richie the Boot looked up from his antipasto and gestured his son to get on with it.

I'll be damned if he doesn't look like he's ready to burst out in song. What comes next, La Donna è Mobile? Debbie thought as she watched Tony Boy push back his chair and take the two gilt-framed photos.

Tony handed off one framed photo to his right and the other to his left, each one making the rounds before Johan and Debbie had a chance to study them, a beaming Richie between them.

"Here's proof that Vittorio's Castle is class with a capital C," Tony Boy bellowed. "There he is, Joe DiMaggio, the Yankee Clipper himself, enjoying the best food in Jersey after closing a deal with my dad for his lucky bride-to-be's engagement ring! And there she is, movie star Dorothy Arnold, sitting with the Clipper right here at this table just a few months ago."

"And he's brought his Yankee buddies with him more than a couple times," his father added, as one waiter cleared his empty plate and another placed a steaming dish of Chicken Marsala in front of him.

It was more than an hour later when all four courses of the meal were completed, and the men and women went their separate ways, the men to his father's office, Debbie and the four women consort to a lounge where they set up camp amid a cluster of overstuffed chairs and sofas specially arranged for them. They were safely out of the way as it should be, caring nothing about the business but enjoying the endless supply of gaudy baubles that came their way. During the next ninety minutes, Debbie learned more about the little tricks that make men happy than she could have ever imagined.

Reports of what transpired in the closed-door office meeting were eagerly awaited in two cities separated by thousands of miles but linked by the same deadly criminal intent.

8

At the presidential palace in Havana, three men appreciated the best rum in the world and a fourth sipped Dewar's scotch from a Bohemian crystal tumbler. They were bound by a shared belief that drugs, prostitution, pornography, loan sharking, extortion, and if necessary, murder, were the branches of an ever-blossoming money tree.

Their confab was hosted by Fulgencio Batista, the strong man for a corrupt military that controlled every aspect of Cuban life and a sure winner in the upcoming presidential election. The sitting president, Frederico Laredo Brù, a puppet in the hands of Batista, was stepping down after four years in office, during which American gangsters had turned Cuba into their private piggy bank.

The meeting was pieced together by Mafia financial wizard Meyer Lansky, the diminutive, soft-spoken, even-tempered scotch drinker who had long realized that Havana's streets were lined with gold. He was joined by

Amleto Battisti, the short Cuban mafia gambling czar, who spoke in hushed tones but was a giant when it came to numbers, profit and loss.

"If everything goes according to plan and we hear the right things about this guy, I think we'll be ready to go," Amleto said to no one in particular, letting his words absorb the lush Cuban cigar smoke and the sweet aroma of rum and scotch that filled the palatial room. "Vito is confident his boys did a good job screening him in Munich."

"This guy has the tools – tall, blonde, blue-eyed, a streak of larceny, family contacts, and a bank that couldn't be better for us," Lansky said, savoring a sip of scotch and the woody chestnut flavor of his Cuban Panetela. "Vito's boys better be right. Fulgencio and I have locked things down here in Cuba for years to come, and we've got five greedy families from coast-to-coast scratching their scrotums in anticipation."

Batista and Brù had been silently listening to Lansky until the military strongman couldn't hold back any longer. He turned to a small man wearing black horn-rimmed glasses and a rakish fedora who had been listening but saying nothing.

"Amleto Battisti, I know you, but do I trust you?" He turned to Lansky, "Mr. Lansky, yes, we've talked but I still don't know you very well," then sat back in his chair to assess the two men. "Are you telling me that things aren't sewed up tight yet? It's not really what you're telling me, is it?"

"Relax. Haven't I always come through for you, of course, with the help of your well-chosen man here,"

Lansky flicked his thumb in the direction of President Brù. "Hotel Nacional, millions poured into the Sevilla Biltmore, how we've lighted up the Paseo del Prado like nothing before. You wanted more land, so we got it and kept your name out of it."

"Son of a bitch, if I don't think that you believe only a little Jew bastard like you could pull it off," the thirty-nine-year-old, slim and handsome Batista threw his contempt directly into Lansky's expressionless face. "Around here, I just snap my fingers, and I have my choice of bagmen."

"I understand. You're talking about Cuba, we're talking global, and with this guy who can travel anywhere with his passports, we have one of the most respected banks in Europe lined up. Let's enjoy our drinks and smokes and not jump to any conclusions until we hear from Vito's guys, get a solid opinion from Richie the Boot, and take things from there," Lansky said. "If we need another bagman, we'll off the blue-eyed blonde and start again."

It was late June of 1940. In four months, puppet-President Brù would be voted out, and an unscrupulous military strongman would join hands with a criminal cartel in the rape of a country. And as far as they were concerned, the Cuban people be damned.

Both sides were so good at their jobs that they were finding it difficult to hide the tens of millions of dollars rolling in both from the mainland and the new cornucopia of plenty, Cuba.

This was only the beginning for Lansky. For six years, he had scrutinized how Hitler, a man he loathed, had been using public works, illegal disarmament, rebirth of the navy and army to transform Germany into a military and industrial colossus. The nation's industrial and commercial elite hated Hitler but loved it when he expressed his loathing of the "bureaucratic management of the economy" and pumped the pulse of German autocrats, friends and foes alike, to heart attack levels when he decreed, "The basic feature of our economic theory is that we have no theory at all." Fat cat greed was the order of the day as smaller competitors were eliminated, tax rates were lowered, and lucrative government contracts were for the taking. This was a financial dream world for Lansky, who had warned for more than a decade that the mafia's lucre had to be hidden or legally invested to keep it from the feds. What better hiding place than Germany's free-booting economy?

More than five thousand miles away and across two bodies of water, Vito Genovese hung up the telephone, removed his thick-lensed, metal-framed glasses, wiped them with his handkerchief, and relaxed his five-foot-seven inch, one-hundred-and-sixty-pound frame into the soft tufts of a green, brocaded sofa and smiled. He had just talked with his second wife, Anna, at her Club Caravan, the centerpiece of the Mafia-controlled queer bars in Manhattan. Vito loved her enough to murder her second husband, Gerard Vernotico, gangster-style, so he could have her. He trusted her implicitly and marveled at how she sized up every situation. He ordered his two goons to funnel the news from Vittorio's Castle through her, and they knew her opinion would govern his decision.

"No doubts? No questions at all?" Vito said, the line to Anna's underground queer haven on West Broadway was surprisingly clear. "It's the second time Giuseppi and Rosario have had a crack at him. Had some doubts in Munich, but no more."

He listened as Anna's controlled voice offered him two imperatives.

"You've got everything I've got. I'll make sure the word gets hand-delivered to Lucky's cell at Dannemora. And if he doesn't trust Mr. Blue-eyes, he can have a couple of his *soldati* check him out. But why?" Anna said. "There's no blood oath here, and if you like, I can…."

"Don't go no further," Vito said, betraying his fifth-grade education in nearby Naples. "I'll get word to Luciano if I got to. And you, *la mia dolce cosa,* you did good. Let's leave it there."

"Do you miss your *dolce cosa?* It's been three years, lover boy."

"You know it. Just grab hold of a couple of the good-looking queers, big mean bastards, to get you out and around, and you'll be okay; I'm not worried. *Arrivederci.*"

"Arrivederci."

He arose and walked to a sideboard along the interior wall of the high-ceilinged room that looked out through two glass paneled doors onto the Alpine forest that spread out for miles below Nola. Despite its Elysium beauty, Genovese hated everything about it. With three-quarters of a million dollars in mob swag, he had returned to his childhood home in 1937 to avoid a New York murder rap for arranging the killing of mobster Ferdinand Boccia.

He opened the top of a handcrafted Dunhill mahogany and teak humidor and inhaled deeply the rich aroma of the very best Cuban Coronas. He then reached for the gold cigar cutter and snipped the rounded head, lifted a gold Dunhill from its assigned place next to the humidor and fired up. To complete the ritual that began almost three years ago, he raised, closely examined and then kissed the simply framed photos of Anna, his stepdaughter Marie, Nancy, his daughter with his first wife, and Phillip, his and Anna's only child.

This was hardly a sentimental gesture by a sadistic thug whose murderous urges had propelled him to the top of the Masseria Manhattan crime family before he and Lucky took it over. Instead, the ritual with the photos honed to perfection his obsession for revenge. His two betrayers, Jerry Esposito and Peter LaTempa, the stoolies who ratted him out to the cops, would never see a courtroom, and the Genovese family would be back together again.

9

It was ten-thirty in the morning of August 20, 1947, when two well-rehearsed but seemingly unrelated events were about to happen. In downtown Newark, newly-minted Police Lieutenant Kevin McClosky was on his way to police headquarters to cry on the shoulder of his former, long-time partner, Captain Nick Cisco, now the head of homicide. In upper West Side Manhattan, Deborah Hammerstein Paasche tooled her Daimler-Benz along Riverside Drive toward the George Washington Bridge and a new but very uncertain future.

"He's expecting you. Go right in," a young, brunette cop nodded at McClosky from her desk just a few steps outside and to the right of the open door to Cisco's office. "There's fresh coffee brewing in the bullpen, interested?"

"That's one hell of a change from the death-dealing sludge we were used to," McClosky said. "If he does nothing else, Nick hit the bullseye with this improvement. Sure, I'll take a chance on a fresh cup of joe."

Standing in front of his desk, Nick was waiting for Kevin, a wide smile creasing his craggy dark features and adding a soft luster to his deep-set brown eyes. He extended his right arm and said, "So you've got something on your mind, old buddy. Spill it, I'm all ears."

Each grabbed one of the two leather chairs in front of the desk, pulled them closer and waited until the pert cop placed two steaming mugs within reach on the desk. *The cups actually look clean,* Kevin thought.

They were about to start when Kevin's replacement, Lieutenant Josh Gingold, popped his head in. "Good to see you again, McClosky. Just can't stay away, can you?" he said but remained at the door. "How's that Intelligence Unit of yours working out? Pretty good, I bet, seeing as you're the Mayor's favorite new toy," Gingold half-kidded, "Just joking."

"Lousy joke," Kevin said, his words bouncing off Gingold's back as he headed to his desk in the homicide bullpen.

"Okay, so what gives?" Nick queried. Like Gingold, he had heard the jabs that had been rolling around almost from the first day the Intelligence Unit took shape eight months ago.

"Shitty remarks like Gingold's hit here," Kevin said, tapping his right thumb on his sternum."

"Just some jealous pissants shooting off, Christ almighty, you're riding the Mayor's shirttails, so just ignore it," Nick said.

"I agree, it looks like a soft gig," Kevin said. "But doing what? After eight months, I'm still not sure who's ass the boss wants me to kiss."

"And the little crew you've put together. I'm not the only one scratching my head over your choices." Nick took a cautious sip of hot coffee and a deep pull on his Chesterfield. "You had a lot to choose from, but Windy Valentine and Frank Gazzi, a little crazy, wouldn't you say?"

"You know I'm a conniving son of a bitch," Kevin said, taking his cue from Nick with two swallows from his mug and a healthy drag from his Old Gold, a time-honored routine of two police interrogators biding time while collecting their thoughts. "You wanna listen or not?"

"I'm all ears."

"Take our old homicide buddy, Sergeant Malcolm Valentine," Kevin said. "His moniker, 'Windy,' doesn't come close. Once he gets started with his bullshit, 'Hurricane' is a better fit. You should know you put up with his lip-flapping for almost a year. And he knew how to cut corners, always one step from losing his pension, just like us, but he got the job done. You looked the other way when Windy dropped signed confessions on your desk, knowing god damn well that broken noses, missing teeth, and cracked ribs were the inducements."

"We were all rogue, still are," Nick said. "I only want homicide cops with bleeding knuckles and broken fingers on their resumés."

"Windy passes muster on all that and more. He's glib, tough, mean as hell when he has to be, knows where the bodies are buried, and nobody messes with him," Kevin said, then drained his mug and shied to the left when a slender hand passed over his right shoulder with a coffee pot and a steaming refill. "Even Gordo's two uniformed henchmen, Gamba and Maroni, kept their hands off. On the mob's payroll, why the hell made waves when they didn't have to?"

"Okay, I got it with Windy, but Christ Almighty, why Frank Gazzi, the most-inept cop on the force? And to top it off, you had the Mayor squeeze the Chief for Gazzi's sergeant stripes. Why, when everything he touched ended tragically? He even accidentally shot and killed an innocent paperboy. So stupid he even busted mob-protected whores, got his ass reamed by family friend Gordo, but kept his badge."

"Yeah, I know all this. Come on, Nick, give me some credit," Kevin said as he stubbed out his fag in the desk ashtray. "Gazzi is a born snooper, as quiet and as innocuous as you can get. Hell, he's almost invisible. You know that as well as I do, or you wouldn't have pulled him from his precinct to gumshoe into Longy and Richie the Boot's punch-out for the Third Ward numbers dodge. He got just what we needed, and that's why he's working for me now, my own fly-on-the-wall."

For the next ten minutes, Kevin unburdened the doubts he had about his job. The unit had run down several tips about suspected internal corruption, some nickel and dime briberies, candy store numbers protection, missing items from the evidence room, nothing big and hardly worth pursuing in a department notorious for its corruption. After all, boys will be boys.

Nick took special note of how Kevin tried unsuccessfully to mask his pique over the demands the Mayor insisted Kevin take care of. It involved a City Councilman who had slapped around his long-time mistress, who wanted to call it quits.

Not a word, not even a hint, would be leaked if Kevin wanted to keep his job, nothing to be put in writing. He was only to look into things, ascertain what was true or just vengeful thinking by the women, and then report back to the Mayor. Gazzi, true to his calling, affirmed everything. The Mayor got his report, barely said a word except for a curt "thank you," and dismissed Kevin, who from that moment wondered whether keeping his lieutenant bars was worth the burn that was eating his guts out.

10

It was noon the same day when Deborah Hammerstein Paasche headed north along Riverside Drive, warmed by the realization that, for the first time in seven years, she was a free woman.

On West Broadway in lower Manhattan, another woman put to rest her long-held suspicion that the numbers fed to her every month had never added up. Anna Petillo Genovese reached for her desk telephone, dialed a number and waited for the tell-tale clicks that indicated a line had been cleared to the *Hotel Nacional du Cuba* in Havana.

"*Ciao*, Vito. Love and kisses from everyone," she purred, and waited for her husband, mass murderer and mob boss Vito Genovese, to reply accordingly. She spelled everything out. An approving smile never left her face as she absorbed every horrific detail of the torture Vito planned for the betrayer. "*Arrivederci, ti amo*," Anna reassured Vito that murdering her husband to get at her was well worth it.

Debbie wound her way through Fort Lee, then to Little Ferry, where she crossed the Hackensack River and headed north to pick-up NJ Route 17 for the final twenty miles to her family home in Tuxedo Park, New York.

It was a pleasantly warm and cloudless day. She was in no hurry and held her vehicle well below the speed limit as she passed estate-size homes, green fields, grazing horses and thick stands of pine. She came to a near stop when she spotted the roadside sign for Mahwah, and just below it, on the same post, a smaller sign, Immaculate Conception Seminary, Archdiocese of Newark. She hadn't been back to this intersection in thirteen years, when as a very proper and well-defined teenager groomed for Vassar, she wrapped her arms as tight as she could around the waist of her cousin, Maria Theresa von Hammerstein, as they bounced along the bumpy road to the seminary for a meeting with a big, tobacco-chewing, communist priest.

He was affable and welcoming and insisted they call him Father Ski. He greeted them outside the church that was the seminary's centerpiece, a twin-turreted, gothic red brick monolith, just perfect for bending innocent young minds.

Theresa handed him a note. "Here, this is for you. All the way from Berlin." He took his time reading the two handwritten pages. He finished with a frown, looked up, studied their faces and said, "They don't give up, do they? I hope and pray that your sister, Marie Luise, and I'm assuming she's a sister to one or both of you, wakes up to the truth in time. A beautiful note; I used to write like this a long, long time ago."

He ushered them to a nearby stone bench and after they were seated, pulled a pack of Twenty-Grand from inside his cassock, tapped out a few cigarettes and offered them. He nodded when they refused, "Don't blame you; you're just kids. They're damn awful but cheap."

The next ten minutes were spent in idle chit-chat, nothing important, with Theresa doing most of the talking and Deborah at a loss to contribute anything more than family stuff. A bell rang from somewhere on the grounds, and Father Ski arose, "I've got a New Testament class waiting to sink their teeth into Christ's Mustard Seed Parable, according to Luke.

"Don't wait for an answer to this," he said, tapping the cassock pocket with Luise's note. "I find Catholic mysticism easier to swallow than Communist voodoo, and I don't have a gun to my head."

"What was that all about?" Debbie said as she and her cousin squeezed in together on the leather seat of the powerful, black BMW R62 motorcycle, the cream of a growing crop of powerful German motorcycles flooding Europe. She wrapped her arms around Theresa and held on for dear life as they roared off to Tuxedo Park.

"I'll tell you about it when we get back," Theresa shouted over her shoulder while steadily accelerating the 750cc machine. "Let's see if we can beat our time getting there."

Theresa knew something about everything, with one exception: Father Ski. Her firebrand sister Luise always played it close to the vest when it came to the German Communist party, never quite sure where her younger sibling stood. Theresa was fed only tidbits that the burly, ham-fisted priest, then known as Peter Majeski, had cracked more than a few heads while mixing it up with capitalist goons on the front line of strikes that spread like wildfire across America in the 1920s.

"I memorized, as best I could, what my sister said when she handed me the note. I saw in her eyes how sad, and maybe even frightened she was. She sent me off with a hug and lamented, *He must get the note. We can't afford to lose men like him and his closest comrade. We knew him in Germany only as Samuel, that's all, just Samuel. A real phantom who came and went as he pleased, and wherever he and Peter showed up, capitalist pigs knew they had a battle on their hands.* For Debbie, that was it as far as the note and Father Ski were concerned. *If it wasn't for her, I wouldn't have known anything.*

Thinking back, Debbie's neurons were crackling at a fever pitch as resentment toward her father grew. *Dad, it was like pulling teeth to get any family truth out of you, only the good stuff. That General Kurt Von Hammerstein-Equord, for me, he was always Uncle Kurt, Chief of Staff of the German army until Hitler and his gangsters took over. He was forced to resign in '34, came back in '38 and became a lackey. Everyone in the family hated Hitler. But hell, you could have told your only daughter that the Hammerstein clan was bursting at the seams with Commies.*

She learned from Theresa that although his hatred for the Nazis was palpable, her uncle refused to join army conspirators plotting the assassination of Hitler shortly after he became Chancellor. *Dad, why didn't you tell me that the family, fearing the worst from Hitler and his gangsters, smuggled Jews out of Germany for years. And if not for Theresa, I wouldn't have known that my eldest cousin, Marie Luise, and her husband, Mogens Harbou, an outspoken Communist party organizer, were hounded by the Gestapo.*

Debbie turned off Route 17 onto Tuxedo Road and slowly idled her way into the gold-encrusted enclave created by tobacco mogul Pierre Lorillard IV. Although long dead, his company minions carried his message far and wide. Old Gold was their latest addiction handed off to an eagerly inhaling America.

Childhood memories accompanied her up Lake Road, past the old race track, now a nature preserve. Just ahead on Clubhouse Road was the fourteen-room Georgian mansion, where she knew that at least handyman Eli, Sophia, the best cook ever, and housekeeper Ingrid would be waiting. They were Jews who had served the family in Berlin, and with the anti-Semitic drumbeat growing ever louder throughout Germany in 1928, it was time to get out. This was no easy thing, but with General Kurt von Hammerstein-Equord pulling the strings, they got the necessary visas, but only after they acted on the advice of Debbie's parents and anglicized their surnames. Eli and his wife, Sophia, were no longer Herr and Frau Greenburg, but Mr. and Mrs. Green, and Frau Ingrid Lupinski was now Miss Ingrid Lindstrom. There were no Jews in Tuxedo Park, and if the family was to gain acceptance of the town's Germanic elite, they had to be squeaky clean.

Debbie had called ahead, hoping her mother would pick-up, but as usual, she was out and around being seen and heard by Tuxedo Park's "right" people.

Her father purchased the mansion in 1926 from a brochure and a long cursive note from Lorillard Suffern Tailer, a successful Wall Street investor, who also had a job waiting for him. The one million dollars in allocated gold certificates he brought with him provided assurance that a big corner office would be waiting.

Polo playing Tailer and Catherine, his social butterfly wife, held nothing back when they greeted Lee and Veronica as they disembarked from the RMS Mauretania in the spring of 1926 with their daughter Deborah, already a tall and angular beauty, in tow with her pet schnauzer. Two Packard Twin Six Touring cars, each with a liveried chauffeur, waited at dockside.

"How wonderful that you finally arrived; we've heard so much about you," Catherine Tailer said with her sweet tonality, so long practiced and perfected to be part of her persona. Her eyes never stopped moving while she fashioned the social box in which to place the Hammersteins. They had to fit in; Catherine's reputation was at stake. She focused on Deborah and gushed, "And look at you! Only ten and already a beauty, who sure as I can be, will have the boys in a tizzy."

From that point on, the welcoming banter became more perfunctory, mandatory handshakes and air kisses, and a brief ruffling of the schnauzer's ears. After they were comfortable in the first Packard, the chauffeur unlatched a small drop-down table from the back of the front passenger seat, popped the cork of a bottle of Mumm and began pouring. The spread included smoked oysters, Camembert, pâté de foie gras, cornichons and truffles. For Debbie, there was Vichy water.

Catherine's guidance firmly shut the doors to the *hoi polloi*. A rich assortment of upper-class innuendo from the homeland and one million dollars in cashable bonds greased their way right into the best seating at dinner parties where malicious gossip was the coin of the realm. They boated and fished at the lake, wagered at the race course and danced at the clubhouse.

11

At six-thirty in the morning, from Monday through Friday, Lee Hammerstein boarded the Erie commuter train to Grand Central Station, took a taxi to Tailer and Company, and except for a one-hour break for lunch, spent seven hours each day at his big mahogany desk in his corner office overlooking Wall Street.

For seven school years on the trip, he was joined by his daughter Deborah. Before heading to his office, Lee ushered Debbie from the incoming platform at Grand Central Station to the taxi stand on East 42nd Street. From there, it was a short ride to the brownstone enclave on West 48th Street, where pampered young ladies at Miss Spence's School for Girls learned the motto, "Not for school, but for the life we learn."

Debbie embraced everything about the school. It was so unlike Germany, where she and her schoolmates were sequestered from the real world because to allow them more than a glance would expose them to the unspeakable.

Debbie loved how mid-town Manhattan pulsated, everything blending into a scherzo that left her breathless in anticipation of more raucous delights.

She needed only a day to discover what it took to fit in, and at Miss Spence's, that's what it was all about, fitting in. Depending on her whim at that moment, her English was a patois that combined the harshness of German, Etonian English, and the in-your-face frankness of the American. Listeners gushed when she spoke. She was the tallest in the fifth grade and challenged Rosemary Pringle and Viola Masterson for the prettiest. Armed with this social ammunition, how could she fail?

She never complained about the rigid rules at Miss Spence's. Compared to St. Bartholomew's Grammar School and its dreaded School Sisters of Notre Dame, her fourteen new classmates didn't know how good they had it. The nuns instilled the fear of God, and that was okay, but when they threw in a long list of forbidden thoughts quite enjoyable to most ten-year-old girls, well…that was just too much.

At Miss Spence's, she discovered, to her delight, that dark thoughts abounded, and there was no trick to finding kindred spirits. At year's end, Debbie, Viola, Rosemary and Juliette Bonet, granddaughter of a former French minister, headed into the summer vowing eternal friendship.

During a three-night summer sleepover at the Hammerstein Georgian mansion in Tuxedo Park, the giggling quartet affirmed and then solidified, with their fingers entwined as they sat in a circle, a naïve sisterhood of the innocent. During the extended weekend, there were no secrets. Each girl sought answers to why their dreams were changing. They were all madly in love with Rudolf Valentino, envied Clara Bow for what the grown-ups called her sex appeal, and yearned to be rescued by Douglas Fairbanks.

Debbie was spellbound when the others described in the smallest real or imagined detail the holiday social mixers with the boys of Collegiate School in Manhattan's Upper

West Side. They wooed and cooed in the wake of Douglas Fairbanks, Jr., the son of the dazzling movie swashbuckler, as he passed among them. It ended after a pillow fight that decided two-to-one with Viola, the outsider, that Junior was more handsome than his father, and he hadn't even grown a mustache.

Debbie's first love was her Shetland pony, Felix, a surprise gift on her eighth birthday. "I cried when I gave him his final carrot and kiss; now, don't laugh at me, promise? There were tears in his eyes, too."

"Where's Felix now?" Viola asked. "I could never leave my Peggy behind. It must be hard for you."

"Sure was."

"I was seven when my dad blindfolded me, picked me up and when I opened my eyes, I was sitting on Andy's back," Rosemary said. "It was love at first sight."

"I believe it," Juliette chimed in. "I'm just like Viola; I can't even think about not having my Bridgette."

Rosemary was the group's veteran equestrian, getting her pint-size, black-and-white Appaloosa lookalike when she was five. "From the first time I saw him, I knew Andy was the perfect pony for me, but I think our time together is up. My dad and our stable hand think I'm ready for something bigger. My birthday's coming up, so I'm crossing my fingers."

The three days ended with finger-entwined friendship rituals, kisses and even some tears before they boarded the early train to Grand Central, leaving Debbie behind. Her father made sure their rides were waiting as they went their separate ways, Rosemary to Upper Montclair, New Jersey; Juliette to Westport, Connecticut; and Viola to Sands Point, Long Island.

Rosemary married a thoracic surgeon, Juliette married into a family that controlled almost half the Connecticut River Valley's broadleaf tobacco acreage, and Viola's husband was a tenth-generation French Count.

At Vassar, Debbie was just another Ivy League Fine Arts major prowling the theatre precincts of Manhattan. Tall, beautiful, blonde and green-eyed, and with Johan's checkbook in hand, she indulged her passion for drama and more recently musicals. The wife of her father's boss, for years a fat cat theatre donor, opened all the right doors. She was welcomed at every insiders' event, a seat at final rehearsals, private parties for people with money, the best opening night seats, and the boozy wait for the first reviews.

Johan was seldom with her, and she explained her husband's absence to anyone who cared that business demands took precedence. She was grateful that never once, during the countless stale and trite conversations that she was never asked exactly what kind of work Johan did. She was introduced to several handsome boy toys, tried out a few of them as arm candy but called it quits. Vodka provided a hell of a lot better companionship.

Ever since the rehearsal party for *Oklahoma* four years earlier, when the deep purple bruise on her neck was her introduction to aspiring actress Bambi Linn, Debbie's life took on a new and bitter dimension.

She knew that her salvation, if such a thing existed, was wrapped inside the entwined fingers of four women who never once had backed away from the vows they made so many years ago at Miss Spence's. True to their word, they never missed the two Broadway theater dinner dates, a week at Saratoga Springs for the running of the Travers Stakes, or renting the biggest house available in Stowe, Vermont, in January for a week of skiing. Perhaps because they thought it was irrelevant, they gave little thought to how all this was paid for -- by their husbands, of course. This was pampered living at its best.

Thinking back to that weekend, it was so many years ago that Debbie's late August 1947 drive home had her questioning for the umpteenth time how she had been so wrong about Johan. There were troubling signs from the start. He was lazy in the way inherited wealth made real work a dreaded phenomenon. He evaded questions about his alleged work for the National Bank of Deutschland, citing instead that his mother was a bank director, and "Let's leave it to that dearest, and get on to those things that are important to us," her abandonment at the Danube River dock, the crazy trip to that monstrous Vittorio's Castle, and his inexplicable trips to Europe and who knows where else.

Her car was visible from the Hammerstein portico for the final half-mile up Clubhouse Road, giving plenty of time for Eli, Ingrid and Sophia, the household staff, to be waiting at the front door, all smiles and warmth for their favorite family member.

"What a big surprise." He studied her face and wasn't fooled by the cosmetic camouflage but stifled his anger as he reached down for her luggage.

Ingrid, the irreplaceable housekeeper whose life was rewarded by her perfection for detail, embraced Debbie, exchanged kisses, and then backed off to a comfortable distance, her smile fading as she labored for the right words. "We will always be here for you. You'll be safe in your very own room with your father and mother; we'll make sure of that. Your bath is already prepared."

Sophia, the household scolded, again spoke her mind. After a hug and kiss, she turned to what was most important to her. "You don't have much time, so get upstairs, take your bath, then come down to your welcome home meal."

Upstairs, Debbie stripped for her bath after laying out her makeup kit on the dresser table. *Gave it my best this morning,* she thought, *and it didn't fool anybody. I just hope to hell that my bastard husband doesn't follow me up here.*

Debbie had no way of knowing that going on at the same time in Manhattan, plans were being finalized in the back office of a homosexual hangout on West Broadway that would indelibly impact her life. She never gave a thought, nor could she imagine that a dimly recalled breakfast with Johan more than two weeks ago was the last time she would ever see him.

Almost immediately after joining their daughter for pre-dinner drinks and seeing her face for the first time, Veronica and Lee Hammerstein began competing for first place on the shock and disbelief barometer. At first, Debbie hesitated, then in measured, softly spoken sentences, described how a marriage made in heaven can easily go to hell.

"My God, how long has this been going on!" Barely in control, her father stepped closer and raised her chin with his right hand for a closer examination. "Tell us straight out; don't lie because if you do, we'll see it in your eyes. This isn't the first time, or the second, or the third, is it? How many times…." He was cut short by his wife.

"I could never have imagined that Johan would hurt you this way, damage your beautiful face." Her mother, in tears, brushed past her husband and, with a cheek-to-cheek hug, declared, "That bastard! That filthy pig! Answer your father…how long?"

"Too long, too many times to describe or count." Debbie, with her mother's sodden mascara and rouge, slopped all over her right cheek, backed off, turned her head in time to rescue her left cheek, and said, "He loved me very much, I'm sure of that. That was in the beginning. Then came the liquor, more of it before and after dinner at home, then at theater parties, to now, always out of sight behind closed doors, always sullen and silent."

"God damn him to hell!" her father's curse came from the nether reaches of his soul. "He loved you, and this is the way he showed his love? And when did he repeat his vows, before, during or after he did this to your face?"

"Please, Dad," Debbie entreated, then turned to her mother, now intent on cleaning up with her handkerchief the mess she had made of her face, "and to you Mom, I'm saying this to both of you. Drop it, drop it right now. I've said all there is to say about Johan. He's history."

All of this had taken place out of sight but loud enough to be heard by Eli, Ingrid and Sophia. The Hammerstein family truce was cemented in place to be honored by the entire household.

Two weeks later, Debbie leafed through the daily mail she'd had forwarded when she came to an envelope postmarked Montclair, New Jersey. It had to be from Rosemary. She tore it open and quickly read the beautifully handwritten pages. She refolded the two pages and returned them to the envelope. None of what she read was good or bad, but she sensed something wrong. After three deep drags on her Benson & Hedges, she stubbed the fag out in her chrome bedside ashtray, then reached for the telephone. Rosemary picked up after three rings.

"Rosie, it's Debbie. Sorry I took so long answering your note; it took two weeks to forward my mail from Manhattan," Debbie said. "Before you ask, I'm back in Tuxedo Park. No details now, but Johan and I are splitting."

"You and Johan are, as the Krauts would say, *kaput*?" Rosemary said. "Hard to believe with your background, the perfect couple. This calls for a get-together; the quicker, the better."

"How quick? I sense we have a lot to talk about."

"Too bad the mail took so long; tomorrow would have been great," Rosemary said. "I was planning an early dinner in Newark, five-ish or so. Any chance?"

"Just tell me where, and I'll be there."

12

On October 28, 1943, U.S. Staff Sergeant Stefano Rizzano had once again pulled off without a hitch, all he had planned. A day earlier, he was transferred from the Third Infantry Division to the Fourth Military Police Battalion of the Sixth Army Corps. The Third Division was refitting for the assault of Monte Cassino, sure to be bloody, and the Sixth Corps was handling security in recently captured Naples, a real soft touch.

To get the transfer, he called in chips he earned when lining up some really fine Italian pieces of ass for his immediate superiors. His fluency in Italian was well past the wop street slang of north and central Newark. He could speak, write, read and even sing it to near perfection; his mother had made sure of that.

Never reluctant to hold anything back, Alicia Rizzano had perfected a swift right-hand slap to the back of Stefano's head every time he messed up. "Our language, it's so beautiful," she constantly admonished, "to read, to write, to speak, to sing and the music, oh the music! So beautiful. It's God's gift, and you must respect it."

Stefano could easily turn the switch from dago gutter

talk to beautiful *bel verso*. He had no trouble with the collegial "Steve" given him by fellow MPs and was grateful that "Fish Hook" and "Schemer," as he was known to fellow mafioso soldiers in Newark, never came out. His new buddies would never understand.

In late 1940, Stefano was one of the street-wise punks who knew that war was coming, and when a twelve-month draft began in October, he figured, *What the hell, why not jump on board? Twelve months, a snap, in and out before Hitler gets serious.*

He never completely unpacked his bags at Fort Dix, no need to; the rat-infested barracks, humidity so high you could drink it, was an easy two-hour drive in his Dodge each weekend, always getting bunkmates to pay for the gas.

Whoa there. Let's not get my balls in an uproar. All the bimbos and booze are just waiting for yours truly. Five more months, that's all. Leave it to other saps to get their asses shot off. And now fucking FDR, a president I really love, Jesus Christ, even voted for, a goddamn double-crosser. Ever comes my way, I'll take that dog of his, what's he call it, Fala I think, I'll shove it up his ass, that's what a double-crosser gets!

Word of the double-cross came while Stefano, now "Steve" to his buddies, was playing pinball in his Company's day room. "Read it and weep," a smiling First Sergeant John Schroeder ("Rocky" to his men) said. Rocky loved to fight with his fists during a barroom brawl, charging the German trenches at Château-Thierry, and emptying one twenty-round magazine after another of his close-to-melting Browning Automatic Rifle (BAR) while shooting to kill from the steps of the American Embassy in Shanghai in 1938. Like ravenous locusts, Jap Zeros swarmed across the Huangpu River, dipped to their left to strafe and murder hundreds of defenseless civilians fleeing along the Bund and hoped-for safety in the International Settlement. Rocky roared at the passing pilots' faces with the obscene anthem of a brave man forced to fight on the terms of treacherous cowards.

"You yellow, slant-eyed, mother fucking bastards! You sons of bitches! If I rip your head off and piss in the hole, it's too good for you. If only, if only, your days are coming, you zippered-eyed freaks."

Rocky was a "thirty-year man," and with twenty-seven years in only three to go, he knew his army fighting days were over. Now, he was babysitting draft-dodging draftees, and he hated it. The punks closed in around him as he finished tacking up the good news. A laughable twelve-month stint was now thirty months in uniform for Uncle Sam, and maybe longer.

Effective immediately.

"He's backstabbing us," Stefano's lament triggered a bleating chorus of disbelief. "That son of a bitch in the White House sucked us in, and now he's got us by the balls for almost three years!"

Thanks to Mama Rizzano's sturdy right hand, things couldn't have worked out better for Stefano, and the irony of his first orders didn't escape him.

I'll be damned. They must really be hard up, he thought as he scanned the details of his assignment to Military Police School at Carlisle Barracks in Pennsylvania. *Me, a mafia street punk, now an Army cop. If they're so damn dumb, there's gotta be ways to work them. They can use a dago who kicks the hell out of good Italian, can even read and write it. Stefano Rizzano, you've got your ticket.*

It took only one phone call from Sam Monaco, underboss of the DeCavalcante family, to Joe Ida, boss of the Bruno-Scarfo family in Philly, to open the door for Stefano. It was only a hundred and twenty miles from

Newark to Philadelphia, so for seven of his nine weekends at Carlisle Barracks, he took it to heart when a smiling Ida clapped his cheek and said, "See something you like, let me know." On the day Stefano shipped out, he had sampled almost every illegal delicacy offered at Mafia joints from the Delaware River west to the Schuylkill. He knew these favors had little to do with him, a low-level shit cleaner, and everything to do with the big bosses of the DeCavalcante family and the powerful Five Families in New York City. And what the Five Families wanted, they got.

The Bruno family was awestruck by the power the Five Families had along the East Coast, and one name that came up over and over again was Vito Genovese.

"He got what he wanted when he wanted it, and you better not get in his fucking way," a reverential Joe Ida said, his voice a nearly indistinct burble over the ice cube he had sucked from his glass of scotch. "Take his wife, Anna; she was married to another Mafioso when Vito got the hots, no problem. He deep-sixed the hubby, and they've been living happily ever after."

"I think I've heard of her. Isn't she the one who runs those queer joints in Manhattan?" Angelo Bruno asked. "Got a thing for the fags?"

Stefano knew that as far as the Bruno-Scarfo family was concerned, he was in exalted company that night at Palumbo's restaurant. Ida may have been holding court, but Stefano easily discerned that Angelo Bruno, quiet most of the evening, was biding his time before taking over.

"I don't think she gives a fiddler's fart for fags, only uses them for arm candy for her nightclub-hopping in Manhattan," Ida said. "And you gotta believe that Vito has given it the nod."

Stefano and the three tightly-wound and carefully-lacquered young ladies who completed the dinner entourage were mostly silent. The three tricks were soaking up booze while he absorbed everything.

Every day on the troop ship to Casablanca was a day of mental self-gratification for Stefano. *Thanks, Mama. Here's my love and kisses for making me slap happy during all those goddamn lessons. Now I'm not a ginney from Newark, I'm a fucking ginney interpreter.*

He had been pulled aside almost immediately after the Third Infantry Division began boarding the troop ship and asked if he could handle Italian.

"Sure can, wanna hear?" he said, looking down from his six-foot-three-inch height at a scrawny lieutenant with a clipboard who motioned him out of line and over to a nearby bulkhead.

"What else, and don't even think of bullshitting us," the lieutenant said. Stefano and two other guys, all freshly minted Privates First Class, were each handed two pieces of paper. One contained a lengthy newspaper article, and the other two paragraphs of an Italian novel. They were separated, each in tow behind an Army Intelligence officer for further questioning. Stefano passed with flying colors and never learned what happened with the other two guys.

As November 1942 drew to a close, half of Morocco was occupied by the Third Division, but Stefano found it hard to find any Italians to interrogate. His work picked up as the division swept through Algeria and Tunisia. In Tunis, he finally questioned the downed pilot of an Italian fighter plane and two infantry captains who abandoned their men for some good food and best of all, maybe a POW camp back in the States.

Except for a few brief skirmishes with Vichy French roadblocks in and around Algiers, the Third Division easily advanced across French North Africa. *The French, the goddamn French, I thought they were on our side,* he thought.

Things moved quickly for Stefano. His immediate superiors, mostly horny first and second lieutenants with a captain or two thrown in, took note. When he satisfied their prurient desires, he was rewarded with a corporal stripe in April, and when the Division stood down to prepare for the invasion of Sicily, he was a Buck Sergeant.

The Division came ashore at Licata on July 10, fought its way across Sicily to Palermo, outraced everyone else to Messina, and by summer's end, the entire island was in Allied hands. Along the way, it was business as usual for Stefano, the pimp. The extracurricular requests were mundane except for one, and that was a real doozy; it went like this.

"Sergeant Rizzano…" a ramrod straight, square-jawed Major Thomas Ulysses Rucker, the MP Battalion Commander, asked as he pulled his Jeep to a stop at Stefano's road crossing.

"Yes, sir," a startled and bemused Stefano replied. He had never before seen his boss talk to anyone below the rank of lieutenant.

"Stand easy, Sergeant. I'll tell you what I want, and you'll have it for me either here in Palermo or in Messina, and if I like your little gift, I can be very appreciative."

Rucker, who Stefano figured to be about thirty and married if you believed his wedding band. The girl couldn't be older than nineteen and had to be pretty with an angelic, innocent look about her, bushy armpits, very hairy legs and the usual elsewhere. Stefano put his Sicilian dialect to work, and in less than four hours spread over two days, he came up with Gabriella, an eighteen-year-old working Messina's dockside streets, and told to expect her biggest payday ever if she could pull off what was needed. Gabriella gave him a choice: did he want St. Cecilia or St. Agnes of Assisi? She could do them both; either one was okay with her.

Stefano had obviously put together a coupling made in heaven. Much to his surprise, Rucker came through with the necessary scribbling in his record-jacket. So, Stefano added a rocker to his three sergeant stripes, becoming, at twenty-four, the Battalion's youngest Staff Sergeant. At six-foot-three, two hundred and ten pounds, he was confident none of the men in his squad would have the guts to fuck with him.

A quick study, Stefano needed only five days to learn the lay of the land in and around Naples. He poured over three outdated maps of the region before tracing the best route to Nola, a steep, winding road around the Mount Vesuvius crater. He had an errand to run.

13

Five hundred and thirty miles north of Naples, Johan Paasche basked in the rare warm late October sun that poked through the gloomy haze enshrouding Geneva, Switzerland.

He had just completed the latest of a long list of very lucrative financial transactions at Lombard Odier, one of the oldest and time-honored banks in the city. With his now empty, beautifully tooled, leather attaché case in hand, Johan's blonde, blue-eyed, square-jawed features broadened to expose the near-perfect teeth of a man enraptured by self-aggrandizement.

Today's money laundering was the latest in a four-year string of mob investments that swelled the coffers of Krupp AG, I.G. Farben, Bayer AG, Topf and Sons, M.L. Kraus, Siemens and other capitalists in bed with Hitler, a man they despised but they loved his huge contracts more.

Johan had one more errand before he could enjoy dinner, dancing and creative sex with Maude Rosenfeldt, a tall, auburn-haired, green-eyed Jew who escaped to Switzerland one step ahead of Hitler's Gestapo. It helped that she brought along her inherited family fortune. Upstairs in his flat on Quai du Mont-Blanc, he freshened up and changed into suitable evening clothes before restuffing his attaché case with more Mafia cash. It was considerably less than the Lombard Odier drop-off, but nice enough for now. He had to be careful. Rico Frenzelli, the mob's New York-based accountant, had already gotten wise to him and was pocketing ten thousand dollars a month in cash to keep his mouth shut, but for how long? It was time for Paasche to start thinking ahead.

He hailed a taxi and enroute along the lake to his Credit Suisse bank on Rue de Lausanne, marveled that the rest of Europe thirsted for gas and diesel, while the Swiss kept right on guzzling.

Ludwig Stein, the bank's stuffy Accounts Manager, had been expecting Johan and, with a blonde secretary in tow, greeted the embezzler as he stepped from the elevator into a mahogany-encased reception area.

"Herr Paasche, so good to see you again," Stein said, extending his right arm, and with a barely discernable gesture indicated that socially mandated amenities were over. "Time is money as we know, neither waits for the other."

"And as we both know, money has no conscience," Johan said. "But it does have an enormous appetite. It's time to talk."

"Very good, always time for a little philosophy," Stein

said.

In Naples, Stefano was about to find out what kind of squad he had taken over. But first, he had to check in with his new Company Commander, Captain Charles Bisnoff, a tightly-wound West Point bully, who by this time had sniffed through Stefano's file.

"At ease, Sergeant," Bisnoff said from the far side of a large wooden shipping crate that served as his desk and platform for a chaotic mess of file folders. "Well, they were right about one goddamn thing, you're one big son of a bitch."

Stefano wondered if this required an answer, thought better of it and watched as Bisnoff went through his four file pages.

"Fluent in Italian, and I can see that includes reading and writing. But right now, I'm looking for muscle, call it patriotic muscle, and the men who know how to use it. Any idea of where I'm going, Sergeant?"

"No, sir, not exactly," Stefano said as he reached for a memo-size sheet of paper handed across the packing crate by the Captain.

"Read it. Memorize every word, then get rid of it," Bisnoff said. "This is your first night out; you have a crew that's gone through it four times already, so just point them in the right direction. You'll recognize some kindred spirits mixed in. Any questions?"

"Kindred spirits, sir? I don't quite understand."

"After reading that page I handed you, Sergeant, you will. The black market has been ripping us for more than a month, and it's getting worse. Penicillin is what they're after right now and as much as they can get. I want these pimps hurt, and I mean hurt bad."

After Bisnoff dismissed him and he had memorized his one page of instructions, Stefano headed to the squad tent and his first "get to know you" meeting with the men under his command. All but three, Buck Sergeant Jim Turco, Corporals Dean Willis and Ray Parma, were younger. All were veterans of the North Africa and Sicily campaigns.

After tossing his helmet on an empty bunk, wiping dirty sweat from his brow, and with studied casualness pulling upright a five-gallon water can for a seat, Stefano said, "Looks like we've got some goddamn babysitting to do." He paused to scan reactions, then added, "No broads, so don't get your balls in an uproar.

"According to this, we've got eight hundred thousand in rags with mouths to feed, no place to live, typhoid breaking out, and the black market carting off all the penicillin they can suck out of our field hospitals." He refolded the single page of notes he had taken at the morning briefing and slipped it back into his shirt pocket. "And nobody gives a damn."

"Even truckloads of C and K rations disappearing like someone waved a magic wand and, poof, they're gone," Willis made no attempt to hide his disgust. "Yeah, I know they taste like shit, but when you're hungry you'll eat anything."

"It's been only about a month, and the bloodsuckers are out in force," Turco said. "Spam, powdered eggs and milk, and Jesus Christ, you know how bad they taste, but for mothers watching their skinny kids with swollen bellies, it's fucking manna from heaven."

"There's two deuce-and-a-halves getting a lot of attention," Parma said. "One is loading up now for a run to Salerno, and from what our new Sarge told me, the second truck is ours. Has the same six bastards every day. It's time to kick some mother fucking ass."

They left the Battalion orderly room in time to catch the first two-and-a-half ton, canvas-covered truck pulling away from a long loading dock looking more and more like a rummage sale gone wild. Staff Sergeant Billy Conklin's squad would be tailing it north, destination unknown.

The tailgate of a second truck was locked in place as six Quartermaster grunts climbed aboard, two in the driver's cab and four in the back, with Stefano's squad following it from a safe distance, it would be traveling south to Salerno.

As it pulled away, Turco, Parma and three younger cops jumped aboard a WC51 ton-and-a-half truck, already gassed and ready to go. Stefano, Willis and the rest of the squad piled into a second WC51. They waited until their quarry was a safe distance ahead before following on the traffic-clogged coastal highway to Salerno.

They drove without incident through Naples, where units of Lieutenant General Mark Clark's Fifth Army were refitting for the push north and the capture of Monte

Cassino. Army engineers worked around the clock to clear debris and vehicles of every size and shape abandoned by Germans who had taken up new positions in the formidable mountains to the north. They approached Torre del Greco, the German's main supply depot reduced to rubble after weeks of Allied bombing.

The MPs were caught off guard when the deuce-and-a-half came to a near stop before turning into a walled-in and virtually undamaged school complex. To avoid detection, they veered into the protective shade of elms that towered along the road and waited.

"Give it a few minutes and we'll take a look," Stefano said, his words punctuated by the clank of the truck's tailgate. They checked their sidearms and carbines, then fanned out, Turco's squad to the right of the schoolyard entrance, Stefano's to the left. They crouched with their backs pressed to the wall and watched as their unsuspecting prey spilled from the truck. Raucous laughter framed the lewd descriptions of the fun and games about to begin. But first the appropriate booty had to be collected and assembled for proper presentation.

Each filled their arms to capacity, their biceps close to bursting with cartons of C and K Rations, spam, cigarettes, matches, coffee, chewing gum, candy, biscuits, and dried eggs and milk. Lifted from wooden crates clearly marked "FOR OFFICERS MESS," were tightly wrapped tins of sardines, ham, veal, chicken and beef. Instead of the four-packs of atrocious Wings and Twenty-Grand, officers' nicotine cravings were reinforced by the perfectly roasted flavor of Lucky Strike.

Stefano inherited a squad of the deadliest enforcers in the Battalion. It couldn't be proven, but it was generally agreed that two murders were stamped with their fingerprints. An Italian colonel who doffed his uniform and put on heavily-mended peasant's clothes fooled no one. His body, with his face and head little more than a bloody stump, was discovered under a mountain of trash in a Messina back alley. The badly beaten body of a Naval commander of a Vichy French destroyer, gussied-up in his freshly starched summer whites and three rows of ribbons was found in the backseat of a Citroën naval staff car abandoned in the dark recesses of the Algiers' quarter.

Stefano's squad, then under the command of Staff Sergeant Rudy Reisman, were ordered to investigate attempts by the two officers to surrender. If true, money, lots of it, would have been de rigueur. None was found, nor was there jewelry of any kind. An inquiry needed only two days for Buck Sergeant Turco, the most literate of the bunch, to determine that the killings were obviously the work of local street gangsters. The report was passed around in triplicate, duly stamped "Investigation Complete, No Further Action Required."

Stefano had scanned Turco's report and didn't believe any of it. He had been sizing up his men for less than a week, but needed only a few bullshit sessions to realize he was indeed among kindred spirits. What a mob of liars, thieves, sadists and maybe even murderers.

Using silent hand signals, he ordered his men to stay safely in the shadows until all of the booty was moved inside. Turco hunkered over and whispered, "What's next?"

"You tell me, you're the experienced hit man," Stefano said. "Till tonight I only translated, left it to the brains in counterintelligence to decide if it was bullshit. Tell me if I saw right, that was a monk, a goddamn priest, who let them in? Right or wrong?"

"Name's Father Buscata, been running the black market around here for years, ever since Il Duce's glory days."

"What can we expect inside?"

"Do you know Dante?" Turco said.

"The only Dante I know is a real asshole back in Newark."

"I'm talking about Dante Alighieri, a real famous guy, a poet, deep thinker."

"How come you know all this?" Stefano was openly impressed.

"Four years at St. Benedict's Prep. You learn Dante, or you got the shit beat out of ya. You don't have to read Dante's Inferno to soak up the disgust he had for the human condition," an increasingly disturbed Turco said. His anger exploding into temple-throbbing pain. "No sense saying anymore, you'll see it when we get inside."

They spread out, five to the entrance and five to the right. They inched up to the waist-high windows to absorb living proof there were no boundaries for human debasement.

14

Stefano watched, stunned, as the tableau took shape through the late autumn sunlight that filtered through the windows. Trapped as a kid in a world ravaged by crime, poverty and incestuous violence, he believed he had seen it all. He was wrong. Eight women, their feeble movements in response to proffered American loot, were little more than zombies shifting into position for their final degradation.

Two piles of stolen supplies were clumped at the far side of the room. There was no item too small for a plump, rosy-cheeked priest to take into account in his notebook. Stefano's disgust was immediate and all-consuming. He had to do something.

"Move in!" Stefano shouted as he burst inside, taking one-half of the double entrance door with him before backing a cowering Father Buscata into a small alcove. In that instant, the priest realized that decades of fascist-supported church extortion was ending. The cleric never saw it coming; a numbing darkness descended when the priest's jaw snapped, and his head bounced off the alcove wall. He spit out teeth before folding into a bloody heap. The sound and feel of the punch landing, and the sticky warmth of blood on his knuckles gave Stefano a sense of satisfaction so complete that it brought a smile to his face. His life would never be the same.

Ringing in Stefano's ears was the loud boast of the young PFC who was still in ecstasy. "Can you believe it! My first dago dream girl and for only a tin of spam. It was wham, bam, thank you ma'am. Too fucking fast for me, but I got more spam, dried milk and eggs left, and baby, that spells more action."

He glanced at the woman he had just mounted, she was pretty and no more than twenty. She had never assisted him in any way, just leaned back in the chair propped against the wall, and only after the blonde Adonis had lowered his pants to his ankles and added the spam to an overflowing box next to her, did she pull up her skirt and spread her legs.

There were seven other women of various ages propped against the wall, each with a cardboard box of booty next to her chair.

"Save the milk and eggs for those two donna matura with the floppy tits at the end of the line." Advice offered by a Buck Sergeant who had already dropped his drawers, erect and ready for his blow job. "Wise up, kid, be careful like me. You don't never want to bring home a dose of clap."

His advice was well taken. The two older women were mothers with mouths to feed. To the PFC's delight, they gave him all that he could handle, but their price was steep. They demanded all of the dried eggs and milk and remaining tins of spam.

Stefano pulled the reluctant Buck Sergeant by the collar to the center of the room, then turned to the PFC and demanded, "You. Over here."

With a nod and shoulder shrug, Turco assembled the other four men and motioned them to join the Buck Sergeant and blonde stud to form a semi-circle before he had them empty their wallets of everything except their ID cards.

Acting on his orders, Corporal Parma and Private Andrew Gordon, the only Jew in Stefano's squad, dragged bloody Father Buscata still on his knees across the floor to the center of the semi-circle. Whimpering Latin entreaties through the bloody handkerchief to his mouth with his left hand, the priest offered for all to see his right hand with rosary beads laced through his fingers, holding four broken teeth. For the first time, the women seated along the wall silently displayed faint signs of emotion. Facial furrows flattened and sun ravaged skin twisted into hopeful smiles. Stefano knew hatred when he saw it.

"Over here, Father," Stefano commanded, but stopped the priest before he could arise from his knees. "Crawl over here, that's right, right there...okay, stop."

During the time Stefano was positioning the priest, Turco had been carefully scanning the faces of the women still seated along the wall. He caught the eye of the oldest woman, probably about forty or so and followed her glance down to her half-empty cardboard box. Before he could put into play the murderous thoughts that had been convulsing him, Turco turned to Stefano, hardly more than a kid but with one more stripe on his sleeve, to hear, "Sergeant Turco, I'll take it from here."

In Italian, Stefano instructed the woman to bring over her box, "Take what you need; don't be shy." Then he watched as the woman, her dress barely holding together, scooped up coins and fistfuls of the coveted military script, the only medium of exchange with any value in Italy since the collapse of the lira, and satisfied she had enough, was about to return to her chair when he put one hand on her shoulder and pointed to the two piles of booty earmarked for the fat pig of a priest and his reverend. With a sweeping gesture of his left arm, a flamboyant bow and a smile, Stefano took in one-by-one the expectant women still seated.

The GIs, thieves and white-helmeted MPs alike were slack-jawed at what they saw. Seemingly docile and weak women became avenging furies. After they tore into and divided the booty, they used their shawls, the remnants of window curtains, and even swaths of their dresses to bundle and place their goods next to their chairs. Once seated, they turned their attention to the whimpering heap on the floor.

"They want a piece of him," Turco said to Stefano, enthralled by what he had witnessed. "What do you say, boss? This is their last chance at him. So what do you say? One shot each, come on."

Stefano turned to the women to have his suspicions

confirmed, just look at them, he thought, no way we can turn them loose. He walked over, gathered the women around him, and in a whisper, laid out the ground rules.

One-by-one each woman pushed or carried her bundle, but not before stopping and, with all the strength she could muster, planting a punch to the priest's face, head or neck. The oldest, not trusting the strength of her bones, removed a shoe and buried its heel in the nape of his neck. He collapsed forward, blood gushing and puke bubbling from his mouth. When it was over, they returned to their chairs with their booty safe.

"Over too quick, these women deserve more than one crack at the bastard," Turco said. "He's where he belongs, on his knees choking on his own vomit."

Two canvas-topped, three-quarter-ton trucks, each with "Military Police" stenciled in white paint on their doors, pulled up outside. A fuzzy-cheeked lieutenant and four enlisted men in white helmets, white Sam Browne belts and holstered .45s got out of each truck and walked inside. They had been handpicked by Captain Bisnoff. Except for the two lieutenants, they were thugs who had done big time.

"What happened here? Who is he, and I hope it's not your handiwork?" one lieutenant shrilled after he spotted the bloody priest.

"His name is Father Buscata, and he's been heading up the local black market. In answer to your second question, those ladies have been waiting a long time, and this was their chance. Check out their bloody knuckles, and you'll see what I mean."

It took about fifteen minutes for the arrested GIs to reload the stolen supplies. Then they were handcuffed and pushed aboard the MP trucks for the start of what would be at least five years of hard labor at Leavenworth.

Stefano signed over the prisoners to the two lieutenants and assigned four of his men, two in each truck, to drive the reclaimed contraband to its scheduled destination. He turned to Turco and said, "Jim, I've got a little errand to take care of. I'll take our three-quarter; it has plenty of gas. Should be back to Battalion by early evening at the latest. You're in charge."

"Sure, you don't want me along?"

"Nope, I'll just be following a hunch, been tipped there's one guy I should put the touch on."

"Been here what, a couple weeks or so, and already pulling stoolies out of your hat. Gonna fill me in?" a surprised Turco said.

"When I'm ready, so don't get your shit in an uproar."

Turco realized that this kid was more than a muscle-bound palooka. And connections, the kid had to have them, but with whom? It was his guess that it was the mafia. He wasn't about to push it with Staff Sergeant Stefano Rizzano.

15

Stefano was a troubled man as he eased behind the wheel of the small utility truck and shifted into gear. The rosary-entwined truisms, largely ignored but still necessary, had taken a massive hit less than two hours earlier at the schoolhouse.

Eight scraggly, odoriferous women, several in flimsy, heavily-mended dresses, and a few more fortunate who had squirreled away one good dress, silently waited. For what? Certainly not for this total degradation at the hands of uniformed thugs. At first sight, Stefano gawked in stunned silence. His years of codified gangster hostility were put to the test. It was okay to whack a rival mobster, cap a knee, break an arm, or butcher a face, all in the name of justice. But with women, no matter she be a bitch, a line was drawn. Like a whirligig spinning wildly in the wind and rain, crazy thoughts swirled between his ears.

He cracked open the pack of Luckies filched from the booty inside, took three deep drags, first gear, second, and a grinding third, as he tooled through the schoolyard gate to Nola.

With folded maps on his lap in the seat next to him, he retraced the route back to Torre del Greco, skirted the mountainous debris and wrecked military vehicles already stripped to their empty carcass and found Via Cavallo, followed it east a few miles to its intersection with the road to San Giorgio a Cremano. From there, it was a few miles on to Via Argine and then on to his destination in Nola.

Passing through bombed-out Ponticelli, he pulled off Via Argine, hit the brakes and turned off the ignition. He had to think, but he didn't know where to start. He was totally at a loss as he watched the cigarette smoke curl along the truck's windshield. Suddenly, as the smoke began to take on shape, his thoughts morphed into a hellish daytime nightmare. The faces of the eight women raped at the schoolhouse emerged from the smoke, glanced accusingly at him for a few seconds before disappearing back into the smoke just as raucous calliope music provided the fanfare for their reappearance of the women. This time, each was sedately riding painted carousel horses, giraffes, lions and reindeer. They were all smiles. With their legs firmly clamped around their grotesque, hideously painted mounts, they reached toward him with both hands as they passed. Each left hand had an mistakable whore's gesture with a finger extended, and the right hand held in turn a can of spam, sardines, cigarettes, K-rations, C-rations, powdered milk and a chocolate candy bar.

And that was the rub. Who the hell were they? The question became as insistent as his heartbeat. His entire family, father's and mother's sides, without exception, were Neapolitan, for God knows how far back, four, five, maybe even ten generations. There were certain to be countless marriages and the spreading of the Rizzano family seed; an inevitable question arose: did any of the trapped, debased women at the school share the Rizzano heritage?

His mother had given him two suburban Naples addresses. One in Barra, where Emilio Rizzano's market on Corso Sirena was for decades a neighborhood social gathering place. It was gone, turned to rubble by repeated carpet bombings. He found no trace of Emilio, his wife or his three daughters. Had they been killed? If alive, where had they fled? With his military police uniform an obvious hindrance, Stefano bribed survivors with cigarettes, spam and K-rations but learned nothing.

It was the same in Mercato, where Stefano's fishmonger, Uncle Giovanni Rizzano and his family were nowhere to be found. Like his brother in Barra, his livelihood and perhaps Giovanni himself, his wife, four daughters and a son had been destroyed by the bombings. Two families with seven daughters, at best roaming the war-torn countryside, or at worst, sharing the same fate as the women at the schoolhouse.

The hallucination was now part of his mental baggage, forcing him to question things that had never given a thought before.

He didn't realize, and probably never would, that his reaction to what he saw at the schoolhouse made him a mafia anomaly. He was unlike other ambitious, low-level mob soldiers who slapped their women around and bragged about it. Danielo and Alicia Rizzano made it clear to their son after they caught him pushing around little Giana Patrino that he had behaved like a coward.

To him, it was simply rough schoolyard play, over in less than a minute. When he yanked on Giana's pigtails, it was not to hurt her but to scare her into laying off with her wisecracks. She might have been small, but damn, did she have a big mouth. He'd never think of doing the same thing with his sister Theresa, three years older and rock solid.

His parents ganged-up on him. "Sei un codardo?" Alicia spat the words at her son, then slapped him as hard as she could across both cheeks. "There are no cowards in the Rizzano family!"

Danielo took over from his wife and grabbed his ten-year-old son by his shirt with both hands, so close their breaths intermingled. "A real man, even the biggest son of a bitch in the world, never lays a hand on a woman no matter what she said or did! Does this sink in? You know what happens if it doesn't."

Danielo and Alicia were serious, God-fearing Catholics up to a point. They never objected when their son spent more and more time at the Salerno Club, a mob hangout over on Tenth. Rosaries, novenas, Ways of the Cross, and masses were, of course, obligatory but only in their places. These rituals soon lost out to the growing wads of cash they found, but never questioned, in the empty kitchen coffee tin that served as the family bank.

Besides, the coffee tin deposits increased with Stefano's

physical growth. When he reached six-feet-one-inch, and still growing at fourteen, mob demands kept pace. From roughing-up a mob soldier with a big mouth or working over a bookie dumb enough to stiff his bosses to lending a helping hand with the stuffing of a body into a steel drum before he was nineteen, he earned his reputation as a bright kid with a strong stomach.

As he sat behind the wheel of his truck in Ponticelli, the effects of the grotesque mirage had taken over. He breathed heavily and felt his heart pumping like crazy as he wiped beads of sweat from his brow with his right hand.

Arriving in Nola, his white helmet and clearly marked vehicle met with silent stares from men and women who, with a few exceptions, were dressed in traditional Neapolitan mufti. The women were all in black shawls, shapeless dresses, stockings and wooden clogs. Likewise, for the men, their only extravagance is a brushed snap-brim felt hat and the shoes, no matter how often repaired, buffed to a shine.

He drove slowly through town past the Orsini Palace, Nola Cathedral, family-run negozi with paltry goods and near-empty shelves, two adjoining caffè with scattered sidewalk seating, and a storefront that could have been out of Third Ward Newark. The windows were painted a billiard table green to six feet from the bottom, leaving two feet of glass open to the light.

Jesus Christ, it's the spitting image of the Salerno Club on West 10th, complete with two goombahs playing their god damn dominoes, he thought after studying the four old men at the tables. Might as well start here. He had barely stepped down from the truck when the door flew open, and he was challenged by a man almost his size dressed head-to-tail in black.

"What the fuck do you want, Mr. MP? We're clean as a witch's tit," he scowled as he took in Stefano's massive frame. His clean-shaven but battered face softened. "You need anything? Just say it. Nothin' around here worthwhile that ain't ours."

"The name's Stefano Rizzano, folks are from Naples, and I mean deep in Naples. Catch my meaning?"

By this time, a second guy, also big and dressed all in black, appeared in the doorway. "Let me in on this, Mike. What the hell is this tin soldier doing here?"

Stefano motioned for them to join him at an empty sidewalk table. They were seated when on cue, three jelly jars filled to the rim with dark dago red were placed in front of them. He introduced himself all around and learned that Lorenzo Stuppi and Mike Creatori, as he had figured, were straight out of the Luciano Family. Ten others, including a cook, a beautiful combination manicurist and barber, and a butcher, had also made the trip to Nola seven years ago from New York. Unlike the men they were protecting, they were not exiled and closely watched and were free to go back and forth periodically. Otherwise, they would have gone stark-raving crazy.

Stefano tapped out three Camels and took one for himself before firing up all three with his Zippo lighter. After two deep drags, washed down with healthy gulps of vino, Stuppi decided to break three minutes of awkward silence, during which they searched for vulnerable openings. The door opener for Stefano was his rapid-fire recounting of his first weeks with the DeCavalcante family. They reveled in their new found camaraderie.

"Son of a bitch, it's just like us. All that bullshit we had to take before we started shelling it out ourselves," Stuppi said. "How about you, kid, remember the first time?"

"Hell, yeah. The Fulton Fish Market. Two dumb sons of bitches came up empty with their vigorish if they wanted to unload their cod. Busted 'em up real good and dumped the cod into the East River. Didn't have to do nothin' myself, just gave the order. That's the first time for me."

After fifteen minutes of blowing smoke up each other's butts, Creatori got serious. His brutally inquisitive features darkened, and he said, "So you wanna see the boss, and if we got it right, for no real fucking reason at all. Just to say hello. That right?"

Stefano laid it on thick. He knew the buttons to push. He recounted those boozy weekends with the Bruno-Scarfo Family in Philly and what a bunch of lunatics they were. But not so dumb to forget that although the powerful Five Families in New York might be a hundred miles away, they called the shots up and down the Eastern Seaboard. He could see that the thugs were awestruck whenever Vito Genovese's name came up. Now here he was, Stefano Rizzano, downing thick red wine with two of Vito's bodyguards while the big man himself was lounging around in his palace just up the hill.

Mike and Lorenzo had left him alone with his thoughts, his fourth jar of wine and an almost-empty pack of Camels, his only companions. Not a single Nola citizen, young, old, male, female, local cops, enfeebled cripples, priests and nuns, studiously paid him no attention. There was not a single word or nod of acknowledgment. Stefano couldn't orchestrate it any better.

Stuppi and Creatori returned to the table. He had hooked them. He had figured it right that their cynical, suspicious and bored boss could use a serious diversion, and who better than an army cop who says he is really a DeCavalcante family soldier? He was either too smart for his own good or uomo pazzo. No one fooled Vito, and in a few minutes, he'd know if this guy was for real or a crazy man.

The two bodyguards waited for Stefano to finish his wine. Then sandwiched him between them for the bumpy walk along a rock-strewn path to Vito's hillside home. He knew this was his only chance with the Big Boss and that he had only a few minutes to convince him how valuable a "Fish Hook" could be to the mob. There was no handshake, perfunctory hug, not even a smile when the two men, like the main characters of the Mutt and Jeff comic strip, Vito at five foot seven and Stefano at six foot three, sized each other up.

They talked for about five minutes when Genovese, now the smiling host, snapped his fingers, and a black-clad housekeeper appeared, seemingly out of nowhere, with an ornate silver tray, two sculpted, gold-rimmed glasses, and a bottle of red wine kept at perfect room temperature in a breezy balcony alcove.

"Didn't know if you'd be worth it. I'm satisfied, at least for now, still need some checking to do," Vito said. He then uncorked the bottle and poured the requisite two inches into each glass. They swirled and sniffed, and the self-satisfied diminutive host said, "A Barolo, 1928. None better."

Stuppi and Creatori, seated out of earshot at the far wall of the adjoining great room, were well into their third snifter of grappa. The potent brandy had predictably blurred their vision to where they failed to notice their boss had leaned closer and in front of Stefano. Shielded by the young punk's massive back and shoulders, they couldn't see what had caught their boss's attention.

At that moment, unless he really fucked up, Stefano knew that his Fulton Fish Market diploma had paid off, and his days as just another low-life mafioso had ended.

16

Four years after Stefano and Vito's 1943 tête-à-tête, Deborah Hammerstein Paasche stretched lazily across her bed in Tuxedo Park to untie the bundle of mail that had finally reached her from New York City. It was September 4, 1947.

These two events, years and continents apart, abolished class boundaries when a common victim provided motivation. Debbie, spoiled, upper class and never violent, would soon be seeking retribution for what Johan had forced upon her: physical abuse. Stefano, a gangster with bloody hands despite his deeply religious family background, didn't know if he could answer the calls for justice of the eight women in that barren schoolhouse outside Salerno. Hallucinations that began on the roadside in Ponticelli were now frequent, unwelcome visitors.

These seemingly unrelated events called for revenge, not mindless, but absolute and pure.

Stefano found just the right time and pushed the right

button when he bragged to Signore Genovese how he had squeezed everything he wanted from the Army and indicated he wanted out; the sooner, the better.

"How soon?" Vito raised his wine glass to his nose and inhaled appreciatively. Stefano wasn't fooled by the barely audible timbre of his short, direct question or his seemingly dispassionate demeanor. It was all by design. Stefano knew the answer would determine his career with the Mafia's New York Five Families.

"So, you want out?" Vito asked that afternoon in Nola, then added, "You got it. Never forget how. Just keep your fucking trap shut." Stefano learned in that moment that there wasn't anyone or anything in the world beyond the mob's reach.

"Grazie, molte grazie," a stunned Stefano replied, searching for the right word to sugarcoat his gratitude but not going too far. "Non dimenticherò mai, mai." He had heard the stories of how Vito dealt with broken promises, always bloody and painful. There was no way in hell he'd be added to the list. He'd keep his mouth shut.

So, without any effort on his part, he was pulled from the MP Battalion in Naples. As Chief Interpreter, Stefano boarded, along with two hundred and fifty Italian POWs, a troop ship to New York and a cross-country train to Phoenix. The prisoners were immediately put to work widening, trenching, clearing and beautifying the path for the Arizona Canal that united Maricopa County.

His job was a breeze. Within a week, it was made even easier when Lola Martini was ushered into his Quonset on the arm of her cousin Captain Carlo Martini, one of the one hundred fifty officers in the POW contingent. They didn't like to work, never picked up a pick, shovel or rake, and pushing the start button on a turbine was beneath their dignity. His interrogations in North Africa and Italy revealed that almost all officers were deserters, abandoning their men to surrender on their own. Lady Liberty offered these lazy, greasy, and obsequious officers the soft life at American POW camps. This left a labor force of one hundred enlisted men, a pitiful lot, to work in hundred-degree or higher temperatures while the officers barked orders from the shade of palm trees.

Stefano wanted to kick some serious ass after a memo from Washington took two weeks to finally filter down to him with a scrawled notation from Lieutenant Colonel Giuseppe ("just call me Joe") Crespi in the margin, "Take care of these creampuffs!" The original handwritten memo was pigeon-dropped from the mayor's mansion in New York by the Little Flower himself. Fiorello LaGuardia reminded FDR that Thomas E. Dewey would be no pushover in '44, and if he wanted to keep the White House, some velvet-gloved political shots had to be taken. He knew the families of many of these politically positioned officers, several having dined with him and Marie at Gracie Mansion. So it would be of no harm to anybody if they could ease their loneliness with family and friends for the duration.

Paperwork bounced around for almost two weeks before it was decided that these arrogant, useless officers had finally gone too far, and their request was denied. Everyone would now endure the same gastric torture in the mess hall and wait in line each evening for showers of green, torpid water from the canal. Rank distinctions mattered not.

A month into his Arizona sojourn, Stefano was ordered to report to Lt. Col. Crespi at Regimental Headquarters. When he arrived, his boss was sharing a smoke with two men under the makeshift parachute awning nailed up over the Quonset entrance to provide a modicum of shade. It was a failure. The shirts of all three men were dripping wet, and the backsides of their trousers were getting darker. For Crespi, a career officer, this came with the territory, but the other two guys were clearly miserable. Their well-tended, gray felt snap-brimmed hats had been discarded, the same for their black silk ties, and their white short-sleeve dress shirts clung to their upper bodies, revealing pot bellies sure to get bigger.

Pinned to their shirts were plastic-encased passes that gave them access to military bases that doled out Uncle Sam's bucks throughout the state. They provided open sesame for Lucky Luciano's thugs to plunder war contracts at will. An agreement with the military, fashioned by Luciano and his suave lieutenant, Frank Costello, had been brokered in New York City. It was cynical wartime expediency at its best. In exchange for a drastic reduction of Luciano's federal prison term for prostitution, the mafia agreed to safeguard transports entering and leaving the Port of New York, but only if the Five Families kept the booty they had been stealing from Uncle Sam's waterfront warehouses for the past eighteen months.

Word of the agreement quickly spread on both sides of

the Atlantic. From Manhattan's Lower East Side and the Bowery to the newly liberated sidewalk cafes of Salerno, Palermo and Naples, pre-invasion fear was transformed into greedy anxiety. Grizzled old men tired of dominoes and matching cards during raucous games of Scopa, young jobless punks, and hirsute young ladies rubbed their hands in anticipation at the thought of all those American ships, planes and trucks arriving with their manna from heaven.

In Arizona, Stefano made a quick appraisal of the two sweat-soaked goombahs waiting with Crespi.

"You got names?" he asked as he came to a stop three feet from the trio, just the right distance to intimidate his mafia cohorts. He towered over them, but size without connections meant little. Stefano had little doubt these guys were somehow mob-connected, but how and to what extent? He noted their unease.

"Never mind our names. We know yours, and that's all that fucking matters," the elder of the two, probably about forty-five, said while wiping his brow with a handkerchief. "God damn, it's hot, so let's make it quick."

He turned to his sidekick, an inch or so shorter and at least ten years younger, and said, "You take it from here. I'm going inside to soak up what those two swamp coolers are pumping out."

"Word is you got to talk to the big boss himself in Nola. That right?" he asked Stefano. The younger punk's question dripped with disbelief that this tin soldier had gone one-on-one with Vito Genovese in the boss's inner sanctum.

"Yeah, that's right."

"Said you were tired of playing Army cop, that you wanted out. Am I right so far?"

"You know it, or you wouldn't be here. So let's stop the bullshit."

This was Crespi's cue to get the hell out of there. He nodded in their direction and, without a word, strode back to the Quonset.

"Let's go over to the car; I've got a little love note for you." The mobster's words were a thinly veiled order. "Let's see how you handle it. Who knows, you could be out of that fucking uniform and back in civvies prima che tu lo sappia."

The job was simple enough; he just had to make Lorenzo Muretti disappear without a trace, not even so much as a pinky ring. The quicker, the better. Clipped to the two-page, block-printed note were the front and profile mug shots of Muretti when he was booked in New Orleans on June 4, 1938. Clearly visible was a three-inch scar revealing the lousy repair work done on Muretti's right cheek and jaw, a throat-cutting gone wrong.

The note concluded with the address and phone number of the De Luxe Motel at 1650 Oracle Road, a great spot where three major highways and important county roads intersected to give Muretti easy access to numerous military bases bulging with recruits and civilian workers.

"He's in cabin 4, and you're in cabin 7, paid up for a month. Don't tell us anything; just get it done, nice and clean. Here's the key."

"The name rings a bell, a real sweetheart. Ran into him

a couple of years ago, passing through on the way to Havana. What was it this time?" Stefano said, flicking his fingers over the mugshots.

"Rape and assault with intent to kill. Got off, and the bitch copped-out and disappeared. Her pimp boyfriend could make it into -- what the hell do you call that cartoon in the newspapers, you know, the one that tells you shit you can't believe but that it's all true?"

"Ripley's Believe It or Not."

"That's it. A record of how many things can happen when you fall down the stairs. His left ear was torn off, nose and jaw broken, wrists snapped like toothpicks, and both kneecaps."

It was obvious to Stefano that this pint-sized thug had orders to watch every move and gesture he made. He had been waiting until the note was read, folded and tucked into Stefano's shirt pocket, lit a cigarette and took a few steps to close the gap between them.

"Wait here, I've got a sweetheart of a toy for you," he said. He went back to the car and returned with a handkerchief-wrapped, fully loaded High Standard HDM .22 LR pistol.

"I bet my ass you never saw this beauty before. Army's had them only a few months, with the silencer no bang, just a little poof.

It required only a few minutes for Stefano to learn why Muretti had to be bumped-off. He was in Tucson on orders from Silver Dollar Sam Carollo, the New Orleans mob boss, who had been eyeing Arizona since the war broke out.

And why not Tucson? Military bases stretching from the Mexican border to the California state line, with all those people in uniform and civvies, an appetizing target for prostitution, loan sharking, and the numbers racket. Carollo had no way of knowing that Giuseppe Carlo Bonanno (Joe Banana) had enrolled his son, Salvatore, with the good Sisters of St. Joseph at the Saints Peter and Paul Boarding School in Tucson, and planned eventually to move there himself.

Joe Bonanno, a member of the mafia's Five Families in New York, with contacts worldwide, wanted no mob trouble in Tucson while his son was recovering from a severe mastoid infection. Mob bosses from California were also finding Arizona interesting as a potential mafia piggybank. For Bonanno, that was trouble.

So, Muretti had to go, sending a loud and clear message to Carollo -- hands off. There was no room here for the New Orleans family.

Two weeks after getting his instructions, Stefano unlocked the door to De Luxe Motel's Cabin 7, walked over to the bed and unpacked his overnight bag, spread his toiletries across the glass shelf under the mirror in the bathroom, returned to the bed and unwrapped the pistol. He had fired off three of the ten hollow-point bullets in the magazine and liked the results. At fifteen feet, it was hushed and accurate to the inch.

It was late Friday evening, and for the rest of the night and the next day, he kept Muretti's cabin under surveillance. It was so god damn easy. In the heat of the desert night, Muretti slept with the front door and four cabin windows open. Shortly after eleven o'clock the next night, he cautiously walked down a narrow space separating Cabins 4 and 5 to the window overlooking the bed. Muretti's head was no more than four feet away. He pumped a bullet into each of Muretti's eye sockets and another in his forehead. He tucked the pistol under his belt in the small of his back, waited until all lights were out in the courtyard, walked into the bedroom at the rear of Cabin 4, and put his six-foot-three-inch package of muscle to work.

He rolled Muretti and his wardrobe onto a large blanket on the floor, emptied the contents of every drawer in the cabin onto the blanket, and made a final inspection. Certain he had gotten it all, he rolled everything into a big bundle and used four of Muretti's belts and the electric wires from three lamps to tighten it up before lugging it outside to the trunk of his DeSoto station wagon. He tooled past the motel manager's office and left his key in the drop box outside the front door.

Less than two hours later, except for Muretti's identification credentials, Stefano had spread everything over a wide area of the Sonoran desert a few miles off the highway back to Phoenix. He stripped Muretti and drove him into the scrub-covered desert, a plump meal for the animals that were sure to close in before daylight.

In three weeks, time enough for all the requisite phone calls and paperwork, Stefano was handed his separation orders by Lt. Colonel Crespi, who shook his hand and said, "God damn, but I'd sure like to know how you pulled this off." Four days later, Stefano was enjoying blackjack at the mafia's Long Branch, New Jersey gambling house.

Drinks flowed, and after his fourth straight losing hand, a wise guy sauntered over, slapped his shoulder and when Stefano looked up, advised with a smile, "Kid, I think that another table is your ticket."

When the night was over, he was two thousand dollars to the good. He knew there was no such thing as good luck in the world of dons, capos, consigliere, and mafia underbosses. Good impressions and the smallest indiscretion never went unnoticed. The word was out that he had shared a bottle of vintage Barolo wine with Vito Genovese in Nola, and it was already paying dividends.

This was well appreciated, but his new-found prestige failed to lessen the growing intensity of the nightmares that awakened him sweat-soaked. These dark dreams made him question whether his bloody eleven-year journey with the mob was worth it. It was a dark and increasingly dreaded universe he knew nothing about.

17

On Saturday, July 26, 1947, it was confirmed for Anna Genovese what she had suspected for more than two years. She leaned back on her swivel desk chair, replaced the telephone receiver in its cradle and turned to the two men seated across from her in her Caravan Club office.

"I never trusted that fucking son of a bitch from day one." Her words a venomous affirmation that she was right and Vito and Lucky had been wrong.

Rosario and Giuseppe, the two bodyguards handpicked by Vito, sat silent and frozen across the desk from Anna. Her profanity-laced temper tantrums were legendary, but this was the first time they had witnessed one, and they had no intention of getting on her wrong side.

She was not exactly beautiful, but pretty enough, ruthless, ambitious and hardly sentimental. Twelve days after her husband, Gerard Vernotico, was found strangled on the roof of a Thompson Street building in Greenwich Village, she could finally marry Vito Genovese, who had openly pursued her since his wife's death due to tuberculosis. Vernotico's murder had Genovese's name written all over it. He was strangled with a sashchord, hauled to the roof of the six-floor tenement, then dragged over to an adjacent apartment house and left for the janitor to find.

The two thugs realized Anna's wrath was not directed at them, so they sat back to listen and enjoy, but not for long.

"About time we see what you two are worth. You, Rosario, is that a goddamn smile I see on your face? Wipe it off!" she scowled. "Now get out of here, the fags at the bar might be looking for playmates. I've got a phone call to make. I'll call you when I need you."

"Anna, it's Saturday; I wasn't expecting your call until tomorrow," a surprised Vito Genovese said as he was about to dig into a lunch of antipasto at Nuovo Villa Tommaro. The Coney Island restaurant was a sentimental favorite of Vito's since his boss, Joe Masseria, was murdered while they were playing pinochle in the dining room in 1931. It didn't escape Vito, then thirty-four, that Luciano had disappeared shortly before the shooting. The tone of her voice indicated a problem.

"What's come up? I got a feeling it ain't gonna be good," Vito said. "No fed bugs have been planted here, so you can talk, give me everything. I'll finish up my work here and be over for dinner on Sunday."

She pulled no punches. For seven years, the Cosa Nostra families, their bosses, members of the Commission, and that fucking Jew mastermind, Meyer Lansky, were being stiffed on a regular basis out of tens of millions of dollars. Today, it was confirmed, during a phone call from Switzerland, that the cache was resting in an untouchable bank account in Geneva. Her suspicions of Paasche were vindicated.

"So, I was just a clever dago broad, too self-important and suspicious for her own good," Anna said. "That if the guy wasn't a fellow wop family member, or blue-eyed and blonde to boot, he couldn't be trusted. Now we know, don't we."

"Sì, ora lo sappiamo," Vito said. "Let's get on with it. I'll get hold of the Jew. No one else right now, got it? Not New Orleans, Philly, LA, Cleveland or Chicago. For now, keep it to yourself."

Earlier that day, it was six o'clock in the evening in Geneva when a self-satisfied Jürgen Müller put down the telephone, arose from the easy chair and walked to the open French door to the balcony.

He stretched, took two deep breaths of the crisp evening air and smiled. It was the easiest half-million dollars he had ever earned. It was like taking candy from a baby. During his just-completed call to Anna Genovese, he had laid out every step taken to find the right pigeon to bribe Ludwig Stein, Accounts Manager at Credit Suisse. Stein was a perfect fit, married with a wife, three kids, a twenty-five-year-old mistress, a growing debt and a dead-end job. It required $75,000 placed in a private Zurich account, separate from Müller's half-million, and the payoff of a Jaguar and Mercedes, two pre-war beauties Stein couldn't afford but foolishly believed would enhance his image.

Müller was an old hand at this sort of thing. If you wanted someone to pry open one of the tightly held Swiss bank accounts, he was your man. The estranged son of a wealthy Bavarian pickled pigs' feet and sauerkraut maker, he had Accountancy and Economic degrees from the University of Bern and the University of Zurich. He was a thief who readily admitted he couldn't help himself. It took years for his father to discover that his son had been secreting withdrawals from the family's accounts and pocketing the money. Out in the cold, it took little time for Müller to stumble across a Banque Cantonale Vaudoise senior bookkeeper with personal and financial problems similar to Stein's.

A plan took shape. Not a cent was ever taken from the targeted accounts, only the names of the accountholders and the amount in each, the very best information for corporate espionage easily put to use by competitors. Along with his brain, Müller had other physical equipment that enabled him to cultivate and eventually bribe the lower-caste bank officers. He was a thirty-seven-year-old bachelor, an even six feet tall, one hundred and sixty-five slender pounds, near-perfect teeth, thick hair, quietly inquisitive blue eyes, erect posture, a carefully firm handshake, and a flawless complexion. Women easily fell in love, and men were eager to glad-hand him.

Today, he hoped the phone call had finalized his first encounter with international gangsters, but you never knew about the mafia, especially mobsters from Sicily and Naples. They were a bloody lot, murder an easy remedy for what troubled them. They could also be extremely stupid. Müller marveled how these narcissistic thugs, capable of every imaginable cruelty, took for granted that no one would ever double-cross them. During the three months since their first contact, he was amazed to discover how Johan Paasche had played them.

He had no way of knowing that the gangsters were certain they had the right man after their meeting at Vittorio's Castle in Newark with Boiardo. Or that till now, Richie "the Boot" had never rubbed shoulders with high-class society. They didn't like Paasche but were entranced by his beautiful wife, Debbie, and coming from the upper class as they did, Boiardo found it impossible to believe that there was even the slightest hint they would swindle the mob. He passed the word along, and even Lansky, who didn't trust his mother, climbed aboard. For Richie the Boot, it was a big step into the stratified air of the elite and privileged.

Paasche, ever the eavesdropper, realized this and, for the first time, weighed his opportunities when he overheard a sotto voce exchange between Boiardo and his son, Tony, as they all headed into the meeting.

"Debbie Paasche, now, she's one beautiful broad with class written all over. Am I right, or am I wrong?" Richie said.

"You're right, Pop, she's class on the hoof," Tony replied, "Now let's see what that pompous ass of a husband has on his mind."

Golden-tongued as usual, Paasche was given the keys to the kingdom. He was anointed transatlantic courier, the sole account holder, negotiator with German capitalists, and a bonus he never expected, the only accountant balancing the books.

Given Anna Genovese's reaction after Müller had laid down to the decimal the years of cleverly planned and carefully executed embezzlement by Paasche, he didn't want to contemplate what was in store for the swindler.

18

It had taken a lot for Rosemary Pringle Volker to send off her handwritten note to Debbie. She did her best to hide her marital problems, but by the late summer of 1947, they had become unbearable. She needed help, but from whom? Her life with her husband had entered a stage that she had only read about in trashy novels. Her dream of a well-deserved life of married bliss for a woman of her station had vanished. During the early years, she hardly noticed that her husband's offhanded criticism was growing more caustic. Could it be that Dr. Millard Dunston Volker, a renowned surgeon who swam in a sea of professional acclaim, was capable of jealousy? Everyone agreed Rosemary was a beauty, a brilliant anthropologist and an accomplished horsewoman who, at the beginning, enjoyed her verbal sparring with Millard, usually after a martini or two.

Perhaps that was it, she thought, when I wouldn't back off during verbal combat and realized that the son of a bitch I married was a bully, pure and simple. Christ, who'd have thought the first time was over something as mundane as politics, and of all places at the Club during a roundtable gabfest with Roger and Pauline and another couple, what was their name? I still don't know how we got so crazy over Walter Edge and Vincent Murphy.

"Just look at his background, and you'll see he was the right man to put in the governor's mansion," Millard said, confident as usual that his assessment would be readily accepted. "Here it is, October of '44, the war's winding down, and we need leaders who are real leaders, not political poseurs."

"Hell, he's over seventy years old," Roger said. "When the war ends, there'll be big changes, not only here in the States but around the world, and that certainly means New Jersey, where we got big problems. He's an old man. Does he have the energy?"

"Like hell, he's an old man," Millard scowled. "Just take a look at what...."

"No need to go any further," Rosemary rebuked, "What the hell does a millionaire and former Ambassador to France know about poverty, homelessness, racism, and, yes, we have plenty of that, too."

"You forget, dearest, he was once our Governor granted it was well before our time," Millard said scornfully, his tone just short of open mockery. "And we mustn't forget his ten years representing our noble state in the U.S. Senate."

"That was then, and this is now," she retorted, "not banquets at the Élysée Palace where guests daintily fingered pâté de foie gras and sipped Heidsick Monopole champagne, wouldn't you say?"

"No, I wouldn't say," her husband, getting hot under the collar, replied. "What does Paris have to do with anything?"

"Everything," she said after another swig of her martini. "Having a valet open your limo's door at the Rue du Faubourg Saint-Honoré curbside is hardly the same as walking into a Father Divine eatery for a ten-cent meal to keep from going hungry."

She had been to Paris twice before their marriage, Millard never. She spoke the language, he didn't and was well aware that his wife trumped him when it came to the social graces. During conversations that evolved into polite debates, either between them or in mixed company, she almost always shied away from putting him on the spot when he was wrong. Not tonight.

Roger, Pauline and the two interlopers sensed that things had taken a bad turn and began shifting about uneasily. Roger took his wife's right arm and nodded to the other couple, "Time to refresh these, don't you think? Hi-de-ho to the bar we go!"

Rosemary was about to join them when Millard grabbed her left wrist and forcibly turned her around to face him. He was sure of his every move, sensing, without even a glance, a safe landing place for his martini on the small round table to his right. As intended, the tightening grip on her wrist was painful. For some unfathomable reason, she made no attempt to pull free or mutter a complaint. She felt his hot breath as he moved in even closer.

"Don't you ever, ever embarrass me again," he hissed

threateningly. "We're clear on this, aren't we, dearest?"

Then it happened. With his right hand, the index and middle fingers extended and rigid, he poked her very hard on the chest between her right breast and clavicle. "Never!" Then another poke, this time hard enough to knock her off balance, "Never!"

It was all over in a few seconds, not noticed by Club members as they turned to the dance floor and began to sway to the silky, smooth rhythm of Artie Shaw's Begin the Beguine, courtesy of Bob Oaks and his Melody Masters.

"What do you say we dance," Millard said, his left hand on her back as he ushered her onto the dance floor. "We'll show them a thing or two."

And they did. The Volkers, both trim and athletic, her a knockout and he with screen-idol looks, were the Club's best dancers, no doubt about it. Other dancers gave them enough room to display their footwork. Rosemary hoped her thin smile over clinched teeth camouflaged the anguish that was consuming her.

Millard had obligated them to take the spotlight on the dance floor. The handclapping of the onlookers tacked together the initial panel of the ominous façade that would become their life. With the pain in her wrist, chest and shoulder now extending down her right arm, Millard had initiated Rosemary into a sisterhood of fear. She was well aware that a community of physically and verbally abused women existed, but it had been unthinkable that she would become a member.

She'd pitied them and wondered why they just didn't get

out, escape, because, after all, this was America. Her essay was awarded an A+ by her Vassar professor, a supportive, very conservative chap and Yale classmate of her father, investment banker Thomas James Pringle.

It was only natural that the Volkers and Pringles would summer at the same resorts and watering holes, in this case, Ocean House, the sprawling Victorian artifact on the Watch Hill, Rhode Island waterfront. It was inevitable that the two most beautiful family specimens would meet and, with their impeccable social and bank account credentials, join in marriage.

19

That was then, and this was September 1947. In the three years since Rosemary was forced to use pancake makeup and wear blouses with long sleeves to hide the black and blue stigmata, she had lost count of the abusive incidents. All by a man who, like his father and grandfather, had pledged to a life of "first do no harm."

His maternal grandfather, Dr. Jefferson Dunston, was a throat surgeon, ever thankful to the tobacco industry that supplied him with an endless stream of rich patients. His father, Dr. Frederick Volker, was an innovator at the forefront of lung lobectomy surgery. With this background, cardio-thoracic surgery was natural for Dr. Millard Dunston Volker.

Rosemary had been slapped, roughly shaken by the shoulders, pushed against the wall, and profanely mocked by Millard during his fits. It was always when they were alone. To the world outside their sprawling Upper Montclair home, theirs was the ideal marriage. He had forced her to accept that their marriage was a charade.

She was not in the habit of asking for help, but the note to Debbie was a first step. Something had to be done, but exactly what and how? David was seven-years-old, Lisa five, and it was only a matter of time before they understood that their parents' confrontations were more than verbal contests. She was certain that her housekeeper Elaine, who had her own isolated living quarters, was aware despite never giving so much as a hint that she knew.

Today Rosemary would be meeting Debbie for an early evening dinner at the Hahne's Department Store Pine Room. Rosemary was introduced to the hoity-toity restaurant by wives in Volker's country club social circle. After learning of her Cultural Anthropology degree from Vassar, they insisted that she join their project to refurbish and restore the Stephen Crane birthplace in downtown Newark. They were all at least twenty years older and she knew she would be doing the heavy lifting, but joined up anyway.

The polite pleading of women with too much time on their hands wasn't the only reason why the restoration of the dilapidated building on Mulberry Street was so appealing to Rosemary. Crane, author of "The Red Badge of Courage" and other realist novels, was one of her cherished favorites. Her decision was made even easier when her research showed that her current hometown of Montclair was once Cranetown, founded by the author's ancestors.

With prompting from Rosemary's father, a few members

of the City's social elite made the necessary phone calls, and the New Jersey Historical Society handed Rosemary the keys to a small fourth-floor, private office with a large window overlooking Military Park, a desk, chair, typewriter, telephone, ornate desk lamp and two leather upholstered visitor chairs. Two large, framed vintage photos of bustling downtown Newark circa 1925 adorned the walls.

Rosemary knew it would be a surprise to Debbie that she had asked a friend to join them for dinner. Grace DeMarco, the first female Chief Clerk of the Essex County Courthouse, would be with her. Grace was filling in for a sick employee at the front counter of the Clerk's office when Rosemary came in for a copy of the police report for the arrest and conviction of the two guys who had burgled and vandalized the Crane birthplace to the tune of fifteen thousand dollars. The document was needed for the insurance company and to pull at the heartstrings of potential donors.

An easy rapport had developed between Rosemary and Grace during the weeks before their dinner with Debbie. For two or three blessed days a week, her office had become her sanctuary from the malevolent inner sanctum that Millard was creating in Montclair.

Except for the few times Rosemary was joined by the country club matrons, she enjoyed lunch at the Pine Room with Grace. They had much in common: good looks, quick wit, college degrees and a gift for conversation that was initially guarded but eventually flowed freely along with their wine. Each sensed that deeply felt personal concerns were being avoided.

This changed a month earlier when Millard was attending a conference of cardio-thoracic surgeons in Chicago, and Rosemary accepted Grace's invitation for Friday dinner at her ten-room Italian Renaissance on Wilden. Except for a cook and a housekeeper, she lived alone. Her divorce settlement four years ago included the mansion, domestic help, generous alimony, and other goodies bundled together by her cutthroat attorney, Chester Bruno.

That evening, the two women, with scotch glasses in hand, toured the first floor admiring an elaborately framed copy of Georges de La Tour's "Penitent Magdalene." But it was a beautifully done oil on canvas of Diego Velázquez's "Las Meninas" on the hallway wall that took Rosemary's breath away.

"Remarkable! I've never seen a Velázquez masterpiece reproduced so beautifully," Rosemary exclaimed as she inched forward to closely study the intricate brushstrokes. "You don't happen to have a master painter on your family tree, do you? I love Velázquez. I consider him to be up there with El Greco."

"No. I commissioned it as a gift for a really great guy I once knew." Grace sipped her scotch and stepped forward to brush shoulders with Rosemary. "He refused to take it with him. 'You should keep it to remember what we had,' he said."

"Where did he go?" Rosemary said as she turned to scan the expensive Renaissance trappings that adorned the hall, parlor and dining room.

"Back to his wife." This stunned Rosemary. She finished off the last drops of her scotch, confident that the heavy-bottomed Haig & Haig glass hid her astonishment. She was only just getting to know her, but there was no way that Grace came across as a homewrecker.

"Want to talk about it?"

Grace's reaction surfaced in the clear and honest expression that crossed her face. "I guess I could start by saying I was a twenty-four-year-old virgin when I married John Fusina, a dentist with a great root canal reputation. He had no problem handling tooth decay and extraction, but he never got to the root of who he really was."

"Did he ever find out?"

"I doubt whether John's ego would ever allow it," Grace hesitated. Had she opened a door better left closed? For weeks, she had sensed that an unspoken special kinship had developed between them. But why? Her father was forced to use the DeMarco family jewels for a down payment on his first optometrist shop; Rosemary's rich husband writes articles praised internationally by fellow heart surgeons. "I had my doubts about John for a long time," she said. "Today, I still wonder how it took only one fleeting moment for the truth about him to come out."

"And that was?"

"That John Fusina was a self-absorbed bully. My epistle was like St. Paul's; no, there wasn't a loud clap of thunder, and I wasn't thrown off a horse. But I did have my bolt of lightning."

"Bolt of lightning?"

"One hard, tight-fisted punch to the face from John. Dazzling brightness and I actually saw stars before everything turned black as I tumbled ass-over-teakettle behind the fireplace sofa."

"And..." Rosemary, stunned, finally sputtered, "Where did this happen?"

They left the hall and started through the parlor to the dining room, where the table had been set by housekeeper Slyvia. Grace tugged at Rosemary's sleeve and directed her attention across the room. "Over there. The son of a bitch clobbered me in front of the fireplace, and I ended up face-down on the floor behind the sofa on the left. That was it, just once. I was out of here in less than an hour and didn't come back until the divorce was final and the settlement erased him from my life."

This revelation was one of several surprises that they uncorked, along with their after-dinner Rémy Martin and espresso. Grace's shared experience was the coup de grâce that severed all restraints. Words flowed freely. Little did they know that more revelations at the dinner to come with Debbie would thrust them into a kaleidoscopic demimonde of characters, places and violence.

20

Tony Boiardo was about to be put on the hot seat. He was seated at his customary place at the bar at Vittorio's Castle and was working on three fingers of bourbon over ice when the bartender replaced the intercom phone on its hook and turned, "Your dad wants to see you. He's waiting in his office."

Tony finished his drink and said, "Hit me again."

"Mr. Boirado sounded like he wanted you in there right now."

Tony found his father deep into a phone call when he entered the office. A reddish-purple flush darkened the Boot's cheeks and jowls, the first sign of one of his father's dangerous moods. He cupped his hand over the mouthpiece and looked across his desk at Tony, now slouched in a padded leather chair, twirling the ice in a fresh glass of bourbon on the rocks. "Put the fucking glass down," he menaced softly in a tone of voice seldom, if ever, used among close family blood. "I don't want that brain of yours floating in booze when we talk after this call."

Tony placed his drink on an onyx coaster at the corner of the desk. He fired up a Camel and studied his father's darkening features. The phone call lasted another five minutes, during which the elder Boiardo did a lot of nodding and very little talking, mostly an oft-repeated. "Non preoccuparti," and ended with "La questione verrà gestita!"

"What's it you'll be taking care of, and who were you yapping with?" Tony asked, his harsh tone moderated enough to keep his father, who was already fuming, from blowing his top. "Come on, Pop, give."

"Rico Frenzelli," the Boot's voice had the accusing ring of an executioner about to quarter and disembowel a victim. "That's right, your cousin Nancy's Godfather. We became made-men the same year. Today, I find out he's been stiffing us."

"Never would have guessed. I thought that Lucky and Vito had set him up in Manhattan?"

"That's the goddamn rub! Frenzelli Accounting and Notary Services did okay with our laundry at first, but then Rico got greedy. The son of a bitch needed a forklift to handle the Franklins we're feeding him each month, which includes our moola, Waxey Gordon's and the DeCavalcante family's here in Jersey. That's right, our moola, all on its way to the Krauts."

"The phone call, that's what changed your mind?" Tony said.

"You got it. Came from Anna Genovese, the most

suspicious goddamn broad in the world. She hated the deal with the Nazi-loving, big-money boys in Germany from the beginning. So she dug in and found out we've been fucked over for the past six years."

"Who would be god damn dumb enough?" Tony said.

"It began when Frenzelli hooked up with, guess who, take a guess…Johan Paasche. That was two years ago, but Anna says Paasche had been at it a lot longer, maybe even four years longer."

During the next half-hour, Richie the Boot stated his bloodlust over and over again. After all, he was the capo who gave his word that the big city mafia families couldn't find anyone better than Johan Paasche to handle their German investments. How wrong could he be?

The Monday, August 4, 1947, phone call from Anna Genovese detailed how, for almost seven years, Paasche and Frenzelli had been skimming money destined for a mafia Swiss account into one of his own, maybe even more than one. How did this happen? The pencil-pusher Frenzelli was keeping a book on it all, or was he?

During that thirty minutes, the Boot put together what would be done. "I only say it once. You get the job done just like I told you. No fuck-ups."

"There's not gonna be any fuck-up."

"He'll be in town tomorrow afternoon. Just convince him why we're talking to him in Elizabeth and not here at my office and a week earlier than his monthly drop-off."

"Nessun problema, I got it all. Pick him up at the North

Elizabeth Station. He always comes in on the Erie noon train from Manhattan for his monthly drop-off. But won't he be suspicious? Christ, I can't even remember the last time, if ever, the swag was dropped off in Elizabeth. It's always been here at Vittorio's Castle."

"Tell him DeCavalcante and Waxey Gordon want to see how their Nazi stocks are doing, maybe increase the profit margin. See what ideas he can come up with. Make it convincing."

"Let's lay it out as fancy as we can," Tony said with a smile that was more of a smirk as he exhaled cigarette smoke from his nostrils. "Give him a great last meal."

Like two men reaching for their glasses of grappa between hands of gin rummy at the club, Boirado and son switched from thoughts of torture and extermination of a comrade to visions of the sumptuous table to be laid out at Spirito's Restaurant.

"His favorite is scungilli and linguini in that sauce he always brags about, olive oil, minced anchovies and garlic," Tony said." I'll phone the Fulton Fish Market to make sure Mario has the scungilli delivered to Spirito's no later than ten."

"Make sure there's plenty for five and that he throws in some mussels, oysters and clams," his father said.

Easily interspersed with the details of the torture and pre-ordained disappearance of Frenzelli were mouthwatering descriptions of the final meal they were preparing for the mob betrayer. The various seafoods, pastries and bread, tomato slices topped with roasted mozzarella, plump capers and sardines swimming together in a spicy sauce, with four different wines.

After dinner, the reckoning would occur at the nearby DeCavalcante enclave a few blocks from the Elizabeth River.

"I'll start working on it right away, have two Lincolns waiting outside the Third Street side entrance to the restaurant," Tony said. "Make sure Benito will be driving the one with you, me and Frenzelli. Carlisimo will have Waxey and Sam in his. Hell, we can almost walk over, but the DeCavalcante's Lincolns add class, and it's all about class with Frenzelli."

"Call home and have Theresa pack an overnight bag for you," the Boot said. "We'll pick you up in about an hour. I'll call Sam; we can expect the same rooms and great meal at his mom's house; God bless her soul."

"What about Paasche? You haven't muttered a goddamn thing about the mastermind." his son asked. "What gives?"

The look on his father's face was enough of an answer to convince him that it was the wrong time and place for his question. Tony quickly jumped into the details of what would be waiting for what remained of Frenzelli after they were finished at the DeCavalcante's.

"I'll make sure the Marcettis have one of their smaller fishing boats tied up at the end of High Street. Couple miles, and it's deep water."

"Never could figure him. Almost the family, Nancy's godfather, even called him Zio, our favorite uncle."

"Remember, he's a made-man, so no fuck ups, like it never happened. Dieci capi di capi has a stake, and if you fuck up, I fuck up."

The following evening, with two muscular mob grunts working in shifts for two hours, the assassins could lay claim to a spreading lake of blood on the basement floor and the bank account number and key where Frenzelli had stashed his part of the take. "Jesus H. Christ, how much? You better not be shitting us!" a DeCavalcante soldier, sleeves rolled above the elbows and both hands bloody, shouted and then looked over to his boss. "Ten thousand Cleveland's a month for two years? That's a quarter of a million!"

That's all they were able to get from Frenzelli, fully aware that the betrayer's loot would be only a fraction of Paasche's. How much more was there? And where was it?

Frenzelli's still-warm body was dumped into the deep channel running past Tottenville, Staten Island, to Sandy Hook and the Atlantic Ocean. Two cement blocks were lashed to the waist, ensuring a feast for crabs and other bottom feeders. As Richie the Boot feared, Tony fucked up. Instead of using chains or wire to secure the cement blocks, he used heavy-duty sisal rope that quickly absorbed the blood that had pooled under and around the body.

This provided underwater scavengers with a tasty appetizer, especially the crabs that quickly clawed the rope apart. The cement blocks sank to the channel floor, and the body popped to the surface, where the swift currents carried it into a muddy marsh on the Staten Island shore. It took only a day for the body to be discovered, now a problem for the New York City Police.

The next afternoon, with the Richmond County Medical Examiner in tow, homicide Lieutenant Mike Shanahan watched as a sheet covered stiff was pulled from its refrigerated slot at the morgue and uncovered. Over the past few years, Shanahan and his partner, Sergeant Stew Rivas, one of only a few homicide dicks with old shields, had developed reputations as the department's organized crime experts. It didn't take much to see this guy was whacked by the mob. The age, how could you tell with its head more like a sliced-up purple turnip? The rest was educated guesswork. The corpse was minus eight fingers, leaving only the thumbs, each stump most probably the result of a question with a wrong answer. His left ear had been cut off, and what was once a nose was split open like a clam shell. The neck was sliced from ear to ear.

"What do you say, Dr. Mendoza?" Shanahan turned to the Medical Examiner, "A mob hit, right?"

"We've been digging them up all over the island for years, but not many like this. I'll have the autopsy report ready in the morning," Mendoza said.

"I'll phone in what I've got. Looks like we'll be here for a while," the detective said. "So will Sgt. Rivas after he finishes up at the discovery site. Hope you have a police budget hotel and restaurant to recommend. I'll take his belongings with me now."

He wasn't sure yet that his educated guess was right on target. And he didn't know that the slicing and dicing was only the first act of mafia revenge.

21

The preamble to the second act occurred two nights earlier. Giulia Frenzelli was not alarmed by the lateness of the ringing telephone. Rico called at any hour, especially when he was out of town. She had not heard from him since early yesterday morning, just before boarding the Erie milk-run commuter to Jersey. Now, he was telling her he was headed to Elizabeth, not Newark, for his monthly drop-off at Vittorio's Castle.

This surprised her, and even more so when she detected nervous uncertainty in her husband's voice despite the noise outside the telephone booth.

"Elizabeth? Hell, how long has it been since you've even been there?" she wondered aloud, making no attempt to hide her concern.

"Not to worry. Boiardo, DeCavalcante and Waxey Gordon have put their heads together and come up with some ideas they want to talk about. Marcello's holding down the fort."

This was all news to Giulia. She had been tempted to call Marcello Vitrioni at the brokerage office, but what the hell would he know? Rico and Marcello were blood brothers, their friendship going back to when they were still burying stiffs in the Jersey meadows. High school graduates parlayed their made-man status with a gift for numbers and gladly exchanged pistols, chainsaws, shovels and axes for pencils and ledgers. When her husband was offered rent-free space in an almost fashionable office building on the mid-East Side with a stenciled Rico Frenzelli Investments, LLC on its front door, Marcello came along with him.

They were often tight-lipped when she asked questions, and she pulled no punches about how much this angered her. Giulia was the daughter of Gino Cappelletti, a third-generation mafioso from Taormina, and god damn it, if that doesn't entitle me, what the hell does! This better be him, she thought as she reached for the bedside telephone.

"Giulia, this is young and good-looking Tony, spero di non averti svegliato," Tony Boiardo purred.

"Damn right, you woke me up! Hell, it's two o'clock in the morning; what did you expect?" she scowled. "Perche tu? Dov'è mio marito?"

"Joe Ida, Don of the Bruno-Scarfo family in Philly, wants in on our meeting. Compliments of Vito Genovese, of course. Rico's going to be around for a day or two longer," Tony said.

"I know Joe Ida and how greedy he is," Giulia said. "Why wasn't he there in the first place? And again, where the hell is my husband?"

"Hey, Joe's not all that bad, and he's a happy man," Tony said, then embellished his lies, "Even muscled up a big yacht in Atlantic City so we can all celebrate, maybe do some fishing."

"Why isn't Rico talking for himself?" Giulia was probing now but carefully.

"They're all headed to South Jersey as I speak. Heard them talking about a stop at Tuckerton. The great restaurant there, great seafood that your hubby slobbers over. Arrivederci."

Giulia heard the click as Tony hung up, not knowing that at the end of the line, he was turning with a smile to others in the DeCavalcante basement bar. "She's home. Got her buttoned-up for at least three days. Knowing that flashy son of a bitch Rico, you can bet their place is quiet and fancy, with a doorman and all. Gonna take some planning."

He focused on two dapper thugs sitting on barstools during Frenzelli's torture and murder. His gaze was met by two silent smirks before they turned to the bartender and motioned for refills. For them, the macabre scene was nothing new. They were there to collect the details, no matter how small, to do their job.

There were seven hangers-on sitting silently at the bar. The only sound in the basement came from the rollers squeezing the last of the blood sopped from the tiled floor into a bucket.

The two hitmen spent the remaining hours that morning in Elizabeth, wining and dining at the DeCavalcante home before spending two nights getting laid at a well-stocked mob whorehouse in a converted mansion with a clear view of the Manhattan skyline. They waited until ten o'clock on the second day before calling Giulia, who, as they had hoped was wide awake, nervous as hell since Tony's phone call.

"Giulia? I hope I have the right number," the shorter, smoother talker said, unsure of what to say next, but her response opened the door.

"You gotta name?"

"You don't know me. I know Rico, actually worked a few cleanup jobs with him, way back when," the thug lied. "Names Mario, Mario Spagnola." Another lie. They never use their real names.

There was a long pause before Giulia's whispered answer, "So what's the call about?"

"Just got in from Atlantic City and have a nice little present from Rico for you. Bet it's expensive as hell, silk ribbon and all."

"A present from Rico, and you're bringing it all the way from Atlantic City?" All the wrong vibrations took over. Giulia was in a state of silent frenzy but managed, "From Rico? I thought he was out fishing?"

"Yeah, damn if he ain't the luckiest paisano ever," he said. "Caught two big ones, tuna, I think, off Cape May. That was in the morning, and then it was the Atlantic City Race Track in the afternoon. Hit three in a row the first day; that's when I bumped into him strictly by accident. Had a few drinks, and he handed me a present for you and said to put it right in your hands to be sure you got it. He wants to see you wearing it when he gets home in a few days."

"In a few days? And he's spending all this time fishing, a man who loves seafood but hates the ocean. He can't even swim." Giulia dabbed a hanky to wipe the snot running from her nose. "It's not hearing from him that's got me," her words were now tentative. "It's ten o'clock now, let's say two o'clock this afternoon."

He put down the phone and, with a smile, shot a thumbs-up at his pal, who responded, "Damn if you ain't the smoothest fucking liar."

They had another errand to attend to that morning before their rendezvous with Giulia. They grabbed a taxi to Nardo and Sons, a Ford Mercury dealership on Bergenline in Hoboken, picked up a black, four-door Mercury Eight and drove it straight from the showroom. The owner, Nick Nardo, had handed over phony registration, legit auto insurance, two sets of keys and his personal phone number. Nick operated three auto dealerships across Hudson County, all of them mob laundering operations.

They drove it through the Holland Tunnel to lower Manhattan, where they got out in front of one of the older office buildings. They nodded to the liveried doorman as they sauntered into the lobby toward the elevators. He let them in without question. He had given them the once over and sized-up that their well-tailored outfits bore either Rogers Peet or Brooks Brothers labels. It was all about details. Their marks were upscale and deserved the finest.

They casually studied the wall directory of occupants and waited for the expected call to divert the doorman's attention to the service phone at the front desk. Sure that a phone conversation had started, the tall mug strolled past the bank of elevators and peered left and right along a dimly lit service hall that ran the width of the building. He confirmed what they had been told, that there was a service elevator to the roof adjacent to the large double door that opened to a loading dock at the rear of the building.

Three minutes later, they stepped from the elevator on the sixth floor just across the hall from Rico Frenzelli Investments, LLC. On the way up, they carefully checked the reinforced pockets sewn into the lining of their jackets for the tools they would need. A beautiful brunette of no more than twenty eyed them with a smile as they stepped through the door. The smile was replaced by fear when the shorter of the two strangers moved instantly to her desk, slammed his right hand down on the phone, lifted his left forefinger to his lips and whispered, "Shush, don't panic. Not a word now, not a fucking word. Just blow, take the day off. It's on us."

They turned toward the inner office door. Their work inside with Marcello shouldn't take long. The one question they wanted an answer to left no room for bullshit.

"Where the hell did you and Rico stash the money?" When Marcello heard the unmistakable sound of two heavy-duty zippers being drawn open, he had no doubt why they were in his office.

Just blocks away, a swarthy man of medium height walked from a public telephone to an unmarked van and joined two other men, who, like him, were dressed in janitor coveralls. The van turned east and circled to a stop beside the loading dock of the building that housed Rico Frenzelli Investments. They were the cleanup and detail team.

This would have to be a quick chopping and sawing job. Their next stop was only a few hours away at a swank, upper-east side they had sized up yesterday afternoon. Everything they needed was there: a service elevator, a loading dock and plenty of parking space.

At three o'clock that afternoon, just outside Atlantic City, valets at Leonardo's Seafood restaurant had two Lincolns and two Packards idling in wait for their occupants to emerge after a sumptuous lunch. Five minutes later, they pocketed hefty tips from the unsmiling chauffeurs, who then slid into the drivers' seats and waited for their bosses.

With his wife, Maria, tucked in beside him, a beaming Leonardo Gamba held the front door open and acknowledged with a handshake the accolades of his departing guests. "Il migliore di sempre," Joe Ida gushed, only to be outdone by Sam Decavalcante's fingers to the lips salute. "La tua lobster thermidor deve uccidere."

Anna's last phone call let them know exactly where they stood, not only with her but with her husband and, most importantly, with Lucky. She made it clear that they were way over their heads and were too damn dumb to realize it. She reminded Decavalcante that this was not just a case of one boss eliminating another who was demanding a bigger slice of his numbers action. Mafia families across the country, including the dumb bastards at the table, were being swindled out of millions.

"I always had doubts about that squeaky-clean bastard," she spit the words into the phone. "And that goes for his wife with a name like Deborah Hammerstein Paasche, the beautiful bitch who gave you all a hardon."

Two days earlier, Rico Frenzelli spilled his guts in the Decavalcante basement. The hitmen who had exchanged words earlier that night with Tony Boiardo silently watched the slicing and dicing from their stools at the bar. Before the week was out, their equally brutal interrogation technique would be put into practice on Rico's wife and his partner, Vitrioni; their pleas for mercy fell on deaf ears. The two killers were convinced that it was a waste of time, that their victims had been kept in the dark from the start. But the money was good and they didn't pick the marks, only blotted them out.

It was agreed that there was no percentage of coming down on Debbie, but she would be closely watched. Deborah's housekeeper was paid-off and replaced with a stooge who reported in three times a week. Anna learned that the couple barely spoke to each other and that Johan had been slapping his wife around. He was last seen by the spy housekeeper on Sunday, two days before the mob's bloodletting began when he left after breakfast with the usual leather briefcase and valise.

Still unanswered were three questions: where and when could they get their hands on Johan Paasche, and where the fuck was the mob's money?

22

Grace DeMarco and Rosemary Pringle worked closely with Margie Bruning, the new manager of the Hahne's Department Store Pine Room, to ensure that the right table was ready for their early dinner with Debbie Paasche that Friday. It would include a chilled bottle of Moët & Chandon to get things started.

Debbie was looking forward to the dinner. Rosemary's high-spirited descriptions of the horse shows she entered and the blue ribbons and trophies she won were always a delight. It was a last-minute decision by Debbie after leaving her family home in Tuxedo Park to detour through Fort Lee across the George Washington Bridge to her co-op on East Riverside Drive. She'd find out if that son of a bitch husband of hers had taken it over or created a pied-à-terre in which to romp with his retinue of roundheels.

"Mrs. Paasche, good to see you; it's been a while," the co-op garage attendant said. "Can I ask, how is your husband?"

"You haven't seen him?"

"No, ma'am. The only one who's been around is your housemaid," he said. "She left without picking up the check you left for her at the front desk."

Debbie expected to spend no more than a few minutes cruising a sprawling space of the twelfth-floor co-op haunted by memories she couldn't dispel. Instead, she was rocked back on her heels when she stepped into a scene of destruction. Every piece of furniture was broken or gutted, and the stuffing of sliced mattresses was strewn through the two bedrooms. The kitchen was not spared during the maelstrom. The safe behind an expensive Rembrandt copy had been ripped from the wall and pried open. It lay on the floor with non-negotiable bonds strewn around it. She gathered her wits and reached for one of the three apartment phones only to find all of their cords severed.

It required less than an hour for her, the manager, the insurance broker, her attorney and uniformed cops to gather and package the details of what had happened and what, if anything, she might know. She signed off where her signature was needed and was told by one of the uniforms that a major crimes detective would be in touch. It was almost four o'clock, and although there should be some traffic, she could still make her dinner appointment in Newark.

The doorman held in wait for her to get behind the wheel of her Daimler and was about to close the door when she stopped him, "Hold on a minute, Otto, let me give you two phone numbers," she said as she handed him a business card with scribbling on the back. "I'll make it worth your while. If my husband or anyone else shows up, no matter who, even the police, leave a message at my number; that's the first one. If you can't reach me, the other number is my attorney. And I've got your number."

From the moment the front wheels of her Daimler pulled onto Riverside Drive, Debbie's mind was a cavalcade of muddled visions. That bastard husband of mine, was this all about him? Where did it begin? When he abandoned me on our honeymoon on the dock of the Danube River?

She reached the Department Store on Broad Street shortly before five, took the ticket from the valet and entered the huge atrium that dominated the four-story building. The Pine Room was the marquee attraction on the first floor, a large exquisitely decorated room with pine paneling from floor to ceiling.

"I'm with Rosemary Pringle. Has she arrived?" she said as she ran her eyes up and down the hostess and easily discerned why the Pine Room was considered classy. Dressed in a well-cut blue serge shift, the very pretty, raven-haired hostess picked up a wine list and menu and reciprocated with an intense perusal of Debbie. A discrete two-strand faux pearl necklace, sapphire brooch and a highly polished brass name tag inscribed with "Margaret" failed to disguise that this rather tall woman came across more as an athlete than a restaurant hostess.

"You must be Debbie Paasche," Margie said. "Rosemary and Grace are already seated; they're waiting for you to arrive before popping a bottle of bubbly that's been cooling."

What the hell is going on here? Never met me before,

but calls me Debbie and Rosemary, just like we're all bosom buddies. And who the hell is Grace?

An ebullient Rosemary arose from her seat at the table, as beautiful as ever in autumn-colored attire, stepped forward and, with a tight hug and kisses on both cheeks, said playfully, "I'm so glad you could make it. But tell me, are you having your make-up professionally applied? You look great!"

"Not quite. We'll have plenty of time to talk about it," Debbie said as she backed off, held her old friend at arm's length, and cast a look both inquisitive and admiring at the woman seated at the table. "And you must be Grace."

Grace arose from her seat and reached across the table to shake Debbie's hand. "That's me, I'm the surprise package. It's all Rosemary's doing, and she insisted we all had something in common. Before we get into that, first let's get into…."

"Unh, unh, unh, this is where I come in," Margie said just as Grace was about to reach for the sweating bottle of Moët & Chandon that had been waiting patiently in the champagne bucket. "Take your seats; I'll do the honors, then get out of your hair. Need anything special, tell the waitress and she'll let me know."

The trio tapped their glasses. "Tchin-tchin!" Rosemary said, followed by "Salute!" from Grace. They took the first sip, followed with sighs of approval.

"Rosemary, you know I'm hardly a snob, but what gives with all the informality?" Debbie said. "What's with all this first name stuff with the restaurant hostess?"

"Call her Margie. She's all class. Treated Grace and me like royalty the two to three times a week we could get together for lunch." Rosemary raised her glass and waited for the others, "Here's to Margie; a friend in need is a friend indeed."

"This is our table. Margie anointed it," Grace chimed in. "She stops by whenever she can. We've come to enjoy her, but lunch is always busy, so it's not very often. Margie now makes sure the table is available during the last half-hour of service so that when she wraps up, she'll be able to share the local gossip."

"And damn, does she have the goods," Rosemary said. "You can't believe how many wives of Essex County's powerbrokers have considered the Pine Room their Tower of Babel. Margie's become a polished eavesdropper, and what a memory."

Debbie no longer thought of Grace as a "surprise package," about to enjoy a long-anticipated dinner with a best friend who obviously had serious concerns about…, about what? Her long friendship with Rosemary opened the door to intimacy, but where did Grace fit in?

Margie pulled out all the stops for a dinner that included cheese-stuffed mushroom caps, endive Roquefort salad, lamb chops, Olivette potatoes, asparagus tips, and peach melba for dessert.

After they had polished off the champagne, they lubricated their early-easygoing chatter with a bottle of California chardonnay. By the time a second bottle was uncorked, their ladylike banter became more probing.

It was now two hours since Grace and Debbie shared their tentative handshake as strangers. During that time, they all shared their journeys down their personal passages into the hellish world of battered wives.

It required a few opening salvos for Debbie to understand the bonding between Rosemary and Grace. They had no idea that she was a member of the same sisterhood. Or did they? Never a heavy drinker, had the wine loosened her up enough to inadvertently drop some clues? If so, were their painful recollections meant to draw her out?

Debbie's admiration for Grace grew when she learned that she had abandoned her wealthy dentist husband after a single incident. A punch to the face knocked her over a sofa and onto the floor, where she landed on her head. There was no explanation, let alone an apology, as he returned to his martini with a smile.

It took only a half-hour for her to gather her personal belongings and leave the bastard behind. She was no longer Grace Fusina but DeMarco, her maiden name.

"She showed me where it happened," Rosemary interjected. "It's at least six feet from the fireplace to the sofa. The son of a bitch really wanted to hurt her." The physical pain was gone, but the memory of Grace's humiliation was her constant companion. She took all she could get, including the twelve-room Italian Renaissance mansion.

"Christ, Grace, were you hospitalized?" An entranced Debbie had been unconsciously twisting the napkin on her lap so hard that her wedding ring was cutting into her finger. Except for the last time, Johan's violent outbursts were slaps to her face and choking. They left bruises that could be cosmetically hidden with makeup.

She tried hard to suppress her next question but failed as the words blurted out, "You don't have to answer, but I've got to know. Did the son of a bitch say he loved you?"

The three women locked eyes before Grace broke the silence, "That's one hell of a question, but yes, John Fusina, God's gift to dentistry, blurted it out for the last time."

"I think I know where the question came from." Rosemary reached over and freed Debbie's hand from her lap, cupped it in hers, and, with tears of concern flooding her eyes, added, "Debbie, I hope I'm wrong. You're not saying, are you that Johan...?"

"It was a combination of his hubris, you know, the kind of stuff – that the great man is never wrong, then mix it with booze and some tough questions he didn't want to answer," Debbie said. "It started with slaps to the face and grabbing my neck until the last time when it was a really hard whack, and his diamond-studded wedding band cut open my right cheek. I never went to the doctor. Oh yes, like the other times, he said he loved me, would always love me."

"Let's take a look," Rosemary said as she turned Debbie's head to examine her right cheek.

Grace leaned forward to join the inspection. "Hardly see anything. Your make-up magician really did a great job. Where'd you find him?"

"It's a long story, works out of a plush apartment in Manhattan. Always on call; I'll give you his number in case you know any lady in need."

"It never got that far with Dr. Millard Dunston Volker, third in a line of renowned surgeons," Rosemary interposed. "He never hit me in the face, but I need a wardrobe of high-neck, long-sleeve blouses and sweaters to hide the bruises. The housekeeper knows but keeps her mouth shut. So do David and Lisa, and god damn it, they're only seven and five, but they know what's happening behind closed doors. They're the only reason we're still together."

Debbie studied the other faces, and the bonding that she saw was open and sincere. She was confused. Why in hell had Rosemary written her? If she needed a shoulder to cry on, she couldn't do any better than Grace.

They arose from the table and were about to leave when Margie stopped them with a commanding voice she uses with troublesome patrons and waitresses, "Sit down. I'm off in ten minutes, and I've got something to say. It's an earful. Cognac and espresso are on their way."

23

Only the Pine Room's wall sconces provided illumination for the cleanup crew and the women's corner table. The remaining waitress dropped off a tray with demitasse cups of espresso, a plate with sugar cubes and chocolate squares, four small cognac glasses, and a bottle of Rémy Martin. Margie did the pouring.

She waited until the other three sat back and took small sips of their cognac. Debbie and Rosemary dropped sugar cubes into their espressos and, along with Grace, tested the coffee. "Skol! A Danish boozer at Todd's taught me that, worked down the line from me and my riveting crew. He could really put down the rotgut after work, of course, but on the clock, he was one hell of a welder."

If Margie wanted rapt attention, she was getting it. It was like hearing a foreign language. What the hell was a Todd? Debbie and Rosemary had no experience with a face-to-face that included words like a welder, riveting crew, rotgut and boozer.

Sure, they graduated from Miss Spence's School for Girls on Manhattan's West 48th Street, but they were hardly naïve. There was no shortage of drunks, bent beggars with their filthy outstretched hands, muggers in wait, and would-be Romeos from Westside tenements waiting for their chance. They and two other pretty rich girls formed a protective quartet. They vowed never to lose touch and kept their oath alive with two Broadway outings a year with Debbie acting as the impresario.

The next reunion was planned for early December. Word was out that director Elia Kazan was gathering a cast that included Marlon Brando, Kim Hunter, Jessica Tandy and Karl Malden for the highly anticipated Tennessee Williams' "A Streetcar Named Desire." Her good friend, Nina Foch, pulled strings to get the four tickets. Debbie's friendship with Nina, the star of "John Loves Mary," developed backstage in a world light years away from Margie's apartment at the corner of Fulton and Rector in Newark, just a block away from the Passaic River's stench.

"I don't know if it caught your attention that I was spending a lot of time with customers at the three nearby tables," Margie said. "I'll be upfront. I was eavesdropping.

"I didn't catch everything, but enough to understand that you were the only one to dump the louse you were married to," Margie was just warming up. "Took only one hard smack to the face for you to pack your bags and get out. That was after you splashed a drink in his face and then tried to crown him with a booze bottle. Do I have it right?"

Grace did not respond and, like Rosemary and Debbie, sat back in her chair and waited for Margie to continue. It was like a tableau torn from the pages of True Confessions. Margie was confident that she was going to be the first one to challenge these women to look in the mirror and truly question what they saw.

"I heard bits and pieces of your story, so now I'll let you in on mine. We're sisters under the skin. Grace, you fled, and that was after only one punchout. Good for you. But don't mistake fear for courage. Believe me, because I've been there." Margie uncorked the Rémy Martin and poured it all around.

"I've never told this to anyone before, so hear me out. I'm not saying that what worked for me works for you. This is a guess on my part that we all loved our guy, and he loved us. In fact, we can't remember how often, sometimes on his knees, he'd blurt out his love and ask for forgiveness, saying it would never happen again. Now, don't say anything; just think about it. Ever think of hitting back just once, a thought that goes pfft in less than a second then disappears? Now that, ladies, is fear."

The darkened Pine Room was silent, the roaches ambling from their recesses in the damp corners of the kitchen to reclaim their territory.

"I don't know if it'll do any good, but let's start by picturing a six-foot-two Marine Gunnery Sergeant, handsome as hell, a solid two hundred and ten pounds and with a build like Charles Atlas. Totally machismo. Dames have their place, and being the breadwinner isn't it."

She wondered if any of this was sinking in. The dim light of the Pine Room failed to obscure the glitter of their expensive baubles. Tiffany's stuff was far out of reach for a woman accustomed to the costume jewelry she could afford. Their carefree wealth on display across the table and Margie's bargain basement accessories defined for her that they lived in two distinctively different worlds. Except for one thing. They had all been slapped around by their loverboys.

"What kind of work did you do?" Debbie asked. "I can't imagine women working on big warships."

"Nor can I," Rosemary said. "Was it office work?"

"The closest I got to the office was filling out withholding forms and signing up for my War Bond deduction. Todd handed me a hardhat, a pair of asbestos gloves, a steel bucket, metal tongs, and in a shake of a lamb's tail, I was a hot-rivet-catcher. I developed muscles, skill and confidence," Margie said, drawing attention with her eyes to how the three-quarter sleeves of her shift were stretched to the utmost by her biceps. "That got me the job as the operator of an overhead crane to hoist and put in place those heavy steel plates."

"I can't imagine any man pushing you around," Grace said. "Are you still together? Is there a divorce in the works? Is he still hitting you?"

"We're still together with no talk of divorce. We're Catholics. Your last question is also a no, and here's why -- every woman on the payroll at Todd's was sex target for the creeps, but I was strong enough to keep their paws off me."

An emboldened Rosemary snuffed out her fifth Chesterfield of the evening; usually her quota for a week, reached for the cognac bottle and poured another round. She lifted the bottle close to the lighted wall sconce, swirled its remaining contents a couple of times and said, "Monsieur Rémy Martin, I love you, but I can see you're about to bid us farewell. Quelle tristesse, quelle tristesse."

Rosemary's mock-serious lament fit the pattern of their conversation during the past two hours. Were they confronting the problem that was wrecking their lives, or were they just feminine gestures of sympathy?

After examining the other three faces, Margie decided she hadn't quite made her point yet. "I gained respect, but there was always one ignorant son of a bitch who couldn't keep his hands off. I knocked him off his stool with a hard right, and he hit the floor like a rock. It was broken up by co-workers and over in a few minutes, but my message went out loud and clear."

"Anything like that happens again?" Debbie asked.

"Never. And damn, did it feel good, that sense of power. A week later, they handed me the controls to the overhead crane," Margie said, then took a sip of cognac. "Made good money, and with overtime, really good money. Enough to surprise Ned when he came back to an apartment full of new appliances and furniture and even put in a modern, flush toilet. Ned hated it all. He couldn't find work and started drinking cheap wine and hanging out with his buddies instead of looking for work. Then I made a big mistake. I showed him my savings account book with seven hundred and fifty smackers in it. Ned never said anything; maybe he even thought I was doing tricks on the side.

"By that time, I was back here at the Pine Room in my old job before the war. Just another waitress working for a pauper's wages and hoping for big tips. Then my dyke boss, a really great lady with an unspoken crush on me, handed me this job and tripled my pay. Even doubled the fifteen percent employee discount for my new wardrobe, couldn't afford it otherwise."

"You talked about fear. Are you still living with it?" Grace said.

"Oh yeah, but not like before. I told you what happened in the saloon, that I could defend myself. Ned's a big guy, seventy pounds heavier and six inches taller. He still has no job and slurps up the rotgut."

"You implied that we can't let them get away with it," Rosemary said, "that we had to fight back. We all know it's easier said than done. Okay, you're Catholic, and divorce is out of the question, so you stay with a brute who can really hurt you, maybe worse. So why do you stay? You haven't said so, and my guess is that he's still slapping you around."

"As crazy as it seems to you, or maybe it's not that crazy after all, it is because I still love him. Two times, without any warning, he bounced me around, cut my nose and bloodied my mouth. The third time, I regained my balance before hitting the floor, and not really knowing what I was doing, punched him in the head hard enough that he had to grab the table to stay up. That was a few weeks ago."

She looked around and discovered shared bewilderment. Margie wondered if she hadn't been wasting her breath.

24

Margie wanted to get on with it and find out how much Tiffany diamonds, big houses and designer duds meant to them. "Any suggestions?"

For the next few minutes, the commiseration was heartfelt but unproductive until Grace finally piped up, "We're getting nowhere. It's clear that we were all badly hurt, and I don't mean the cuts and bruises. It comes from the inside, the anxiety, fear and helplessness. Nothing we talked about tonight is new, and men have been kicking women around for centuries.

"As County Clerk, I see every marital abuse filing, those that go to court and those that get dismissed. It didn't take long to see that the dismissals had big bucks and some big names attached, and not even a whisper got out. There are a lot more of them than you'd think.

"It's easy to see why the poor, frightened women with kids in run-down tenements drop their complaints. They need a breadwinner."

Margie turned from the table to an alcove twenty feet away and out of earshot of the waitress tending the noisy espresso machine, and in a raised voice, said, "Doris, we're just about wrapped up. Before you leave, can you spare us a few minutes? Over time, of course."

"Never turn my back on a few extra bucks," the petite black woman, about twenty-five years old, responded. Margie handpicked Doris for her replacement after hearing her story during the job interview. Five minutes later, out of her waitress uniform and into street clothes, an obviously angered Doris strode to the table.

"This might cost me my job cuz I know why you called me over. But I ain't playin' it your way," Doris peered directly at Margie. "Thought I couldn't hear, but I did. Everything. What crybabies. Don't mean you, Mrs. Bruning, and maybe not you County Clerk DeMarco. I read the papers, hear the radio and know who you are, a strong lady.

"But you other two, I see who you are, fine and pretty, and lookin' at what you're wearing, don't come cheap either. A lot of comfort, but I'm not seeing much else."

This wasn't what Margie was hoping to hear; she glanced at the others. Grace had fired up a fresh Chesterfield, Debbie was fingering her cognac glass on the table, and Rosemary was just sitting there.

"Any suggestions? And no, you're not losing your job," Margie addressed Doris, who had declined to take the empty seat at the table. She gazed from face to face while propping her worn, heavily repaired Naugahyde purse on the back of the empty chair.

"No suggestions. Just a little story, that's what you were looking for, wasn't it Mrs. Bruning?" Doris said. "My man's name is Oliver, handsome as hell and a gambler. A full-time loser suckered into any shaved dice or stacked poker game he could find. Married him anyway. Got discharged but couldn't get his truck driver's job back; driving a truck was all he could do. Didn't look much for work, a good for nothin' layabout who gambled on anything, even nigger's pool. That's right, the numbers racket, a dime or quarter every day and never a winner."

She had captured their attention. Each woman awaited in silence what came next.

"Oliver came home from the war. Gambling is in his blood, so he had no savings and didn't send anything home with what I had stashed away from Defense work and his severance pay for him to dip into, jobs, well that never crossed his mind. I hated it but went along because I love him and believe he loves me. That was before I caught him forging a check to draw a hundred dollars from my savings account.

"I grabbed for the checkbook, but he pushed me away, and for the first time ever, I cursed at him, 'You useless bastard, now you're even stealing from your wife!' I saw his fist coming. It was like, what do they call it, hypnosis, and I just froze. His punch caught me on the chin and knocked me down hard over the kitchen chair. He turned the chair over, and when I was on the floor, he kicked me. I don't know how many times. My back, my side, my butt, everywhere. He bent down and screamed over and over again, 'You bitch, you bitch! Who the fuck you think you're talking to!'"

Doris snapped open her purse, reached in and pulled out a black, plastic-encased, grip-shaped object about six inches long and extended it in the air over the table. There was a slight click when she pushed a small button, and a four-inch, stainless steel blade snapped into place. She leaned across the chair and, in a circular motion, waived the switchblade over the table. Another click and the blade snapped back into its handle.

"Bet you never saw one before. The next time I was ready. It was over money. He wanted another check. When I said no, he grabbed me and slapped me across the face. I pawed around in my purse like I was lookin' for my checkbook. Waited for my chance, and it came when he turned and reached for something on the table. He was about to learn that his days as the boss man were over."

"Make it out for a hundred and fifty bucks," he said, turning from the table with his right arm extended and the fingers wiggling 'gimme, gimme.' "I reckon you have that much and a lot more left in your account."

"Did you reckon this?"

Her spellbound audience remained silent as Doris, in machine gun fashion, without a hint of emotion, showed how she pulled the switchblade from her purse, snapped it open before Oliver could react, pressed its needlepoint under his chin hard enough to draw blood, then reached over with a kitchen towel and pressed it over the wound to staunch the bleeding.

"After that, no more punching, slapping, kicking or switchblade clicking. That was two years ago. That's all I want to say. It should be easy enough to see how you and your men compare. Why don't y'all start with, 'He says he loves me.'"

Doris dropped the switchblade into her purse, closed it and strode toward the entrance door. Over her shoulder, she threw out loud and clear, "Still have a job? Hard to put me out on the street knowing we are sisters."

"Yeah, Sister Doris, we're sisters, and you still have a job, maybe a pay raise," Margie echoed across the Pine Room. 'I'll take care of your timecard."

The echo increased as the other three women, in near-perfect unison, said, "We all be sisters!"

Grace waited for the giggling to end, leaned forward on her elbows and said, "I've got an idea. You might think it's absurd, but if you want your pound of flesh without getting physically involved, you can have it."

"And we'll not be involved?" Debbie said. She scanned the table and saw she was not the only one with the question. "That doesn't work for me. I'm dropping Johan; an annulment is in the works. I don't need his money."

"Don't you think paybacks are in order?" Grace replied. "It will take some doing, a lot of it on the dark side, but I believe I have the contacts to pull it off. If I do, are you willing to listen? Our targets will be the rich, well-connected winners who leave the judge's chambers with a smile and a handshake and maybe even an invitation to join the judge and his wife for dinner."

"Wow, this is almost comic book stuff," Margie chimed in, "superwomen bringing down Gotham City's rich and powerful wrongdoers. But I have to fess up; I can't fly."

"I like that, Margie; lightens things up," Debbie said, then turned to Grace, "Johan's history, but when you mentioned the dark side, my ears perked up. I'm willing to listen."

"Same for me," Rosemary said.

"I'll get on it right away. I should know more by the end of this week." Grace arose from the table and added, "Same time, same place, same table next Friday. In the meantime, think vigilante."

It was half-past seven when Margie punched out Doris' timecard, padding it an extra half-hour. She nodded to the cleaning woman who had been waiting patiently for them to leave and headed out the door to her 1940 Nash; she had picked up dirt cheap from a G.I. down on his luck. Debbie in her Daimler and Rosemary in the family Packard followed Grace's Studebaker to her home where they'd all be spending the night.

Fifteen minutes earlier, homicide detectives Rizzo and Melnyk pulled their unmarked car to a stop at the bottom of the driveway leading to a sprawling Victorian mansion on East Elmwood Avenue. Farther up, an unoccupied police car was parked at the steps leading to an artistically-tooled portico entrance. Two uniforms stood to either side of a tall, attractive, stone-faced woman. She seemed unaware of the handcuffs that held her arms in front of her.

"What do we have, Sarge?" Melnyk asked the older cop, in deference to his stripes.

"Got the call when neighbors reported hearing three gunshots. In a neighborhood like this, they must have sounded like canon blasts," Sergeant Solerno said. "When we got here, she was standing right over there in the open door. Never said a word, just handed me this." He handed over a handkerchief-wrapped handgun, careful that his fingers never touched the weapon.

"A Colt .32 caliber pocket pistol," Melnyk said after carefully unwrapping the handgun and smelling the muzzle. "Less than an hour, I'd say."

"That seems about right," the younger cop said, eager to be included while positioning himself so the nameplate on his shirt was clearly visible.

"And you are?" Rizzo stepped in closer to the woman, careful not to intimidate her.

"I'm Maureen Whitaker Sherry," the dark blonde woman, about five feet eight inches, slender and beautiful, said in a bored monotone. "The dead man is, or should I say was, my husband, Dr. Felix Franklin Sherry, Chief of the St. John's Hospital Neurology Clinic. We were alone like always when he decided to turn from healing to hurting."

She fixed her gaze on the Colt pistol still unwrapped in Melnyk's hand. "First time I used it, it surprised me that I even knew how. The bastard's in our bedroom, the first door at the top of the stairs."

25

On Thursday, September 11, Newark was enjoying uncommonly good weather, sunny, clear, and warm enough for Captain Nick Cisco to doff his jacket. It had been almost a year since he had taken over Newark's Homicide Division, and he was getting restless. The City's body count had not gone down, but Lt. Josh Gingold, his second in command and once a light heavyweight title contender was keeping the homicide squad in line. Competing mafia crime families were still collecting beach houses along the Jersey shore; they had to put their dirty money somewhere. With Thomas E. Dewey, Mr. Crime Buster, the sure bet Republican nominee for the Presidency next year, the mob wanted Harry Truman and the Democrats in the White House, everything normal with headlines at a minimum.

He reached for one of the two phones on his desk to accept a call put through by his secretary and smiled when she said, "It's from New York. It's a Lieutenant Mike Shanahan."

"Mike, I'll be god damn. It's got to be at least two years. And congrats to NYPD's new gangbuster. Must be doing one hell of a job to get a mention by Walter Winchell and a blurb in the Daily News. Even won your captain's bars." Shanahan didn't take the bait.

"How about you? Your secretary made it clear that she'd see if Captain Cisco was available. Enough with our ass-kissing," Shanahan said. "A few things have come up here, one in particular that I'd like to talk to you about. First, any rumblings between the Jersey families that you know of, Richie the Boot, DeCavalcante, and Waxey Gordon on your turf, or the Bruno-Scarfos in Philly? How about Longy? Have his boys shot anyone lately?"

"All members of the Genovese family," Cisco said. "We know it's been business as usual, but on the quiet side, ever since, Vito's been cooling it somewhere in Italy courtesy of the feds. Mike, it's been a long time, but I still know you well enough that your call isn't about any of the above. So, let's talk Rico Frenzelli."

"Bingo. Word about recently departed Rico has even crossed the river into Jersey. Any thoughts?"

"Not really. Frenzelli has been out of sight and out of mind for, I don't know, at least a couple of years. This call's on your dime."

"Ever hear of Johan Paasche?" Shanahan asked.

"Nope, never heard of him. Sounds like a Kraut composer."

"Moving on, here's another outstanding citizen I'm sure

you'll remember, Marcello Vitrioni."

"Hell, yes. Long before my time, but Christ, stories about him and Frenzelli go back to the late twenties and early thirties. Talk about playing your cards right; they were contractors for Maranzano when he and Masseria were shooting it out for control of the Big Apple. Both became made men, bodies all over the place. Turned out to be a waste of time and bullets. Enter our old friend Lucky and say arrivederci to Maranzano and Masseria; our two hitmen now had a new boss."

"Damn, that's quite a memory. Let's get to it," Shanahan said. "I believe the handle the mob gave them, the Two School Boys, is in play right now."

"How so? It's been years since I've seen their names on a sheet," Cisco said. "Word is that when Lucky and Vito discovered they had two high school graduates who were great with numbers on the payroll, they took their guns away and gave them pencils."

"There's the rub," Shanahan said. "Frenzelli has been running a brokerage firm on the mid-east side, Rico Frenzelli Investments. Very legal, licensed by the state and feds, very expensive, cash upfront, and you know where that came from."

"So, you've got a laundering operation on your turf nothing unusual about that. Hell, they've even moved into Cuba."

Taking him step-by-step, Shanahan ushered Cisco through what he knew or suspected. "Let's start with Frenzelli's brokerage office. Except for a neat little secretary, Rose Lupina, it's deserted. She said she hadn't seen Frenzelli since August fourth, when he stopped by to pick up his train ticket to Elizabeth."

"Rose Lupina? The name rings a bell. Isn't she the daughter of...." Cisco was cut off in mid-sentence.

"A loud bell. You got it. Joey Lupina a mob enforcer until he had his brains splattered outside Gamba's Ocean Fish joint in Rockaway. Still unsolved."

"She's a plant, of course," Cisco said. "I bet she's on the phone with her boss every day, even when there's nothing to say. They don't trust anybody, not even their own. What gives with Vitrioni?"

"Here's where it gets interesting," Shanahan said. "Two days after the boss took the train to Elizabeth, Rose was scared enough to wet her pants when two well-dressed, cigar-smoking thugs showed up. She never saw them before and they didn't give their names. Told her to take the rest of the day off. She did, and here's where things get blurred. Returned the next day and every day after that just like nothing had happened."

"I think I can fill in the rest. She's all alone there every day, no Frenzelli or Vitrioni," Cisco said.

"Nothing subtle here. Two thugs, both made men, pop up on my turf with federal and state brokerage licenses, open a fancy office, hire a mob-connected secretary, and sure as shit start laundering."

"I don't figure Frenzelli and Vitrioni to be the brains, you agree? You've dug Frenzelli out of the mud; what about

Vitrioni? I've got a pretty good guess, but fill me in."

"Exactly a month ago, we got the first call from the cop shop on Staten Island. A body, or what was left after the crabs had their fill, had washed up in a muddy marsh. Nothing there to involve my squad until a call the next day from the Richmond County Medical Examiner indicated it was a mob hit. That's when I headed over. A visit to the morgue left little doubt. Eight fingers had been chopped off, but enough of the two thumbs was intact for forensics to get prints. Coroner figures he'd been in the water two to three days, putting us back to the last time he was seen in his office."

"That's god damn well and good, but where's Vitrioni?"

"This is all hush-hush; can't be blabbed anywhere. Don't want the media parasites all over it. It's also where Johan Paasche comes in. Remember, it was a month ago that the two killers scared the hell out of pretty little Rose, then disappeared. So did Vitrioni. Four days later, a gasoline drum stuffed with his chopped-up body was caught in the net of a boat seine-fishing off Sandy Hook."

"Get anything out of their families? This sounds like business as usual."

"Vitrioni was single, a real whore master disowned by his family a long time ago. We hit the Frenzelli co-op on the Upper East Side with everything overdone in typical mafia fashion. Hold on a minute."

Cisco heard the click of a Zippo lighter and waited for him to enjoy a few deep drags.

162

"I'm well ahead of you, Mike. The place was empty. Talked to the neighbors, and nobody had seen anyone coming or going for at least four days. His wife, the neighbors never knew her by name or otherwise, was gone. Never saw her leave or when. Am I right?"

"Name's Giulia, daughter of Gino Cappelletti, a boss with the Bonanno family. You're right. Nobody had seen her for four days. Nothing seemed to have been disturbed. She was just gone. We're still looking, but I'm not about to start digging up the Jersey Meadows.

"Enter Johan Paasche. It wasn't easy to pry anything out of Rose Lupina; it took three weeks of questioning and threats to learn that a blonde, blue-eyed, handsome man by the name of Johan Paasche showed up at the brokerage office once a month to pick up a package from her boss. Oh yeah, she swore she didn't know what was in the packages."

"Real name? Real person?"

"Yes, on both counts. Not only that, he was in the phone book. Sometimes, police work can be so enjoyable. His humble digs were on the twelfth floor of a Riverside Drive co-op. Bear in mind that for the tenants of this palace, privacy and security are birthrights. Without a warrant, we had to sweet talk past the building manager. Once inside, it was like a tornado had blown through. Nothing was intact, not even the wall safe."

"When was that? Did you find Johan Strauss tangled up in the debris? How about a wife, was he married?" Cisco said.

"That was August 24. Yes, there is a wife who goes by

the name of Deborah Hammerstein Paasche. She left four days earlier, indicating to the doorman she'd be gone for quite a while and to have her mail forwarded to her family home in Tuxedo Park. Paasche had left two weeks earlier."

"Mike, you're like a raccoon going after roadkill. Don't know when to quit a case even when there's only a sniff of the prey to gnaw on," Cisco said. "It's okay if you want the goddamn lid buckled down. Just give me a hint why I should be worried?"

"By luck, the gods of law and order smiled down when we were about to take our final look-see at the Paasche co-op," Shanahan said. "Sergeant Rivas and I were headed to the elevator when this hard-looking dame entered the lobby and confronted the doorman with a question that was more like a threat. We heard it all. 'Thought I'd forgot, didn't ya. Hand it over. It's your ass if you cashed it.' You could see the guy was scared. He pulled a sealed envelope out of the top drawer of the concierge stand and gave it to her. She ripped it open, inspected the check, and we heard her say, 'Real nice, even put in a little bonus.'"

"We caught her at the door, pulled her inside, identified ourselves, sat her down in a far corner of the lobby and began digging," Shanahan said. "She had the right credentials - housekeepers union card, Local 58, which immediately rang a bell. The Local is mob. Her name is Ida Maria Santos, a real sweetheart with a sheet that includes whoring, forgery, B&E and A&B. No surprise, she didn't do a day in the slammer. Nothing current. Now this is a tough mob skirt, had her answers tattooed on her tongue until...."

"I take it that there's a point here somewhere," Cisco interrupted at his sarcastic best.

"Convinced her she could forget about Class B and C misdemeanors, charges that a Ward Heeler's phone call could fix," Shanahan said. "When my partner took out his cuffs and dangled them in front of her, and I rattled off charges that included felonious destruction of private property and busting open and looting a wall safe, there was a helluva big change in tough girl Ida's attitude. Ida's lip-flapping began."

"What the fuck you talking about?" a red-faced Ida Maria Santos spit out. "I didn't even work there when the place was busted up." That was a mistake, and she immediately knew it.

"Not so fast, give me a fag," she said as Shanahan was about to return his pack of Pall Mall to his jacket pocket, an obvious attempt to collect her wits. "And polite guy that you are fire me up."

"If your ass was canned and you didn't work there any longer, how the hell did you know when the Paasche apartment was broken up and looted?" Sgt. Rivas demanded. "And it just slipped your mind to hand in the apartment keys?"

"So, I forgot to turn in the fucking keys, so what? Is the best you assholes can do petty larceny for stealing keys?"

"Always amazed me how gangster frills can lie their asses off without blinking an eye," Shanahan said.

"This time, she knew we weren't bluffing; she had to give

us something if she wanted walking papers. Oh yeah, she's married to a Bonanno soldier doing a nickel at Dannemora. It took some hard coaxing by Rivas to get it out of her. It seems that Johan Paasche had been smacking the hell out of Deborah Hammerstein Paasche for several months. Ida swore that she saw it all, even raised her right hand. A break-up was coming."

"And did it?" Cisco asked.

"It did. Got the exact date from the doorman: August twentieth. Her mail was forwarded to the family homestead in Tuxedo Park. We asked state troopers to keep an eye out whenever they can, and as of today, she's still bedding down at home."

"Think she's connected in any way?"

"I doubt she knows anything. This gal's draped in velvet, very, very posh - Miss Spence's School for Girls, Vassar and a millionaire father. Probably never met anyone like Paasche before, swept off her feet."

"How does this spill over to Jersey?" Cisco asked.

"Coughed it out of the Lupina broad, you know, the one it took three weeks to get anything worthwhile. Same bullshit as usual. We protected her, wouldn't repeat a word she said, who'd she trust more - us or the thugs who made her piss her pants, and finally, the nonsense of a long list of charges if she didn't talk. After we convinced her we wouldn't rat her out, she finally gave us something. It turns out that Paasche visited the brokerage firm once a month, always the final week. Stayed only long enough to pick up his package of goodies, then headed over to Newark for a stop at Richie the Boot's Vittorio's Castle. Does this give you enough to do some snooping? Very discreet, of course."

"I've got a messy case on my hands. The press, radio and even the newsreels can't get enough of it. A blueblood dame pumped three .32 caliber slugs from her pearl-handled Colt pocket pistol into her rich husband. It seemed he'd been slapping the hell out of her for quite a while. The brute was Dr. Felix Franklin Sherry, a renowned neurosurgeon. This is pulp fiction stuff hardly believable to the upper class, but enjoyable as hell to tabloid readers on buses to work each morning."

"Were you satisfied or surprised?"

"Surprised, maybe. I had to decide what made Maureen Whitaker Sherry do it. I made some calls yesterday and came up with a shrink who threw the Messiah Complex at me."

"And?"

"Raises a lot of questions. I know a lot of this crap goes on in the Big Apple. Got a few more minutes?"

Cisco had more than an inkling of what prompted Maureen Whitaker Sherry to murder her husband. But was it murder? During his three-year adulterous affair with Grace DeMarco, he learned it didn't take continuous verbal and physical abuse to shatter a marriage.

26

Cisco intercommed his secretary that he wasn't to be disturbed and placed the call on speaker. He tapped out a Chesterfield and removed the sterling Dunhill from its usual spot next to the onyx ashtray on his desk. It was the only gift that he had retained from the many that Grace had given him during their torrid affair.

Two deep drags burnt off a half-inch of his cigarette. He tapped off the ash, raised the cigarette to his mouth, thought better of it, crushed out the butt in the ashtray and waited for Mike to get on the line.

"You there?" Shanahan asked.

Cisco heard the familiar click of a Zippo, the universal tool of nicotine fiends on every police force. Shanahan began, "I still don't know who Johan Paasche is, and other than his monthly stops at the Boot's Castle, don't see a Jersey connection."

"Here's what we got so far, all of it from Interpol. He's from a German brokerage and banking family and has U.S.,

Swiss and German passports. He got what he wanted by using his family's peace-loving connections known to the Red Cross in Germany, Austria and Switzerland. He was named plenipotentiary for *World Without War,* a Nazi-approved tripartite group that gave him diplomatic immunity with no travel restrictions. And Christ, did he do a lot of traveling. Not much to Germany, but enough back and forth between Switzerland and the U.S. to coincide with what Rose Lupina told us about his visits. The son of a bitch traveled well and seemed to be in no hurry until real fighting began in '40. Luxury cruises out of Buenos Aires with a female companion, not his wife, of course. Get this: one of those cruises, possibly more, was directly to Naples during the time Vito Genovese was holed up there to escape federal murder charges."

"So, you've got Paasche, a wife-beating money launderer, Richie the Boot, and Vito," Cisco said. "If you have them, you have the Luciano family, and if you have Luciano, can Lansky be far behind?"

"Something big is happening here. Anything I can get from your end, you'll receive *míle rud maith* from the good Lord, as my granny from Limerick would say."

"Can't use uniforms for this, but there are two new men in Homicide who could fit, moved up from the Vice Squad; you can't get better than that if you're looking for snoopers. I'll cut them loose and keep you informed. Now, let's get back to Maureen Whitaker Sherry and the late Dr. Sherry."

Shanahan took over and admitted he knew very little about spousal abuse, only that with no official word on where to place these messy cases, they fell in the lap of NYPD Homicide.

"Unless they're bragging, you know how talkative Homicide is," Shanahan said. "Big stories are leaked to the press first, and kudos are passed from one gold shield to another, while wife beatings in hell's kitchen are who-the-hell-cares items that rarely make the blotter."

"What gives with Deborah Hammerstein Paasche?" Cisco asked.

"Oh yeah, she's a blueblood also from a brokerage and banking family, this one on Wall Street. On two of the State troopers' look-sees at Tuxedo Park, they found her galloping around the town's racetrack. Too bad it's closed now, had some pretty nice stakes there once."

"Rich bitches and their horses, all Elizabeth Taylor wannabes, all riding the pie to fame and glory."

"Give it a break, Nick," Shanahan said. "Somehow, and I don't know why, I think she could be a key."

Their phone talk ended with Cisco promising to snoop around Jersey and the acknowledgment by the two detectives they were not the only ones tracking down Johan and Deborah. If the mob is the winner, things could get very messy.

He reached for his Dunhill and Chesterfields, cursing how the job he had coveted for so long had turned him into a two-pack-a-day weakling. He spread open a spiral notebook and began studying the pages of scribbling he had compiled during his interview with Dr. Moishe Andrew.

Less than a mile from where Cisco was in his office attempting to make sense of his shorthand, Grace was sitting across the table from Chester Bruno in a cozy niche at the Broad Street Club. She would have to wait to see if the confidence she placed in him would be rewarded. To make her crazy scheme work, she needed a shady, brilliantly successful criminal attorney with mob connections, and there was none better than Chester Bruno, Esquire.

"Not only is what you just described pure insanity, but it's also illegal," Bruno said after listening for fifteen minutes as Grace unfolded her blueprint for collective revenge. He smiled and glanced over the top of his martini glass to the face across the table. He wasn't surprised that his gaze was met with the same volcanic look he encountered when Grace laid out her plan to financially castrate her abusive husband in their divorce four years earlier.

"You're smiling. Is it because after what I just described, I should be hauled off to the looney bin? I've seen your clients, most of them guilty as hell and straight from the cesspool," she smirked. "You got most of them off, some with barely a slap on the wrist. I've said nothing about murder, and the only thing I want from you is...." She got no further.

"To be an accomplice. That's right, asking me to team you up with, let's call him an acquaintance, and four hate-filled women who, from my perspective, are on the very edge of insanity." His words were soft and, to her surprise, reassuring, impeccable lawyer speak. "Just to give you a name or two could cost me my license."

"Jesus Christ, Chester. If you haven't lost your license by now, you never will. This lunch is on my dime, so are you going to give or not?"

"Just so happens I was taking in cool ocean breezes at Long Branch last weekend when I ran into an acquaintance. He's little more than a kid, maybe twenty-five or so. Been a Genovese soldier since high school. He's a killer, a made man. Want to hear more?"

"I told you what we were looking for, quite clear about it." Grace jiggled the ice cubes floating in the remainder of her Haig & Haig and admonished, "Is this fuzzy-cheeked killer the best you can do?"

"Believe it or not, he's likeable as hell. A B+ graduate of good ol' Barringer High, All City tight-end, a great hammer thrower and shot putter in '39, and, oh yeah, he's schizophrenic."

"Schizophrenic? First, you describe him as a Mickey Rooney type and as an afterthought as a guy adrift in a world of make-believe. And he's at the top of your list?"

"Perhaps calling him schizo is a little too much. At the same time, and I've never seen it before, he's melded Boy Scout wholesomeness with mafia deviance and done alright for himself.

"He's the only Genovese soldier who willingly signed up for FDR's military draft, not like his mob cohorts who chopped a pinky-toe or punctured an ear drum to avoid serving. Earned Staff Sergeant stripes with the Army MPs, became a top interpreter in North Africa, Sicily and Italy, and got an early discharge, probably with Genovese pulling the strings."

"How is it you know so much about this schizo, who isn't really a schizo at all, but merely a criminal deviant and a murderer? I never saw a file on anyone like this. Am I right, no arrests?"

"No arrests, not even a bicycle violation. Answering your first question is kind of complicated and maybe an eye-opener for you. I kind of adopted the kid after his mama and papa were my chief witnesses in a burglary and beating case. Nice people, always on the fringes of the mob, who never questioned why their boy spent more and more time in goombah clubhouses than with his school buddies. Badly needed cash found its way to their kitchen table, no questions asked."

"Adopted? That doesn't sound like you. We've known each other since the third grade, and I never once detected a soft spot. Tell me I'm wrong, that there wasn't a devious reason for adopting, and that's your word, not mine, a kid genetically programmed for violence."

"Christ, did I hear right, genetic programming?" Chester said, a lopsided smile of mock disbelief exposing perfect teeth.

"That's right buddy, don't forget I'm a New Jersey Women's College alum, top ten percent, in fact. Psych 102 sorted out a lot for me, but I never bought completely into Freud and Jung. They'd have a field day with a heartless courtroom beast like you. So, what gives?"

"I tried to pry the kid out of those storefront dago domino parlors, you know, the ones with the green painted windows," he said. "Even had him working at my law office as a would-be intern. Money wasn't as good as the mob's, but just fine for a teenage kid. It was a no go, lasted about six months."

Chester motioned for another round, and she agreed. They sat back in their cushioned seats, sipped, lighted up with him doing the honors, then a few more sips. Grace waited for the kicker, knowing him well enough that one was coming. Then it came.

"Imbed in your mind that only cowardly sons of bitches hit women!" Chester said. It was the first time his voice rose above a polite conversational level.

"It's a dictum handed down from the kid's grandparents who shared family digs with his parents, sister and him whenever he's not shacked up. We're not dealing with a saint, but still a guy who's never been charged or convicted of anything," he said. "We talked in my office just before he graduated high school; at the time, I was handling a domestic violence case for a cousin."

"Mr. Bruno, I can't imagine anyone striking my sister Theresa or cursing her in the face with filthy words like 'fancullo.' If I ever caught a guy doing that, you'd have to hold me back from killing him. And this goes for any dame, young or old."

"Is he a looker?" Grace asked. "We're not looking for a palooka with cauliflower ears; the kind cops stop for being in an upper-class neighborhood. Does he have a car? Hopefully, not a fancy, bulletproof mob chariot with dark windows."

"Movie star looks, I'm not kidding. Has his own car, and

he's off the streets. Vito ordained him with a plush job, liaison between the gangster unions that control most of the labor in New Jersey. He's never in the news."

"He sounds like what we're looking for. When can I talk to him?"

"Slow down; we don't know if he'd even be interested. I'll pass on your contact number only if he is. I've got only one more guy that I could call, and that's it for me." Bruno stood up, "Craziest god damn idea I ever heard. Wish you luck. *Arrivederci,* Grace."

27

It did not come as a surprise for Captain Cisco to learn that domestic abuse was handled the same way. Unless it involved important people, married or not, it was swept under the rug. In Newark, the Old World mentality that a man only struck a woman when she deserved it still ran rampant among inner-city immigrant families. He opened the middle drawer of his desk and scratched around for a newspaper clipping given to him by his former partner, Lieutenant Kevin McClosky. It contained a comment by radio comic Fred Allen on his nationally syndicated show, much admired by FDR and John Steinbeck. Self-righteous, holier-than-thou editorials blossomed across the land when Allen brought his live studio audience and millions of his faithful to laughter with the advice, *"A gentleman is any man who wouldn't hit a woman with his hat on."*

Grace never mentioned that her bastard husband was wearing a hat when he floored her with one hard punch to the face. John Fusina was Newark's Crown Prince of Dentistry, who with that one violent act, showed that he was also a coward.

Now Cisco had a homicidal rich dame on his hands who came from a class even higher than the Fusinas. Maureen Whitaker Sherry had pumped three bullets into her husband, Dr. Felix Franklin Sherry, Chief of the St. John's Hospital Neurology Clinic. That was a week ago, and since then, Mrs. Sherry had not experienced a courtroom, let alone the clammy dampness of a jail cell. At the suggestion of the Mayor, she has been under house arrest with the complete domestic staff at her bidding. Monday's grocery deliveries contributed to her deprivation with tins of *pâté de foie gras* and jars of artichoke hearts, but she resolved to make the best of it.

Three days after the shooting, this happy ending for Mrs. Sherry came when Dr. Forest Whitehead, an internationally renowned disciple of Sigmund Freud, showed up. With the support of her powerful friends across New Jersey and tacit approval by the District Attorney, the shrink took over a second-floor bedroom at the Sherry mansion to determine the state of Maureen's mind, conscious or unconscious, during the shooting.

Cisco knew if he put together a case that led to the conviction of Mrs. Sherry, it would be a feather in his cap that might include the Police Chief's gold bars. But he was ignorant when it came to handling sexual abuse cases; that's Vice Squad territory. He decided to go directly to the source, St. John's Hospital, where doubtless there were whispers about the Sherrys among the staff. He fished around for two days until it was suggested he contact Dr. Moishe Andrew, Chief of Psychiatry.

Dr. Andrew returned his call in less than an hour, not from the hospital but from his downtown private practice.

"Captain Cisco here," he said after his secretary handed off the call.

"Dr. Moishe Andrew. I recognize your name from the headlines. Very nice job solving those Nazi Bund murders. What can I do for you?"

"I'd like to talk about domestic abuse, and in particular, where it can lead if it's prolonged."

"And you're calling me?" a puzzled Dr. Andrew said. "Don't you have one of the country's most renowned dream merchants in town? Whitehead's a talker; I suggest you give him a call."

"There's no chance. The D.A. says he talks to no one, not even Homicide, until he's finished probing her psyche."

"You're looking for answers but don't know where to look. It's like Cheshire Cat's advice to Alice, 'If you don't know where you are going, any road can take you there.'"

The phone was silent, enough time for Dr. Andrew to assess Cisco's motives. "We can talk, but only in generalities. Dr. Sherry was a colleague but hardly a friend. For the Sherrys, it is the Montclair Golf and Hunt Club; for us, the Altacrest Country Club out in Bergen County."

This left Cisco questioning whether he had sought out the right source. There was a built-in animus in cop shops toward shrinks, especially those who collected hefty fees to sabotage the prosecution. Of course, everyone knows these swamis are as loony as their clients.

"I'm like a babe in the woods with this case, so generalities will do just fine. You've seen the headlines and heard the radio; the media hyenas are having a feast. Are you willing to give me some time?"

"Just so happens I've got an hour open this afternoon at two," Dr. Andrew said, "how does that sound?"

"Expect me at two," Cisco replied. He was given the address by the doctor's receptionist, not surprised that the office was in one of the city's swankiest buildings.

Cisco was greeted in Dr. Andrew's outer office by an auburn-haired, grey-eyed beauty who gave more bounce to the ounce in her simple blue dress than a designer could hope for. The nameplate on her desk read, "Patricia Grosser." Her wide smile left him wondering if she had discovered the tooth fairy. She reached across the desk and said, "Captain Cisco, I presume? You must be important. I can't remember the last time Dr. Moishe opened up an hour without an appointment."

"You presume correctly," Cisco replied with a smile while taking in the expensive trappings, not too plush, just discrete enough to put troubled clients at ease. Meanwhile, Patricia had pushed the button on her intercom and Dr. Andrew entered the outer office.

"Come right in." Dr. Andrew ushered Cisco into the office with an extended right arm and handshake. He was a swarthy man of about fifty, perhaps five-foot-ten, slender with graying dark hair and penetrating hazel eyes. His charcoal trousers were razor-creased, and an open, button-down collar of a white shirt was layered by a loosely buttoned forest green cardigan sweater. Black, highly polished loafers completed the shrink straight from central casting.

Cisco led the way into an office resplendent in what he knew was original fine art interspersed with glass-framed sheepskins from universities here and abroad. Brown leather was everywhere: a tufted couch, two high-backed armchairs on casters, an inlaid coffee table, two side tables, a large cherrywood desk, also inlaid, and an office chair on casters making it easy for Andrew to swivel between his desk and a corner reading table stacked with files. A brightly colored, tightly woven Egyptian rug was the centerpiece of a well-buffed hardwood floor.

"Take a seat. Patricia will have coffee in a moment," Andrew motioned Cisco to one of the high-backed armchairs while he took the other. "An hour passes quickly. Your main reason for seeing me would be…."

"The Sherry shooting is at the crux," the homicide chief said and then took in the file folders on the corner table. "You can understand that the average cop avoids domestic abuse cases like the plague. Not just domestic, but any of the 'she said, he said' sexual variety unless the physical evidence is quite clear. Most cops have kids, so when the abuse - sexual, verbal or sadistic beatings – occurs, they're out for blood. We, and that includes me, have no ground rules."

"If you're looking for me to supply them, I'm uncertain what I can do for you," the psychiatrist said, his eyes never leaving Cisco's. "I'm a doctor who happens to be a shrink entrusted with reams of privileged information, some life or death for my patients."

"I'm just looking for some helpful pointers. Here in Newark, and from what my research over the...don't laugh now...last three days have shown, police departments routinely dump these cases in the laps of homicide."

"Why is that?"

"I haven't asked, but is it a problem if I take notes," Cisco said as he pulled a spiral notebook and pen from an inside jacket pocket.

"You won't be getting any privileged information, so go right ahead."

"I don't think the higher-ups give a damn unless, of course, something like the Sherry case comes along and makes them nervous." Cisco opened his notebook and tested his pen. "Class has its privileges in this town. My former partner, Lt. McClosky, who works directly under the Mayor's office, says there are a hell of a lot more well-heeled bastards who kick their wives around than you would think. You know where I'm going with this; no coincidence that they're either friends or political backers of the Mayor. Hush, hush all the way, and if a charge is filed, it's taken care of in the judge's chambers."

"Here's what I can do." He took a sip of the freshly brewed coffee that Patricia brought in on a tray with sugar cubes and cream. "I can give you a few anonymous cases, composites based on my clinical experience. Would that help?"

"Much more than I expected. I'd like to start with Dr. Felix Franklin Sherry. He was world-renowned, and at the same time, he was physically and verbally abusing his wife.

This just doesn't fit. Wasn't he pledged to 'first do no harm'"?

"In my work, it's often referred to as the *Messiah Complex*," Andrew paused for a sip of coffee, at the same time judging the effect his words had on the detective. Cisco's facial expression revealed nothing. "My guess is you've never heard that expression before. Correct?"

"Never. Are you suggesting that this Messiah Complex comes into play in the Sherry shooting?"

"I'm not suggesting anything, just describing a troubling pattern in the medical profession, especially among surgeons, who are god-like figures in the operating room but mere mortals at home."

"I'm guessing that Dr. Sherry fills the bill and that you can only speak in generalities, no names, no cases. I've got twenty detectives under me, more than half of them barely making it through high school. Three of them have cases where severe physical pain that comes close to torture was inflicted. Every case different. A whore, cigarette-burned by her pimp until she admitted skimming part of his take for tuition to keep her son off Newark streets and in an upstate boarding school. My guy admits having no love for the prostitute but would gladly strangle the pimp if the law allowed."

"Understandable, and the others?" Andrew asked.

"A sad story heard over and over again since the end of the war. In this case, a discharged Navy Petty Officer can't find work, drinks too much and with no mustering-out pay left his wife threatened to leave him and return home to her parents. He threw a frying pan with sizzling bacon grease in her face. She might be scarred for life."

"And the next case?"

"Two love-doves until they started cheating on each other," Cisco said. "The husband was deferred because of his wartime job. He was a numbers man for the Price Stabilization Board, not much muscle. At the same time, the little lady was developing shoulders and arms of a weightlifter down at Arthur Kill docks as a forklift operator, even filled in when she was needed to load fifty-five-gallon drums. Well, they got into a punchout. She broke lover boy's jaw and sent him to the hospital with a fractured skull. He's still there."

"Let's hope so. What kind of help do you want from me?"

"Some guidelines. We've got a handle on the inner-city domestic mayhem, the Friday night beatings when the wife finds for the umpteenth time her husband's pay envelope half gone, down the drain with rotgut rye and screw-top wine. I need a tutorial, if I can call it that, that I can pass on to my men on how to handle a Sherry shooting. Up til now, this has been a no-trespass zone. How do they proceed when class, privilege, money, political clout and a rigged legal system is involved? They all want the satisfaction that comes with a collar, and that's the problem: how to button down the collar."

"I'm sure I can come up with a few pointers."

28

"Despite what you see around this office, I first practiced at a free inner-city psychiatric clinic," Andrew said, then reached forward to refill their coffee cups. "Those file folders you eyed earlier, one out of five is *pro bono,* same clinic only twenty years later."

"Twenty years ago, I was a rookie pounding the bricks in the Central Ward. There was the usual street garbage to deal with; that was expected. And then there were those trapped on the first, second and third floor of every tenement. They needed only one weapon to break out, but rarely, if ever, found it," Cisco responded.

Andrew leaned forward and asked, "What was the weapon?"

"Hope." Cisco drained his cup, looked at his watch, and added, "It's meaningless when it's out of sight. I've lost count of how many kids didn't have a chance in this land of the free, boys or girls; it makes no difference when all they see around them is despair. All they want is an escape route."

The psychiatrist kept his eyes on Cisco, "How about a helping hand?"

There was a sudden hardening of Cisco's flushed features and a deepening of the corrugated creases that spanned his forehead.

"First, let's agree that hope is not a packaged commodity," each word stung like a needle in his tongue. "It's amorphous and shapeless, invisible and intoxicating. A poor tenement kid's wish for new or well-mended shoes for Christmas never comes true. A small crushed hope, to be sure, but along with it comes the first pangs of despair. I helped a kid like that once when I was a rookie. Then there was Joey Bancik, a good kid who chose the wrong escape route, running numbers for the mob. He ended up dead in the basement of a swank apartment house, a cop's bullet in his chest."

"So, it was the police who chose Joey's escape route." Again, the psychiatrist quickly realized he had gone too far.

Cisco leaned forward in his chair and, with his elbows pressed deeply into his thighs, spat out, "Jesus Christ, and here I was thinking you were different."

Andrew sat back in his chair and waited for Cisco to collect his thoughts.

"Escape? How do you help a kid whose hope diminished in lockstep with the shrinking meals at the kitchen table," Cisco said. "He was a first-generation American in a Montenegrin émigré family who barely handled English.

The father hurt his back, lost his job and couldn't find another. The family lived on the dole. It was no secret to neighbors, the walls of tenements no thicker than cardboard, that Joey's mom was slapped around whenever she complained. Hardly the clients that walk into your office."

Cisco pulled a pack of cigarettes from his jacket pocket, tapped one out, and, without waiting for approval, fired up, and took two deep pulls.

"Here, use this," Andrew reached across the coffee table and proffered his saucer.

"I wasn't the only one who held out hope for Joey. His assistant pastor, Father Terry Nolan, also tried. Both of us were heartened to see that he had lucked into a *Star-Ledger* paper route, only to discover it was a cover for the numbers that he was running for the mob."

"So, he was bringing in real money for the family," the shrink interjected, "I know the story well; remember, I started at a free clinic. Many Joeys passed through."

"Passed through!" Cisco shouted, lowered his head, took a deep breath and rubbed both temples before looking up and accusing the doctor. "Tell me, Dr. Andrew, how many of these kids' homes have you actually visited? You know, the firetrap tenements with the condemned 'proceed at your own risk' warning posted at the bottom of every rotting outside wooden staircase."

"None."

"And that's the difference, Doctor, I can't forget any of

the domestic violence calls I answered. You kicked them out the door for rookie cops like me to deal with. A drunken son of a bitch husband snoring it off in the bedroom while the wife, nursing a black eye or broken nose, waited on the outside landing with her terrified kids for me and my partner to arrive and cuff him."

The psychiatrist absorbed what he was hearing. He couldn't think of any other time he was taken down a peg or two, probably not since his internship when ass-chewing was a daily rite of passage. Today, it was by a pissed-off cop seeking his help.

"Right up 'til two days before Joey took a bullet in the chest, we were trying to steer him straight. My partner, Sgt. McClosky, and I were a few minutes too late. So I don't need any blowback from you, only some useful advice. In a world where famous radio comedians like Fred Allen joke about the correct way to slap a lady around, it's only a matter of time before we hear from a lot more Mrs. Sherrys."

"Hold that thought; I have to touch base with Patricia. Look around; there are two books on deviant behavior in that stack on the table. You can take them if you want."

Five minutes later, Dr. Andrew returned and handed Cisco a note with three names along with addresses and phone numbers.

"I decided against meeting with your guys at the station. Here are three names that will do just as well, one you're familiar with. It took some convincing from the other person. You're set to go; just give him a call. If you want to touch base with me again, I'm here. I think I got more out of this past hour than you did. Thanks, and good luck."

They shook hands, and with a wink and a nod to Patricia, Cisco passed through the outer office and gently closed the door behind him.

In the office of a fenced warehouse complex out near the Newark airport, a nervous Albert Cervi, founder and president of Cervi Trucking and Storage, Inc., fidgeted with anything in arm's reach on his desk. Two guys suited more for the loading ramp than his office sat across from him, silently chain-smoking and bored. They claimed to be union reps, never naming the union, only that the time was right for him to join up. Everything would be explained when the head man arrived later in the day. Cervi had sense enough not to ask the names of the boss or his union.

Cervi's company was one of three in the complex, like many others in northern and central New Jersey that were either padlocked or close to bankruptcy since the war time gravy train came to a halt. He knew this day was coming. Mob union organizers had laid back during the war years; it wouldn't look good roughing up Uncle Sam's suppliers.

At that moment, Stefano Rizzano was at least a half-hour away after lunch at Carmine's Restaurant, the mob favorite where Fulton Fish Market mafia boss Joseph Lanza, held court. It was at Carmine's three months earlier that Stefano was formally taken off the streets, surrounded by others, who like himself, cut their mobster teeth with the Fulton Market Watchman and Patrol Association and the United Seafood Workers Union Local 202.

He came away bruised from rib-crushing hugs and back-pounding when Vito Genovese's underboss, gambling czar Willie Moretti, declared that he was the new head man of the enforcers who provided muscle for mob takeover of established New Jersey unions. Now, he was in a white collar with an office in downtown Newark and a black Lincoln Continental Cabriolet, a gift from Vito to tool around in.

"Hey, Stefano, before you leave, you gotta show it to us," bellowed a lubricated voice in the crowd at the bar. "You know what the fuck I'm saying. Ain't that right, *paisanos?*" Several loud voices were raised in affirmation.

Moretti sat back in his chair at the table he shared with Lanza and Stefano. "Go on, show them. I'd like to see it myself," he said.

Stefano nodded across the table and reluctantly removed the black and white sports shirt he was wearing, accompanied by a few raucous shouts of, "Take it off! Take it off!"

Exposed were two half-inch, hard purple scars at the front and back of his right trapezius muscle about midway between his neck and shoulder. The scars were smooth and rounded, looking much like two marbles embedded in his flesh. The wound occurred just down the street at the Fulton Fish Market when a nineteen-year-old Stefano attempted to stop the unloading of cod from a Swedish boat whose master refused to pay the extortionary fee of two hundred and fifty dollars for the privilege.

Stefano and three others on mafia Watchman Patrol attempted to board the boat, only to be met by a large and very angry deckhand waving a nine-inch, cast iron cargo hook in their faces.

"No more you come," the ape-like deckhand roared. "One more step, and you get this!" The commotion had not yet aroused other crew members who were busy at the stern and bow holds.

"Put that fucking thing away and fork over the money," Stefano demanded at the same, reaching for the leather sheath belted to his right hip and pulled out a wood handled cargo hook. "Here is my toy, you bastard. You want to play, or you want to pay?"

The two men were arm's distance apart when the deckhand lunged forward with a large left-handed sweep of his cargo hook. It caught Stefano by surprise, and before he could react, the hook passed through the front of his right shoulder muscle and emerged with a spurt of blood from the back. The big Swede then attempted to pull the hook completely through Stefano's trapezius, tearing it completely from his shoulder. It was a mistake. Stefano's hard, football-toughened muscles resisted for the two seconds needed for him to embed his hook into his attacker's left biceps, forcing him to let loose of his grip on his weapon.

With the nine-inch cast iron hook dangling and his blood spurting everywhere, he flattened the Swede with his left shoulder, jumped on him, and battered his face with his left fist. Blood from the now unconscious deckhand and a barely conscious Stefano mixed into an expanding red lake.

Watchman Patrol cohorts pulled Stefano to his feet and

supported him to the gangway. "Jesus Christ, look at that," Tom Graziani marveled as he watched the hook's heavy oak handle sway back and forth from the ever-widening wound. "Gotta get it out. Ready if you are."

"I'll break your arm if you touch it," Stefano, barely able to stand, warned. "I'll pull it out, but not on this fucking boat."

A wobbly, blood-drenched Stefano was assisted into the glass-enclosed office of one of the Fish Market's shipping bosses. A pushing and shoving throng had gathered around the cubicle for a better vantage point to see if what had been described was actually true.

Stefano was oblivious to it all. Shock was setting in when he suddenly reached for his shoulder and, with his left thumb felt the point of the hook that had emerged from the bloody, jagged wound. He smiled as mindless delirium took hold.

"A toy, just a toy," he giggled. "This kind of fun is my daily vitamin." His childish humor turned somber as he slowly removed the cargo hook from his trapezius before he passed out. The legend of the nineteen-year-old "Fish Hook" was born.

That was seven years ago, years during which Stefano was never asked to whack anyone, only rough-up malcontents who bitched about the way business was being run. Everyone wanted a larger share, especially from the expanding heroin market and high-rise construction in Manhattan controlled by the mob's tight-fisted "Concrete Club."

Today, it was business as usual at Cervi Trucking and Storage. It took only fifteen minutes for him to remind Albert Cervi that a mysterious fire had destroyed fifty percent of an uncooperative competitor in South Amboy. He left with a handshake after introducing the two thugs who would share office space.

Outside in his car, Stefano once again confronted the mixed feelings that had been growing for some time. It was all so goddamn easy how fear could diminish a decent, hardworking, self-made man like Albert Cervi. The intensity of his nightmares didn't help. In fact, they had forced him to question the lifestyle he had yearned for since sharing pinochle and dominoes with neighborhood goombahs as a teenager.

It started three years ago in Long Branch. With four big ones stuffed in his pocket courtesy of rigged blackjack and crap games, he was comp'd with a top-floor luxury suite at the Berkeley Carteret Hotel overlooking the boardwalk and ocean in Asbury Park, courtesy of Joe Bonanno.

Lillian, a beautiful mob call girl from Philadelphia, was brought in to service him. Stefano sensed there was something different about this tall and athletic, brown-eyed brunette. She loved her work and performed with quiet and intense enthusiasm. They spent the night and most of the next morning nakedly skirmishing from king-size bed to couch, finally meeting the morning sunrise at the big window overlooking the pier.

Twice during the night and morning recovery periods, Stefano pulled away from Lillian when the unwelcome, sexually abused women in the Italian schoolhouse invited him to join them on their grotesque carousel. Cans of spam, packets of coffee, chocolate and cigarettes that were once offered as friendly bribes were now thrust at him, accompanied by a cacophony of ribald jokes and hand gestures from grim-faced women demanding he understand. Each time, he leaped from bed only to be followed by Lillian, who, after the second time, put her arms around his neck and pulled her body in close, "Hey, you're great. I could probably fall for you if you hadn't scared the hell out of me twice tonight. Buster, you really need help."

Countless times, recall of that night with Lillian flashed past in vivid detail. As he drove from the Cervi parking lot toward Newark, Lillian's probing brown eyes once again searched for answers that were beyond him. She was right, he needed help. But from where and from whom? Her beautiful, imploring face floated past, only to disappear like the grotesque carousel into the clouds. Was she the only one who understood what he was going through, his hooker soulmate? He looked her up a year later only to find she had overdosed on heroin.

The final image of Lillian faded away as he turned into heavy stop-and-go traffic, and reached into the Cabriolet glove compartment for cigarettes when he found a memo he had scribbled during his meeting with Chester Bruno. It was the craziest, goddamn thing he'd ever heard. He glanced at the memo and found the telephone number, no name attached, and whispered to himself, *What the hell, could be good for a laugh.*

29

It was only three days since his meeting with Dr. Moishe Andrew and Captain Nick Cisco had had it up to here with the Sherry case. The press' bloodlust for anything true or imagined about the Dr. Felix Franklin Sherry killing only increased when it was learned that Maureen Whitaker Sherry's house arrest was more like life at a sultan's palace.

Jerry Saunders, the *Star Beacon's* hatchet man, exaggerated as usual in his above-the-fold front-page story, "How many readers would turn their backs on a feast at home that included Dom Perignon, *pâté de foie gras*, a Burgundy Chablis for lunch, and a Saint-Émilion Merlot with dinner? Throw in escargot, and the only thing to worry about is gout."

The *Clarion's* Joe Lucio described "The delights of being a home-confined convict" and admitted, "I would be a hypocrite not to admit I'm jealous."

The newspapers were spread on Cisco's desk and would be added to a pile on a nearby table that included scathing stories from the *Afro-American*. One reporter introduced the racial element when she noted, "Maybe Mrs. Maureen Whitaker Sherry might try some real food like collard greens, fried okra and chicken."

Rizzo and Melnyk, the two detectives he had assigned to the case, had become little more than babysitters. They reluctantly admitted to Cisco they were out of their league after the brief questioning of Sherry the night of the shooting and a subsequent interrogation attended by Sherry's attorney and a shrink, who is a close friend of the family.

Cisco pulled his two men off the case and sent them back to the homicide bullpen. Around-the-clock babysitting was taken over by the uniform division with strict orders that no one, rich, famous or whatever, entered the mansion if their name was not on a list approved by him, the District Attorney or Mayor.

His former partner, McClosky, chimed in with a message from the Mayor, "Have the DA or an assistant listen to everything that Sherry and the shrink have to say. To hell, that's privileged information. Let's see now, here it is; her name's Dr. Marsha Seavers." McClosky reached over and snubbed out his cigarette in Cisco's onyx ashtray already filled to the brim with stubs. "His Honor believes the Sherry dame is a troubled woman whose abuse forced her to crack; no hint of class distinction and privilege is allowed."

"We know where the pressure is coming from; your boss might have thought he left his plumber tools behind when he was elected," Cisco said, "he was wrong. He'll always be viewed as a handyman by the political powerbrokers who anointed him, grateful for the job and useful for stopping leaks and unplugging toilets."

"Politics in this city has always been in the toilet," McClosky said. "Give the Mayor credit, at least for now keeping it from overflowing."

"And now, thanks to Maureen Whitaker Sherry, it's getting close," Cisco said. "Saunders and Lucio are pulling out all stops."

The meeting lasted about fifteen minutes, their conversation turning into harmless family banter. It concluded when Kevin's gaze rested on the framed photo of Muriel, Cisco's beautiful, blonde, blue-eyed adopted daughter.

When the spring-loaded office door finally closed behind McClosky, Cisco unfolded the paper he had been carrying in his wallet, picked up his phone and dialed the first of the two names that Dr. Andrew had scribbled.

"It's been a long time, Nick. How's my old classmate doing?" Mishap Township's Police Chief, Ned Gillespie, was expecting Cisco's call. The two men were at the police academy together and finished first and second on the Sergeant's exam, with Cisco edging out his friend by five points. Until Gillespie skipped town for the suburbs, they had been close friends but still managed to keep in touch. "Congrats on getting your second silver bar. It was too long coming."

"I was surprised when Doc Andrew gave me your name," Cisco said. "Can't imagine domestic abuse being a problem in Mishap, a land of honey, big lawns and horse lovers."

"Close, but no cigar," Gillespie said. "He and I worked together on a case that makes your Sherry killing look clean and straightforward; just bang, bang, bang, and it was over."

"Nice, if it were true. When a Maureen Whitaker Sherry knocks off her renowned surgeon husband, and when the story leaks out, it's god damn manna from heaven for the press," Cisco said. "No place else to put it, so the Chief dumped the whole fucking mess in homicide's lap. It's a political plum just ripe for picking by the Mayor's enemies."

"Nick, you're not going to tell me some greasy, faceless politicians are putting the heat on? Not in Newark, that's not the Newark I know," Gillespie sarcastically quipped, then added, "You probably never imagined being on a call that involved a thoroughbred filly with a black eye, bruised jaw and smoking pistol."

"I love it when a former East Ward street punk uses fancy horse country jargon."

"When in Rome, do as," the Police Chief said. "The good doctor found out we went back ways and wondered if I'd be willing to discuss the case I already alluded to, so here we are."

"I don't need names, just what happened, how you handled it and what the courts decided to hand down."

"I've got a couple of files for you to look at. Give me a date and time, and I'll make myself available."

Two days later, Cisco washed down a bagel heavily loaded with cream cheese and lox with his second cup of coffee, arose from the kitchen breakfast nook, and set in motion the daily Cisco family workday routine. With hands on both of her shoulders, he kissed his wife, Connie, tenderly on the lips, then reached down and lifted their daughter Muriel for a nose-to-nose rub and forehead kisses.

"Auf Wiedersehen," Muriel, now back on her feet, said. Her smiling German farewell was in sharp contrast to the language tutorial forced on her during her year as a ward of a rich, neo-Nazi, abusive couple. A dislocated shoulder and fractured arm were part of the learning process.

He decided to leave his unmarked police sedan and instead took the family's Pontiac on the pleasant forty-minute ride through rolling hills to Mishap, then south to Monmouth County and Tumult Village.

His first stop was Mishap, where Police Chief Gillespie greeted him at the door to his office in the quaint, colonial-style City Hall that also housed the City Clerk's office, two-cell jail, and City Recorder with the Municipal Court.

"Have a seat," he said as he pushed a folder across his desk. "It's heavily redacted. The only thing I'll say is that the bastard is a surgeon." The Chief leaned back in his upholstered swivel chair, fired up a cigarette and watched as Cisco silently leafed through the initial report of the arresting officer, Patrolman Michael Fitzsimmons. "When you've read all you can stomach, you'll want to strangle the son of a bitch."

After silently going through the police report, Cisco

looked up and scowled, "Jesus H. Christ. A naked woman, beaten black and blue with a pool cue. Renowned surgeon or not, this son of a bitch is a sadistic animal. Even wanted his kids...."

The Chief interrupted him and waved for someone in the doorway behind Cisco. "Mike, this is Newark Homicide Chief Nick Cisco." At the same time catching Cisco's surprised reaction to the informality. "We're informal around here. I've got twelve uniforms, two detectives and an assistant chief, now on vacation, on the payroll. We're all on a first-name basis, never in public, of course, or during official meetings with the suits upstairs."

The patrolman, unaccustomed to being in the Chief's inner sanctum, cautiously stepped forward, shook hands, removed his hat and waited.

"Mike, I know it's been two years since the pool cue arrest," the Chief said. "Captain Cisco has a similar case on his hands, and it'd be helpful if you could tell him your first reaction to what you discovered on patrol. The condition of the victim, what she told you, and all that led to putting that son of a bitch in handcuffs."

"Take your time, Mike. I read your report, like a good cop, you kept your emotions out of it. Don't hold back about your feelings toward the victim's husband; that's why I'm here."

"Well, Captain, you have to remember that was my rookie year on the force, and even separating two Great Danes screwing on the Bigelow's front lawn made me nervous," the patrolman said. "You still want my stuff?"

"I've got sixteen detectives who never confronted anything like the case we're handling now. Your reaction to Doctor Pool Cue could help me if we get another Maureen Whitaker Sherry case. You no doubt have seen the headlines: a rich, pampered dame from a blue-chip family who pumped three slugs into her surgeon husband who had been kicking the hell out of her for years. Start anytime you want to," Cisco said.

The Chief arose from his desk and lightly punched Mike on the shoulder as he walked to the office door and closed it. He turned and took a Chesterfield pack from his shirt pocket and offered it all around. Three deep drags later, Mike was ready to go.

30

The young cop began, "It would make it a lot easier for me to spill it out if I used names. The Chief filled me in that anything I say would never leave his room."

"That's right," Cisco said. "Let it fly. I'll probably stick my nose in as you go along. This isn't about procedure; it's how you responded to what you heard and saw."

"I was making my usual six o'clock patrol through the Upper Fork neighborhood when I heard sobbing from the roadside hedges of the Wilkins estate. I pulled over. At first, it was kind of dream-like. It was dark and kind of spooky when the bushes were parted enough to expose a naked woman hiding there. She was no more than maybe five or six feet from the curb; my cruiser obscured her. There was no traffic. What she said next set the tone for the evening, a trip into never-never land."

"That's hardly police terminology," Cisco said.

"I know that, Captain. As close as I can remember, this is what she said after she stopped sobbing, 'Thank God.

Don't talk too loud; I know he's looking for me.' Before I could say anything, she whispered, 'Thank God it's you, the police and not a neighbor who's discovered what's happened tonight.'"

"She used the word *discovered*?" Cisco asked. "Hardly what you'd expect, wouldn't you say?"

"Right. It was as if she was more worried about neighborhood gossip than being rescued. At this point, I still didn't know what was going on. "I told her to stay put while I returned to the car and grabbed the blanket from the backseat. She partially stepped from her hiding place in the hedge, and when I put the blanket around her shoulders, I saw that it was Mrs. Wilkins. I also saw for the first time the black and blue welts across her buttocks and the back of her thighs. I helped her into the backseat and asked who's looking for her."

"She answered, 'My husband.' This shocked the hell out of me, and I asked her where he was now. Remember, Captain, this was two years ago and memories get dim, especially those so bad you just as soon not remember them."

"You're doing great," Cisco said.

"She told me she didn't know for sure. She just hoped that Brent and Melissa were safe and that he hadn't hurt them. I was scratching everything down as fast as I could, and at this point, I asked her if these were her kids and if she thought her husband might hurt them. She replied, 'I don't know, I just pray to God they're okay. They saw everything he had did to me, then he handed them pool cues.'

"I've got to tell you, this really stunned me, and I said, 'I'm not sure I understand Mrs. Wilkins.'

"I had to back off at this point; her sobbing made it hard for her to go on. We were still in the back of my patrol car. Her crying stopped, and she said, 'The children weren't expected home so early from a friend's birthday party. He was in the middle of beating me with the pool cue when they walked in. Brent is only twelve, and Melissa is nine. They must have been horrified seeing me spread across the pool table, naked.

"'*Mommy, mommy, what's daddy doing to you!* Melissa screamed. Brent is big and strong for his twelve years; he tried to grab the cue but was pushed away. My husband blocked the door so they couldn't leave.'

"I asked her what happened then, she replied, 'I tried to get off the pool table, and he handed my son a cue and said that it was their turn, that I deserved it, and I liked it.'

"Looking for the right question, I asked Mrs. Wilkins if her children had also hit her. I was relieved when she replied, 'They never had a chance. My husband had turned his back on me, and I was able to get off the pool table and escape upstairs to our bedroom through another door and locked myself in.'

"By this time, I believed her husband was off his rocker and dangerous as hell and asked Mrs. Wilkins if he was hunting her down. Her answer surprised the hell out of me. 'No, thank God, not at first. I'm sure my children were holding him back. The last thing I heard was my son shouting, *Run, mother, run. We'll hold him!'*

"I asked if this had ever happened before? She said, 'Never with a pool cue. Raymond always uses his hands and, one time, a leather belt. My children might have guessed what was happening but never knew for sure. They were never even spanked. But who knows if they're in danger tonight. Raymond has completely lost control.'"

Cisco and Gillespie realized they were watching a young cop put together details of a nightmare. Beads of sweat found their way into his eyebrows, the armpits of his shirt dampened, and he nervously fidgeted with his hat.

Gillespie's secretary knocked on the door, partially opened it, peeked in and asked, "How about some coffee?" She returned a few minutes later with three mugs on a tray. Mike eagerly accepted one, took three sips, followed by a deep breath before placing the mug on the corner of the Chief's desk and lighting a cigarette of his own.

"I saw that shock was setting in, and her sobbing intensified as she began to shake. I told her to keep the blanket wrapped around her. I planned to call for an ambulance to meet us at her home and for backup in case her husband was still crazy.

"I checked the time; it was 6:04. The interrogation had lasted four minutes. I was turning into the long driveway to the Wilkins home and was about to put through my calls when Mrs. Wilkins began pounding on the protective grill behind me and shouting, 'Don't you dare make any calls! And turn off your headlights! There's never been a police car at our home, and the neighbors don't miss anything. I don't need a doctor.'"

"So, we have a rich dame who first kissed your ass for rescuing her, and once back on her homestead, she didn't want you around or any evidence that you had been there," interjected Cisco.

"So, I didn't make the calls, and we drove silently up the drive and parked in front of their mansion. I got out and saw why she didn't want my patrol car there. It could easily be spotted by neighbors from some distance away. I made sure Mrs. Wilkins was wrapped in the blanket. She was very unsteady when I assisted her to the front door.

"The house was silent and completely dark except for a light in one room. His wife, who had already escaped once, had fled up the stairs when I headed toward the lighted library. It was the library where I found Dr. Wilkins seated in a large, leather wingback chair. He welcomed me with a smile, and I thought, *It's like I'm joining him for a chess match and a cognac*. It was a big house, but you could still hear the sobbing reunion with her kids upstairs. I knew the smiling bastard sitting in the chair heard the same thing, but there was no reaction, not a hint anything was wrong."

Gillespie could see that Cisco was getting exactly what he wanted from the young cop, bridled anger barely kept in check. Cisco nodded appreciatively in response to everything Mike had to say.

"Dr. Wilkins wasn't a big guy; I'd say maybe five-nine, five-ten and slender. I'm six-two and could have easily smashed in his smiling face. That's when I said to myself, *Whoa, buddy, slow down and be a cop*. His first words to me,

205

and I know I have them exactly right, were, 'I lost it, completely lost it. Can't remember anything. Put in a call to Doctor Burroughs, a good friend who knows my problem, and he'll make sure my wife is well cared for. My son and daughter are in their rooms, quite safe I assure you. Everything is back to normal.'

"I told Dr. Wilkins that it was clear a violent act had occurred and that a formal complaint would be filed. I told him that anything he said could be used as evidence against him. He just sat there and didn't say a thing, sort of like I was a big annoyance."

Mike was uncertain whether to go on. He wasn't even sure why he was relating details of a case more than two years old. The Chief only said that the NPD boss thought a talk with him could be useful. After studying their faces for any sign that he was giving Captain Cisco what he wanted, he asked, "Am I being any help?"

"There's no right or wrong; I didn't drive up here to pass judgment on how you followed the rules. Just wanted your reaction and how you handled it," Cisco said. "Keep going. Let's get into the wife and kids. Did they come down?"

"I think they were afraid to. Found out that while I was downstairs with the good doctor, she was using the upstairs telephone to call her sister and brother-in-law. I used the library phone to call headquarters. They all arrived at about the same time, seven o'clock."

"What was going on in the meantime?" Cisco asked.

"Nothing. She stayed upstairs with the kids while the

husband strolled about the library. The good doctor asked if it was okay to play some music while they were waiting. I was dumbfounded. 'It's Beethoven's Seventh in A Major, one of my favorites,' the son of a bitch said.

"Off the record, when the music started playing and remembering what the wife's bottom and thighs looked like, I wanted to take my nightstick and beat the hell out of him."

"That's about it, Mike, you did great," Cisco said. "More than half my bullpen has never handled a domestic or sexual abuse case that made the headlines. Just routine, and I hate to use that word, just tenement punch-outs, razor blade slicing when a hooker was pushed too far, or ice pick stabbing usually over money or sexual cheating."

"So, I can go? I'm finished?" Mike asked.

"That's right. Unless Captain Cisco has anything more," Gillespie said.

"Nope. You made the forty-minute trip to Mishap worth it. Thanks," Cisco said as he extended his hand, and he and Gillespie walked Mike to the door.

31

The Police Chief waited until Mike closed the door behind him, walked back to his desk and motioned Cisco to take a seat.

"Nice job by the kid," Cisco said. "I can guess, but tell me anyway, how did it all end up?"

"Misdemeanor charges. The hearing behind closed doors in the judge's chambers. One year probation, weekly anger management sessions with a psychiatrist, who happened to be one of the accused's best friends. I tried but couldn't prove that the sessions petered out after three months however, the shrink's reports kept coming in."

"And the wife and kids?"

"They're all back together again, one happy family. Remember, no one gets beaten black and blue in Mishap."

He reached into the lower left drawer of his desk and removed two bottles and two glasses. "Sour mash or single malt?"

Cisco reached for the two bottles and examined their labels as he placed a half bottle of Jack Daniels and a well-used bottle of ten-year-old Laphroaig Islay on the desk.

"If you're an upper-crust drinker in Mishap, status symbol booze is the only thing that dare pass your lips," Gillespie said. "Far cry from the old days when ten cents a shot rotgut rye chased by a nickel glass of suds did the job."

Cisco---- nodded toward the two bottles, "Scotch for me, make it stiff."

Gillespie poured four fingers of Islay into one glass and the same amount of sour mash into the other. They reached across the desk and tipped glasses.

"How old are we now? Early forties and we're already old guard," Gillespie said. "Mike is the new breed. Put his ass on the line in the Pacific and saw things that two stay-at-home essentials like us can only imagine."

"The whole afternoon's mine," Cisco said. "Something bothering you, Ned? Or am I just imagining that there is?"

"You wouldn't think so in a town where the Police Chief has it soft and sweet. Millie and Brenda, hard to believe she's eighteen, are both medal-winning equestrians. Never knew what the hell dressage was until they came home with ribbons."

"Can't believe a tough nut like you is bent out of shape," Cisco said, "because your wife and daughter know how to saddle-up and prance around an arena on horseback."

"Give me your glass, looks like you could use another splash," Gillespie said.

The two veteran cops tapped out cigarettes, fired up, and then washed away the smoke with healthy gulps of eighty-proof elixir. Cisco waited for the Chief to get the ball rolling.

"Ever wonder why I jumped ship?" the Chief asked, his eyes inquisitive slits. "Getting my sergeant stripes on the first try didn't sit well with the paisanos who had rigged the exam. I should have been a smart cop on the way up, but instead, I was a dumb Mic who didn't play their game. I had to be watched, never any chance for invites to homemade meatball and linguini dinners."

"Some of us talked about it and decided to throw you a get-away bash to be proud of," Cisco said, then arose from his seat and walked to a large picture window overlooking a manicured lawn that edged along a bubbling stream. On the far side were neatly trimmed and perfectly spaced trees and shrubs. Two boys were targeting stone throws at a large, rounded boulder jutting from the stream, and further down, a woman in slacks and sweaters was walking two leashed collies.

"This burg could be a million miles from your old precinct in Newark's Ironbound. Ever miss the adrenaline rush, never knowing if your next call could be a shooting, knifing, rape or a pimp in the gutter with a bloody single-edged razorblade nearby?"

"Nope. But it wasn't the Ward's daily home brew of crime, misery and hopelessness at the edge," Gillespie said. "I jumped off the edge all by my lonesome. It was three murders that didn't even make page eighteen or grist for the radio lip-flappers. Made the cursory rounds, precinct to precinct. It was Jim Sweeney who put his loud, dirty mouth to work behind his sergeant stripes and squad boss power that did it."

"Jimmy Sweeney, what gave with him?" Cisco circled back to his seat, reached for the bottle of Laphroaig, poured a healthy one, sat back and waited.

"Remember the case," Gillespie said. "The bodies of three working ladies, the oldest only twenty-one, found in a garbage dumpster, a back alley and river riprap? All had cutthroats and were sliced up pretty bad."

"Where does Sweeney come in?"

"On Vice, Sweeney came to know all three of them. He gave them street corner and curb privileges only after they spent some time in the backseat of his patrol car. He said the youngest was the best, and he was sorry to see her go."

"That's what pushed you over, bragging from a son of a bitch like Sweeney?"

"Not just Sweeney. I knew the youngest hooker. Her name was Nancy Czarobski. The kid was only thirteen when she was arrested giving a blow job to a Marine in a back alley. Turned her over to juvie court. From time-to-time caught sight of her working the streets around Penn Station. Hers was the usual 'never had a chance' story.

"My disgust was coming for a long time. Not because of the filth on the street but because of the rotten sons of bitches wearing blue badges and carrying guns.

"A sap like Sweeney figured the rules from the get-go. I never did.

"Heard about the Mishap Chief's job on the grapevine and jumped for it before it went public. So here I am, but only after the go-ahead from Millie and Brenda."

Cisco knew his old boyhood friend well enough to know that there was something more to come. He reached forward and poured healthy splashes in first the Chief's glass and then his own.

"It didn't surprise me that homicide had closed their books," Gillespie said. "Nothing new there, but Jesus Christ, Nick, the thought of Nancy Czarobski, a kid who never had a chance, lying in a pool of her own blood really got to me. Started gumshoeing on my own. I saw that the suits working the murders never correlated their notes. Jumping out was the fact that each victim was on her back, legs straight and together, and arms outstretched to form a cross. The work of a religion-crazed nut with a knife."

"Were the three hookers churchgoers?" Cisco asked. "Wouldn't surprise me if they were. Can't recall how many criminal types, even mob soldiers, who had a gun in one hand and a rosary in the other."

"All were Catholic, and all were regular at their parishes," the Chief said. "Nosed around and discovered that there were several frightened young ladies at St. Dominic's with the same story. A slightly older religious creep kept bugging them for days, even promised long country rides in his bakery delivery truck. The girls were right; he was a religious nut who made mass and communion every day, every novena and Way of the Cross, and passed the collection plate around during high mass on Sunday."

"So, I staked out Saturday afternoon confessions. St. Gregory's is a huge Gothic horror, complete with flying trusses and gargoyles. A huge mausoleum with confessionals along each side aisle. It was late in the afternoon, and confessions were winding down. Only one dark box had its 'open for business' red light still on. My hunch was right; the church was deserted when my mark came in, genuflected and entered the right side of the confessional, closing the curtain behind him. I waited about three or four minutes and entered the left side. Their voices were low but distinctive enough for me to catch almost every word. The son of a bitch was asking for the priest's blessing and prayers to shield him from the next murderous temptation he felt coming on."

Cisco knew it was best not to interrupt.

"I waited until he received his blessing and penance from the priest and began his act of contrition before sliding out of the confessional and hiding in an alcove with a bigger-than-life statue of St. Anthony. I jumped him, and with one hand crushing his larynx and the other smothering his mouth, I dragged him into the first box of the next row of confessionals. I have to make it clear, Nick: I wanted to kill him. I pushed him onto the priest's bench and began punching and punching. Don't know how many times."

Gillespie had placed his glass down and, with a twisted motion, was rubbing the knuckles of both hands. He bent forward and, with his elbows digging deeply into his thighs, began rubbing his face. He looked up and studied Cisco.

"And that's it. I was out of uniform, and I'm sure he

never got a clear look at my face. I left him slouched and bleeding on the priest's seat in the confessional, blood flowing and teeth in his lap. Thanks, Nick, for sitting through all this. But getting this off my chest with a friend who knows where I'm coming from, well, what can I say? It's been a long time coming."

On his way back to the Cisco family Pontiac, Nick took in the surrounding landscape. The beautifully trimmed trees, the park benches, the well-manicured lawn, the brook, and what the hell else he could feel and taste. It was invisible but yet palpable…life as it was meant to be.

As he drove off, he was glad that he had stifled his temptation to compare notes related to that chaotic moment when, as a young sergeant, hatred had also pushed him close to murder. It took time for him to reconcile that if it wasn't for his partner, he would have drowned the animal who had beaten his wife and young daughter to death while in a drunken rage. He had pushed the husband's head into the toilet and held it during flush after flush until McClosky stopped him with threats that the son of a bitch wasn't worth ending his career for.

McClosky was right. As a team, they had climbed countless condemned tenement steps only to discover where the true condemnation belonged. For more than ten years, the two men formed a bond unique for the Newark police department. He knew more than Cisco did that this was what their life as cops would always be. Get with it and move on.

32

Cisco decided to avoid the major highways and take the fifty-five-mile scenic route from Mishap to Tumult Village through the gentle rolling hills of the northwest into the industrial ugliness that defined much of the northeast. He crossed the border into Warren County and stopped at a two-pump station for a fill-up. While the gas jockey was at work, he walked over to a public phone, pulled out the note from Dr. Andrew and called Martha Tremaine Featherstone. After five rings, a cultured woman's voice, unmistakably shaped during years of polished consonants and vowels in European finishing schools, purred into the handset.

"This is Martha Featherstone. To whom am I speaking?"

"Captain Nicholas Cisco, Newark Police Homicide Chief. Dr. Moishe Andrew said that you've consented to speak with me off the record and anonymously. Would this afternoon be possible?"

"Yes, I did, but only after Moishe told me what you were

up to, and it intrigued me."

"How so?"

"That a big city homicide detective would want to learn how to manage upper-class wife beating. How surprising. The small-town investigators we have around here were only interested in itemizing my physical wreckage in snapshots."

Cisco had learned from Dr. Andrew that Mrs. Featherstone had been fighting a divorce for almost two years. She didn't want one. Why not? That would be useful information for him and any of his homicide crew who would find themselves working another Maureen Whitaker Sherry case.

"Can you spare some time this afternoon?" Cisco asked, relieved by what he had just heard. Mrs. Featherstone had obviously given considerable thought to her current situation, but how much detail would she be willing to share? "So, is now a good time? I'm no more than a half-hour away."

"I'll be waiting, sixty-seven Sweet Refuge Drive, a big house up on the hill."

Cisco pulled his car to a stop at the end of a crushed-stone driveway and appreciated how precise her directions were. The hill was the highest in the neighborhood; the driveway handled its steep slope by meandering west to east on its way to the top. Stepping from his car he approached the sprawling, Gothic fortress that Mrs. Featherstone now had all to herself. He was halfway up the twelve-wide steps when the huge oak door opened, and she stepped out onto the six-column portico to greet him. When he reached the top and took full measure of Mrs. Featherstone, a thought crossed Cisco's mind, a wispy notion that quickly disappeared.

"Captain Cisco?" she said, sneaking in a thin, forced smile that set the stage for what was to come. She would be direct, feign friendliness and never lose control. "You were right; it didn't take long for you to get here."

He took her extended, velvet-smooth right hand, and when she clasped her left hand over his, he couldn't fail to notice that her ring finger was adorned with an emerald cut diamond, in tribute to F. Scott Fitzgerald's *The diamond as big as the Ritz*.

Dr. Moise Andrew was right; she would never accept a divorce.

She led him down a long hallway, surprisingly bright in contrast to the mansion's somber, almost forbidding exterior. "You like madeleines? They're my favorite cookie, savory and not sweet."

"Had them a few times at art exhibits. I like them."

"At art exhibits? Very interesting. Did you have aspirations?"

"A long time ago, not as an artist, but as a critic. I'm not here to talk about me."

They arranged themselves in matching maroon, Queen Anne wing chairs on opposite sides of an oblong, glass-protected coffee table with all the goodies.

"Do you smoke? I do, but won't if you don't."

"I do. Brought my own and a lighter just in case," Cisco said. "Mine are Chesterfields, pretty strong stuff."

"How wonderful, so do I!" she gushed, reached for the butler bell on the table and when a primly dressed Mexican girl appeared at the door, commanded, *"Carla, tráeme mis cigarrillos y dos ceniceros, por favor."*

Cisco was questioning a woman who was obviously in full control of her emotions. She offered him another cup of coffee, which he refused, poured one for herself, and then casually lit up. Mrs. Featherstone could well have invented the word "composure." Her high breeding was on display. She was so unlike his highly intelligent wife, Connie, and college-educated Grace DeMarco, who had been his mistress for three years, both with humble Italian immigrant backgrounds.

During his mild contretemps with the shrink, he learned that the Featherstones never wanted children, making it possible for Martha to focus entirely on Spencer, every unfathomable whim, temper tantrum, loss of control, to tight-fisted punches everywhere. These were all considered expressions of love.

He decided to get straight to the point. "Can you recall the first time he hit you?"

Her answer was immediate, as though the two had been going through a well-rehearsed scene. "It was six years ago. We had just returned from a fundraising dance and auction at the country club."

"Where did it happen?"

"Here, just as soon as we walked through the front door. It seems he couldn't wait."

"That's what you sensed? But first, tell me about your husband."

"Dr. Spencer Featherstone is the best of the best, and he lets you know it. He's a urologist renowned for his research into prostate cancer."

"So, out of the blue, when you walked into your home, he smacked you?"

"Not out of the blue. During the evening, I danced three times with an Army Major from Fort Dix. A handsome man in a full-dress uniform with all of the braid that goes with it. Spencer was never a dancer; you needed a loaded pistol to get him on the floor."

"So, it was the jealous rage? Was it a slap, a punch, or a hard shaking of the shoulders?"

"A slap to my right cheek. It just as well could have been a cannon shot. I fell backward and sent a stack of mail flying when I grabbed for the entrance table. He grabbed my shoulders, tightened his grip and began shaking me uncontrollably. With our faces nearly touching, he spat out words I'll never forget. 'So now you've become a dancehall bitch!'"

"And that was it, one slap to the face and some shaking?"

"You're kind of new at this. That wasn't all. It took more than a week of applying make-up to hide the black and blue. Then, a couple of months later, like the first time, it was after a fundraiser. After that, I began spending more and more time with my new friends."

"New friends?"

"Helena Rubenstein, Max Factor, Elizabeth Arden and Dorothy Gray were always ready with a helping hand. When it comes to camouflage, only the best will do."

"So, this went on for six years. Pardon my English, why in hell did you stay?"

"Because I love him, and I know in my heart that he loves me. I still do, and I'm certain it's the same for Spencer. He only has to come to his senses and return."

This was new territory for Cisco. How far could he push it before she considered him impertinent and ordered him from the house? He decided to go for it.

"And if the beatings return with him, you'll accept the package just as it was before?"

As if she hadn't heard Cisco's question or heard it and chose to ignore it, she replaced her coffee cup on the table, leaned back in her chair and fixed him with a wide, blue-eyed gaze. "We are both members of prominent Catholic families; there's a bishop and two monsignors on my side of the family and an archbishop and a Benedictine abbot on Spencer's. Divorce is out of the question."

Since his days as a uniform on the streets, he was aware that there was a litany of resignations shared by battered women in the inner city. It was a religious prop that rationalized every righteous slap, punch and kick, often in front of children. Each was a manifestation of *amor in extremo*, a reminder that the man she married had vowed before God to protect her and would only strike her if she deserved it.

Cisco couldn't remember how many times he was called to witness the results of catholicity gone crazy. Where would a humiliated woman, used for years as a punching bag, turn for help if she pressed charges? Payroll checks were never issued from jail.

"Let me get this right: are you saying it is Catholicism that keeps you together?"

"We are both vain and self-indulgent. Spencer was tall and handsome, what they called a 'dreamboat,' and I was tall, blonde, blue-eyed and smart. He had just given a paper at the University of Chicago's Pritzker School of Medicine, and I was finishing my senior year across town at Mundelein College."

"Obviously, money has never been a problem, or is it?"

"I'm what you call a trust-fund baby, so money will never be a problem. Spencer is comfortably ensconced with a new paramour, a passing fancy that I'm sure won't last. I'm a patient woman, Captain Cisco."

Is it possible that this rock-solid woman, so sure of herself, had just let loose an underlying note of pleading for something that will never happen again.

"May I ask how often your husband hit you or pushed you around?"

"It is not like those others, the poor women in tenements who have no choice when their drunken husbands slam them around." She stiffened and barely controlled her pique.

Her answer surprised Cisco. It was glib enough to have been rehearsed.

"How often did Spencer assault you in any way, verbally, physically or sexually?"

"Verbally, quite often. He had trouble with verbal give and take. I was an English Lit major and the top performer on the Mundelein debate team. He couldn't compete. It was often a slap, a shove or twisted arm that expressed his point of view."

"Did Dr. Andrew ever discuss the *Messiah Complex* with you?"

"No, he did not. What is the *Messiah Complex*?"

"As I understand it, the complex emerges when a massive ego's control is challenged and, lacking verbal skills, strikes out physically. Surgeons fit the pattern. How many times have your verbal skills put you in Spencer's crosshairs?"

"Too many to remember. Spencer isn't the only one with a temper. There were times when I had it up to here," she said, placing her right hand on her neck, "and let him have it, and it didn't matter who was within earshot."

"And this will all change when he sees the light and returns to you?" The wonder of it all was an educated, beautiful, intelligent woman who intentionally provoked her hot-tempered husband, knowing the consequences.

"Possibly not. You notice I said, 'possibly' and not 'hopefully.' It may shock you to know that Spencer and I shared the most incredible sex after our encounters." She sipped her coffee and enjoyed the surprise reflecting in his eyes. "You asked me how many times? Well, I can tell you, in retrospect, not enough."

33

She motioned him to stay seated as she turned and walked to a mahogany cabinet nestled between two tall bookshelves against the only unadorned wall in the drawing room.

Martha Tremaine Featherstone might be a forty-two-year-old woman, but it was obvious that she had worked hard to make four-plus decades as physically perfect as possible. Despite his twenty years of face-to-face experiences with the guilty and innocent, he realized he was now in alien territory. He wasn't alone.

Sergeants Quentin Rockford and Dan Thibadeau were transferred from the Major Crime squad, which often dealt with the city's elite. Cisco assigned them the Maureen Whitaker Sherry case because he assumed a higher degree of sophistication from them. It was an assumption gone astray. Five days into their investigation, they were clueless about Mrs. Sherry. "Can't make her out," Rockford said. "Don't get me wrong, she's not hostile, just doesn't want us around."

Thibadeau's latest report was just as befuddled. "I still can't get a handle on Mrs. Sherry. She's just as remote now as she was a few hours after she pumped three bullets into her hubby."

Cisco was about to see how class aloofness developed and how it was destroyed. It was an area where, except for the one punch to the face of his mistress, Grace DeMarco, he had very little knowledge.

Mrs. Featherstone had removed a thick, leatherbound album from the cabinet's top drawer and now placed it on the table in front of Cisco and said, "Here, take a look, and you'll see what my problem is."

Cisco took the album, opened it and began leafing through page after page of newspaper clippings and photos, with each page in a clear, protective sleeve.

On the first page, there was a forty-point headline that chronicled *BALLET GETS NEW BOARD PRESIDENT*. The first paragraph of the story noted the vote for Martha Tremaine Featherstone was unanimous. The text went on to say it was the first non-profit foundation office that the wife of renowned urologist Dr. Spencer Featherstone had held….

Another album page headlined *ORPHANAGE BOARD APPEALS FOR PUBLIC SUPPORT*. The second paragraph of the story quoted Board President Martha Tremaine Featherstone, "St. James Orphanage has been a blessing to this community for more than fifty years. Now, it is in dire need of public support. Demands for bed space have been drastically increasing. The Board needs everyone's helping hand...."

Deeper into the album, readers learned that, *FEATHERSTONE UNOPPOSED IN BID FOR CITY PARKS SEAT*. The Evening News reporter, Roslyn Longly, gushed, "It should come as no surprise that the first woman to hold a seat on the City Parks Board is Martha Tremaine Featherstone. Her volunteer service is legendary...."

He sensed that her eyes never left him as he looked through one sheet after another. *The woman sitting across from me isn't just another rich, beautiful woman; she's a public monument.*

"You're not hiding a pair of angel wings under your dress, are you? What's the problem?"

"Loneliness."

He studied her face and no longer attempted to hide his surprise. "Loneliness?"

"Did you happen to notice the dates of those stories? Everyone is dated before Spencer, and I separated."

Then, the silence began as she refilled both coffee cups and waited until they dragged deeply into their Chesterfields. It lasted for an excruciating ten seconds. "The last date sets in stone when telephone calls steadily decreased to where only a few of my closest friends invite me to lunch or anywhere else. Now, these invitations are fewer and fewer."

"Any explanation?"

"It became increasingly apparent that I am not only Martha Tremaine Featherstone, but most important that I am Martha Tremaine Featherstone, wife of the nationally renowned urologist, Dr. Spencer Featherstone. His name was the door opener for everything. His family has been a cornerstone of local high society for generations. And I might be beautiful and smart, but I'm still an outsider from Chicago."

"Has any of this helped you to understand why you and other rich, talented and beautiful women allow yourselves to be kicked and punched around?"

"I'll answer your question with some questions of my own. I know this isn't the way it usually works. I'm guessing this won't take much of your time and will be informative."

"Okay."

"Do you know how many of us have our own names on our credit cards?"

"I have no idea."

"How many of us have title to the cars we drive?"

"Again, no idea."

"And checking accounts, how many are ours?"

"No idea."

"How many share title to their homes?"

"Again, no."

"Or can still enjoy family escapes, you know aboard the sailboat or yacht, up in the country cabin, or the bungalow at the beach?"

"No."

"Are you surprised?"

"Quite a bit," Cisco replied. "Are you saying that all the luxuries that have defined your life come to an end with a divorce?"

"Remember, Spencer and I are not divorced, just separated. There's not even an annulment. I know how several of the other marriages ended, an insidious process much like Chinese water torture. In the end, the victims can still share in the goodies up to the point agreed to by the bastards they married, if, and only if, they keep their mouths shut."

"You haven't mentioned child custody," Cisco said. "Not all of the kids turn out well. In fact, while I was still in uniform and out on the street, there were more than a few rich kids who showed up in juvie."

"I know that, and it's the reason Spencer and I decided against kids. There are a lot of rich little monsters floating around, kids who have stolen their neighbor's Bentley, broken into mansions, dealt drugs, and even motored off in their neighbor's fifty-foot yacht."

"Are you saying there's no limits to the hush-hush?" Cisco asked.

"Let me give you an example, and then we can end this interview."

Cisco finished his cigarette, sat back and waited. He was tired and grudgingly admitted to himself that he'd like to get it over with.

"This kid, a seventeen-year-old honor student and

athlete at an elite prep school, where his father is a big donor, is a case in point. We know the family very well and are among the few aware of the facts. It seems the boy was in love with pistols and amphetamines. Both were accessible at a school founded almost a century ago to instill strength of character.

"It was as though the parents had to tell somebody. They were not seeking answers but needed to unburden themselves. The boy was only fifteen when his father got him out of his first big jam. It was at school when he got one snort of cocaine too many, pulled a hidden pistol and had his roommate and two student visitors jumping for cover as he wildly shot into the ceiling and out the door into the hall. A one-hundred-thousand dollar gift kept everyone's mouth shut, and the boy remained in school."

"Did the kid learn his lesson?"

"I'll just say before his eighteenth birthday, his parents discovered that their son's old habits were hard to break. This time, they and the domestic staff jumped for cover as he ran through their mansion, shooting enough to reload twice, according to his father. Empty cartridges were spread throughout the halls."

"So, tell me, how did it turn out?" Cisco asked.

"No one was hurt. The boy passed out, and a doctor was called. He was secluded in his room for the rest of his vacation and as though nothing had happened, jumped into his little convertible and returned to school. You'll see their house when you drive home; it's on a smaller hill about a mile west of here."

"Well, that should do it, Mrs. Featherstone. You've been a big help, and I can't thank you enough for giving me so much of your time," he said as they walked to the front door. She went no further than the threshold, and as he headed across the portico to his car, she said, "I'm not delusional, Captain Cisco. You understand that much, don't you?"

He descended the twelve steps to his car without turning to answer and drove away. No, he didn't understand. As he merged into highway traffic on his way back to Newark, his thoughts turned first to his wife Connie, a bright and caring woman who could never fathom what he had just been told, and to Grace DeMarco, who knew all too well.

Five miles out of Tumult Village, Cisco pulled off the road and parked in a shaded rest area, fired up a Chesterfield and questioned his motivation. Was he on a fool's errand? He pulled the paper given to him by Dr. Moishe Andrew and wondered whether it was necessary to visit the third person on the list.

His thoughts went back to the morning before when he watched unnoticed from the doorway the uniform shift change. It was the second day the unit would be on twenty-four-hour watch at the Sherry mansion.

"Musselman and Dolan, you're back to a life of leisure." Sergeant Fogerty worked hard to suppress a smile.

Cisco kept his eyes on Musselman and Dolan when they turned to leave. As they reached the exit when another officer cried out, "Here da-da, and daddy number two, don't forget your ammunition!"

They turned to catch a tightly wrapped package of cotton diapers and a box of safety pins. Musselman snatched the diapers, and Dolan just missed the box before it hit the wall, burst open and shot pins in every direction.

"Go fuck yourselves, and here's something to wipe up with afterward!" Dolan shouted back and, with a football quarterback pose, tossed the package of diapers back at the pack of guffawing officers. They were all smiles when they drove off in their squad car.

It reminded Cisco of his days in uniform when blue tribalism made daily encounters with filth bearable. But today's scum of the earth wasn't his problem.

Before roll call, Cisco studied the jackets of his sixteen homicide detectives to find that all but three had never handled a case involving the rich and entitled. They were a close-knit bunch, and after hearing Rockford's and Thibadeau's complaints that they were no more useful than farts in the wind, the squad room echoed with ribald remarks and mockery.

Despite their cynicism, these were the hardboiled guys Cisco had to deal with, and he would not trade a single one of them. He decided to follow a crazy hunch.

34

Fifty-seven miles to the southeast, just outside Metuchen, the huge kilns of Mario Riati & Son Cement blasted at 1450 degrees Fahrenheit as Stefano Rizzano, Mario, his son, Jack, and two thugs met. The office overlooked the heaps of gypsum, limestone and clay that found its way through the heat of the kiln, then through the grinding teeth of the mill to be mixed with water and finally to the company's six cement-mixing trucks with their bulbous churning mixers.

The meeting had been punctuated with shouts of protest as Stefano explained that the rules had changed for the Teamsters Local 91 and Cement and Concrete Laborers Union Local 39.

"I'm not handing out bullshit when I say the Unions are getting bigger and stronger," he said. "And we'll need an increase in Union dues to pull it off. Your paychecks won't get smaller, only bigger."

"When I see the numbers on my paycheck getting smaller in order to get bigger, now that's a goddamn miracle, and I don't believe in miracles," jeered a tall, muscular worker leaning against a cement mixer.

"Let's everybody cool down," Stefano calmly replied. He then held up both hands, palms out and said, "Things are falling into place. Jimmy Hoffa just got back from some heavy organizing in Michigan. Hell, he's a Trustee on the General Executive Board. And you'll get to know real well these two guys next to me. Have anything to bitch about, take it to them."

Stefano felt thirty pairs of eyes boring into the back of his head as he drove away in his open Cabriolet. He motored across Newark, picked up Park Avenue as it entered Branch Brook Park, drove east through the park, turned onto Lake Street, passed four large homes and into the driveway of the fifth, a ten-room Victorian that he bought for his parents.

His older sister, Theresa, loved the place, with an *en suite* that included a bedroom, full bath and large lounge area all her own. Their parents, Danielo and Alicia, had to be literally dragged from their home of thirty-five years on Mount Prospect to their new upscale surroundings. Two years earlier, Stefano employed some softer-than-usual mafia extortion tactics to convince the former owner that it was time to move out at a mob-approved price. Following his sister's example, he put together a comfortable trysting place that had its own second-floor entrance on the opposite end of the house.

"Stefano! Just in time," his mother, Alicia, bellowed loud enough to be heard throughout the ten rooms, then greeted him with a kiss on the cheek as he entered the kitchen. "It's time for the sauce, so get out of that tie and jacket and start chopping. Here, take this." She removed one of three aprons that hung from hooks near the pantry, handed it to him, and pointed to a cutting board covered with mushrooms, garlic cloves, fresh Roma tomatoes, thyme, basil, hot red peppers and a large white onion. "You take care of that, and I'll handle the antipasti."

"Where's everybody?" he asked as he slipped on the apron and reached for a large mixing bowl on the top shelf of the cupboard.

"Upstairs. Your father's taking his daily *riposo pomeridiano,* and Theresa is putting on her face for dinner. And you know how long that takes."

At twenty minutes after six, Danielo and his son were in the parlor sipping their second glass of grappa. "Where's Theresa!" He hoped his rich baritone reached his daughter upstairs. "She's pretty enough not to need all that goddamn junk Pietro Lupo gives her. But if the lady wants, the lady gets."

"How's Pietro doing? I hear that he's moved up in the world," Stefano said, alluding to the gossip that his sister's boyfriend had been taken off the street and made a collector by one of Richie the Boot's underbosses.

Alicia joined them, taking a seat on the Davenport and methodically fluffed and re-fluffed its two large throw pillows. Stefano studied her face and then his father's and sensed he had opened a subject they'd rather not discuss.

"He gonna be here tonight for dinner?"

"Not tonight. It's just the four of us," his father said.

Stefano wondered what the hell was going on. Theresa always had boyfriends over for the family's big bash on Sunday. They came, and they went. Pete had been his parents' favorite, to the point where marriage hints were jokingly passed back and forth across the dinner table.

There was an awkward silence, so rare in a family that loved to talk, when Theresa called down, "I'm coming."

Once she was seated, Stefano understood his parents' reluctance to talk about Pete. Theresa wore a white, high-collared, buttoned chiffon blouse that failed at its job. Despite the skillfully applied pancake makeup and the blouse's high collar, bruises in their green and yellow healing stage could be seen on both sides of her neck. Someone with strong hands had grabbed her in a vice-like grip that Stefano knew from experience had left her breathless. From the color of her bruises, he figured the attack had occurred at least a week earlier.

Despite the two bottles of Chianti, there was very little talk at the dinner table. Everyone knew that Stefano was thinking the unthinkable, that a female member of the Rizzano family had been attacked. The dishes were washed and put away with little attempt at the friendly banter that went with the chore. There were kisses on the cheek and *buona nottes* all around to conclude the early evening.

Stefano waited until he was sure that Theresa had settled in before he knocked on her door and asked, "It's me, Terri. Can I come in?"

Silence. Without asking, he turned the door handle, saw

that it was unlocked and quietly stepped inside. He had closely studied his sister's face during dinner and saw clearly that she was hurting. *Why? Was it Pietro Lupo, the flashy, low-level Boiardo thug Terri calls her boyfriend? Better not be.* He distrusted him with his big mouth and unfounded bragging. Stefano sized up Lupo as one of those Al Capone wannabees who, just like he had, competed for Mafia attention as a teenager.

"Terri, come on out here so we can talk."

Theresa stepped from her bedroom into the sitting room. She was barefoot and clad in short-sleeve, collarless, powder blue pajamas. The bruises on her neck were larger than he had imagined, and there was another bruise on the biceps of her right arm. His older sister was his hero during his pre-teen years; she had never backed off when they were threatened during playground disputes. It was clear that the mother-fucker had pinned her down with his right hand on his sister's throat while his left hand pinned down her right arm.

Theresa joined her brother on the plush divan, where he waited with his arms folded. The look on his face frightened her. *Jesus, Mary and Joseph,* she prayed, *don't let it happen.* She had witnessed how his two violent daytime nightmares took control of both mind and body. He was only twelve years old when three classmates were needed to pull him off a wiseass punk who had said the wrong thing at the wrong time. The second she witnessed from the grandstand during a timeout at an East Side High football game. Instead of joining his team's huddle, he raced to the other sideline and plunged with fists flying into the other team. He was ejected, but not before the East Side players kicked the hell out of him.

"You wanna know, so here it is. Lucy Nigro, you remember her, don't you? Good looking tramp with big tits, plenty of dough and a fancy car. Nice to have a papa with three numbers parlors." Stefano reached over and cupped both of her hands in his. She studied his hands, then moved to his face, still amazed at how good-looking, big and strong he had become.

"We were doing fine for about three months when I caught Pietro and Lucy over on Avon. Don't ask me why I was there, and no, I wasn't spying. She was giving him a blow job in the backseat. I tapped on the window lightly at first, then hard with my knuckles. Like two deaf mutes, they kept on going. I didn't stick around."

"And then what?"

"We went face-to-face two days later. We were alone at his place. I let it all out, and he had the balls to say that I was his one and only and that Lucy's pipe cleaning was a mistake. And yeah, he did get in that he loved me, and it would never happen again."

"God damn it, Terri, I'm sorry. I didn't realize," Stefano said as he removed his hands from hers. He had unconsciously tightened his grip. Her fingers were completely numb. As she watched her brother's features darken, his eyes now opaque and sightless, and his jaw tighten over clenched teeth, she feared the worst.

Stefano rose and assisted Terri to her feet. He bent over and peered into her eyes. Her eyes were cleaved into two imploring orbits. The sister who had protected him during his early school years was now silently asking him to back away from revenge.

"Don't worry, Terri, I won't lay a hand on Lupo," he kissed her forehead. "One big favor though, get rid of all that shit lover boy's been giving you. You don't need it; you're beautiful."

"We both know that right now, I'm anything but beautiful," she replied with a forced smile that instantly faded when she saw the furrows above his eyes deepen. "It scares me what this has done to you. I've seen you at your darkest, but promise me not this time."

"I won't touch him." Stefano threw his sister a kiss and left.

Back in his room, he poured himself a healthy scotch, added two cubes, walked over to the bureau to retrieve his wallet and got comfortable in a leather lounge chair near the window. He removed the small scrap of paper given him by attorney Chester Bruno with the suggestion that he might want to call the scribbled phone number to hear the craziest scheme ever hatched.

It was a Newark number, not much travel involved and hell; it might even be good for a laugh. He placed the call, and the woman's voice at the other end had a no-nonsense, professionally-tuned quality.

"I talked to Bruno. So, we know who our connection is." Stefano said.

"No sense wasting our time then. Do you have strong

opinions, pro or con, about men beating up women?"

"That only cowards do it."

"That's the right answer. Before we go any further, there is no money involved, only satisfaction. You can think of your time as a donation."

Stefano realized that Bruno had it right. Nothing could be crazier than a mafia hitman being asked by an unknown woman to donate his services. "I'm willing to listen. Just give me a time and place, and I'll see if I can make it."

He took down the information and was about to hang up when the woman chimed in, "Oh yes, this is the name you use to get past the receptionist, Bill Collector."

35

It was the Monday after Debbie's meeting with Grace DeMarco, Margie Bruni and two former classmates that she decided it was best to remain in Newark to hear Grace's scheme.

From his brokerage office on Wall Street, her father had called in some due bills and in less than a week, she was ensconced in a fully furnished luxury apartment on High Street. The owners had left for five months in Europe. She also inherited the housekeeper/cook, Jenny McGuire.

She made ample use of the three telephones, keeping in daily touch with Grace and Rosemary Pringle, another prospective schemer. It was shortly after noon of Wednesday, October 1, when after an insistent ten rings she answered the living room telephone. It was Ingrid Lindstrom's voice, always assertive but now reduced to a tearful mumble, "Madame Deborah, we have trouble. I called your father, and now I call you. Big trouble. A doctor is needed...."

Eli Green, the caretaker of the Hammerstein mansion, was busy in the three-car garage when he heard a thud. Something heavy or someone had hit the floor directly overhead. He sensed that someone had entered the mansion. The thump and the first discernable words from his wife, Sophia, broke what obviously had been a softer-spoken conversation.

"Warum haben Sie mich geschlagen, Herr Paasche? Ich habe dir alles gesagt. Ich wusste nicht, dass sie ein geheimes Versteck hatte."

"You see what happens if you lie or keep secrets. Does Madam Paasche have a secret place where she keeps her special things? Tell me in English, or do you want more of this!" Paasche said as he kicked Sophia's feet from under her as she attempted to pull herself up from the floor. She had braced herself on a heavy wooden carving block on casters. With both hands, he pushed the cutting block across the kitchen, causing Sophia to fall to her knees. He placed his right foot between her shoulder blades and shoved her head first against the wall. There was the unmistakable crack of breaking bones.

Housekeeper Ingrid Lindstrom was polishing silver in the dining room when she heard Sophia's cries. She raced to the kitchen door and fought for balance after stumbling over Sophia, blood flowing freely from her nose. "My God, what have you done!" She looked up at a smirking Paasche standing with crossed arms against the kitchen sink.

"We know nothing about secret hiding places!" Ingrid

screamed, tears cascading down her cheeks. Johan reached forward, grabbed her blouse with his left hand and was prepared to hit her with his right fist when Eli stumbled into the kitchen and saw his unconscious wife on the floor, blood pooling around her head.

"Sophia, Sophia, what has he done to you!" He was about to bend over his wife when Johan hurled himself across the kitchen and rammed his shoulder into Eli's chest. The older man lost his balance, fell backward and tumbled down the stairs. His head bounced off the heavy plank stairs, and he was unconscious when he hit the floor.

Johan turned to Ingrid, who was cowering in a far corner of the large kitchen. In her hand was a large carving knife. He knew he'd have no trouble taking it from her, but why bother? She would be useless, pleading ignorance or lying.

He descended the stairs and, reaching the bottom, pushed Eli aside with heavy kicks to his ribs and head. He stepped to the floor and paused before exiting through the garage door to glance at the carefully polished black BMW R-62 on its kickstand to his left. He hated the machine and the corrosive memories of his once-perfect marriage to Debbie. Johan resisted the urge to take one of Eli's heavy ball peen hammers and destroy the black machine that mocked him as he exited.

The powerful machine was Debbie's treasured memento left behind by her communist cousin, Maria Theresa von Hammerstein. Debbie used it infrequently but had given strict orders to Eli that it must be kept dust-free, polished to a mirror finish and in perfect running order. She was certain Theresa would come back when her work for the Party in Europe was completed. She prayed for her return.

Johan walked to the black Chevy Fleetmaster parked out of sight behind bushes fifty yards down the road. The car was a straight no-cash trade for his pre-war, silver Mercedes convertible. His inability the past few days to reach his partner Rico Frenzelli or his wife Giulia, and a late-night visit to an obviously abandoned brokerage office told him it was time to get out. A flashy, rare German convertible would be easy to spot. Not so an everyman's car priced at less than two thousand dollars.

By the time he got behind the wheel of the Fleetmaster, Ingrid had made her calls to Mr. Hammerstein and his daughter Debbie, the State Police and for an ambulance.

Hammerstein raced to the Hudson River Yacht Basin, where his brokerage firm's converted Navy PT boat was berthed. A two-man crew was waiting to take him the thirty-miles upriver to Nyack.

Debbie had a hard time digesting Ingrid's frantic message. One thing was certain: she had to get back to Tuxedo Park. She would miss the long-anticipated meeting with the man she, Grace, Rosemary and Margie had dubbed the *Bill Collector*. She grabbed her car keys and purse and raced to the elevator. She wasted no time in the basement parking garage and, with a full tank of gas, headed the thirty-two miles to Tuxedo Park.

Hammerstein had called ahead for a taxicab for the twenty-one-mile drive from Nyack to Tuxedo Park. The cabbie was excited by the promise of a one-hundred-dollar tip and twice came close to side-swiping other cars on a curve five miles from their destination.

Debbie dangerously floored her Daimler during the drive from Newark, three times running red lights and even frightening a newsboy peddling papers on a street corner so much that he dropped the papers and ran for cover. The two cars reached the road to the family mansion only minutes apart.

When they arrived, they found their property crowded with four State Police patrol cars, with State Patrolmen halting all traffic at the bottom of the driveway.

"I'm the owner, Lee Hammerstein. The woman in the car behind me is my daughter, Deborah," Hammerstein said. "Who's in charge?"

"Captain Tuttle, he's up at the house. The housekeeper, I believe her name is Ingrid Lindstrom, is with him. She's the one who called us," patrolman Fisher said, reaching for a war surplus walkie-talkie strapped to his waist and waited for it to be picked up at the other end. "Captain, this is Fisher. The owner and his daughter just arrived, and I'm sending them up."

Tuttle was waiting for them at the front door, then ushered them into the parlor where Ingrid was seated on a sofa, trying unsuccessfully to stop her sobbing.

"Thank God you have come," Ingrid said when they entered the room. "*Es war schrecklich. Johan war ein Biest.*" Debbie left Tuttle and her father at the parlor door, ran to the sofa, wrapped her arms around Ingrid, turned to Tuttle and asked, "Where are Sophie and Eli?"

"They've been taken to St. Anthony's in Warwick; the ambulance picked them up an hour ago. The husband is in the operating room with a fractured skull. It doesn't look good. The wife has a crushed nose and broken cheekbone but is in stable condition."

"Did our housekeeper tell you what happened?" Hammerstein asked.

"In great detail, as expected, when two close friends are beaten in front of her. She waved this around to protect herself," Tuttle said as he unfolded a towel wrapped around a six-inch carving knife.

"What about my bastard husband? Are you tracking him down?" Debbie, with her arms still around Ingrid, asked.

"A statewide stop and arrest teletype went out an hour ago," the Captain said. "Ingrid noted he's tall, blue-eyed and blonde, well-built and with an easy smile. He drives a silver Mercedes convertible. She didn't know the license number. Give us the numbers to reach you, and be assured we'll be in constant touch."

Debbie was a driven woman. Johan had destroyed her world. It was a year in coming, but never had she fathomed the depth of his cruelty. Was there anything left for her to rekindle memories of her protected life before Johan?

"Give me a moment or two. I'll meet you at the car," Debbie said as she and her father were about to descend the stairs to the driveway. "Don't worry, I'll be right behind you." Lee Hammerstein motioned over the cabbie as he reached for his wallet. She quickly turned and climbed down the stairs from the kitchen to the basement garage and found what she badly needed: reassurance.

The black BMW sparkled under the strong workshop light Eli had installed. She walked over and ran her hands first over the handlebars, the beautifully tooled black leather seat, and the perfectly polished body of the machine. She spotted a can of Simoniz wax, a bottle of leather preservative and a stack of shammies on the shelf.

Father and daughter left the mansion and with Debbie behind the wheel, sped off to St. Anthony's Hospital, a sixteen-mile drive over country roads. Tuttle called that they were on their way. Doctors Dennis Johnston and Raymond Turri ushered them through the hundred-bed hospital. First, to the post-op intensive care room where Eli was recovering from emergency surgery. Except for his eyes, nose and mouth, his head was completely swathed in bandages, oxygen tubes in his nose forcing air to his lungs, and in three other places tubing ran from his body to beeping monitors. The tube inserted into his skull above and behind the left ear conveyed ominous portent.

"How bad is he?" Debbie asked the two doctors who were reading the meters and studying the charts. "He's a beautiful man who never hurt anyone. Tell us what it is you're doing to save his life?"

"Neither of us is a neurosurgeon," Dr. Johnston replied. "So we did the best we could. The nearest neurosurgeon is sixty miles away in Poughkeepsie."

"Screw the distance to Poughkeepsie, and there's no

neurosurgeon around. What the hell have you done to save Eli's life?" Debbie demanded. Her father looked on in astonishment, hearing for the first time vulgar language from his daughter.

"Eli's in a coma right now with a cracked skull and severe cerebral hemorrhage," Johnston said. "We've drilled a hole in the skull to drain the fluid that surrounds the brain. This will give room for the hematoma to expand without damaging brain cells. Now, all we can do is wait."

"Wait, wait! Like hell we'll wait," Hammerstein said. "Where's the phone? I'm putting a call into New York for Dr. Bauer, the best neurosurgeon in the city and a personal friend. It's your job to keep Eli alive until he gets here."

A nurse ushered them out, and two doors down the hall, they were in Sophie's room. The family cook of more than twenty years was sedated and asleep. An oxygen mask had been lightly secured over her nose and mouth to prevent further damage to her face. A pressure bandage covered her right cheekbone, where X-rays had revealed a hairline fracture below the corner of her eye.

"She's stable," the attending nurse said. "Doctors are waiting for her vital signs to return to normal and for the trauma she has suffered to lessen enough to permit surgery. The way she's progressing, this could be late this afternoon."

The Hammersteins went to Sophie's bed, and Debbie bent over to kiss her on the forehead.

They left the room, and when they reached the lobby, Lee answered the call from Dr. Bauer, who had just come in for him at the reception desk. The doctor was about to cross the river to Teterboro Airport, where he and his surgical nurse of many years would climb aboard his Bellanca Cruiseair fast enough to cover the forty miles to Warwick Municipal Airport in about twenty minutes.

Bauer worked his magic. Eli would live but with a drooping left eyelid, drooping mouth and paralyzed left arm. With hours of therapy and practice, his slurred speech was expected to return to normal. His wife Sophie's nose and cheekbone were repaired, and she waited for Hammerstein's plastic surgeon golfing partner to arrive to complete the cosmetic work.

Sophie, Eli and Ingrid would always have the Hammerstein mansion roof over their heads. Only three days after his operation, Eli was working hard to recover discernable speech. Debbie looked into their hospital room to find Sophie gently wiping away bubbles of saliva oozing past his numb lips and onto his chin. She turned away in tears.

36

On October 1, the day Debbie and her cohorts were to meet him, Stefano dodged the mid-day traffic on Broad Street. He strolled across Military Park and crossed the street to the four-story building that housed the New Jersey Historical Society.

In the lobby, he was greeted by a pert woman of a certain age sitting at a switchboard sorting a bundle of incoming mail. Stefano approached her, overcame his reluctance and said, "I'm the *Bill Collector*. I'm expected for a one o'clock meeting at the Historical Society."

"Oh yes," the woman said, "they just called down that you were coming. The Society is on the third floor, the entire floor, in fact, and I apologize we do not have an elevator."

Stefano did some heavy breathing before reaching the third floor. Since early childhood, he had trouble breathing through a chronically stuffed left nostril. Waiting at the third-floor landing, a good-looking, olive-complected woman of about forty stood with her left hand on the banister newel and her right hand on her hip.

He recognized her immediately, Grace DeMarco, every woman's heroine, the first female to hold down the influential Essex County Clerk's office. If you believed her press clippings and news photos, pundits predicted a bright future. Stefano saw that photos did not do her justice; she was much prettier, and some would even call her a hot number. They shook hands when he reached the top of the stairs. Obviously, well at ease they smiled their way through the double-glazed door to the Historical Society.

Inside, two women who had been seated at an eight-foot, oblong table arose with outstretched hands to greet him. Both were eye-catching but in different ways, the brunette could even be called beautiful. He guessed her to be about forty, give or take. A heavily-loaded diamond engagement ring and a wedding band adorned her left hand, and her two-piece blue suit wasn't pulled from a store rack. "I'm Rosemary," she said with a practiced smile.

The other woman caught him by surprise. At least ten years younger, there was not an ounce of softness in her features. Her emerald green eyes had the hard edge that came with experience. Her hairdo was professional, and her dark brown, one-piece dress with white piping, although not bargain basement, was well designed but not in the same class as Rosemary's. As if on cue, she said, "I'm Margie." When he shook her hand, he noticed that a plain gold wedding band was on her right ring finger.

Turning to Stefano, standing awkwardly on the opposite

side of the table, Grace said, "We already know each other." Stefano nodded affirmatively.

Grace casually turned her gaze from Stefano to her two cohorts to appraise if this big, handsome thug, no more than a kid, was the right guy for what they had been planning.

"So far, you fit in, that is if you want to. Do you?" Grace said.

"Into what? So far, you've only given me a new name, Bill Collector, but haven't said a word about who the hell I'm collecting from and what I'm collecting."

"You're collecting with a punch and maybe a kick to the balls if needed," Margie said, her deadly green eyes leaving no doubt she meant every word. "You'll collect from bastards who never had to pay up."

Margie didn't care that her language was over the top and liked the reaction of the others.

"I have a question for Stefano, our ersatz *Bill Collector*," Grace said, looking across the table at the young thug. "That's right. You're Stefano here with us and a collector when you meet up with the bastards we'll be telling you about. Explain why you believe any man who abuses a woman, and for that matter, a child, is a coward?"

What the hell was he to say? It was ingrained from early childhood by his parents, who supported his rise from streetcorner punk to a white-collar Union enforcer for the Genovese family.

Or was it the paralyzing nightmares that originated in

an obscure Italian schoolhouse? The nightmares always ended the same way, with a blast of calliope music and the hideously smiling rape victims riding past on a carousel. Even the garishly painted wooden animals they were riding smiled lasciviously.

Or was it that slimy bastard Lupo with his beloved sister Terri?

What was his answer to these three women? They waited expectantly for him to affirm Chester Bruno's recommendation and their first impressions that he was the right guy.

"I don't think you want a lot of details. That could get ugly," he said. "I had choices, but advice to stay clean rolled off my back as a kid. Instead, I got into the slop the mob offered, the green getting greener the deeper I dug. I bought in, but not all the way. Had only contempt for the wise guys who bragged about how it only took a few slaps, punches, and kicks for their women to keep their mouths shut. You don't want to know what I saw as an Army cop in North Africa, Sicily and Italy."

The women who had been hanging on Stefano's every word were startled when he swiveled from the table with his coffee cup, walked to the Hamilton Beach on a small service table in front of the office's large window and poured himself a refill. He peered over to Military Park at *Wars of America,* a colossal bronze monument with forty-two men in combat and two riderless horses. For sculptors Luigi Del Blanco and Gutzon Borglum, Mount Rushmore's creator, it was their call to arms dedicated in 1926. The mammoth heroic gesture provided a safe haven for the homeless veterans, who with their meager belongings, bedded down around it each night. The cops, most of them veterans themselves, let them be just so long as they were gone by daylight.

But Stefano knew nothing about the statue's history and what it had become in Newark's downtown land of plenty. Now, it was a night time flop for men, who, like the bronze brothers above them, had answered the call to arms. He turned from the window and returned to his chair. "What the hell are you dolls asking?" Stefano said, his words now harsh at the edges. They replied with an awkward silence that gave him time to study their faces. Polite concern was evident. It was not the troubled anxiety that ruled the inner-city sidewalks he had known as a kid. They were strangers, and it was quite possible he was a misfit. It was time to find out. "Give it to me straight."

"Here it is," Grace said after Margie and Rosemary silently handed her the gavel. "I only know that Chester Bruno suggested you, that you have the background for the job we want done. To collect the outstanding bills owed by rich wife-beaters who believe they are untouchable."

"And what exactly is the bill I'd be collecting?"

"Pain," Margie put her elbows on the table and leaned forward to study his reaction. "Real pain, but no black eyes, split lips or bruises. Everything below the shoulders. We want them out on the street suffering in silence like the ladies they've been using as punching bags." She never took her eyes from Stefano's, "Are you up for it?"

The three women nervously kept busy as they waited for Stefano's decision. There was chair-squirming, pencil-tapping and coffee-sipping. He took it all in and decided to slow things down.

"Whoa, let me take a breath before you go on with this. You're asking me to go out and beat up rich guys who have been slapping their ladies around, wife or mistress; makes no difference. Do I have it right? Who are the marks, and how do I find them? If and when I find them, what then? You want evidence of a beating not to show. What the hell is your motive?"

"That he's a cowardly son of a bitch. That there's payback for beating women, too," Grace said. "We don't want the world to know, only him."

"Women beaters at that level don't go around bragging, 'Jonathan, ol' boy, another martini to celebrate how I slapped Roslyn around tonight,'" Stefano asked. "Where do the names come from?"

"I'll get you the names and addresses," Grace said. "We can start with four, all right here in the greater Newark area and see what happens."

"Who was it that hatched this up? Convince me it'll work."

"A street-smart guy like you needs convincing? Our good friend, Chester Bruno, doesn't pony-up names easily, and yours was at the top of the list," Grace said. "As Court Clerk, I've seen the paperwork too many times to count. Cowardly misfits are cuffed and pulled from their cold-water tenements to do six months slammer time for battering their wives, girlfriends, hookers and even children. These outrages rarely make the news. We want headlines.

"We're after the upper-crust bullies," Grace studied the faces at the table. Stefano's gave nothing away. "The wealthy jerks we've targeted are so well connected they seldom, if ever, see the inside of a courtroom. Their cases are amicably heard in the judge's chambers and end with a sealed verdict, usually six months' probation, smiles and handshakes all around. Meanwhile, the woman this louse had vowed *to love and to cherish* was still in hiding while her wounds healed." She suppressed the nervous tick in her left eye. She saw his detached features harden. She was getting to him.

"I hope that this makes it clear where we're coming from. Chester Bruno was well into his third martini when he guessed that you may be a kindred spirit. Are you with us?"

"If you are, here are four names to start with," Rosemary said. "Take your time. Do it your way, but remember everything below the shoulders. You'll also get a woman's first name and a phone number to call after you've finished each job. Then we'll see you back here at three o'clock the next day."

"What do I do with that?"

"Memorize it, then get rid of it. Never let him see your face. That will be difficult because when you're finished, you'll whisper in his ear, 'This is a payback kiss from...' the woman whose name we have given you. The phone number belongs to the Pine Room at Hahne's. It's open every night except Sunday until eleven. Just say, 'I want to make a reservation for two tomorrow evening at seven. Table three.' Anything goes wrong, it's table four. Call Grace the next day," Rosemary drew a breath.

Talk about planning; these gals have put an awful lot of work into how best to beat up some rich palooka without getting directly involved themselves. He was uncertain whether he was a good fit until he and Margie locked eyes, and a slight smile of approval crossed her face.

Turning to Grace, Stefano asked, "Over the phone, you said four of you were involved, but there's only three here. Where's the fourth? Does she agree with all of this, or is she not here because she has some doubts? If she's on the outside looking in, it's not hard to imagine her blowing the whistle."

"Her name is Debbie, and she's way ahead of us wanting her pound of flesh," Grace said. "I'm certain she'll agree that we've found the right *Bill Collector*."

"Give me the names," Stefano said. Margie reached across the table and handed him a sealed envelope, their fingers touching. Once again, their eyes met, and he could see she was probably the only one with whom he shared anything in common. He slipped the envelope into his right inside jacket pocket, shared nods with all of them and silently left the office.

Stefano descended the three flights of stairs to the lobby, still unsure why he agreed to this lunatic dodge. Was this penance for him to pay? For what? Was it for playing the pimp for officers in Morocco, Sicily and Italy? Or for doing nothing to the American GIs who turned an Italian school into a whore house?

He stepped from the lobby, crossed over to Military Park and casually took a seat on the low wall surrounding Borglum's massive bronze statue. He knew he was being watched from the third-floor window. He tapped out a Chesterfield, and after a few deep drags, he had his answer. It was the bruised body of his sister Terri. She protected a younger brother still in knee britches, often taking the kicks and hard blows meant for him. When he saw the widespread nature of the bruises, it was clear that she hadn't only been slapped around, she had been beaten. How could she ever call Pietro Lupo her boyfriend?

It was only Terri's plea for restraint that saved that cowardly bastard. He promised not to lay a hand on her greasy lover boy. This would not be the case for the four targets chosen for payback by women with whom he had only one thing in common: revenge.

37

That wednesday, Stefano wasn't the only one wondering about Debbie. Rosario and Giuseppe had failed miserably as mafia gumshoes, and their asses were still burning after the blistering attack by their boss Anna Genovese. Because of their loyalty, she had pulled them from their bodyguard jobs at Club Caravan, the queer joint she ran on West Broadway, and given them a job that would make or break them with the family. Johan Paasche had been on the loose since late August.

"You just missed him. Is that what you're fucking telling me?" Anna was holding it as best she could, but the steam had to let loose. "That son of a bitch Paasche has left a trail wide enough for a truck to drive through, and you just missed him?"

There was a long pause and heavy breathing at the other end. Anna smirked, knowing her guys had both been listening in on the call and were about to shrug out an answer to save their assess. Rosario got the short straw.

"When Paasche was shacking up with his favorite whore in Manhattan and tooling around in his silver Daimler, it was easy as hell," he said. "Then the screwing stopped, and the Daimler disappeared. Ain't many of them around, so Giuseppe checked with his brother, who has three dealerships, and found out it had been traded straight across, no cash, for a new Chevy Fleetmaster."

"He knew we were on his ass," Giuseppe said, "and that was the end of highways and county roads; he even used a long gravel and dirt road that emptied into Sleepy Hollow. Asked around but nobody knew or saw nothin'. That's where we lost him."

"So, you assholes fell asleep in Sleepy Hollow."

"Nobody fell asleep. This guy is slippery as hell and a smart shit too. Figured something was up; he was gone. Fuck the millions he was handling, he was gone, pfft, just like that. He disappeared until we tracked down the Fleetmaster."

"You had my written instructions simple and direct, so even you two *manichini* could understand them. Did you throw them away and use them to light your cigars? Whatever happened to them?"

"We're not *manichini*," Rosario said. "Your note is right here in my hand. Even lifted a gas station roadmap. The Tappan Zee Bridge across the river to Tuxedo Park, where all hell had broken loose. *I poliziotti erano ovunque!* Couldn't get near the place; police roadblocks all over. So we asked around and were told Paasche had kicked the hell out of the domestic help looking for his wife and other things. We missed him by a few hours."

"*Mi è mancato, mi è mancato,* that's all I've been hearing from you. So, after your third miss, I started snooping around the Club. Deborah Paasche is looney about the Broadway stage, a big contributor. Her husband also kicked the shit out of her. You don't need any details, just the name, address and phone number of the guy who fixed her up. You know what I want." Anna, like her husband Vito, had mastered the art of the oblique threat.

Rosario and Giuseppe had rehearsed what to do when they reached apartment 3B on the sixth floor of the very expensive apartment building on Manhattan's Upper Eastside. Their experience at the Giulia Frenzelli apartment would be their ticket. Everyone welcomes an unexpected present delivered to their door. It worked then, smooth as silk, so why not now?

They were breathing hard after ignoring the ornate Greco-Roman entrance to the building with its liveried valet, walked to the delivery door in the rear past the service elevator and began their climb. They reached the apartment just as two newspapers were being pulled under the door. They decided to wait until things settled down inside.

Reginald "Reggie" Rouge was in good spirits on Friday, October 3, when he gathered the *Daily News* and *Daily Mirror* from under his door. That week, he was able to fit in time for two expensive face repairs along with his scheduled make-up work on the hit Broadway musical *Oklahoma.*

When it came to baseball Reggie was a pathological

gambler. The fourth game of the World Series was scheduled for that afternoon at Ebbets Field. The Yankees had taken the first two out of three games, and this was a must win for the Brooklyn Dodgers. He had made a killing on the first three games, picking all three winners, even a 40-1 longshot on the total runs scored in the Dodgers' nine to eight third-game victory. He was flush.

He returned to his bed, plumped two large pillows against the headboard, and was about to spread out the sports pages when the doorbell rang. He arose and angrily pushed his perfectly pedicured, soft white feet into his slippers. "Who the hell is it? It's not even eight o'clock!" Reggie's falsetto at its shrillest.

"I have a present here for a Reggie Rouge beautifully wrapped in red with a gold ribbon," a man's voice replied.

Reggie quickened his steps to the door in pleasant surprise that at least one of the rich bitches he has been patching up was grateful. He undid the three-door locks and was turning the knob when the heavy, ornate door was forced open. He was slammed against the entrance table, knocking two porcelain bowls. Shards were flying everywhere, with Reggie plopping down in the middle with a big, high-pitched, "Oh God, I'm stabbed!" A dagger-like shard had penetrated one-half inch into his left buttock, blood was oozing and he was close to crying. He rose to his knees, pulled a perfumed handkerchief from his robe and thrust it to the wound.

Still on his knees and with his head bowed, he cautiously raised his eyes from the mirror shine on a pair of black

Cordovans. He then took in the whole picture. Two expensively dressed men in black suits, white shirts, black ties, tri-tip handkerchief poking from their jacket pocket, and directly above were menacing faces that softened into tight smiles that mocked what they were seeing on the floor.

"Cry, baby, cry. You ain't gonna die, and here's somethin' just for you," Giuseppe sneered and, with a flourish, tossed the package on the floor in front of Reggie. "Don't open it now. We got business."

"Business? What business?" Reggie asked. With his hand holding the blood-drenched hanky to his left buttock, he used his right arm to push up from the floor eliciting a stream of "ouch, shit, shit." Porcelain chips were embedded in the knuckles of his right hand.

"Take it easy, Reggie, take it easy," Rosario soothed as he pulled an afghan from a nearby chair and tossed it to him. "Throw that bloody rag away and take this for your ass."

With the two thugs on either side, Reginald "Reggie" Rouge was gently guided to the fireplace sofa. With the afghan folded and refolded to form a cushion, he took a seat, leaving behind a rivulet of blood on the thick, pale blue carpet.

"I need a doctor. Even you guys can see that" his voice hardened; this was a painful mistake.

"You guys? You guys? Is that what you said? Who the fuck do you think you are, and who the hell do you think we are?" Giuseppe leaned forward, braced his left hand against the back of the sofa, and with all the strength he could muster, slapped Reggie across both cheeks. His head bounced off the back of the sofa, first to the left and then to the right. A stabbing pain shot from the base of his skull to his shoulder.

Giuseppe stepped back, pulled a chair in front of the fireplace and sat down as Rosario took a seat next to Reggie.

"Let's talk business. You give us answers, then we're gone, and you can call your sawbones," Rosario said, his tone not menacing like Giuseppe's but soft and reassuring. "Let's start with the name. Deborah Hammerstein Paasche. Know her?"

Their faces were twelve inches apart, close enough for Reggie to inhale the tobacco and cheap wine stench of Rosario's breath. He still didn't know who these two thugs were and why in hell they were hurting him, hurting him very badly. How did the Paasche woman fit in? He hadn't seen her since last August. There was a phone call to confirm she was using the cosmetic kit he had given her, and that was it.

"Yes, I know her, but only as a client," he said, adopting his most sincere voice, the one that always worked with his clients and hoped would keep the two thugs at bay. "My last contact with Mrs. Paasche was almost two months ago."

"Tell us about it." Rosario was no longer reassuring; his dark eyes widened, and his face hardened. "What did this fancy broad tell you about herself and the guy who slapped her around? Here's a reminder: his name is Johan Paasche, and we've been looking for him."

Over the last few years, Reggie had bumped shoulders

backstage with underworld types who were boffing chorus cuties, but these two brutes were a different breed. He had no doubt that more pain was in store if he failed to make them happy.

"Two months ago, you sure of that?" Giuseppe moved to the front edge of his chair and, with his elbows on his knees, said, "The housekeeper worked for us, but she couldn't hear everything they said. That's where you come in. You patched her up enough times to get to know her. Was she a talkative dame, blabbed to you like you were her priest? Maybe your grease paint opened her up?"

"They were connected real good in Europe, took vacations there. How'd they get there with a war going on? She talks about it?" Rosario said. "Give us what we want, and we're on our way."

"Would the name of a steamship line help?"

His inquisitors silently traded glances, and Giuseppe gave him a "keep going" gesture with both hands.

Reggie's ass was no longer bleeding like an overturned ketchup bottle, and his hand was wrapped in a linen doily he grabbed from the back of the sofa. The slightest movement was painful. A sharp, dagger-like pain stabbed his neck and right shoulder. A postcard from Mrs. Paasche could be his meal ticket out, but it had to be retrieved from a desk drawer and there was no way he could get it.

"After her first repair job, she phoned me to say that she and Mr. Paasche had patched things up, and they were going abroad for a vacation that was to be their second honeymoon. I received a postcard two weeks later. It's in an album in the right-hand drawer of my desk."

Rosario jumped from the sofa to the desk and pulled out a leatherbound album; a few seconds later, he was back on the sofa. "Is this it? If it is, read it."

Reggie took the card. It was a picture of the Swedish-American Ocean liner *S.S. Gripsholm* sailing past the Statue of Liberty on its way to Gothenburg, Sweden. It was dated early May 1944, with their return voyage on the same ship in late May. The sailing was uneventful. This surprised her, but not Johann, because Nazi submarines and Allied warships were constantly on patrol. This was Johan's fourth voyage on the *Gripsholm*, dubbed "the Mercy Ship," for the safe passage it had provided thousands of refugees, including Jews.

"This is it, all you have? You sure! Come on, out with it," Giuseppe dangled the card in front of a terrified Reggie, who feared the worst was yet to come. Rosario grabbed him by the neck, a large glob of phlegm gathered in his throat, forcing him to gag out, "That's all I have. I swear it. Please, please, believe me!"

They studied his face and saw what they had seen many times before: terrified dread. Rosario released Reggie's throat, allowing him to cough up gobs of sputum and entreat, "Please, whoever you are, you can see I'm telling all that I know."

They never fully believed what they heard and saw until they were told to do so. Giuseppe walked to the bedroom and picked up a thing of beauty he'd spotted when they first entered the apartment: a vintage, white and gold Western

Electric Imperial telephone. He'd take it with him when they were finished with the cosmetic man.

Anna Genovese took his call at the office desk of her Club Caravan. She scribbled down everything he said and asked, "You better be goddamn sure that you got it all, everything he knows. Tell me again the name of the ship they sailed on? Spell it out."

"This crumb would give away his god damn mother if it would save his ass," Giuseppe said. "We think we have everything the perfumed bastard has to say."

"I never told you to think, but I'll buy what you told me," she said sarcastically. "Hold on to the postcard and let your friend know that if he opens his mouth, you'll be back."

Anna hung up and pulled a phone book from the upper right drawer of her desk. "This is the Havana operator. To whom should I place your call?"

Meyer Lansky didn't say much, but the pounding veins in his temples and the deep redness of his face told all. "The *Gripsholm*, during the war it was called the Mercy Ship," he said from his penthouse throne atop the Hotel Nacional de Cuba. "I know its owners well. Helped them roundup Jewish refugees one step from the gas chamber and sailed them to safety. We still keep in touch."

It was too late to do anything today; the *Gripsholm* had already sailed, its first stop Lisbon, then on to Gothenburg, its homeport in Sweden. Anna's call set off a speedy interchange of cables that spanned the Atlantic, the Caribbean, the Mediterranean and the North Sea. The first phone call was to the Swedish-American Line's Chief Purser in New York. The passenger manifest placed Johan Paasche in a first-class cabin. It was fifteen days to Lisbon, and if they missed him in Portugal, mid a barrage of profanity Anna made it clear they better not lose him in Gothenburg.

After Lansky got what he wanted, his face softened, and his temple veins went back into hiding. Say what you want about the son of a bitch; Paasche had class even when his ass was on the line.

38

Except for the traditional Sunday Italian feast at home, Union Boss Stefano Rizzano had cleared up what little work he had over the weekend. The christening of Steamfitter Local 49 Treasurer's daughter on Saturday and on Sunday, the thirtieth-anniversary party of the longest member of Sanitation Workers Local 90. His office staff of five did the rest and proved that with the right bloodlines and contacts, nepotism works. He had little to do.

At nine o'clock on the evening of Monday, October 6, former Newark Councilman Jeremiah Jerome Fulton had just taken the elevator down from the thirteenth floor of the National Newark and Essex Bank Building after enjoying a five-course dinner at The Broad Street Club. Stepping from the lobby, he took a few deep breaths to enjoy the cool autumn air, then walked a short distance to his car on a darkened side street. The fifty-five-year-old Fulton long suffered from chronic back pain, and he was about to get more.

He bent to insert the car key when a rough cloth was thrown over his head and twisted tightly behind his neck. A heavy blow, probably a knee, was delivered to his right kidney, slamming him against the side of the car. He fell to his knees and, on the way down, banged his head on the driver's door. He was pushed face down on the street when a clear, low voice said in his ear, "Here's another one for good measure." The next blow was a hard punch to the left kidney. Stefano leaned down, assured that Fulton had not passed out and said, "These are payback kisses from Janice."

Stefano arose and drove his right foot between Fulton's shoulder blades. "Don't even think of getting up or pulling the blindfold off for at least three minutes." He removed his foot from the back of a man who was now gasping for air under the coarse cloth.

Fulton waited until he heard a car drive away before he pulled off the blindfold and rose to his knees, a move that made him woozy. He spit out blood and was close to vomiting.

Luckily, his car key was still in the door. In his semi-conscious condition, finding it anywhere on the dark sidewalk or in the gutter would have been impossible. He unlocked the door and painfully dropped into the driver's seat, switched on the ignition and slowly started the five-mile drive to his new home in South Orange, acquired after his divorce from Janice. The divorce ended his political career.

After twenty minutes, during which Fulton endured searing pain and unthinkable thoughts, he parked in the driveway of his empty house. His live-in girlfriend was visiting her parents, his two grown sons were long gone, and Monday was his housekeeper's day off. He stumbled to the bathroom and bent over the toilet to watch his rack of lamb, potatoes au gratin, baked asparagus and crepe suzette disappear. After a final dry heave, he staggered into the bedroom and, without removing his clothes, collapsed on the bed.

His sleep was disturbed by a persistent thought: *where did Janice fit in? She's gentle and refined but also resourceful and selfish. But Christ Almighty, there's no way she would pay a thug to almost break my back, or could she? Whatever, it has to be kept quiet.*

When the National Newark and Essex Banking Building disappeared in Stefano's rearview mirror, his mood, unlike Fulton's, was exuberant. They'd all think, even Terri, that he was on some kind of drug high.

He hadn't eaten dinner, so he decided to devour the poor man's filet mignon served at the White Castle - four sliders topped with sliced onion and pickle that he smothered in ketchup before encasing the small, square hamburgers in a soft roll, ten cents each, hot, freshly brewed coffee five cents, and for dessert a wedge of apple pie, ten cents. He paid with a dollar bill, and when his server spread the forty-five cents change on the counter, he said, "It's all yours; just give me a refill while I finish my cigarette." The server, probably no more than seventeen, quickly picked up the coins, hoping that this large tip wasn't a mirage.

Stefano drove home with one big question on his mind: could it be possible that none of the four guys he plants with payback kisses never open their yaps? No noise, no headlines. Like the tree falling in the forest with no one around, did it happen?

Three days later, after he had worked over the chief legal counsel handling the city's contracts, he got his answer. One angry, profanity-laced phone call from Ferguson Flutie Dickenson, III, was enough to harangue Mayor Paul Simpson into action. Simpson skippered an efficient and well-run City Hall, but in close quarters with a canon pointed his way, he was not what you would call a brave leader.

"God damn it, Paul, I masterminded your campaign, and what was it, a vow that street crime was about to end in Newark," Ferguson shouted. "So, what happened at ten o'clock last night at the driveway mailbox? Right in front of my house, I was jumped from behind by a thug who had been hiding in the hedges. Goddamn, if the first thing he did was to throw a big rag over my head and, at the same time, drive a knee into my lower spine. I thought my back was broken. I fell to the ground, and for good measure, he kicked me on the left side. I could barely breathe, couldn't breathe as a matter of fact, when he bent down and said, 'this is a payback kiss from June.'"

It had been more than a year and a half since Dickenson had even given a thought to June Travers. Dickenson never married, and it was known in confidential circles and among Newark's pimps that he was addicted to the rough trade. Reciprocal pain, dishing it out and taking it, was what the whores were paid for, but there were limits. June was driven to number 14 at the far end of the single row of rooms that composed the *Just Like Home Motor Lodge*. Dickenson was waiting inside. His car was parked two blocks away on a pitch-black street devoid of light poles and unwanted questions. Two hours later, the pimp returned to find June lying naked and unconscious.

There were bite marks on both her breasts, neck and shoulders. Severe groping between her legs and buttocks caused internal damage and bleeding that left half the bed blood-soaked. The pimp, Arthur Anthony, Jr., tried unsuccessfully to revive her. He put his ear to her chest and discovered her breath was shallow but steady. He was confident she would live. He used the room phone to call for an ambulance, hastily picked up two hundred in bills from the nightstand, wiped his fingerprints from the doorknob and fled in his blue Buick convertible.

June Travers survived and, with her pimp calling in all debts adding to an already bulging bankroll, hired Chester Bruno. The lawsuit was filed minutes before Grace's office closed when newspaper reporters had quit filing their stories for the day. On Monday, it was filed away unnoticed except by Grace and Dickenson. Two days later, Grace was ordered to personally bring a file, Case Number 47-446798, Travers v. Dickenson, to District Attorney Silo Cranbon.

Two weeks later, at a hush-hush, closed-door meeting at Bruno's office, a three-hundred-thousand-dollar money order drawn on a large Philadelphia investment bank changed hands. The bank's president, Dickenson's brother, okayed the blood-soaked deal. After Bruno and Anthony got their share, June walked away with a hundred thousand dollars.

Dickenson barely remembered what happened that night at the *Just Like Home Motor Lodge*. More than a handful of beautiful and expensive whores were shoved his way, and until the Travers slut's lawsuit, none had opened their mouths.

The Mayor never said a word during Dickenson's tirade. When it ended with, "There's an election coming up. Need I say more!" He pushed a red button on his intercom. In less than a minute, Lieutenant Kevin McClosky and Sergeants Frank Gazzi and Windy Valentine were in his office.

"My special Intelligence Squad," the Mayor smirked, his ears still burning; decided to fire up his own barbecue, and a threat was not a bad place to start. "You like your jobs? Been at it for almost a year now. Cleaned up two departments, four convictions and more to come." Their response was a smiling shrug of the shoulders.

"Your smiles tell me you want to keep your jobs, your cars and that cushy office down the hall," he said. Their smiles disappeared, replaced by reluctant memories of their uniform life on the streets. They were shocked into the present when the Mayor, in a raised voice, said, "I promised an end to street crime, and you're going to keep that promise for me, and...."

McClosky stood up and said, "Your Honor, I know I'm out of line, but you said our job was to uncover and choke-off the crooks running the city, nothing about street crime."

"Now it's changed. I've been hearing that beatings and robberies, especially beatings, are no longer confined to the inner city but are now a threat uptown as well. Find out why. I'll expect timely reports," he said, then sent them on their way with a lazy wave of his right hand.

A short walk from City Hall in his downtown office, Stefano Rizzano studied a scribbled note with the itinerary of Sergio Simpliano, owner of six auto dealerships throughout New Jersey. At last count, seven women were driving around in top-of-the-line Ford and Dodge convertibles. The women, all young and beautiful, had done their four to six months parading around on Simpliano's arm. Everyone knew he was rough, so what if they collected bruises along the way, just so long as a convertible with title, registration and insurance in their names was waiting.

Francie Turlock wasn't one of them. She had fallen in love with the divorced Simpliano and become a loudmouth pest and embarrassment. Sergio wasn't embarrassed easily, but she had to go. His threats had no effect. Then, one night, she drove through the guardrail of the Pulaski Skyway. It was a big drop to the railroad tracks below. A suicide note was found in the wreckage.

Simpliano had two sweetheart contracts with the City and County; no less than thirty of his Fords, Dodges, upscale Chryslers and Lincolns went out each year without competing bids or disapproving whispers.

Sergeant William Shiner headed the traffic investigation

of the suicide. Francie Turlock's note complicated what appeared to be a routine accident fatality, a driver losing control and driving through a bridge barrier. He faced hours of paperwork before turning the case over to homicide. Francie nosedived off the Pulaski in a red Dodge convertible, a kiss-off gift from Simpliano. Shiner knew her sexually-charged confessional note was headline material. A phone call could make the suicide note disappear and send a very expensive thank-you gift his way.

The coverup would have been a complete success if Shiner, who knew better, hadn't pointed out his new toy, a black Ford coupé convertible parked in a police slot outside the Essex County Courthouse. Grace DeMarco heard his bragging from her office and walked to the window overlooking the parking lot. She knew that Shiner always had his hand out. His three-bedroom, two-door garage Vailsburg home wasn't the result of monopoly money collected after getting out of jail free. After an afternoon of well-aimed inquiries, including Francie Turlock's mother and sister, Simpliano's name made it onto Stefano's list.

Simpliano was a little guy who hated he was only sixty-six inches tall, so he added two inches when he was told by many that he was a living, breathing example of Napoleon. "He was only five-and-a-half feet," Simpliano snickered, "I've got two inches on him." If any of his three hundred employees were detected smirking at the remark, they were out on the street.

Stefano made easy work of the car dealer. He caught him shortly before midnight the following Wednesday after he had been working alone on the books at his Central

Ward Chrysler dealership. Stefano was surprised at how frail his target was and was careful not to break his back. When he whispered, "This is a payback kiss from Francie," it felt that Simpliano's ribcage had collapsed. He heard the downed man's breath filling the hood. The *Bill Collector* casually arose, knowing there was no hurry. The slimy bastard he was leaving behind would be on the marble floor for a while but with enough breath left to choke out, "That filthy bitch, that god damn filthy bitch."

The next day, Simpliano conducted a bitch-a-thon at the offices of the Mayor and Councilman Holden Upt, keeper of the City's transportation budget. The Mayor was clean but still had to endure a thirty-minute verbal barrage centered on a central theme, "Where the hell was the police when I was attacked last night in my dealership in the center of the city? Almost had my back broken, can hardly walk. Talk about walking; a lot of your people, especially the cops, aren't doing it thanks to the wheels I've given them at a god damn good price! A notch on your belt, an election day plus."

Mayor Paul Simpson sighed, "Mr. Simpliano, you have my promise that the police will be pulling out all stops."

With Councilman Upt, it was a different story. For the past six years, he had grown his reputation as a white-collar guy who was savvy from the start about how the city was run, graft. He made sure there were no effective bids to counter Simpliano. Hidden were the original costs and annual trade-ins for the Chryslers with all the goodies that Upt and his wife drove. Simpliano ended his harangue when he simply stated, "You and the missus each have a rolling palace, air conditioning, leather seats, and got you Presto-Matic, when even I didn't have semi-automatic transmission."

"What can I do?" a chastened Upt replied. "Newark's always had street thugs; it's been getting worse since the war ended, but inside your Chrysler dealership, who would have thought?"

"Well, god damn it, start thinking!" Simpliano sniped. "Every department in this burg has a year-to-year budget. We all know that; you just salt the budget enough to make everyone happy."

It had been more than a week since the *Bill Collector* had been in action, and while panic and accusations roiled behind closed doors, the four female schemers were still looking for their first public headline.

39

Stefano kept the fourth name on his list until last, and it had nothing to do with his female cohorts or the beating his sister had taken. It was the deep wound inflicted by Stan Pafkoski that would fester until he set things straight.

Pafkoski had come a long way since chopping huge ice slabs into manageable blocks on his father's horse-drawn cart, then hauling them up tenement stairs where refrigerators were still a dream. At fifty-five, he was a ruthless anomaly whose brutal tactics transformed Pafkoski Hauling into the last family-owned trucker able to compete with the giants. His preferred weapon was a sawed-off baseball bat, and the cab of every truck had two Louisville Sluggers within easy reach.

Long before settling into his new job, Stefano had absorbed the nuances of upper-level gangster singularity: expensively tailored clothes, handmade shoes, discreet, very expensive baubles on their fingers, wrists, lapels, and tie clasps, and carefully brushed and blocked fedoras.

Stefano put the word out that he wanted well-dressed and socially acceptable mob muscle to spearhead his forced entry into organized labor. Refusal to join up was a no-no, and the threat of violence was always there. Renato Ponzi and Alfonso Prieto fit the bill. Well-dressed with dark, swarthy good looks and having just turned thirty, they had climbed from the gutters of north Newark through the ranks to made-men soldiers. Pafkoski Hauling was their first target.

"We thought we had Pafkoski locked up," Renato whispered from his bed at Queen of Peace Hospital between bandages that swathed his broken nose and cracked jaw. His left arm was in a cast. "The big bastard didn't say much, had his secretary taking notes, let Alfonso and me do all the talking. We made our pitch, how he needed our Union to help him kick ass if he wanted to beat the big carriers moving in."

"What did he actually say?" Stefano.

"He asked the name of our Union Local, when I told him Teamsters 51, he said he never heard of it. That's when we came in strong. Told him he needed a Union behind him or no way he'd keep the big carriers from sucking away his customers."

"A lot to think about," Pafkoski said and dismissed them with a casual wave of his right arm, a Cuban panetella firmly between his index and middle fingers. As they arose from chairs in front of Pafkoski's desk, he added, "As I understand it, you want me to join a wop Union that doesn't exist, and I'll be sitting at the top of the heap taking orders from dagos like you."

This stopped Alfonso and Renato in their tracks, but before they could turn to face their Polack nemesis, he cautioned, "Don't turn around. I've seen enough of your greasy faces."

He waited until the two hoods closed the office door behind them, reached for his intercom, pushed the button and said, "They're coming down. You know what to do."

Stefano pulled his chair closer to the bed. It was the first time anything like this had happened during the year he held his job. Yeah, there had been plenty of profanity and finger-pointing and a few times grabbing the other guy's lapels to make a point, but never anything close to using baseball bats. Stefano was boiling over, but he wanted to hear it all.

"How many were there? You and Alfonso have any chance at all?"

"Four of them, big sons of bitches. Wore leather gloves. Jumped us in the hall at the bottom of the stairs. Alfonso got it first, three, maybe four whacks to the head, shoulders and back. Hit the floor like a rock, and when he didn't move, they turned on me. The bastards knew their business."

"Then what?" an infuriated Stefano asked. "Couldn't get much from Alfonso. He's got a concussion, and Richie the Boot made sure he got the best doctor in town. He's resting at his sister's, spitting out a lot of gibberish that made no sense. How the hell did you guys get out of there?"

"They kicked the hell out of me, but I still had a good

right arm. I grabbed Alfonso behind the collar, dragged him into the DeSoto and got our asses out of there."

"And that's it, you just drove away?"

"Yes and no. There were at least twenty mother-fuckers waiting for us out in the lot. Baseball bats again, this time pounding on the car, cracked three windows, both headlights and pulled off the radio antennae."

Stefano arose, patted Renato on his right shoulder and said, "Your job will be waiting." He stopped at the nurse's station and made it clear that Renato Ponzi in Room 37 got everything he wants, immediately if not sooner.

Pafkoski had to be handled, and a hard kick in the ass won't do. He had been getting increased heat from the Five Families, and he knew that being Genovese's golden boy saved his ass. The Five Families were getting impatient. During a meeting in Manhattan, Joe Profaci let him know the Colombo Family liked his work so far, but when a son of a bitch like Pafkoski showed no respect, he knew what must be done.

It still amazed him that Stan Pafkoski's name was among the four handed him by Margie Bruning the first of October. A three-month stretch during which he did little to avenge the beatings of his hand-chosen men while being sucked into a crazy scheme by four broads who were complete strangers.

Margie was at her station greeting early supper guests at the Pine Room when the telephone rang. "The Pine Room, this is Margie. How can I help you?" She waited for two highly discernable deep breaths to come and go and repeated, "This is the Pine Room. Can I help you?"

"It's the Bill Collector. I know you're busy, so I'll make it short. I'm calling it quits with you and your girlfriends. The three jobs I pulled off got the attention you wanted, not the headlines you were hoping for, but with enough juice to cause a lot of squirming and sweating. It had to be fun watching the scared rats chasing their tails."

"What about the rotten SOB who bragged that every one of his women needed a good slapping around to know their place?"

"Let's just say he'll be taken care of," he said.

His crazy relationship with the ladies had lasted only two weeks, more than enough time to take care of the first three marks on his hit list. At their insistence, he reluctantly met with them at the Historical Society to describe how each beating was administered. He had never talked so much in his life. The smallest bloody detail triggered whoops of triumph, and from Margie, a congratulatory toast, "Here's to the best goddamn Bill Collector in the world."

On Saturday, October 25, Stanislaus Bali Pafkoski's ornate mahogany casket was carried from St. Stephen's Church to a waiting hearse on Ferry Street, deep in Newark's Ironbound ghetto. Here, among his own kind, he had brutalized his way to the top of the Polish hierarchy.

It was standing room only inside. A crowd of three hundred Ironbound citizens spilled from the church's entrance onto Ferry and Wilson streets, causing a traffic jam of epic proportions. They were there to pay a final homage to a man you either loved or hated as the Ice Pick Man, who took shit from no one, supported three Polish parishes, and anted-up for an eight-bus convoy of kids to Rockaway Beach for fun each summer. The hearse inched its way through the crowd on the way to the Harrison Avenue Bridge and once across the Passaic to a memorial service at Our Lady of Czestochowa.

Mid-morning four days earlier, Homicide Lieutenant Josh Gingold had just finished reading the one-page, perfectly typewritten report of rookie patrolman Dennis Twining. It was a fatal truck accident. The report made it clear to Gingold that the kid didn't recognize the name. It could have been taken from a Police Academy instruction booklet:

Name: Stanislaus Bali Pafkoski; Age: 52; Witnesses: None; Accident Date and Time: Monday, Oct. 20, approx. 9:30 a.m.; Occupation: Owner Pafkoski Hauling; Family: Divorced, grown son and daughter living in California; Driver involved: (1) Michael Simpliski.

After going through the rest of the report, it wasn't hard for Gingold to piece things together, especially when it came to the cause of death. The victim was knocked to the ground by one of his trucks loaded with heavy steel construction bars as it backed from the company's loading warehouse. The tailgate had not been locked to allow for a final count of the bars before delivery. One of the bars slid off the truck and, with its hundred pounds and possible help, hit Pafkoski in the neck, killing him instantly. There were no witnesses during a time of day when the company's loading docks were mobbed with activity. Simpliski was a company driver.

"So, they finally got him," Gingold said loud enough to perk up detectives fighting off late morning ennui at nearby desks. "Had to know it was coming. Tough son of a bitch on borrowed time. He gave the mob paisanos some heavy grief."

"What's that all about?" Sergeant Bevo Simvietta queried from his adjoining desk.

"I've seen your jacket, you blottered him five times, and he still has a lily-white police sheet. You booked him for kicking sweet, young ass in the Tenderloin and the upscale, curbside cuties along broad. If you take your nose out of the comics and god damn sports pages and take a glance at the front page, you'll learn something," Gingold said.

"Give me the goddamn paper," Simvietta said, reaching over to grab the *Beacon* from Gingold's desk.

40

On October 27, after two weeks of snooping around the Sherry mansion on East Elmwood Avenue, Jerry Saunders was about to close his deal with a one-hundred-fifty-dollar bribe with the mark plucked from the household staff.

It wasn't easy. There weren't many beat-up Dodges like his sharing the rarified air of this socially elevated neighborhood. A weeping willow with filigreed branches tickling the ground provided an ideal place for him to park while he observed Mary McDonough. He parked his car, separated the thin, reedy branches of the tree and walked the fifty yards of beautifully cared for lawns to the bus stop where Mary sat waiting on the bench. He sat beside her and pulled a sealed, legal-size envelope from the inside pocket of his rumpled suit jacket. She reached for it only to have the *Beacon* reporter pull his hand back and, much like a dog owner waving a treat, cooed, "Uh, uh, uh, Mary. No trick, no treat." He put the envelope back in his pocket while she reached into her purse beside her and removed a similar envelope.

Mary was nobody's fool. She was thirty-two and, before reaching her privileged position of cook at the Sherry mansion, had spent thirteen years at one greasy spoon after another, some with cynical titles such as "Mom's Kitchen," "Food at Its Finest" and at her final job with its neon enticement, "European Cuisine for American Taste."

"You open yours, then I'll open mine. I want to see your green before I hand anything over."

Like two greedy parvenu reaching for even the smallest brass ring, they turned and carefully unsealed the envelopes, with Saunders exposing the corners of three fifty dollar bills and Mary producing a pink sheet of stationery embossed at the top with Maureen Whitaker Sherry.

The cook, whose biggest tip had been a two-dollar bill left by a whiskey-drenched sailor on shore leave, plucked the envelope from Saunders' hand, made sure the bills were safely inside, and then placed it into the deepest pocket of her purse. Meanwhile Saunders' smile broadened as he poured over his prize. It was the complete menu prepared for the September 28th dinner at the Sherry mansion, only two weeks after Dr. Felix Franklin Sherry was shot and killed by his wife. At the bottom were the names of the two guests, the Essex County District Attorney and his wife.

"I'll be god damned," Saunders said, "Is this an example of all her guests?"

"Hey, honey, you paid for one menu, and you got it," Mary said. She arose as her bus glided past the willow tree and was about to pull to a stop. Saunders stood and headed towards his Dodge and the twenty-minute drive downtown to the *Beacon* Building.

Saunders headed east and stopped at the first phone booth. "I should be there in fifteen minutes," he said, and after a lengthy reply, added, "It's about as good as it gets, signature and all."

Beacon owner and publisher David Goldman was pleased as he returned his office phone to its cradle. Ruthless and unforgiving of even the smallest slight since his boyhood days in Manhattan's Hell's Kitchen, he knew hunger, cold water, kerosene-heated tenements and, despite his small size, how to use his fists when the bullies on Delancey Street called him a *kike, sheeny,* or *yid.*

The *Evening Clarion,* the news platform for New Jersey's upper-crust elite, once referred to a *Beacon* editorial as "journalistic buffoonery." The WASP-owned competitor had thrown down the gauntlet. Thirty minutes later, with Saunders sitting quietly in the background, his paper's legal counsel, city editor and the engineer who kept the presses rolling had their marching orders.

On Friday morning, *Beacon* readers couldn't miss Jerry Saunders' story with a six-inch photo of a handwritten dinner menu prepared and signed by accused killer Maureen Whitaker Sherry. It was emblazoned with a 32-point headline: *A DINNER TO DIE FOR.* Followed by a smaller two-line deck: *OUTRAGEOUS PROOF THAT PRIVILEGED KILLERS ARE CODDLED.*

Saunders' byline story followed, outdoing his earlier poison pen articles about the Sherry murder case.

For two months, newspapers, radio news outlets, and even

magazines speculated about what transpired in the Sherry mansion since Maureen Whitaker Sherry pumped three bullets into the back of her renowned neurosurgeon husband, Dr. Felix Franklin Sherry, and left him for dead in their second-floor bedroom.

I'll digress here to describe how police officers called to the scene were met at the front door by a tall, beautiful woman who calmly handed over a .32 caliber, nickel-plated, pearl-handled pocket pistol. The toy-like gun is commonly given to rich women by their spouses for protection, an accessory rarely used. Sherry admitted as much to the officers, stating, "Until tonight, I didn't even know how to use it, not even how to pull the trigger. I was really startled when it exploded in my hand." One officer commented to reporters it was as though an unfortunate accident had occurred that she didn't quite understand.

Since the Sherry killing in early September, and let's not forget it was a killing, not an accident, there has been a flood of rumors purported to describe how a pampered killer endures her house arrest while awaiting a trial date. It isn't necessary to reveal more than just one aspect of the life Maureen Whitaker Sherry has been enjoying. The report will be brief and to the point, just long enough to define unrestricted privilege. You, the reader, can judge for yourself whether class discrimination is alive and well in America.

During my thirty-five years as a journalist, mostly as a police reporter, I was mired in the dark depths of Newark. Countless times, I was sickened by what I saw in tenement after tenement across this city. No guesswork was needed as to the cause of death of skin and bone black infants with bloated bellies or what caused the blue skin of white tots forced to breathe the noxious fumes of anthracite-burning stoves and heaters. And there were the heartbreaking scenes of sobbing mothers bold enough to confront city officials who were told they must wait their turn.

After some hard digging, I was able to obtain all that was needed to illustrate the wide chasm between our nation's haves and have-nots. A single piece of paper written in beautiful cursive by Mrs. Sherry. It outlines, for her help, a full five-course dinner menu served at her mansion two weeks after she shot and killed her husband.

Like me, I doubt many of my readers have ever been served a dinner of squab, or for that matter, even know what squab is. Well, here it is, ten-to-twelve inch pigeons killed when four weeks old to ensure the most tender meat. It should be roasted and continually sauteed with herbal sauces.

Having had the patience to wade through my angry sputtering, let's talk about what you'll find when you turn to the large adjoining picture. It's an enhanced photo of Mrs. Sherry's September 28 dinner menu; the guests are none other than the District Attorney and his wife. You're undoubtedly asking the same question I am: aren't visiting hours for the criminally charged limited to one, and on special occasions, two hours a week? Here things begin to play out like Gothic fiction.

Remember Dr. Forest Whitehead, the Freudian dream merchant, who for two months has been telling the D.A. and the judge that Mrs. Sherry is not mentally sound enough to be arraigned?

Saunders pulled out all stops, going so far as to imply that New Jersey prosecutors might have a soft spot for female killers.

His article went on for three full columns, two on page eight amid a picture of twelve-year-old Jimmy Austeen holding aloft the yellow and black Bumblebee sphere that won him the 1947 City Marble Championship. Among the two hundred entrants were thirty-seven competitors over forty years old. Jimmy pocketed fifty dollars, and runner-up Fred Boros, a thirty-nine-year-old unemployed steel worker, took home twenty-five dollars. Times are tough when grown men knuckle down in the dirt with kids.

Despite its length, the Saunders story was macabre enough to keep readers' attention. He and his boss believed it would lead to a public outcry condemning class privilege and demanding that Mrs. Sherry be pulled from her sumptuous dinner table and thrown behind bars. For the *Beacon,* it was a big disappointment.

The Newark police and County sheriff's cadre generally found the column amusing. "Have to give the son of a bitch credit," Sheriff Sergeant Willard Thompson said as he tossed the paper across his desk to another deputy at the County lockup.

"Took some digging. Never knew there was a Lucrezia Borgia of New Jersey, and would you believe, right here in Newark, named Mary Frances Creighton. Seems everyone knew Lucrezia used arsenic to knock off her brother, but she was acquitted. Moved to New York, and when arsenic-loaded bodies started piling up, the Creighton grad was arrested and fried in Sing Sing."

It took a while for the other deputy to finish the Saunders piece, commenting along the way. "Did you know there hasn't been a dame executed in Jersey since 1881? Name was Margaret Meierhoffer. She and her handyman lover knocked off her husband at their West Orange farm.

They shared the same gallows."

Reaction in Homicide was immediate and hardly ho-hum. Cisco's telephone rang off the hook. The Chief demanded to know why Detectives Thibabdeau and Rockford, Mrs. Sherry's original babysitters, were pulled off the case, "I gave you full reign, and you fucked up!"

"Chief, you know damn well it was politics. The minute the Mayor, the D.A., and a court-ordered shrink took over and determined Sherry wasn't a complete wacko; it was out of Homicide's hands."

"What in the good Christ's name have Thibadeau and Rockford been doing since you pulled them off?" the Chief demanded. "Tell me I'm wrong, but they have been checking in daily at the Sherry mansion, at least to see that the two uniforms aren't sleeping on the job or helping themselves to dinner leftovers. Someone had to be nosing around before going public with that broad's menu."

"At least a dozen people, including delivery men, come and go every day. We're blottering every one of them."

"Here's a warning, Captain: I'm not the only one who has you and your division in the crosshairs."

After that eighty-proof howl, Cisco slammed his phone down in disgust. Lieutenant Gingold had just entered Cisco's office as the Chief's rant ended. He sat a cup down in front of Cisco, took a seat and sipped his joe while his boss' forehead furrows deepened. Cisco pushed over the *Beacon*. "Have you read it yet?"

"For me and the bullpen, it's the same fucking anti-police and class hatred shit Saunders has been slinging for years. But that's us. There are hundreds, maybe thousands of lunatics out there who believe, like Saunders, that the war didn't change things at all. The rich get richer while the poor watch their children die of starvation and toxic fumes."

Cisco, who had been enduring the lieutenant's sermons ever since he replaced Kevin McClosky as Homicide's second in command, was about to reply when the intercom buzzed. It was Sergeant Charlie Dolan from his desk in the bullpen. "Chief, you have a few minutes? I see that Lieutenant Gingold is with you. I think what I have to say interests you both."

Cisco took in the bullpen through his open door and saw Dolan sitting expectantly on the corner of his desk. Less than a minute after getting a nod from Cisco, the detective was in the office and had taken the chair offered by Gingold.

"Okay, Charlie, what do you have?"

"Can I speak frankly?" and after getting a favorable reaction flipped his right thumb back over his shoulder toward the open door to the bullpen, "Me and a lot of the guys out there know the Sherry case is eating at you. Geez, you even needed time off. You're not alone. The big boys have been handing homicide the shitty end of the stick for years. Now we have a rich woman, for years her husband's punching bag, who decides enough is enough and pumps three bullets into him. The first case of its kind for any of us, including you and the Chief. Rockford and Thibadeau, two of your best, haven't been able to talk to her since the shrink decided the beatings had made her looney. We all know she'll get off, spend some time in therapy and rejoin her country club friends."

"Charlie, you and your buddies have in-baskets overflowing with murder and manslaughter files you haven't gotten to but have enough time to gossip about my taking a day off for a nice trip in the country. So, pass it along with your next cup of joe that the trip was to pick some brains."

Cisco reached into the bottom right drawer of his desk and pulled out a file folder with a sheath of handwritten notes. "These notes go into a memorandum, hopefully, to be on everyone's desk by the end of next week. Until the Mayor and Chief decide that a well-trained special team is needed, battering cases for rich and poor alike will be dumped in our laps. Anything more, Sergeant?"

"Until recently, I haven't given much thought to battering cases until a pinochle game got me thinking," Dolan said.

"Pinochle? This better be good, Charlie," said Gingold.

Dolan saw that his two superiors were getting impatient and knew that the Captain could be verbally hostile if he thought you were wasting his time. He would give it his best shot.

"An incident last year in the duplex Colleen and I were renting put the problem in focus. It's amazing how an innocent game of pinochle can turn hostile. By ending the evening with two winning hands, Colleen and I unwittingly severed a friendship that not only included the couple but their families as well."

They were now listening intently, and the Captain was scribbling notes.

"For sure, they were the better team. On this Friday, it looked like another rout, then the wife made a stupid mistake, and we won by ten. The point I want to make is that this just wasn't a pinochle game for the husband."

"So, you're finally getting to the point," Cisco said.

"They left for their apartment in the duplex we shared. It was old with a lath and plaster wall separating our flats. Hardly soundproof. Within seconds after their front door closed, he was punching her hard enough that her head thudded off our common wall. All the time, he shouted, '*Stupid bitch, stupid bitch!*'

"There were a few moments of silence before she was pounding on our kitchen door. We let her in, Colleen took her to the bathroom and fixed her face as best she could. It was really a mess, black and blue, swelling all over. I shouted across for him to stay put if he knew what was good for him. He did, although a steady stream of verbal filth kept us awake all night. She stayed with us two days under lock and key, and on the afternoon of the second, while we were out, she went missing.

'We waited until dinner time, expecting her to be back, when their front door opened, and we heard laughter from him and high-pitched, forced giggling from her. She had returned to the man who only forty-eight hours earlier beat the hell out of her. They brought home Chinese take-out. *Nice combo,* he said loud enough for us to hear through the wall, *Cantonese for me and Szechuan for you.* They moved out after spending the next week completely ignoring us, not a single nod of acknowledgement, a hello or how are you. A week later, their parents called Colleen's mom and dad, and mine as well, to say it was best to end the friendship. Forty years, our families were friends. Shame has no boundaries."

"And how powerful it can be," Cisco said.

"If there's any shame at all," Gingold said. "Can you, me, Charlie and everyone in the bullpen honestly say that the bastards who prey on the helpless are ashamed?"

"And it takes little or no provocation," Cisco said.

Pinochle.

Cisco and Gingold watched Dolan saunter back to his desk, knowing full well that the Sergeant's pinochle story was a thinly disguised job application.

"He put a lot of thought into his pitch," Gingold said. "But he's a dreamer, actually believes that the Mayor and Council are ready to take the blinders off and a special abuse detail is around the corner."

"If his dream comes true and he's still around, I'll keep him in mind," Cisco said, then pushed a folded copy of the *Beacon* across his desk and tapped on Saunders' article and squab menu. "This rag's been on the street for six hours now, and still no crazies pro or con have surfaced."

Cisco hoped this was more than wishful thinking, and if there were any demonstrations outside the Sherry mansion, they would be handled by the uniform crowd control division. He tried hard to believe this was not his concern, but he couldn't dispel his strong feeling of foreboding that the present situation was about to change.

41

His apprehension persisted as he and Gingold strode into the bullpen to find business as usual. Sergeant Sid Rosen flagged them down and handed Cisco the two-page report he'd just completed. "Nice timing, Captain. Could be a mob hit, really strange. Haven't heard a peep from Boiardo, Zwillman or DeCavalcante for a while; maybe they're getting restless. Do you want me to file it or sit on it? Don't need more for the press to turn it into the start of a gangster war."

"Tell me why it's so strange," Cisco said and, without reading the report, handed it over to Gingold. "What's your gut telling you?"

"Right now, my guess is revenge," Rosen said. "The mark is twenty-nine-year-old Pietro Lupo, a low-level collector for one of Boiardo's underbosses. Flashy dresser, flashy car and a fucking braggart ran into him a couple of times while working Vice. Two twenty-two slugs in the back of his skull while sitting in the front seat with his lady love, a chemical blonde, naked from the waist up, two enormous boobs, each with several hickies. She also took two in the back of the head."

"Now, let's get to the surprises," Gingold said.

"First, it wasn't his car but hers, a red Buick convertible straight from the showroom floor. Didn't need her driver's license to I.D. her. Lucy Nigro, the mob's bombshell nympho who shared the wealth with the big boys, even Tony Boiardo. Mystery to me, she would mess with a low-life like Pietro Lupo. Christ, she's the daughter of Jimmy Nigro, a made-man and longtime Genovese underboss. A gang payback? If so, who lent the contract? That's it so far. Where do you want me to go with this?"

"Sit on it for now; Lieutenant Gingold will get back to you," Cisco said. "Nice work, Sid."

They waited until Rosen returned to his desk and then went back to Cisco's office. Jessie Landry, his newly-minted civilian secretary, was waiting with two mugs of coffee. Cisco planted himself behind the desk just as his intercom rang. It was Jessie about an incoming call from Kevin McClosky. "He says that Sergeant Gazzi has uncovered a bombshell. 'Heads could roll,' he cautioned and added, 'nothing's out there yet and won't be unless you say so.'"

Cisco knew Kevin could really lay it on, lie, cajole, exaggerate, sympathize, threaten or just plead ignorance. It depended upon his target. "What's up, partner?"

"Grace DeMarco. But not over the phone. It'll be me, you and Gazzi. We'll set something up."

"Thanks for your input," Cisco said.

To dispel Gingold's suspicion that he might be hiding something, Cisco became jocular on the phone, "Connie's been asking where the hell you've been and, of course, Muriel is convinced that Uncle Kevin doesn't love her anymore. After all, it's been two weeks. Give Connie a call."

Nothing escaped Gingold. He hoped this was enough to assuage Gingold's suspicion that something was brewing. He turned his attention to the front page of the *Beacon* and thought aloud, "Wonder what Joe Lucio and the *Clarion* will do with this? Their bulldog hits the street in about an hour."

"Probably not much. The two owners hate each other, and the less said, the better. Giving Saunders any free publicity would be a case of 'cutting off your nose to spite your face.'"

Cisco buzzed Jessie for coffee refills. She daintily minced her way across the bullpen to the coffee maker, knowing full well that her smile, tight red skirt, matching heels, white ruffled blouse and auburn hair had set off a libido explosion.

Like the others, Sergeants Thibedeau and Rockford watched her sway to the coffee before leaving for another mandated trip to the Sherry mansion. With Maureen Whitaker Sherry comfortably incommunicado, all they did was poke around with their meaningless search warrant, question the help and get next to nothing from the two babysitting uniforms, Officers Musselman and Dolan. It was a damp and overcast day, with the temperature dropping to forty degrees by five-thirty that afternoon, so the cup of coffee offered by the cook was accepted without hesitation.

"Time for our walk-around," Dolan said as he and Musselman rose from the smallest of two kitchen tables. "My turn around the grounds. You've got the inside."

"We'll take our time. Damn, but that cook makes great coffee," Thibedeau said.

The kitchen, with its four doors wide open, was the only first-floor room still with lights on. All of the help had left for the day; the last to leave was Mary McDonough, the cook who pocketed one hundred fifty bucks for a purloined dinner menu that motivated what happened next.

Five minutes after she left, the two uniforms were still on patrol, and the detectives were about to leave when all hell broke loose. Two pistol shots echoed through the funereal mansion, followed by a shout from Musselman, "What the hell was that! Where the fuck did those shots come from?"

The two detectives sprang from their chairs and, with pistols drawn, crouched their way to opposite sides of the room. Thibedeau took a position beside the door leading to the dining room, foyer and the main entrance, where the ornate door was wide open to the portico. Rockford quickly switched off the main light and, in complete darkness, crawled out of the kitchen and headed to the curbed staircase.

The silence was broken when Dolan rushed from the front portico into the foyer and, with his weapon drawn, shouted, "Partner, you okay?"

Then, another gunshot from deep within the house

dropped Dolan to his knees. A searing pain enveloped his left calf, the bullet passing cleanly through before bouncing along the marble floor. "I'm hit!" Dolan shouted as he dropped straightened his legs and eased himself into a seated position against the wall about ten feet from the front door. "Jesus Christ, what the fuck is going on!" With his left index finger, he felt the wound, relieved to see it was a clean hit.

"I'm okay, upstairs with Sherry and the shrink," Musselman said. "How bad were you hit, and where the hell are you?" Musselman's voice echoed into every corner of the cavernous mansion. "And the two badges, where the hell are they?"

"Left leg, just soft tissue. I'll stay put, got the front door covered," Dolan said.

"We're in position," Rockford said. "Won't say where and tip off the fucker with the gun."

"Let's stop all this goddamn talk; what better tip-off is there!" Thibedeau, the senior cop on site, ordered.

Musselman had his .38 Smith & Wesson and was crouched against the wall at the far west side of the second-floor landing.

"Mrs. Sherry, you okay? Dr. Whitehead? Were you hit?"

"Not hit, just scared out of my skin!" Mrs. Sherry responded.

"Same here," Dr. Whitehead said. "I was just about to...."

"Shut up! Not another word," Musselman shouted.

"The shooter wants to know your location and no better way than tracing your goddamn voices. And no lights."

Two more shots. The bullets whistled past his head, shattering an ornate porcelain vase sitting on a table three feet away, the second destroying a medium-sized mirror to his left. The shooter had zeroed in on him. He dropped to his knees and crawled to the opposite side of the landing, which ran the full width of the house, accessing four bedrooms and ending at a glass-door sunroom overlooking the front lawn and the only light an entrance lamp on the driveway.

Sherry and the shrink were sequestered in two of the bedrooms. This still left plenty of room for the shooter to maneuver. The shooter could be anywhere, prone on the floor of the landing or going from one room to another, even the sunroom. Musselman could hear one of the badges edging his way up the stairs. So could the shooter. A bullet shattered the staircase balustrade, another bullet taking with it the lobe of Rockford's left ear.

"My ear, my fucking ear, he got my ear," Rockford screamed and stopped in his tracks and emptied his revolver in the direction from which the shots had come. The bullets splintered the door of the utility room and buried themselves in the towels, washcloths and sheets. Wrong door.

Musselman caught the flash of the gunman's second shot coming from the far bedroom door and was just about to fire when a figure emerged and promptly disappeared into the darkness. He could hear the gunman discard an empty magazine from his pistol and insert another one. Musselman had what he wanted: the probable position of the shooter. He fired three times. Silence. Then, the metallic sound of a gun hitting the floor followed by the unmistakable sound of a falling body.

"I think I got him; get some lights on!" The doors of the Sherry and Shrink's bedrooms opened, flooding the landing with light. In the middle of the landing, a well-dressed man of about thirty laid on his back. He was still alive, but barely. Musselman saw he was trying to speak and bent close enough to hear a barely discernable whisper, "We don't give up." His last words then closed his eyes and silence. A gold Star of David hung prominently from his neck.

Sherry and the shrink cautiously left the safety of their bedrooms and grouped beside Musselman over the body. They could hear Thibedeau on the downstairs phone. "Thibedeau at the Sherry mansion. Two men hit, and the shooter's down. Medics and backup, now!"

Within ten minutes the estate was ringed by five patrol cars with dome lights flashing, ten uniforms, two with shotguns, the others with revolvers at the ready on the grounds. The driveway was crowded with two ambulances, a meat wagon from the morgue, and two unmarked police cruisers.

"Spread out! I'm going inside. You three button down the front area," Gingold ordered as he and three homicide detectives raced up the stairs to the front door, their guns drawn. "No happy trigger fingers, that's all the fuck we need right now."

A few feet inside, he spotted Dolan stretched on a gurney while two medics treated his wound. Dolan saw the lieutenant, pushed up on his elbows and quipped, "God damn, you homicide dicks are fast." The lieutenant ignored him as he headed to the stairs.

When Gingold reached the crowd around the body, Musselman had already pulled a wallet from one inside pocket of the dead man's windbreaker and from another folded pages from that morning's *Beacon*. Thibedeau knelt beside him and, with a pencil through the trigger guard was examining a strange pistol with a long barrel. "So this little fucker's been causing all the trouble. Never saw anything like it before," he said. He passed the pistol to Gingold, who used a handkerchief to pull the gun off the pencil to get a closer look.

"It's Japanese, a Nambu. I've heard of it. As I recall, it's the only eight-millimeter handgun ever made. A souvenir from the Pacific. The perp is obviously a veteran. What did you find in his pockets?"

Benjamin Shapiro's credentials were typical during a time when wounded veterans questioned just about everything. His I.D. from Brooklyn Naval Hospital listed his age as twenty-nine, with no permanent home address, was attached to his scheduled appointment card listing five upcoming visits to the massive facility and a signed and stamped receipt from the downtown YMCA on Halsey Street, room 310, five dollars a week.

Musselman fished into his other pockets and came up

with a small notebook, a room key, a smaller key to Shapiro's YMCA gym locker, ninety cents in change, a USO gift card good for four coffee and doughnut sit-downs at the counter in the lobby and forty-seven dollars. Gingold flinched when he heard the dead man's name but said nothing.

By eight o'clock that night, no one was immune from the finger pointing and accusations. When it was learned that Shapiro had a copy of Jerry Saunders' article with him during the shooting spree, the focus narrowed but to no avail. The *Beacon's* legal counsel pointed to the Second Amendment, that Saunders was one of its top reporters just doing his job. Everyone was to blame and no one was to blame.

The Mayor threw punches in every direction. McClosky, Gazzi and Valentine were called into his office, shrugged off a ten-minute tirade and returned to their desks for business as usual. The Police Chief, Mayor, three council members, the D.A. and an aroused clergy burnt the lines to Cisco's office through the early hours of the next day, running out of steam at four in the morning.

Cisco made no apology. He controlled his anger enough to pare down a rote reply repeated dozens of times that night. "It was a wounded veteran, crazed by what he read, driven to do our job for us. A killer enjoying squab dinners with her personal shrink in her own mansion with the blessing of the D.A. and court. It's god damn easy to understand."

It was a threat from Police Chief Patrick Riley that sent

Cisco off the deep end. The Chief was an eighty-proof imbiber who barely survived the Mayor's purge of the police department four years earlier. "Get rid of them," the Chief, already deep into his cups, mentioned no names. "They keep their stripes and time and grade, but they're out of homicide and back in uniform."

"What the hell are you talking about?" Cisco said. "Which of my men am I putting back on the bricks?"

"Rockford and Thibedeau."

"Is this a joke? Who put you up to this? The Mayor or the D.A.? Dan and Quent are two of my best men. You know, god damn well, it wasn't my decision or theirs to be part-time babysitters. You've read their dailies; they still had a real job to do, and they did it: five homicide arrests in two months."

"So, you're ignoring my order?" the Chief said. "Losing your job makes no difference? It's not just me involved. Put up a fight, and it'll go public, a goddamn mess that nobody wants. I'll get back to you."

Cisco was confident that he had heard the last of it. He replaced his phone in its cradle, knowing the last thing the Essex County power elite wanted was an internal police squabble centered around the privileged treatment of a killer from their own class.

42

Later that morning, Cisco was informed by the County Hospital that Dolan would probably be released that evening. Rockford's severed earlobe was on ice, and plastic surgery to reattach it was scheduled later that day. He let Gingold know he would be out for a few hours and that he should hold down the fort.

Gingold had the dead man's personal belongings spread out on his desk along with Musselman's report. He squirmed when he read Shapiro's last words, "We don't give up." Years earlier, the two of them were up-and-coming fighters during a time when Newark's Jewish boxers were making a national reputation. Light heavyweight Gingold won three straight main events at St. Nick's, two of them early knockouts. Middleweight Shapiro, a bruising puncher with both hands, broke three knuckles of his right hand during a ten-round main event at Newark's Laurel Gardens. He came close to flooring his trainer, who was about to throw in the towel. Using only his left hand, he scored a knockout in the tenth round. It was his last fight.

Bruising Benny Shapiro had it all at one time and now this.

He reached for Shapiro's small notebook and stopped scanning when he got to the name of the Hospital Chief Corpsman Kenneth Belman. There were two phone numbers for Boysenberry, Iowa and a third from Letterman Naval Hospital in San Francisco. The war was long over so he decided to call the second of the Iowa numbers.

"Name's Josh Gingold. I trying to get hold of Kenneth Belman. Do I have the right number?"

"Sure do. What's up Josh?"

"Did you ever treat a Marine by the name of Benjamin Eli Shapiro? From what I see in his notebook, the two of you traded quite a few phone calls."

"Yeah, I did. I still have nightmares. It was on Guadalcanal during a bloodbath at the Bonego Coconut Plantation. I was just a kid, and this was my first real battle. Me and another medic were following a platoon skirmish line entering the coconut grove when Jap mortars zeroed in. I saw Benny go down, and the two of us crawled over with our field kits. When I saw his head, I almost puked. I know I started to cry. A piece of Benny's skull had been blown away, along with a large chunk of hair. The hole was almost two inches. I could see the brain; it was pulsating like it wanted to escape the skull. I put my palm over the wound and applied pressure.

"I remember shouting to my sidekick, 'Give me every compression bandage we have and morphine. I've got the wound; you handle the joy juice.'"

"You saved his life, and he's never forgotten," Gingold said.

"Exactly right. God damn, if he didn't research the entire Navy to get my name. Finally tracked me down at Letterman. He's one brave son of a bitch. You know, living with a steel plate in his skull for five years and the headaches that never go away. I've only seen him four times, at the coconut grove and twice each at the Brooklyn and St. Alban's Naval Hospitals. You might find it hard to believe but he is the closest friend I have. Now, can you tell me what your call is about?"

It was the first that Gingold learned about the metal plate, having not yet seen the autopsy report.

"Bruiser Benny was shot and killed during a gunfight with police while attempting to track down and shoot an upper-class woman living a life of luxury after killing her husband."

"Jesus fucking Christ. Benny, Benny, how could you do it? I know how you'd been hurting, and I also know you're no killer. Benny, Benny, I'm going to miss the hell out of you."

It took fifteen minutes for Cisco to pull rank, take over the police cruiser of two pissed-off uniforms, and drive to City Hall for the hush-hush meeting with McClosky and Gazzi. Seeing no need for preamble, he said, "What's this about Grace DeMarco that couldn't be **said** on the phone?"

McClosky appeared ill at ease. How do they approach a

colleague with felonious information about a woman with whom he had carried on an adulterous three-year love affair? He decided to turn it over to Gazzi.

"Captain, it was sheer chance. It was about three-thirty in the afternoon on the seventh of this month and I was doing my due diligence downtown in and around Military Park when I saw Grace DeMarco and a male companion, over six foot tall, leave the New Jersey Historical Society building. Right behind them three well-dressed women emerged, chatted a minute or two then went their separate ways. Meanwhile, there had been a lot of hand gesturing by Miss DeMarco during her sidewalk talk with the big guy. When it was over, she went to her car parked half a block away, and he turned, crossed the street and headed directly towards me. I couldn't believe who it was, Stefano Rizzano. He might be off the streets as white collar labor muscle for the mob right now, but as a made man, he's also a murderer. We almost brushed shoulders, then I followed him across Broad Street, where he bought a ticket at the Capital Theater to see "The Unfinished Dance." Maria and I took it in on opening night. I thought it was corny, but my wife thought it was great."

Gazzi was the master of minutiae. Cisco marveled that McClosky and Valentine, the third man of the unit, had kept their sanity. McClosky shifted his weight several times and was about to light an Old Gold when he decided it was time to take over.

"Is that it, Frank? You tail him to a movie, a movie that you hated and your wife loved? Did he buy any popcorn?"

Gazzi was on a roll and ignored the wisecrack. "I went back to the Historical Society and learned from the lobby receptionist that it was the second time Rizzano had joined Miss DeMarco and the other ladies in the third-floor society offices. She took notes on everything, a lot like me." He waited for the sarcastic guffaws.

"Anyone wanted to get in had to sign her register. It was meticulous right down to the visitors' phone numbers."

"The names, god damn it! Let's have the names and the numbers," Cisco said. His tone suggesting that Gazzi could be pulled off his sweetheart's job if he didn't get on with it. No more cars, no more Mayor's office.

"Grace DeMarco, of course, Margie Bruning, Rosemary Pringle, and Deborah Hammerstein Paasche. Here's their addresses and phone numbers."

Cisco looked it over and asked, "And that's it? Better tell me you've got more. You're implying that the County Courthouse Clerk is a felon. Do I have that right?"

"Not implying anything, Captain, just telling you what I've come up with. The morning of the tenth, a pissed-off Mayor called us into his office. His red face was a sure sign that someone had just chewed his ass over the phone."

"You know Ferguson Dickenson, the third," the Mayor said. "He's the guy who signs your paychecks and approves your raises. Well, he had the shit kicked out of him last night by some big son of a bitch who almost broke his back. Right in front of his house. He wants action, and so do I! Got a ten percent raise coming up, and I better get it."

The three detectives had gotten to know the Mayor well enough to recognize an implied threat when they heard it. Gazzi was excited; he was putting things together. Could Dickenson's attacker possibly be the large and muscular Rizzano?

"I've got a hunch I want to run down," Gazzi said. "I'll let you know this afternoon if it pans out."

He bought the final edition of the Beacon and the Clarion's bulldog edition and drove to his favorite White Castle. There was no mention of Dickenson's beating in either paper. With plenty of time on his hands, he went through four sliders, three coffees, and an apple pie. By the time he scanned the comics and sports pages of both papers, it was time to go.

Gazzi parked his easily recognizable cruiser two blocks from Military Park, casually walked to the monument and waited. His hunch was right, and he began to sweat beads of perspiration that, along with a smile, convinced him he was as shrewd as ever. It was three twenty-eight when they emerged from the Historical Society Building. As on the seventh, DeMarco and Rizzano paired off and the three other women bid their farewells and went their separate ways. By the time Gazzi returned to the squad's City Hall office, McClosky and Valentine had left for the day. The following morning, Gazzi's hunch was never mentioned.

On the morning of the sixteenth, McClosky's squad endured another of Mayor Simpson's tirades. This time, he was blistered by Sergio Simpliano, the rich auto dealer who supplied Newark's political bigshots with upper-end Lincolns, Dodges and Fords in exchange for lucrative City and County fleet contracts.

"This time, it's Sergio Simpliano, and only a few blocks away from my office at his Chrysler dealership. What do you guys have to say about it, if anything?"

"Say about what?" a dumbfounded McClosky said. The other two detectives, who were just as puzzled, hunched their shoulders and rolled their eyes.

"Not what, who! Simpliano finished his books and was about to leave when a big gorilla came out of the shadows, never saw his face, threw a hood over his head and beat the hell out of him. The son of a bitch left him on the showroom floor, panting for breath. Thinks he has a few broken ribs."

Simpliano never mentioned the message his attacker had whispered in his ear, "This is a payback kiss from Francie."

"When was this, and where do we look?" McClosky said. "Not the best-loved auto dealer in town. It seems like every year, he's in court fighting fraud claims. Won them all. We can start there." A grim Mayor Simpson silently nodded them out of his office.

Gazzi was now certain that his hunch was right. A search of Civil Court records would be a waste of time. It was lunchtime. The three detectives worked well as a team, but their divergent personalities made breaking bread together beyond their call to duty. Their cruisers left the parking lot in different directions for the usual two-hour break.

Maria Gazzi had been hounding her husband to start their holiday shopping early. The extended family was big and widespread. He picked her up at their house and dropped her off at Bamberger's, making sure she had enough cash for lunch and the taxi ride home.

"Expect me for dinner," he said with a kiss on her cheek. "If Bam's restaurant still has orders to go for their hoity-toity customers, pick up some lasagna; it's the best."

After a short drive to Military Park, he took up his customary spot at the monument and waited. Three-thirty came and went, and the only activity at the Historical Society was the coming and going of other tenants. Where were they? He was certain his hunch was right; the Simpliano beating was proof positive. But was it? By four o'clock, doubt had turned to despair, and he was about to return to his car when they finally appeared. But unlike before, Grace remained with the other three women and Stefano walked to his Lincoln Cabriolet parked at the end of the block.

Gazzi was great on details. Nothing had escaped him on the sixteenth. He remembered everything he saw, even the name on the dealer's medallion. But he was no mind reader. If so, the decision Stefano finalized as he fired up the Cabriolet would have surprised him.

Two weeks later, Gazzi closed his notebook. He was finished telling Cisco and McClosky all that he knew or thought he knew. "You're my superiors and can do whatever you want with the information. From my end, I'm coming away convinced that the strategy for the three beatings began in the Historical Society office. Given what we know so far about the four ladies, my guess is Miss DeMarco was the leader of the pack. They put together a crazy scheme and were able to suck in a mob thug to do their bidding. That's all I got. I'm handing you no proof, just strong suspicions." Gazzi sat back in his chair and waited.

Cisco and McClosky exchanged knowing glances that some action had to be taken. They understood that the beatings were not the problem. The problem was Grace DeMarco. Gazzi was now clearly an intruder, and he knew it was time to go. He was about to return his notebook to his inside jacket pocket when McClosky said, "Great job, Frank. Leave your notebook with me so I can go over your notes." Gazzi doubted he would ever see his notebook again.

Cisco waited until Gazzi had closed the door behind him. Then put it directly to his long-time friend and former partner, "Kevin, I'm asking a favor. I can imagine how the Mayor and his big-time buddies have been squeezing you. But a straight yes or no, will you sit on Gazzi's info for a day or two?"

"I knew that was coming," Kevin said. "I'll give you a long weekend. Let's say Tuesday evening at six at the Pamplona for tacos and beer."

43

Grace was pleasantly surprised to see Nick leaning against her Studebaker as she descended the courthouse steps at four-thirty Monday afternoon, a half hour earlier than her usual quitting time. She wondered how long he had been waiting. She ignored his grim expression and planted a soft kiss on each cheek. Old habits never die.

"How's Connie and that adorable little daughter of yours?" she asked, backing off a few feet to study his face.

"Both are doing great," Nick said. "Muriel has the Cisco family under her thumb. Got us all learning German. And you?"

"Lonely at times but bearing up quite well," she replied. "Been quite busy the last few months; as much as you think you're getting ahead, the court docket never gets smaller."

"It's the last few months I want to talk about. Let's sit inside."

Grace unlocked her car, took the driver's seat and then

reached over and unlocked the passenger door for Nick. He waited until they were both settled and asked, "Ever hear of a mug by the name of Stefano Rizzano?"

"Who's Stefano Rizzano? The name doesn't ring a bell."

"Are you sure? Maybe the three dates I'll throw out will jog your memory. All at the same time of day and at the same place, the Newark Historical Society office across from Military Park."

What Grace had feared but never actually imagined would happen was about to take shape—the discovery of the crazy scheme that had pulled in three other women as accomplices. Her body tensed as she white-knuckled the steering wheel and waited.

"Let's go back to October 7," Nick said. He described in detail everything he had learned from Gazzi and asked, "You still insist you don't know anyone named Stefano Rizzano?" He didn't wait for an answer.

Grace was silently looking through the windshield, several times acknowledging passing co-workers as they headed to their cars.

It was as though Nick was reciting a rote exercise as he went through what Gazzi had seen and heard on October 10th and 16th. When finished, he asked, "You still insist Rizzano is a stranger?"

Grace gathered her wits and answered with a sigh of resignation, "He was our bill collector."

"Your bill collector. What the hell does that mean? You had to realize you were dealing with a member of the Vito

Genovese crime family, an alleged killer. You knew that, didn't you?"

"We knew and appreciated him only as our bill collector, not a killer. A man who came highly recommended to carry out what we wanted: revenge."

Nick studied Grace's face and found no sign of remorse. For the first time, it dawned on him that the three men Rizzano had stomped had two things in common. They were public figures known to be physically abusive to women. Charges were never brought. Could it be that this was behind it all? That the women would have their bill collector do what the three abusers with all their power had kept the D.A., Mayor and judge from doing their duty.

"The four of you roped a mafia thug to do your dirty work, then sat back and waited for a reaction. None of this ever made the press, so what good was it? You know that you have all become felons. I'm not talking here three to six months in county jail, but a year or more of real prison time in Trenton. What was your motivation? Was it that punch in the face from your husband?"

"Only partly. I know that you and your homicide badges have never heard of Clarissa Bagnel and neither had I until my secretary threw her name out. Clarissa was her neighbor. She told me that the weekend before was the sixth time Clarissa was badly beaten in front of their children by her husband. She ended up in ER, got patched up, had the son of a bitch arrested, but after a night of cursing him as a loser and acknowledging him as the family breadwinner dropped the charges the next morning."

"I had my staff do some research and discovered there were three hundred and seventeen similar arrests the previous year, with two hundred and forty of those charges dropped. Only twelve were serious enough to get press mention. It was clear that if beating up women was ever to be a public concern, big names were needed."

"Ever since your rich, dentist husband almost destroyed your face, then returned to his Gibson and smilingly asked you to join him, this endemic has been on my mind." He reached over, pulled her right hand from the steering wheel, cupped it in both of his and said, "This isn't a homicide case, so I'm not involved." Raising his eyes to hers added, "I'll see what I can do."

Grace watched as Nick slid across his seat, opened the door and left. She failed to fight off her tears as her gaze followed him across the parking lot to his car. He was history, an uncompromising lover who gave her the three happiest years of her life.

Cisco returned to homicide and with Gingold went over the three new cases added to the tote board hanging near the entrance to the bullpen. "Jesus Christ, they just keep coming," he said, turned and went to his office.

Seated at his desk, he rummaged through the top drawer and came up empty. He knew the piece of paper was around somewhere, but after rifling through his three right-hand drawers was about to give up when he found it crumbled at the back of the bottom drawer. He flattened it on his blotter and traced the three names the psychiatrist

Dr. Moishe Andrew had written, stopping at the one he had never found time to interview, Hillary Thorne.

The traumatic half-hour he and Grace had spent in her car left him confused; he needed more, more what? That kicking the hell out of women was wrong? That four privileged women who had taken the law into their own hands was right? He was certain of the first but needed convincing about the second.

It was not yet six o'clock, still early enough for a phone call. He picked up the phone. "This is Hillary. Who's this?" The voice, once sweet had taken on the husky edge common to middle-aged women.

"Captain Nick Cisco, Newark Police Homicide Chief. Don't be scared off; I got your name from your psychiatrist. I convinced him I was concerned about abuse of all kinds, and he thought you would be a lady worth talking to."

"Oh yes, yes. I recall now, but that was almost two months ago. I gave up waiting for your call," there was a long pause on her end as she collected her thoughts. "So, what prompted you today?"

"It wasn't that I didn't want to talk with you, but things got very busy. Murder has almost become a rite of passage in certain neighborhoods. I know this is very short notice, but can you free up an hour tomorrow morning or afternoon so we can talk?"

There was another long pause on her end. "I'll say yes, only if you assure me I won't be blindsided."

"I really don't know the exact questions only that Dr. Andrew would not have given me your name if he didn't think you could enlighten me."

"I take that to mean my former stepfather and how he treated me and my mother. How much did Dr. Andrew tell you?"

"Nothing. All I have is a piece of paper with your name on it."

"Their marriage lasted eight years. There were signs from the very beginning that he was crazy. Over the years, two psychiatrists and my school counselor advised her to leave him. Before we go further, I want your assurance that if our talk is useful to you, no names will ever be mentioned."

"You've got it. I have an open window until three tomorrow afternoon; you set the time, and I'll be there. Give me an address, I'll be driving in from downtown Newark." He was relieved when she gave him an address in Maplewood, an easy drive less than seven miles from headquarters.

44

Exactly at noon the next day, he parked his unmarked cruiser in front of a sprawling two-story, brown brick Georgian colonial, got out and surveyed a street of equally expensive and well-kept homes. His cop instincts told him he was being watched. A long cobblestone path led to the front door that swung open as he was about to reach for the doorbell.

"Right on time, Captain. And I was led to believe that cops were never on time," a well-tended, handsome woman of about thirty said. Her dark, gray-streaked hair fit well with her hazel eyes and sculptured, angular features. She was tall and ample in all the right places. "Come in; you've got as much time as you need."

She ushered him into the parlor, where they took seats in two heavily-tufted wingback chairs in front of a large casement window overlooking a broad expanse of lawn. A silver service with coffeepot, sugar and cream was waiting. After taking their first sips of coffee in silence, they sat back in their chairs.

"First, let me say that I've been curious why a school counselor was involved?"

"I was twelve and doing poorly at school because of what was happening at home. I was a bright kid. The counselor had me in her office three or four times. It didn't take her long to realize she had a scared and very confused adolescent on her hands and beyond the help she could give. She phoned my mother, I believe it was at least four times, but got nowhere. Mom was a very private woman."

"Are you comfortable talking about the situation at home?" Cisco asked. "If so, you can start by filling me in where your mother and stepfather are now."

"As I told you on the phone, they were divorced after eight years. Mom's fifty-eight now and married to a great guy in California. A lifetime nurse with all the credentials, she can't stay away from doctors. He's a thoracic surgeon.

"And your stepfather?"

"He's in a loony bin in Montana. His family, in denial for years, finally acknowledged what mom and I had known for a long time: their son was crazy. They finally committed him five years ago. After your phone call, I rehearsed what I wanted to say. If your questions fit, I'll answer them."

"You said crazy, that's hardly a medical definition."

"The terms experts used to describe my stepfather included: megalomania, schizophrenia, psychopath, amoral, and I could go on. There was one face he presented as Chief of Surgery at a big hospital, and another face hidden behind a mask of deviant behavior."

"Deviant behavior?" Cisco asked.

"Illegal abortions, dozens of them. Before the hospital found out, we knew. For years he had forbidden us to even approach the door to the farthest wing of our house. One day, when he was attending a medical seminar, we had the guts to go in. The wing had a separate basement. We found an operating table complete with stirrups and instruments needed for abortions."

She poured more coffee into her cup, offered the pot to Cisco and sat back. "Mom opened one of several wall cabinets and what she found, I'll never forget it, caused her to scream, 'Oh my God! Oh my God!' I was only thirteen but strong enough to keep her from fainting. In the cabinet were twelve large, sealed glass jars, each containing a fetus preserved in alcohol and labeled with the date and time the abortion was performed. In another cabinet, we found two stacks of large glossy photos showing exactly the same thing: women's breasts. That was the first time we had evidence we had a crazy man in the house."

"Did you ever confront him?"

"Are you kidding! You don't challenge a nut case."

Cisco nodded in agreement and asked, "Was there any physical or sexual abuse?"

"He never physically abused me; it was always sexual. It started right after their marriage. Remember, I was only six and wanted to please him. The sex was always oral, with him purring sweetly during the act. Then, a kiss on the forehead after it was over. Any time we were alone, it could happen. I never told my mother."

"No wonder you were having trouble in school. You just described sexual abuse of a minor that went on for years; why didn't you tell your mother?"

"I wanted everyone to be happy. My mom was slapped around two or three times a week and seemed to be always crying. It didn't take long for me to realize, even as a kid that every time I went down on my stepfather, his attitude towards mom changed, and the beatings stopped at least for a while."

Cisco was stunned. "I'm having a hard time with this. You just told me you were providing therapeutic sex to make your stepfather happy enough to stop beating your mom."

"That's a polite way to put it."

"How often did your father force you to perform your therapy?"

"Over the years, more than a hundred. I'm no genius but I did enough research to see that it was all about power. He was a very careful megalomaniac. That one medical text described a case that could have been my stepfather."

Cisco waited patiently for Hillary to reveal stupefying details and after topping off her coffee, did not disappoint.

"He was always careful not to leave any visible bruises. A hospital's Chief of Surgery must have his little secrets."

"Megalomaniacal, I can't even spell it. But abuse of power that I do understand. How did you reach that conclusion?" Cisco asked.

"I've never been able to forget those preserved fetuses. You might think I'm crazy that I believe my lunatic stepfather was convinced that ending dozens of lives and then preserving them forever in jars of alcohol was the ultimate power. Years of beating my mother and having oral sex with me completed the picture."

"I'm having a hard time understanding why your mother didn't leave and take you with her. Was she so shamed by your stepfather, so frightened of him that she was scared of what he might do if she threatened to leave?"

"We did leave twice, to Denver and to Salt Lake City where, as Mormons we had plenty of friends. She easily found a good nursing job. He followed us and sobbed and whined his way back into her heart and out of her job, and we returned home to Maplewood. After a few months, we had enough and once again we took off, this time to Utah. He followed. He was a pathological liar who could sell ice cubes to Eskimos. In Salt Lake City close relatives, distant relatives, close friends and acquaintances all believed him when he said he had never laid a hand on my mother. So, it was back to Maplewood.

"Two more things very quickly to give you a more complete picture. Every time he beat my mother, he begged forgiveness. It was so theatrical. He got us together in the living room, knelt down and began to sob. Tears flowed, first his and then my mother's. I never cried. His 'please forgive me's' seemed endless. It was pitiful."

"You said there were two things you wanted to mention

to complete the picture."

"My stepfather was a closet bisexual. He made little effort to hide his affairs with women, but there was no hint that he had sex with men. That ended when a good friend told mom that he had been propositioned during a fishing trip, and a male patient switched doctors for the same reason. He described my stepfather as a sick and dangerous man."

"I think I've heard enough," Cisco said. "You and your mom have shown a remarkable amount of courage."

They arose and walked to the front door. He was surprised when she took firm hold of his right hand and held it until they reached the porch. He turned and encountered the smile of a woman who had learned the hard way the value of human understanding. "Thank you, Captain Cisco, thank you very much." She released his hand, turned and went inside, gently closing the door behind her. He retraced his steps down the cobble path to his car.

At six that evening, he entered the Pamplona to find McClosky sitting in a corner booth with a pitcher of dark beer, an extra glass along with chips and salsa. "Qué pasa, señor!" McClosky said as he filled the second glass to the top.

"Had a very interesting afternoon," Cisco said as he poured himself a brew, "and I need to ask a favor of you and Gazzi that could cost you your jobs."

McClosky drained his glass and, while carefully refilling it turned and asked, "It's Grace DeMarco, right?"

"We've been partners for almost twenty years, so you know that what I'm about to ask is tearing me apart..."

"No need to go through the blood brothers' speech; just spit it out."

"Burn Gazzi's notes and bury the investigation."

Kevin was deep in thought as he used his sweating beer glass to make rings on the table. "Nick, it's not really my decision; it's Gazzi's. After all his career fuckups, he never dreamed he'd be working directly under the Mayor. His wife would kill him if he lost his sweetheart job and hit the bricks again."

"Can you scare him out of his notes and to shut his mouth?" Cisco said.

"So, you want me to order Frank to suborn criminal evidence?"

"Yes." Nick reached for his Chesterfield and fired up as Kevin continued to make circles on the table, silently weighing the consequences. They had never hesitated to put their lives on the line for each other, often bending the law. This time Cisco was asking his former partner and Gazzi to jeopardize their careers and even do jail time if a cover-up was discovered.

"I'm not going to threaten him; he's worked his ass off mostly on his own time and deserves better," Kevin said. "He's been insecure, paranoid even, about his future since he panicked during that arrest and shot and killed the Bancik kid."

"I knew that there was less than a 50-50 chance that you'd go along," Cisco said.

"I have to feed his ego."

"From where I'm sitting, that's a total repair job," Cisco said.

"He'll head up our meetings with the Mayor and City Council while I sit back and listen," Kevin said. "I'll make sure that at least half the press releases have his name on them."

"He'll go for that?"

"If not, I'll remind him that it only takes one phone call for him to be back on his old city dump walking beat. Then there's Maria to face every day."

"Let's keep our fingers crossed," Cisco said.

"Relax, Nick. I know all the right buttons with Gazzi and the Mayor has backed off. He's put the word out he wants Acardo's vacated State Senate seat and he's looking for money. Doubt if much else is on his mind. You can call Grace and tell her it's a done deal."

They tipped their refilled glasses just as Pamplona's specialty, a large combination platter with an overstuffed chile relleno, beef and chicken tacos, two cheese enchiladas, rice, small salad and refried beans, was placed in front of them.

45

At the same time Cisco and McClosky were burping down their massive meals at the Pamplona, four women were taking seats at an out of the way Pine Room corner table. It had been reserved for them by Doris, the black waitress who, like them, was a member of the abused woman's sisterhood. At their initial meeting two months earlier, Doris opened their eyes to the harsh realities of inner-city life. She had four champagne flutes and an ice bucket with a bottle of Mumms waiting.

"I know why y'all here, and it makes me sad. Maybe this'll help," Doris scanned the faces at the table as she popped the bottle. "Sure hope you didn't take as gospel that you best be carrying a switchblade for protection. That's my world, not yours."

"I was sitting at the edge of my seat when you gave your little demonstration," Debbie said, "and I think the other ladies were just as fascinated. Just a little click, there's not a woman-beating coward who'd raise a fist. I know the others think the same." She returned to seating patrons with reservations at their tables.

Their first glass of Mumm's disappeared quickly; they were well into their second when Grace said, "Be nice if the bill collector was here. I haven't been able to reach him since the Simpliano beating. I searched as far back as juvie. No arrests, no records."

"So, you know his real name and kept it from us," Debbie said, her disappointment clearly showing.

"Right on all points. No sense giving you information that could be pried out by police if we were arrested," Grace said. "Only one other person knows him by name and there's absolutely no chance he'll talk."

More bubbly to wash down their Oyster Rockefeller appetizers, the specialty of the house. Their early chit-chat was mundane as they savored the main dish of Halibut Florentine, another richly flavored house special. The side dish was roasted asparagus dipped in olive oil and encrusted with bread crumbs, parmesan romano cheese and garlic.

The table was cleared, more champagne poured and as they waited for their dessert of Black Forest cake to arrive Grace said, "Well, it's over. We gave it a good run but never got the attention we wanted. It was exciting. The bill collector cashed in three long overdue debts and the lords of the manor began to sweat. Now what?"

"For me, things are looking good," Margie said. "Thanks to you, Grace; I'm waiting for final court approval of my annulment. Ned isn't fighting it. He called it quits after months of hopeless job hunting and with his near perfect Marine Corps record, he was welcomed back with open arms. He left me a one-line farewell, 'Like you wanted, the annulment is yours.'"

"So, you have an empty nest," Rosemary said.

"Not exactly. I never talked about Eduardo Solano, a co-worker at Todd's Shipyard during the war. When tonight's farewell party is over, he'll be waiting at my Rector Street apartment. From the start, he was my guardian angel, you know living in a dangerous neighborhood with a husband who slapped me around."

"You were still with your husband?" Rosemary asked. "How'd he protect you?"

"He gave me a stiletto and taught me how to use it if Ned got rough again. Thank God I never unsheathed it. Now Eduardo uses it to clean his fingernails."

"You've got yourself a live-in boyfriend," Grace smiled.

"We're together on weekends and one day during the week. He supervises the flotilla of mothballed Liberty Ships anchored up the Hudson at Stony Point."

"Sounds like a great job," Rosemary said.

"That's only the beginning. He's been tapped to manage mothball and salvage operations across the nation, eight of them. I'm packed and ready to go."

"I guess this is a good time for me to chime in," Rosemary said between forkfuls of Black Forest. "Getting to the point, yes, I'll continue to stay with my husband in Upper Montclair until Lisa and David are off to boarding school and away from their father. They're five and seven now, so that's years away."

"What about your families," Margie asked, "are they in on it?"

"The Volker family has known for decades Millard has a dual personality and as long as their upper-crust friends didn't know it was all to the good, everyone kept their mouths shut."

"Rosie, I know you well enough now and have seen the bruises. Quite frankly, I've never been able to understand why you stay with him regardless of his family's renown, his personal fame and the magnificent mansion." Grace tried hard to hide her distress but failed.

"I realize it's impossible for a strong woman like you to understand. One punch from your husband and the marriage was over." Rosemary pushed away her dessert fully aware the others were waiting for an answer. "He never physically hurt the children. If he does, divorce papers will be filed immediately. I've endured his violent outbursts because of them."

The Pine Room, as usual, was overheated. Rosemary used her napkin to dab at her forehead. She described in detail how it took three years for her to confront his family with her bruises. No Volker had ever been divorced, and none ever would be. A family meeting in the Poconos without her and the Gordian knot was cut. Millard's verbal abuse became less harsh and he had not physically abused her since that meeting.

"I have my work with the Historical Society, love my

anthropology consulting at the museum, and my horses and the blue ribbons to prove I'm one of the best women riders in New Jersey," she said, then turned to Grace. "There's our growing friendship, Grace, and the children."

"It is with deep love and understanding that I value our friendship," Grace said. "Sure, after a torrid, adulterous love affair of three years that split two religious families, I'm without a man. For how long? I have no idea. In the past year, I dated enough arrogant and presumptive creeps to swear off men. For now, it's my job that consumes me, and maybe later, I'll take a look at politics."

"Hell, we all know about men," Margie said, then turned to Debbie. "Don't you agree? You've been through a lot. Tell us what's next for you."

"First, I'm giving up the apartment a good family friend has let me use and plan to spend some time at our family home in Tuxedo Park. Our jack-of-all-trades handyman, Eli, who goes back to our years in Germany, is very sick. A head injury we all thought was healed has come back. He's the beloved uncle who was always there when I needed him. Right now, he's all I think about."

"So, your husband is history?" Rosemary said, "or is divorce still up in the air?"

"I haven't seen him since August. Abandonment papers have been filed."

The dinner ended shortly after nine o'clock with an emotional cognac toast. They had earned the trust of lifelong friends. They could count on each other for anything.

At ten that evening, Grace and Rosemary were about to settle in for the night at the DeMarco home when the telephone rang. Along with Debbie and Margie, they had spent a champagne-fueled three hours at the Pine Room, bidding "adieu pour toujours" to their crazy scheme. Rosemary, never much of a drinker, was in no shape to drive to her home in Upper Montclair.

"Rosie, will you pick up the phone," Grace said. "I'm popping the cork on a bottle of bubbly. A nightcap's in order. I wonder who's calling at this hour?"

"Yes, she's here. Who's calling?" Rosie paused before offering the phone to Grace, not at all sure she wasn't an intruder, "It's Nick Cisco."

Grace reached for the phone, uncertain what to say to a former lover who only the day before, warned that she and the others were felons. "Yes, Nick?"

"It's taken care of. You can all breathe easier now," Cisco said. "Don't thank me, thank Kevin for the cover-up. He put everything on the line, a twenty-year career, and if it ever gets out, there'll be some jail time for suborning evidence."

Grace was at a loss for words. During her three years with Nick, she recognized the deep bond between the two men and was equally aware of Kevin's disapproval of the affair.

She was still enjoying the champagne glow and having trouble with the complexity of Nick's words. Why did he take this enormous chance? And how could she express her gratitude? As if reading her mind, Nick came to her rescue.

"Here's what I want you to do," he said sternly. "You're going to invite him to your mansion for dinner. Just the two of you and it's going to be a feast, everything but the kitchen sink. He's also a scotch drinker, so Haig & Haig Pinch is a must. He loves jazz piano, Teddy Wilson and Art Tatum. If you don't have them, get them. You can take it from there." The phone line went dead.

It was midnight when the two women tucked in for the night. Twenty-five hundred miles across the Atlantic, the S.S. Gripsholm dropped anchor less than a mile outside Ponta Delgada. It was three in the morning, and the ship's manifest did not include a mercy drop-off to the Azores of two large wooden crates loaded with badly-needed medical supplies.

Johan Paasche learned of the detour during the after-dinner cognac he shared with the Gripsholm's purser, Erik Svensson, at the Waldorf's Starlight Roof with Xavier Cugat's sweet testosterone-laden melodies filling the air. Paasche hated the place, but had gotten to know Svensson well enough after four voyages that the celebrity-spiced nightclub was an easy choice.

"It's a shame your beautiful wife, Deborah, could not make it," Svensson said. "Such a wonderful dancer. Give her my regards."

"She's doing very well, thank you," Paasche replied. It required only a few minutes for him to lay out what he wanted from the purser. During one voyage Svensson noted his rising expenses and static pay level, hinting he was available for what he called "special requests." This evening

Paasche made one such "special request" and pushed an envelope across the table to ensure it was carried out.

For more than ten years Svensson had broken bread at the Captain's table with an endless array of Europe's boring but very wealthy elite. This private contact was worth ten times its weight in gold. There would be no haggling over money; Paasche made it clear he would beat any price.

Even in the dark, moonless night of Ponta Delgada, it was easy to choose the vessel Paasche had bargained for, the sixty-foot luxury trawler Branca. The purser knew it was a matter of speed, not delicacy. Within seconds after dropping anchor, the deck crane had swiveled over the water to lower a cargo net with two large crates onto the deck of a waiting tug boat. A few yards aft of the crane, a heavy rope ladder was thrown over the rail to the deck of the Branca. Two deckhands secured it as Paasche began his descent. Within arms-length, another rope was lowering two large leather suitcases. In less than fifteen minutes, the Gripsholm had hoisted anchor and disappeared into the darkness to complete the nine hundred miles to the port of Lisbon.

The tug boat with its precious cargo secured on deck returned to Ponta Delgada. The owner of the Branca came forward and extended his hand, "Senhor Paasche? Johan Paasche?" His smile was genuine, "I am João Pereira. The Branca is my pet. I am certain its comforts will more than meet your needs." He turned, looked up and nodded to the captain in the pilothouse. Two powerful diesel engines were throttled and the yacht began its journey to Porto harbor, one hundred seventy miles north of Lisbon on the Atlantic coast. Its speed would be almost twice that of the Gripsholm getting it into port a day before. Paasche was the only passenger. Once ashore, he would lay out his future. He had evaded the Genovese Family hitmen, but for how long?

46

By noon, November 5, 1947, mafia Boss Meyer Lansky doubted the day could get any better. He was just assured by Portuguese dictator Antônio Salazar that his secret police chief would be waiting when the S.S. Gripsholm berthed in the Port of Lisbon. Johan Paasche would be arrested when he stepped ashore, held overnight, and then turned over to mafia soldiers. From then on, it was out of his hands. The two men had never met except by phone and had expressed mutual admiration over their handling of the Jews. Before and during the war, Portugal had an open door for Jewish refugees fleeing the Nazis, and Lansky financed several voyages of the Gripsholm, taking Jews out of occupied Nazi territories.

Lansky planned to use this friendship to further the plans he had for Portugal. The country's underworld was a loose collection of gangster mobs with no leadership. He knew that with its long unprotected coastline at the tip of Europe the country was a natural conduit for the growing drug trade.

But first, the matter of Johan Paasche had to be resolved. He had to be hunted down and killed for his eight-year theft of millions, not only from the mafia but also from Cuban dictator Batista and his criminal cohorts. His death would be long and painful. In two days, four of the best and most brutal Sicilian hitmen would be waiting at dockside in Lisbon. A twin-engine Beechcraft would be fueled and ready at the airport.

Anna Genovese was apprised by phone and cable of every move. Her hatred for the Paasches, especially Deborah had long been evident. Was it jealousy? Anna had heard how Deborah's class and beauty had a sexual stranglehold on Richie the Boot Boiardo during that first meeting at his Vittorio's Castle. Despite Anna's heated objections, it was decided that Debbie was no more than window-dressing for her husband and no longer of any concern.

It was shortly after noon when a disturbed Debbie checked the locks of the three suitcases she was taking back with her to Tuxedo Park. She had just received a surprise phone call from her father not at his Wall Street office but from their home. He had sped by car to join his wife Veronica and the domestic staff at the bedside of Eli Green, Debbie's beloved adopted uncle, a family member for almost three decades who had fallen in and out of consciousness for more than twenty-four hours.

The diagnosis of the Nyack clinic doctor was cerebral thrombosis. When Eli's wife Sophie described the head injuries inflicted by Johan, the doctor was certain, even without x-rays, that a massive blood clot had formed.

When Debbie arrived shortly before five, one of New York's top neurosurgeons, a close friend of her father's, had been called and was only two hours away. Debbie joined the group at Eli's bedside, immediately stricken by his labored breath escaping from under the oxygen mask. She made no attempt to stop her tears.

"What the hell have you done, if anything! He can hardly breathe and you're just standing there like empty-headed-statues!"

The nurse recoiled at her words but the doctor stoically waited for her to vent.

"Do something, please! You cannot, I repeat cannot, let this dear man die!"

Her father strode quickly to her from the opposite side of the bed, wrapped his arms around her shoulders and pressed her head to his chest. "Doctor Stacy and his nurse Lucy have been working non-stop for more than an hour to save Eli. Any minute now, an ambulance should be here. A large powered yacht is waiting at Nyack dockside. Another ambulance and operating room will be waiting at the Vassar Brothers Hospital in Poughkeepsie."

"In Poughkeepsie! Damn it, Dad, that's across the river. How long can Eli go on like this?"

"It's only three miles; we'll have him across in minutes. I'll alert Dr. Bauer to go directly to Vassar Brothers Hospital."

Dr. Edwin Bauer had never lost a patient. He arrived at the hospital and after studying the x-rays, saw that Eli's chance for survival was at best five percent. Two holes were drilled in the skull to relieve the pressure, only to find that a massive clot had caused a cerebral hemorrhage that turned Eli's brain into bloody mush.

Eli Greenburg, alias Eli Green, a Jewish refugee, died on the operating table far from his beloved homeland at exactly 8:23 p.m. on November 5, 1947. In death, he was no longer an anonymous, closeted Jew and his wife Sophie made sure of that. Within two hours of his death, and after accepting condolences from the Hammerstein family, Sophie called Rabbi Zimet and arranged for services at the Temple Beth-El and burial at the temple's cemetery east of the city.

The Tuxedo Park landowners and staff were invited to attend his funeral at the cemetery outside Poughkeepsie.

"Temple Beth-El Cemetery?" a surprised Ethel Stanley asked. "That's a big surprise. He's been in and out of our home dozens of times fixing things and I never suspected. My God, Eli was a Jew."

Mrs. Stanley's unspoken but inherent racism was echoed throughout Tuxedo Park. Except for the Hammersteins, their staff, two highway patrolmen who had befriended him, and Captain Tuttle, the State police cop still pursuing Johan, no one else attended.

Two days later, Debbie was trying to put it all together. She was never much for hatred and revenge. Her thoughts were transcendent, reaching back to her childhood in Germany when Eli took her in hand and gently ushered her into adolescence. He became what she never had: an uncle who steered her without judgment. Today she had the mansion to herself. Sophie and Ingrid were due back that afternoon, and her parents were squaring things with Dr. Bauer and the hospital across the river.

She dumped her three suitcases on her bed which, as usual, was waiting for her neatly made by Ingrid. She was unlocking the first one when a memory caught her eye: the reading lamp on the bedside table. It seemed like only yesterday that she sat on the bed and watched Eli replace the lamp's faulty socket. "Now it will be much nicer for you; just pull the chain. No more little switch to search for in the dark."

She reached across the bed and pulled the chain, pulled it again, again and again. She squeezed the end of the chain between the thumb and index finger of her right hand. For her, there could be no better testament for Eli than this thin string of scalloped metal. She rose, shed her jacket and began to wander until she reached her target, the door to the basement garage and Eli's workshop. An irresistible instinct pulled her down the stairs.

She found the light switch and was found her way to the center of the large, cold and dimly lit room. The family's two cars were gone, the Packard with her mom and dad in Poughkeepsie and the LaSalle Touring car was under repair in Warwick. She strode to the west side of the garage, and with an easy pull of the handle Eli had rigged, a brightly lit room came to life. There was the high stool where she had often sat watching him at work with the vast array of tools hanging in their proper places from a pegboard above his workbench. In the far corner an electric drill press, a miter saw with its menacing nine-inch blade, a router and a large table saw occupied forbidden territory. She was never allowed across the border.

Two framed photos, one on each side, bordered the pegboard. On the frame to the right was a small brass plate inscribed "Berlin 1926." A prim and proper ten-year-old Deborah sat in a garden chair with Eli behind her, Sophie and Ingrid to either side. Everyone was in their Sunday best.

The brass inscription on the photo to the left was simply dated 1934. The photo was taken on the driveway in front of the Hammerstein mansion. The centerpiece was a black BMW R62 motorcycle, the cream of the BMW crop for almost a decade. Debbie's cousin, Maria Theresa, was at the controls with both hands on the handlebar with Debbie on the saddle seat behind her, both arms wrapped around Theresa's waist. They were in traditional full black leather, their smiling faces cocked toward the camera. An obviously proud Eli stood behind them in his daily work clothes.

Debbie walked to the terminal mounted between the two garage doors, pushed a button, the doors opened, and the driveway lights went on. She turned her gaze to the far side of the garage, knowing quite well what she would find. The BMW R62 had become Eli's pride and joy and he pampered it endlessly. She could only guess how many times he had buffed the shiny black surface, checked the air in its tires, the fuel in its tank and polished the rearview mirror. It was waiting for her and she was ready.

In less than ten minutes, she returned from her bedroom in black leather and black boots she hadn't worn in years. As always, Eli had left the ignition key ready to be turned. Debbie didn't believe in magic, but from the moment she took the seat, she couldn't shake off the mystical feeling and demanding urge that enveloped her. She had to do this.

She turned the key, felt the powerful surge, waited a few seconds, then revved the gas three times and roared down the driveway to the street that would take her to the old race course. The black stable hands were shaken from their early evening ennui when Debbie roared across the surrounding lawn to the track and with full throttle, did the first of five circuits around a one-mile oval. Then, as quickly as she had startled them, she disappeared into the growing darkness.

Back in the garage, she accepted what she had to do,

walked over to Eli's workbench and reached into what had always been forbidden territory.

"Dad, Mom, I'm a mess," she said over breakfast with her parents the next morning. Her father drained his coffee cup and placed it on the table. Her mother finished her orange juice and dabbed her lips with a napkin. Neither said a word. This was not like Debbie, always buoyant and cocksure of herself.

"I haven't slept a wink since Eli was buried. Eli is everywhere. So much of what we have is only because his hands and tools made it right," Debbie said. She pushed away her breakfast plate, looked across the table, found what she expected and said, "I have to get away. I'm taking the BMW. I've already attached the tool box just as Eli always wanted it, to the rear wheel bracket. The two large saddlebags will hold everything I need and I have plenty of money."

"You're taking the motorcycle? Why?" Her mother's incredulity shaped her response, "A bike to get away from us, and I mean all of us, Sophie and Ingrid?"

"It's a token of my love for Eli and I know he would have wanted it. His niece and his pet together. Relax, mom. My first stop will start the trip just right, the Immaculate Conception Seminary just up the road in Mahwah."

"Why?"

"Way back in '34, during cousin Theresa's visit, we stopped at the seminary and she introduced me to Father Majeski, a wonderful man known to everyone as Father Ski. We spent more than an hour together and when he found out that we were almost next-door neighbors, he jokingly made me promise to come back and see him again. It took a long time, but I'll finally be keeping my promise."

"Again, why?"

"Just a great way to start my journey of discovery," she said. "Looking back, he was so open and friendly with us. I had a teenage crush. I checked, he's still there and I have an important question for him."

"And we can't answer it?" her father asked, his features stern and probing.

"It's not something I would ask you or mom."

Until his question, her father had listened in silence but was fully aware of what was happening. Debbie was devoted to routine; she never came to the breakfast table without washing her face, brushing her teeth and applying her makeup. This morning, there was no makeup and he noticed during their conversation she ran her right index finger over a barely discernible thin white line that marred the otherwise flawless complexion of her cheek.

João Periera recognized a hunted man when he saw one. Johan Paasche might exude the persona of a privileged man without a care, but João knew better. During the war, he had encountered many formerly wealthy Jews fleeing the Nazis who hid their fear behind the friendships they had to develop if they were to remain free. Did Johan fit the mold?

After the Branca was secured in its berth at Porto Harbor, Periera startled Paasche when he asked, "Are you looking for a secret place to stay?"

"Where the hell did that come from!" Paasche blurted as he spun from the gangway to the dock. Then turned to the yacht owner and as he had done his entire adult life, changed the atmosphere with a smile and smooth reply. "You're a very smart fellow."

Johan's smile brightened as he edged to a comfortable distance from Periera and said, "What do you have in mind?"

"Do you know Coimbra?"

"I do. A few years ago, my wife, Deborah, and I passed through Coimbra on our tour of Portugal. It was the day university students with their black berets and capes serenaded in front of the chapel seemingly endless Fado melodies. We were entranced."

"Then it's settled. Coimbra it is. I have a secret little place on the banks of the Mondego. Get yourself a room; I'll make arrangements and let you know when all is ready." They shook hands and headed down the gangway.

Periera waited until the two suitcases were in the trunk of a waiting taxi and bent over as Paasche took the rear seat and was about to close the door. "I don't know who is after you but I can assure you they are not alone."

"Is that a fact or an assumption?" Paasche held the door open and studied Periera. Neither man was smiling.

"The Gripsholm is scheduled to dock in Lisbon tomorrow morning. You are expected to be aboard. Every foreign visitor, regardless of passport, who enters Portugal is watched by Salazar's Secret Police. Your dossier will describe a rich investment banker who is nowhere to be found. Salazar will be informed and a search will begin."

Periera, despite his contacts, had heard nothing about the assurance Salazar had made Lansky.

"You're saying the Secret Police will be tracing my every move. I can't understand that out of nowhere, you've become my guardian angel," Paasche said, "Are you somehow untouchable?"

"Let's put it this way: one uncle graduated with Salazar from Coimbra University and have been close friends and political powerbrokers ever since. Another uncle was briefly engaged to Salazar's oldest sister. Today, I have three cousins who are Salazar insiders."

"That's great but it still doesn't tell me why you're involved, hell I'm a complete stranger, or am I?" Paasche asked.

Periera hesitated as he was about to close the door and said, "Perhaps because I hate what is happening in Lisbon, or maybe it is just because I am bored. In any case, you will have two weeks at my Mondego River hideout to decide how to escape."

At noon the next day, Lieutenant Lucas Silva led a contingent of armed PIDE secret police agents to ring the Lisbon harbor berth where the S.S. Gripsholm was off-loading. After a thorough search, Johan Paasche was nowhere to be found.

"Your manifest has Senhor Johan Paasche listed as occupant of First Class Suite 3," Silva confronted Purser Erik Svensson, "where is he?"

"At his request, we dropped him off at Ponte Delgado. He said his plans had changed and Lisbon was no longer part of them."

"Your manifest does not include a stop in the Azores. Are you telling me you detoured just to drop off Paasche?"

"That's a ridiculous suggestion, of course not," an irked Svensson replied. "We never made port in the Azores, just dropped anchor long enough to unload badly needed medical supplies along with Paasche. He boarded a yacht he had arranged for."

"And the yacht's name?"

"It was a cloudy night with zero visibility I never saw the yacht's name."

Silva realized this was as much as he would get from Svensson, as smooth a liar as any he had encountered. He could only imagine how big the purser's payoff was.

Watching the commotion in and around the Gripsholm were two tall, well-dressed hitmen for hire admired throughout Europe's criminal cliques. Few knew their identity. Their contracts were completed by phone or cable and finalized with increasingly large deposits into a Swiss bank account. Fluent in several languages and dialects, they mixed well when tracking down their target. While Paasche was still on the loose there would be no bank deposit.

"I have a bad feeling about this job," the taller of the two said as they returned to their Daimler for a short ride to the Hotel Império to await further instructions.

Paasche wasted little time to look for a well-conditioned, fast car in Porto and on Periera's recommendation, he decided to test the burgeoning black market. He quickly found a black Ford, four-door Super Deluxe sedan, beautifully kept by the former chargé d'affaires at the American Embassy in Lisbon. The price was outrageous but he wanted out of Porto now.

47

That November the police shooting and killing of Benjamin Shapiro, a wounded and decorated ex-Marine, added another layer of public anger over the handling of the Maureen Whitaker Sherry case.

Unlike earlier outbursts of public disapproval that led to plenty of bitching but no action this one was different. Sincere Sister Sara had been chosen by Father Divine to put forth his message. Simply stated a wronged woman no matter how harshly treated should not seek redress but offer forgiveness. A coalition of Catholic women from parishes throughout the city marched on City Hall were met at the entrance by the Mayor's Praetorian Guard: McClosky, Gazzi and Valentine while Mayor Simpson watched from above.

McClosky accepted their one-page, typewritten proclamation. It stated the lack of concern by City Officials and police about the endemic marital abuse in the inner city. Cases were noted, then filed away and forgotten.

Abusive behavior within the marginalized must be endured while the rich and connected lived in a different world. The final paragraph made everything clear.

It denounced how Kathleen McGuire was serving a five-to-seven-year prison sentence for stabbing and wounding a husband who had been beating her and her three children for years, while Sherry enjoyed lavish meals with her court-appointed psychiatrist after shooting and killing her husband.

The public outcry over the McGuire and Sherry cases was the last straw for Jonathan Eagleton, the senior partner of Eagleton, Jefferson & Clink Law Firm and Treasurer of the Essex County Republican Party. He and other GOP powerbrokers had begun burning phone lines within hours after Catholic women, at the urging of their pastors, marched on City Hall. The growing anger of this important voting block could change the outcome of the upcoming election that he and other deep-pocket stalwarts figured was in the bag. Paul Simpson's rise from Mayor to State Senator had been well-greased and made him a near certainty in the upcoming election. Barring any cosmic screw-ups his future residence would be the Governor's mansion.

"What the hell was that simpleton D.A. thinking? We don't have a problem on our hands but a major fuck-up," City Commissioner Stuart Bowlen shouted during a conference call that District Attorney Silo Crandon get his ass in gear. "Shares a squab dinner with Sherry. Okay, she's our class but Jesus Christ, allowing daily delivery of delicacies ninety percent of voters can't afford, then letting a famous shrink move in telling the world that pumping three bullets into her husband was the result of dreams she couldn't control. We're a laughingstock."

"I'll take care of it," Eagleton said.

At ten o'clock the next morning, D.A. Crandon had just taken a seat at his office desk and was reaching for his first cup of coffee when a call was put through by his secretary.

"Crandon, this is Eagleton. Listen closely. We've decided how you'll handle the Sherry case. We don't want you to fuck it up any more than you have already. That pampered bitch goes before the grand jury. Put the call out today."

"And the charge?" Said Crandon.

"Involuntary manslaughter. You'll make it work. Six of the jurors, including the foreman belong to us, you'll know how to play them. And unless you trip over your ass again, we'll make sure Maureen Whitaker Sherry's name will be no more than a footnote during your run for mayor. Any questions?"

"No questions," the District Attorney replied. Aware more than ever of his subservience.

Two hours later, A.D.A. Ellen Pafko, a close confidante was hit with the news when she entered his office with a handful of briefs.

"Involuntary manslaughter! My God, she pumped three bullets into her old man."

"Simple enough. She shot him when he reached for a heavy vase to bash her with. I'll get my guy on forensics to back it up. Let's set the jury for nine o'clock Monday morning, the seventeenth. Short notice, I know, only eleven days to prepare. This will be a short one, no more than a day, maybe even just the morning," Crandon said.

He knew this grand jury well. He'd called it up six times during their tenure and found it to be a pliable bunch. Now that he was assured by Eagleton that six were in the bag their only uncertainty would be when they would be handed their envelopes.

In less than four hours, they learned she was a wounded sister, fearful of yet another beating, who had shot and killed her husband just before he bashed her head in with a heavy vase. They agreed with the men that she couldn't just walk and that some slammer time was necessary. They compromised. Involuntary Manslaughter was justified. They compromised that at least a true bill of involuntary manslaughter was necessary.

Orchestrated leaks of the grand jury's closed-door banter were on the street a few hours after Crandon thanked and excused them.

News that the en chambre trial before Judge Rodney Hampton drew attention as expected and street protests paled in comparison to hand-to-hand combat for the dwindling supply of Thanksgiving turkeys in the city's markets. Diving to grab hold of a dead turkey's neck pulled many housewives into battle.

Ten days earlier, Meyer Lansky was enjoying a light breakfast in his luxury suite at Hotel Nacional in Havana when he received the bad news from Lisbon. He was livid. Never profane and always composed when hearing bad or threatening news, he came close to losing control when he was told that Johan Paasche was on the loose.

He listened and said, "Salazar himself assured me that Paasche would be taken into custody. He is a friend and a man of his word. Obviously, Paasche was not aboard when the Gripsholm made port. Talk to me."

The two assassins explained that Paasche's preparations were fastidious. Paasche found out about the uncharted stop at Ponto Delgado and seized it as his chance to disappear. A yacht was waiting to take him aboard when the Gripsholm dropped anchor. He learned that this was an uncharted stop of a half-hour at most and a chance for him to disappear. A yacht was waiting to take him aboard when the Gripsholm dropped anchor.

"We greased several hands to get the name and ownership of the yacht and where it was headed but got nothing," the short man said. "Our guess is that the ship's purser set things up and he vanished right after clearing customs."

"You have a contract. Find him and kill him. I'll want photos," Lansky said. "Until then, there will be no deposits." The phone call was brought to an end.

By this time, Paasche had reached his destination, a beautifully furnished home on the Mondego River just outside Coimbra. The Ford surpassed his expectations covering the seventy-six miles over a good road in forty minutes. He wasted little time in sorting things out and he was soon on the phone planning his escape from Portugal. In four days he had covered five hundred thirty-three miles across Spain and the northern end of the Pyrenees to Saint-Jean-Pied-de-Port in France.

At the Hôtel de Pyrénées an obliging concierge gladly accepted five hundred dollars to complete a very simple task. Paasche would call him within a week to learn if he was being followed.

After a harrowing seventy-six-mile drive along the French crest of the Pyrenees, he reached Pau, checked into the Hotel Bristol and made his telephone call. "Will you please tell your concierge that he has a phone call from Monsieur Paasche? He's expecting it."

"Ah, bonjour Monsieur Paasche, I was awaiting your call. And yes, there has been an inquiry about you, a very interesting one. Two well-dressed men, very much urban types asked for you. They said because of an unforeseen problem they had failed to meet you in Porto as had been arranged. This is what I found interesting, they both spoke perfect Basque, but obviously were not from Catalonia. I told them you checked out two days earlier but had no idea for where. They stayed one night. Is this what you wanted to know Monsieur Paasche?"

"Exactly, Merci beaucoup."

Paasche had carefully mapped out the obscure roads he would take to his sanctum, the family hunting lodge overlooking the Rhine in the Outre Forêt. An agent immobilier in the nearby hamlet of Hunspach was outfitting the lodge for his arrival. Electricity, telephone, water, cleaning, provisions including liquor and wine enough for a month, and notice to the postmaster that Madam Ellen

Witting, his mother's maiden name, would arrive at the lodge within a week. The lease to the lodge was her wedding present, but she never removed her name from it.

Two days after Paasche checked out, the doorman and concierge at Hotel Bristol compared notes that they had never seen the two men approaching the lobby entrance before. A bellman had taken their luggage from the trunk of their silver Daimler and led them inside. They were well-dressed with obviously tailored made pinstripe suits, the taller in black, his companion in brown. Their silk-lined overcoats were draped over their shoulders. As they neared the front desk, Bruno Passieu judged them to be big city dandies possibly even lovers.

"A room, your very best," the shorter man said in perfect French. "A chilled bottle of Bollinger sent to the room immediately and an early dinner reservation."

"Oh dear, you exasperate me. Once again, you fail to say we always sit by a window with a view."

"It will be taken care of," Passieu assured them with a wide smile certain the scent of subtle men's cologne wafting his way promised a big franc bundle.

In their suite, with jackets off and loosened ties, the two men shared a smile as they watched the server pop the champagne cork and pour the bubbly into two flutes. After the obligatory first sip the shorter man said, "Very nice, very nice indeed. Now tell me young man, what is your name?"

"Michel."

"Michel, I know you wouldn't mind answering a few

questions," the taller man said. "You see we arrived here a day or two late. We were to rendezvous with an old friend we had not seen in years. We simply got our dates wrong. His name is Johan Paasche. Here is a picture. Very handsome, very handsome indeed you would agree."

"Oh yes, he was here. Checked out two days ago, a very nice man, very generous. I checked him in and out."

"Did he say where he was going?" the short man asked.

"No. He only wanted me to make sure he had a full tank of petrol. He had no visitors. Stayed in his room and I was told he tied up one of our two long-distance lines for hours each day."

"Thank you, Michel. Here, this is for you," he said as he handed over two twenty franc notes. "By the way, what was he driving?"

"A very nice black Ford sedan."

"Did you notice the license plate number?"

"Only that it was Portuguese."

"I believe we pulled it off beautifully," the taller man said in preferred English when they were alone. "They'll always remember us as two light-footed pansies who swished through and were gone the next day."

The two assassins changed personas to meet the needs of each contract. The day before their Paasche agreement, they had rigged the murder of a communist labor leader in Antwerp to appear as an accidental drowning. For two weeks they wore rough, well-worn worker's clothes, went unshaven, and spoke only Flemish slang at dockside bistros and bars while setting up their victim.

Who would ever mistake two harmless queers on a lovers' tour of France for killers hunting down their prey? But where the hell was Paasche? They had a reputation to uphold.

"This fellow Paasche is good, very good," the short man said. "We accepted a job from American gangsters because it was short and really sweet, one hundred thousand U.S. dollars. So here we are in beautiful downtown Pau more than five hundred miles from our wives and families in Milan. We don't know where the son of a bitch is and France is too big for two killers playing blind-man's-bluff. So...."

"I think we're both leaning the same way," the tall man said, waiting for his partner to gulp the last of his bubbly. "The Paris mob, that smelly bunch came through once, so why not now?"

"Everything has changed. Gang des Tractions Avant still drives their trademark Citroën. Once sited, can a violent crime be far behind? Our contact with the Gang was gunned down during a robbery," the short man said. "So, we'll be dealing with Émile Buisson the new Caïd."

"We know Buisson. He's been on the loose since his escape from the Loos-Les Lille prison. Problem is he was under lock and key in the prison's ward for the criminally insane. Thirty murders, a hundred robberies and nobody's chasing him."

"I say we give it a try," the short man said. "Let's put the word out in the Pigalle that we want to meet him."

"The Gang des Tractions Avant knows who we are, that we payoff as promised. I'll put the word out that we want the meeting with Buisson the sooner the better. Let him pick the spot. We prefer an obscure Pigalle bistro with good food and privacy," the tall man said.

"Don't hold your breath."

48

As much as Lansky hated the glib Paasche and wanted his head on a platter, he admired the thief who made dreamlike amounts for the Five Families while skimming millions. His choice of Dresdner Bank to spread it around was clearly an insider's move.

With the Lombard Odier Bank now in step with the Dresdner Bank, there was no further need for the Lombard Odier Bank in Geneva to disperse funds. Swiss bank accounts were secret, but for how long? Anna Genovese knew there must be no hint that Cosa Nostra money had sifted across the border into Germany. The Internal Revenue Service had for years pressured the Swiss to open them for scrutiny. With everything going so smoothly, the IRS on their ass was the last thing they wanted. Ludwig Stein must go.

"I'm no killer, and I'm not about to become one," an astonished Jürgen Müller blurted in response to Anna's thinly veiled order. He had been well paid for exposing the intricate scheme Paasche had put together, but that was as far as he would go.

"God damn it another German pussy!" Anna said. There was silence on Müller's end. She took a deep drag on her cigarette, exhaled through her nostrils and in a softened voice said, "Okay, so you're no trigger man. There'll be a couple of guys looking you up, give them the info they need and you're out of it."

"How much?"

"You'll still be walking around when they leave. Ain't that enough?"

Two weeks later, Swiss papers and radio stations reported the murders of Ludwig Stein, Accounts Manager at the downtown Geneva branch of Credit Suisse Bank, and thirty-three-year-old Freda Schafer in the front seat of his Jaguar sedan. They were shot twice in the back of the head. An autopsy confirmed the forensics team's findings that they were killed by different guns, most probably twenty-two caliber American-made Colt pistols.

"As expected, neat and clean," Vito Genovese responded from his table on the colonnade of Havana's Hotel Saratoga. Warming up for a rare appearance at the hotel was the all-female band Anacaonas, his favorite. His wife had patched him in from her queer bar in Manhattan that their Swiss worries were over. "And you're sure about Müller that he knows what happens if he opens his trap?"

"Calmati, mio caro. Müller è un codardo intelligente," she assured him, "and clever cowards stay alive by not fucking with the rules."

"I have your word, that's enough. Now I have another job for Stefano Rizzano."

"Your golden boy? What more can you do for him?"

"And that's why we want him over here. Half of all Cuban workers are members of a communist union. We want the Reds out and Batista in complete control. Havana's our cash cow and getting fatter every day. For the first time Commie union members are everywhere shouting 'social justice, honest government, and political freedom.'"

"Where does Rizzano figure in?" Anna said.

"He's young, handsome, handles Spanish pretty well, has no police record and has a nice touch for union takeovers. We want a piece of everything in the four districts inside the Malecón, hotels, whorehouses, nightclubs, strip joints and casinos. All are unionized."

"Vito, Vito, mio caro, remember me? I've never been there. What the hell is a Malecón?"

"It's a five-mile wall that runs along the waterfront. Now, with Batista getting fifteen percent of the action, it's in our hands. Get hold of Rizzano at his office. Tell him Lucky's Family, meaning us and at least eight others, have bought into what the little Jew calls an endless gift-wrapped bonanza. That's only if Batista stays in power."

"So, what do I say?"

"He's been promoted. Book a first-class seat for him on the next plane to Havana. We'll expect him here before the holidays. La Navidad sucks in thousands of well-heeled tourists to Havana, where vice control is a laugh, we'll make

362

millions."

"Who takes Rizzano's place? He'll want to know," Anna said. "He's giving up his seat on the gravy train and won't want some dumb-ass soldier to take his place."

"He's already picked. Did one hell of a job in Michigan. Jimmy Hoffa. He'll be in Rizzano's office by the end of the week to get the lay of the land."

After a full day going over the books, Rizzano and Hoffa spent two days touring the Locals. Hoffa's intensity, how he never lost eye contact and demanded no-bullshit answers, made it clear a new boss was in town.

Even more time was needed to convince Danielo and Alicia Rizzano that they were not losing a son but would now have a son sharing a table in Havana with the most powerful mafia Dons. "You know you will always be right here," Stefano placed his hand over his heart and as the tears flowed added, "You'll hear from me every week. That's a promise."

The next day Rizzano boarded a National Airlines DC-4 at La Guardia for a five-hour flight to Miami. During a stopover at Amelia Earhart Field, he was greeted by Santo Trafficante Jr. who had just visited his family in Tampa and was returning to Havana.

"Ciao, Stefano, benvenuto nella nostra miniera d'oro cubana" Junior purred with a tight hug and kisses. "I sindacati dell'Avana hanno bisogno di un uomo buono come te."

"I hope Lucky, Vito and your father are right that I'm

the man to clean up the commie labor unions," Stefano replied in English.

"Pops sent me out last year to see if I'd be useful. Tampa is already ours and we're always on the lookout," Junior said, "and with just a little muscle, let's call it persuasion, here I am operating Sans Souci Cabaret and the Casino International, oro, oro puro!"

"We don't want any reds chipping away our streets of gold," Stefano chuckled.

"Bravo! A tough guy with a sense of humor," Junior said in English and couldn't resist giving another hug and kiss on both cheeks.

Also boarding was Carlos Marcello, the mafia boss in New Orleans. His greeting to Stefano was a perfunctory handshake. He squinted behind sunglasses at the tall young man who was an army cop in Arizona at the time his former boss, Sam Carollo, had sent his top underboss, Lorenzo Muretti, to see if the Joe Bonanno state was ripe for a takeover. Muretti was never heard from again and his body was never found. Marcello and his small entourage waited for the other gangsters to board. He never took his eyes off Stefano.

Stefano's first week in Havana was an eye-opener. At the airport, he was provided with a showroom-perfect green Chevy Fleetmaster convertible along with a Luciano soldier to be his tour guide and Lucky's canary. While driving through the Vedado a few blocks from the University of Havana, they rolled past a scene he never expected to see on Havana's streets of gold. About a dozen students had been caught in President Ramōn Grau's secret police round-up after a massive anti-government demonstration. They were ringed by soldiers with their American-issued garands at the ready. Eisenhower often declared that the rifle in the hands of GIs had won the war. Stefano squinted in the bright glare that bounced from the fixed bayonets now used to suppress demands for freedom.

"What happens to them?" he asked the Luciano snooper sitting beside him. He was answered with a silent shrug and facial expression that clearly implied who knows and who cares. He realized for the first time it wasn't just the commies to be eradicated. These kids with their bruised faces and blood-stained shirts were from the country's elite.

Two days later, during dinner with upper echelon secret police officials he heard for the first time the name Fidel Castro. Castro had escaped capture during the attempted overthrow of Dominican Republic Dictator Raphael Trujillo by a poorly-organized and well-publicized invasion force of twelve hundred Cubans and Dominicans. Castro was back in Havana working with the anti-Batista Socialist Revolutionary Movement.

"He's a rich, pampered son of a bitch but dangerous," Secret Police Captain Alfonso Sanchez said to Stefano in a low hard voice. "Only twenty-one but people listen when he hands out that fucking bullshit of his. He's got the ears of the intellectual students right now and with the commie bastards gone, the unions come next."

"He won't get far with the unions while I'm here," Stefano boasted. He was surprised by the Captain's hatred-laden profanity. The two men were joined by four middle-echelon officers, the guys who did the dirty work, at a sumptuous dinner at the Sans Souci.

Drinks were served by very young, inviting ladies who centered their attention on Stefano. The prettiest took him by surprise when she reached over his shoulder and almost cheek-to-cheek, made sure he could see deep into her cleavage. There was no mistaking her smile.

"Get used to it, Señor Rizzano, you've seen only two scoops of the pudding," There was laughter all around and even the Captain cracked a smile between pulls on his Corona.

It started as a tiny image at the bottom of Stefano's half-full martini glass and widened as it rose coming into full view on the surface; crazily painted spinning carousel with cackling women offering cigarettes, chocolates, dry milk, and C-rations. From their purchase of wooden horses, zebras and cows, they admonished him for looking down at the girl's bosom.

It had been more than a month since his last recurring nightmare. Lillian, the tall, beautiful and sexually athletic prostitute from Philly, arrived unbidden in his mind to bring back the cold sweats, pounding temples and aching stomach. They were still pounding it out when he jumped out of bed to relive the horrible curse that was haunting him. A naked Lillian followed him to the window and put her arms around his neck. "Hey, you're great. I could probably fall for you if you hadn't scared the hell out of me tonight. Buster, you really need help."

He had to leave the restaurant before he lashed out in response with his fists. There were no pillows or walls to punch and the cadre at the table was off-limits.

The ribald banter came to an abrupt end when Stefano arose and apologized, "Lo siento mis amigos," he said. "It's my stomach. Nothing serious, but it's better that I return to my room. Many thanks for allowing me to get to know you."

Outside, he waited until a valet delivered his Chevy convertible and his shadow emerged from the lobby to join him in the passenger seat.

Sitting at a nearby table, New Orleans mafia boss Carlos Marcello watched Stefano rise, give his apologies with a bow all around, turn and walk from the dining room. He immediately motioned over his right shoulder with a click of his fingers and two swarthy, tall and bulky men from a nearby table discretely followed Stefano. They would join a third member of their assassination team who was waiting in Stefano's Hotel Saratoga suite with his favorite toy, a made-to-order garrote with two wooden handles attached to a workable length of piano wire. The handles were decorated with thirteen notches. A promise Marcello had made to his former boss, Silver Dollar Sam Carollo before he was deported to Mexico, was about to be kept. A heartbroken woman in New Orleans would be revived.

Marcello turned his attention to the cabaret entrance and was pleased to see his two soldiers had waited until Stefano had pulled away before jumping into their car to follow him at a safe distance.

Stefano drove silently to the hotel. There was nothing

wrong with his stomach, it was his pounding brain that forced him from the table. At the hotel, he turned his car over to a waiting valet and motioned disdainfully for his creepy canary to get lost.

"Buonanotte, signore" the Luciano snitch said as he walked to his Dodge roadster. "Domani mattina alle sei."

The two assassins remained in their car and watched from a safe distance as a stumbling Stefano grabbed a wrought iron entrance railing for support before going into the lobby.

"This should be easy," one of them said. "Remember what the boss said, no blood. Everything clean as a baby's ass. If I know Al, he can't wait to carve another notch."

They pulled their car to the rear of the hotel and parked in a space between a large dumpster and a row of fifty-five-gallon overflowing trash cans. The car was screened from sight of the loading dock and rear service entrance.

They emerged from the car and walked back to the trunk, removed a large, tightly-wrapped bundle of tarp, a hundred-foot spool of hemp rope, two heavy-duty butcher shears, three forty-ounce hand-forged battle-tested meat cleavers and headed to the service entrance.

Two hours later, Cecilia Muretti awoke to the demanding ring of the bedside telephone in her mansion on St. Charles Avenue in New Orleans' opulent Garden District. She had remained close to her roots as a third-generation Sicilian wife who basked for twenty years in the growing power of her husband as he gained caporegime rank in the Carollo Family. The clock showed 11 p.m.

"Can't you see the hour? Who is this?" she demanded.

"Cecilia Muretti?"

"Who else would it be."

"It's done."

The two words stunned her. Could this possibly be the message she had hoped and prayed for since the day her husband disappeared more than four years earlier? She knew the rules and asking for even the smallest detail was forbidden, but she had waited so long and decided to take a chance. "Was it long and painful?"

"It's done," the husky voice repeated and the line went dead.

Cecilia knew this would be the only message she would receive that her husband's death had been avenged.

She immediately dropped to her knees and painfully made her way to a corner table she had transformed into a shrine to St. Cecilia, her martyred patron saint. "God bless you. I never lost faith that you heard my prayers for justice."

She reached across the table and removed a beautifully framed oil on canvas copy of Raphael's The Ecstasy of St. Cecilia. Her kisses moistened the canvas as she vowed that in return for her long-awaited revenge every mass, novena and Way of the Cross would be dedicated to the heavenly spirit that made it possible.

49

At six the next morning, Luciano's stooge lowered himself into an overstuffed leather chair in the lobby not far from the elevators and waited for Stefano to emerge. Fifteen minutes later he was still waiting. Another fifteen minutes and still no Stefano. He motioned for a telephone and put in a call to Room 316. Ten rings and still no Stefano. He voiced his concern to the manager. When they got no response to the manager's heavy knocking on the door, he used his passkey to enter. Following hotel protocol, he motioned the mafia soldier to wait at the door while he walked inside.

"Signore Rizzano, are you here?" his voice modulated to be heard throughout the suite. No answer. "Signore Rizzano, are you here? This is the manager, can I be of help?" His voice was no longer professionally tempered but edgy with growing concern by the silence and the pristine condition of the suite.

The complimentary bowl of fruit centered the coffee

table, and the two vases of fresh flowers were exactly where they were placed the afternoon before. Pillows on the matching sofa and two wingback chairs were fluffed, everything was spotless as if the maids had just passed through. Toiletries in the bathroom and clothes and shoes in the bedroom walk-in closet were the only evidence that Stefano had been there. The massive bed had not been touched.

After getting an okay from the manager, the wise guy made a complete appraisal of the bedroom and realized his job had ended. He left the manager to deal with the police and returned to the lobby. The call to the Hotel Nacional elicited no surprise from the Luciano underboss who answered. Word would be passed on, everyone knew that debts must be paid.

On November 14, it was almost two weeks since Danielo and Alicia Rizzano and their daughter Theresa had heard from Stefano. They suspected the worst. He promised to call every week and during his final meal at home, pulled from under his shirt a small sacred cloth scapular that vowed endless devotion to the Blessed Virgin Mary and Our Lady of Mount Carmel. His parents and sister made the sign of the cross while Stefano sealed his promise with a kiss to each image on the scapular.

Only death could erase this sacred pledge. Late in the afternoon, Danielo steered his immaculate 1941 Nash Coupe to the curb in front of the Sicilian Club on Tenth. His teenage son, with his encouragement, began his mob career in this very room hidden from outsiders by a six-foot shield of green paint on the window. It was his first return in six years. Nothing had changed.

"Gesù Cristo, guarda chi è, Danielo Rizzano!" came a shout from a four-handed gin rummy table.

The click of domino tiles ended abruptly at another table when a bent, silver-haired gumba exhorted, "Benvenuto! Welcome, Danielo! You look great! And Stefano?"

"Stefano è il motivo per cui sono qui." Danielo was not there to reminisce with old Sicilianos. He came to discuss his fears for Stefano with Luigi Bonini the club president.

He needn't have bothered. He laid everything out in full detail for Bonini and in return received a few grunts and an occasional raised eyebrow. He left after gulping an obligatory glass of grappa, his throat burning as much as his temples.

Danielo was stonewalled wherever he went that weekend. He accepted that he was no more than an outsider now posing irrational questions that even a made man would hesitate to ask his Don.

His final stop was Fulton Fish Market, where Stefano earned his reputation as the fearless Fish Hook. Certainly, if anyone had followed his son's career, it would be Caporegime Joseph Lanza, whose bloody control of the fish market went back twenty years. Seated at Lanza's favorite table at Carmine's Restaurant, he was once again met with empty cordiality that included the elaborate seven-fish dinner traditionally served during the holidays. Wine and grappa flowed freely and Lanza's current girlfriend served the antipasto. After hearing Danielo's story, Lanza, like the others, pleaded ignorance.

Late at night and deep in his cups, Danielo finally realized that he was a pariah. From that weekend on it was understood that any mention to him of Stefano would be met with painful consequences.

It was after midnight when Danielo walked slowly across Fulton Street and got into his highly-polished Nash, replete with whitewall tires and sparkling chrome. Together they formed a perfect ironic metaphor, he never questioned where Stefano with no visible means of income collected the cabbage needed. Did he care? Of course not. Stefano was doing just fine rising to middle rank among Richie the Boot Boiardo's soldiers. The shadowy origins of his son's growing stash were of little concern to him and Alicia. Theresa's questions were largely ignored when the family moved from their cramped flat on Mount Prospect into a ten-room Victorian on Lake Street. God damn it, if life wasn't great, he often marveled as he basked in his new surroundings only to be shushed by Alicia.

As he drove through the Lincoln Tunnel that emptied into Weehawken, then across Bergen County on his way home, Danielo was tortured by self-accusatory thoughts.

The first-floor lights were still on when he pulled into the driveway. He turned off the ignition and was about to open the driver's door when a thought stopped him. Any mention of his son during the past three days was met with the Sicilian codice del silenzio. He knew now that his family would never see Stefano again.

For years he expressed the growing pride he felt when Stefano reached the exalted status of mafia made-man. His rise to white-collar union organizer added icing to the cake. His first-class flight to Havana, where he would rub shoulders with Lucky Luciano, Meyer Lansky and Fulgencio Batista, my God, could it get any better? His elation obscured the Cosa Nostra pledge that the killer of a caporegime would never have an open casket funeral with a face so destroyed as to be unrecognizable.

He was about to open the front door to the Victorian splendor that awaited inside when he acknowledged for the first time that without his and Alicia's tacit approval, Stefano's rise from street corner numbers runner to soldier, the meeting with Vito Genovese and golden boy status would not have been possible. Unquestioned acceptance of the lifestyle Stefano provided had made him a coward.

For the rest of his life he would suffer with the thought that it wasn't mafia-wise guys who killed his son, that by not nipping a bloody career in the bud, he was the murderer. God help him.

In Newark things were humming on several connected fronts during November. Grace DeMarco had listened intensely when Nick Cisco advised her that she owed a big thank you to Kevin McClosky for jeopardizing his career and facing possible slammer time for getting her and her cohorts off the hook. She nailed him in her office with a kiss on the cheek and an offer he couldn't refuse, a home-cooked classic Italian dinner at her mansion, a building he had never entered during her three-year affair with Nick. He readily accepted as much out of curiosity than for the promise of a great meal.

"Then it's Friday at five," she said. "A strong aperitif in front of a burning fireplace appeal to you? I seem to remember hearing that your drink is Scotch, but only the best."

It was easy for Kevin to wonder what the hell was going on here. He barely knew this woman.

"For dinner, we'll have Barolo Red and a chilled pinot grigio, Conte Fini. The meal is simple enough, Veal piccata, and for the pasta, cacio e pepe, dessert is tiramisu."

Exactly at five o'clock, Grace took Kevin's overcoat and hung it in the front closet then ushered him to the cocktail cart between a roaring fireplace and the large window overlooking Wilden Place. Using ice tongs, she dropped three cubes in crystal tumblers and added a three-inch pour of Haig & Haig Pinch. They tipped glasses and after the first sip she said, "That street corner across the way where you always waited, it's the closest you've ever been. I hated when it was two or three in the morning."

"Just doing my job, dear lady," he said with an Irish brogue that perfectly fit his blue eyes, manly features and an unruly mop of auburn hair. He took a healthy sip and added, "Just another police minion making sure that mansion dwellers remain safe and secure."

She saw how his wide smile could easily camouflage the probing questions that challenged suspected criminals.

"The meal's warming in the oven, want to look around, only take a few minutes?"

She added a finger of scotch to each of their glasses and to his surprise, reached for his hand and led him to the west wall of the parlor. "It's a Georges de La Tour, the Penitent Magdalene."

"Quite a piece. Rarely hear much of de La Tour these days," Kevin said. She studied him openly surprised. He took a step closer to the picture and added, "It's a shame, I love Baroque art and music."

She led him to the hall and switched on a light mounted above a large, beautifully framed oil painting. "I'm sure Velázquez would approve," she said.

"Las Meninas. Christ, once you see it you never forget it."

"You know art, I'm impressed."

"Art appreciation 101 and 102. Night school at Rutgers several years back."

"Same thing here, difference that it was mandatory at Douglas. I'm sure you got a lot more out of it than I did." They appreciated the effort each was making to omit Nick from the conversation.

She left him seated in one of the two overstuffed fireplace chairs. "I won't be long in the kitchen. When everything is ready, I'll give you a whistle."

Grace walked to the kitchen door, turned and struck a seductive Lauren Bacall pose straight out of the movie To Have and Have Not, "I do know how to whistle, I'll just pucker my lips and blow."

Kevin's laughter was hard and deep enough that he

almost swallowed an ice cube.

Seven minutes later, there was a soft tweet-tweet from the kitchen. A few seconds later another tweet-tweet and finally a loud repeat that sounded more like a crow's cackle wafting above a barnyard corn crib.

They seated themselves at the dining room table, the veal piccata in a heated chafing dish and the linguine cacio e pepe steaming in a silver bowl complete with **matching** serving tongs and spoon. Without asking, Kevin arose and draped his large damash napkin over his left forearm and with his right hand carried the Barolo Red to Grace. He poured enough for her to taste. She nodded appreciatively. With a broad smile and courtly bow he became a French sommelier, "Madam, ou est-ce Mademoiselle? Avec votre permission, puis-je?"

She reached forward with her glass and he poured to an acceptable level. He bowed and returned to his chair. She waited until he was seated and cracked, "Very nice, unusual but very nice. A French sommelier with an Irish brogue."

Grace served on Royal Doulton she hadn't removed from the china cabinet in almost a year. Kevin did the honors by filling the beautifully-etched Bohemian crystal glasses with water. He realized she had pulled out all the stops but why? She hardly knew him. Throughout the dinner they groped for common ground. He loved fiction and leaned heavily toward Fitzgerald, Hemingway and James Cain.

"F. Scott and Ernie are my guys as well but Cain is too rough for me. Ever read John O'Hara?"

And so it went for almost two hours, plenty of non-intrusive banter that skirted an invisible barrier each was loathe to breach. They were well into the tiramisu when Grace decided what the hell, let's give it a try.

"This has all been nice but let's fess up who's really been on our minds, Nick. He's the reason we're sitting here. Even played matchmaker touting you as a rare specimen who put his career on the line to keep me and my loony girlfriends out of jail."

"Don't forget the Bill Collector. Damn, if you ladies didn't reach deep into the city's netherworld to pull off your crazy scheme."

"Netherworld? Been a long time since anyone unloaded that phrase. So, you really do read."

"Lassie, I sadly abjure your remark," his Irish brogue thickened, and their smiles widened.

"Nick never once talked shop with me. Give me one shared incident that gives me insight."

"We worked robbery-burglary before homicide and one of our first calls after prohibition was an early morning break-in at Shuman's Fine Whiskeys and Liquors. Every city and county official, cop and fire chief with muscle relied on Shuman to quench their thirst. In return, a pipeline set up by the mob and bootlegger Joe Kennedy, yeah I see the look on your face, our former Ambassador to Britain, was pumping in the very best from Canada, the Volstead Act be damned.

"At Shuman's the alarm was off and two uniforms were

waiting. We found a smashed front window and two bottles of Canadian Mist missing from a Christmas display of the shop's very best. A rock that had to weigh at least six or seven pounds shared space with the broken glass. We gathered the uniforms' notes and the search began."

By this time, the tiramisu was gone and after double espresso, they headed into the living room for cognac by the fireplace. Kevin added two oak logs, bellowed up the flames and joined Grace on the sofa. After their first two sips of Rémy Martin he resumed, the bottle conveniently placed on the mahogany coffee table.

"Not to our surprise we found Jumping Jimmy Sullivan splayed on the grass in front of the statue of George and his sturdy steed in Washington Park. One bottle of Canadian Mist was unopened the other was drained to about four inches from the bottom. He took a big swig and with hiccups and a gap-tooth smile, he offered the bottle around. 'I 'members you in uniform way long ago, hiccup, hiccup.' A big stomach convulsion and we backed up a few feet to avoid the vomit.

"Jumping Jimmy heaved and heaved but nothing more came up, then he looked us over and said, 'What's you here for? Done nothin' but enjoy myself after near breaking my leg on that rock in front of Shuman's.'

"Breaking your leg?" Nick asked. "How?"

"Here I was minding my business, ya know me, peaceful as hell. Didn't see that fuckin' rock in the dark and I tripped. Pissed me off. I kicked at it hard as hell. Like it had wings, it flew through the window."

Kevin saw how a smiling Grace, now leaning in his direction was enthusiastically taking in the ludicrous story. At least an inch possibly two fingers of cognac was the needed lubricant for him to continue.

"At this point, I followed Nick's lead and crouched down on the opposite side of Jumping Jimmy. To my surprise Nick accepted the whiskey bottle proffered by Jimmy. He took a healthy swig then handed the bottle to me. It didn't take long before we had an empty bottle and were working on the second.

"Nick and I were no longer crouched but had plopped on our asses as the bottle was passed around with increased frequency. Robbie Burns Scotland's Ploughman Poet arose and without thinking I began my father's favorite, O, whistle, and I'll come to you, my lad. Come down the back stairs when you come to court me, Come down the back stairs, and let no body see, And come as ye were na coming to me. O, whistle, and I'll come to you, my lad.

"I know what you're thinking, yeah we emptied the second bottle, and I couldn't shut off my brogue. We threw the empty bottles into a trash can and delivered Jumping Jimmy to his home. A cozy nook at the bottom of the abandoned cellar stairs of Schraft's."

"Obviously, you reported in and got home okay. But no charges? And increasingly tipsy?" Grace asked.

"No charges. Jumpin' Jimmy and Nick went all the way back to his walking beat on Bloomfield. He lost most of his hearing during a German artillery barrage only weeks before the Armistice. For Jimmy, scarce jobs became no jobs. His rap sheet was long but all petty stuff. He loved military surplus stores. This continued until 1944 when his body was found in an alley off lower Bloomfield, stripped of the combat boots he stole. A search of his body disclosed a sealed envelope sewn into the lining of his jacket that contained a bronze star with an oak leaf cluster, a purple heart and their official citations earned in battles along the Meuse. A few feet away was the bloody lead pipe that cracked his skull."

"That's it? That's all?"

"Not even close. When Nick got the time and date for the Potter's Field burial, he searched Jimmy's military records and discovered he was a Catholic. As the rough pine casket arrived, Nick, a priest in full cassock and surplice, was waiting with an altar boy swinging a brass incense burner. It took some bucks to get the priest and altar boy there and Jumping Jimmy's clustered bronze star and purple heart had earned him a respectful farewell."

"After all these years I've finally gotten to see the other side of Nick."

"No, you haven't. not at all. You have no reason to do so, but if you ever visit that terrible place tucked in beside Route 1 and Haynes Avenue, there is a marble headstone with Marine Staff Sergeant James Gilroy, 1900-1944, and under it is an epitaph that only Nick would think of, 'A true war hero who deserves God's everlasting peace.'"

"Thank you for that," Grace said leaning over and brushing his lips with a gentle kiss.

Grace hesitated before removing his coat from the closet

and asked, "The front door or upstairs?"

He reached forward and with his hands over her ears, gently drew her toward him and whispered, "Upstairs."

50

Superior Court Judge Rodney Hampton rearranged his calendar for December after a working dinner at the Broad Street Club with County Supervisor Michael Composto, City Councilman Stanley Brodski and Cornelius Dark, President of the Summit Bank & Trust. Wednesday, December 10, was decided for the en chambre hearing in Judge Hampton's chambers.

The following day, the Christmas season would awake from its year-long sleep when Bamberger's, with all its dough, assembled its cornucopia of holiday delights for its two-mile parade from Fairmount Cemetery to Military Park. Santa, with the touch of a button, would ignite the store's high-voltage window display that sent every kid in town into near hysteria. The buying season would begin, and Christmas trees would crowd empty lots and storefront sidewalks throughout the city. Wreaths of all sizes would appear out of nowhere.

At the same time, behind closed doors Judge Hampton

waived the need for a preliminary hearing which was followed by a not guilty plea from Maureen Whitaker Sherry's high-priced New York attorney.

After hearing testimony and reviewing evidence, the judge decided that Sherry was guilty of involuntary manslaughter. He noted in his decision that she feared for her life when she shot and killed her husband, that she had been physically and verbally abused for several years, often in public, and had developed a deep psychosis that diminished her sense of reality. Dr. Forest Whitehead testified she no longer knew right from wrong. The judge decided that Sherry was to spend one to three years at the newly built Honeysuckle State Sanitarium for the mentally ill in Gloucester County. She would be fined for one day of court costs and the extraordinary police overtime at her mansion.

The County's GOP tribal leaders waited until Sherry was safely ensconced in her rubber-room universe before trekking to their pow-wow chamber just outside Vernon. The Fernwood Country Club and its two championship courses sprawled over land once sacred to the Lenape, a friendly forest tribe who watched helplessly as the white man destroyed six thousand acres of trees for the charcoal needed to fire-up pig iron furnaces. The forest was gone and soon the Lenape.

As usual, there were plenty of self-righteous hee-haws by council members during the eighty-proof confab at the club. The late lamented Dr. Felix Franklin Sherry, a GOP stalwart and the tribe's worst golfer, was mourned by Assistant Party Chairman Isaiah Spanky because "He was worth a hundred bucks a round." And Union County Party Boss Cyril Dorchester intoned, "We did the best we could for Maureen. When she gets out, she's a celebrity."

The speed of the decision took everyone by surprise. The Beacon's Jerry Saunders and the Daily Clairon's Joe Lucio were absent from the press room and only the Afro-American's cub reporter Nate Theobold was hanging around. Radio reporters were strung along the parade route picking out targets to interview. Theobold couldn't believe his good luck having a big story like the Sherry killing all to himself, at least for now. He replaced the phone in its cradle after getting the news from the court bailiff and never having dictated a story to the City Desk broke into a sweat. He got it off after composing himself enough to answer the editor's questions and before hanging up meekly asked, "Mr. Josephson, you'll be giving me a byline, right?"

He got his byline but the front page scoop in the Afro-American, with its feeble circulation, got little attention. Josephson called it into the wire services and in less than fifteen minutes the United Press, Associated Press and the International Press teletypes were in full swing. The first story and immediate follow-ups in the Beacon and Clarion carried wire service logos causing Lucio to explode, "The fucking Afro-American! It's our story and here we are with shit on our faces."

Cisco and McClosky were not surprised by Hampton's decision, only that it might have been the fastest example of judge and jury tampering in a county where everyone and everything could be bought and sold. "Wonder how much green was involved," Cisco said. "There's no way Hampton lines his pockets, it's too easy to trace. My guess he held out until promised a sure-thing consideration for either a state appellate or supreme court seat."

They were seated in the living room davenport safely out of earshot from Connie, who with the help of seven-year-old Muriel, was in the kitchen completing preparations for dinner. They tapped their half-filled tumblers of Haig & Haig Pinch. If ever there was an elixir that bonded them, it came from the Pinch bottle. It had been almost a month since McClosky's dinner with Grace. There were two other visits to the mansion and McClosky's unease about tonight's meal was washed slowly away as he sipped his scotch.

Cisco swirled the ice cubes in his glass, took a healthy hit and said, "Something's been bugging me since you bribed Gazzi to bury his investigation of Grace and her sisters in crime. His notes nailed them all, except for Deborah Hammerstein Paasche."

"What about her?"

"I believe it was more than a coincidence that a few months back, I got a call from our buddy Mike Shanahan. He's come a long way since jumping the Hudson into Manhattan. Got his captain's bars and heads up homicide. Asked if we had a handle on Johan Paasche, a former German aristocrat, now a citizen who's wanted for two brutal beatings in upstate New York and most probably connected to three mafia hits on his turf."

"Where does Deborah Paasche fit in?" McClosky said.

"Johan Paasche is or was her husband. The upstate beatings occurred in Tuxedo Park. Almost killed a guy with his fists. Mike says there's evidence of him beating his wife before they split in late August. He's nowhere to be found and here she is in our laps in Newark."

"So what did Mike want from us?"

"Nothing specific, just nose around to see if Paasche's name surfaced. It didn't."

"Paasche is Mike's problem, not yours. By the way, where is Deborah Paasche now?"

"At the family home in Tuxedo Park. Broke off contact here when a longtime household retainer beaten by her husband had a massive cerebral hemorrhage, and later died. Murder charges are pending."

Sergeants Kalicki and Nusbum, the two homicide detectives sniffing around for Paasche, returned to the rotation in September after two weeks of coming up empty. Both were big men handy with their fists. They had two cases on the board, one of them getting daily attention from the Beacon and Clarion, the double mob hit of Pietro Lupo, an up-and-coming soldier in Richie the Boot's entourage, and Lucy Nigro, the daughter of Genovese underboss Jimmy Nigro, a made-man. Both papers thirsted for a mob war and increased circulation.

The two detectives exhausted their Sicilian and Calabrian mafia contacts convinced that the contract for the twin killings did not come from the upper reaches of the local mob. They needed a time-tested informant on the fringes, headed deep into the Third Ward and pulled to the curb at the Peace barbershop on Spruce Street. The shop was a front for three black bookies posing as disciples and members of Father Divine's International Peace Movement. It was the most lucrative gambling spot in the Ward and would remain that way as long as they were ready and willing to be police-peepers. Perhaps this time a little more convincing was needed.

Wilber Fontaine, alias God's Tall Timber, arose from one of the three swivel barber's chairs and leisurely walked to the front door. He opened it but failed to react when a big, hairy fist headed his way. Unable to keep his balance he stumbled backwards and fell into the lap of Buck Barton, alias Darn Good Disciple, seated in the middle chair.

"What the hell you doing! Jesus Christ, man, we play straight and narrow with you and now you take pokes at us!" John Travers, alias Righteous Reckoning, shouted as he rose from his chair.

"Just making sure you're still good little snoopers," Nusbum said. "Let's see now, it's nine in the morning. Plenty of time to smell out the Pietro Lupo and Lucy Nigro killings by late afternoon. We'll get back to you. Make sure this line is open." He pointed to one of the three telephones on a long counter against the back wall where bets were taken and rare payoffs became vigorish for future wagers.

At five, God's Tall Timber called to confirm that the hits were by a contract killer hired and paid for by an important mafioso. Behind green-painted windows of precinct clubhouses throughout the city retired goombahs mused they had seen it all before. From Salerno and Naples, across the Strait of Messina to Palermo and Catania the face of revenge never changed. The bloodier, the better.

Nusbum listened intently and held out the phone so Kalicki could also hear God's Tall Timber, a smooth and accomplished liar, assure them that he and the others as disciples of Father Divine had worked every mob contact they had and come up with only one useful tidbit.

They learned that Lupo was an incessant player with a harem of girlfriends. One of them was Theresa Rizzano, the sister of Stefano, Vito Genovese's golden boy and untouchable.

"You thinking the same as me?" Kalicki said.

"Yeah, and just as disgusted," Nusbum said. "We know who ordered and paid for the hits but it ain't going nowhere."

"Got-cha," Kalicki said.

"Fish Hook has come a long way since the Fulton Fish Market," Nusbum cracked. "The East River stink is long gone and after some heavy-duty union busting here in Jersey, he's doing the same thing with Luciano and Lansky in Havana."

"This useless report to the Chief is yours, I got the last one. Two more mob murders under investigation but don't hold your goddamn breath waiting for arrests."

Nusbum cranked a sheet of paper into his typewriter and started his report with the date December 12, 1947. He and his partner had no way of knowing that Stefano Rizzano was last seen alive in Havana on November 7. Disappearance of the gangster handpicked by the mob with Batista's blessing to rid Cuba's labor unions of commies and political agitators aroused suspicions. Inquiries from reporters who'd met his plane from Miami encountered massive waves of silence from every level of mafiosi, the secret police and Batista minions. The U.S. Embassy was useless.

When a reporter was able to get someone to talk, the response began with a few moments of silence, a puzzled look and perhaps a cloud of Panetela smoke.

"Stefano Rizzano? Are you sure of the name? Because I never heard of him."

The one-time Bill Collector who hated to see women beaten but had no trouble shooting and killing a man was a puzzle to the very end.

On November 9, Deborah had taken care of obligations she felt necessary before her BMW cross-country trip. Thanking the Bill Collector for his heavy-handed justice was impossible. She didn't even know his name. Phone calls to Grace and Rosemary were more like trips down memory lane as they laughed their way through their crazy payback scheme and promised to keep in touch. She knew Margie's quitting time at The Pine Room and caught her just before she left. Unlike Grace and Rosemary, Deborah was never able to span the chasm society had placed between them.

51

It was five in the evening on November 16 when the assassins' Daimler pulled to the curb on Boulevard de Clichy at the corner of Rue des Martyrs, a street notorious for its beautiful prostitutes and the bistros and brasseries favored by Paris' deeply entrenched criminal element, Le Milieu.

Although they had successfully completed several assignments in the dangerous Pigalle, and knew its streets well they were unfamiliar with the bistro chosen by Émile Buisson for their meeting, Le Suprême de Chocolat.

It was Sunday and throngs of Parisians and tourists crowded the narrow streets in search of sinful delights. They realized but They didn't really care that they would be fleeced by professional gamblers in games of Faro and Rouge et Noir. Because it was Pigalle, the whores were beautiful and the high price was worth it for the bragging rights it gave the happy lechers.

The two assassins climbed out of their car and went into

a series of stretches, knee bends and body twists needed after a nine-hour drive from Pau. These were warm-up exercises that preceded the daily body-strengthening torture during their first months with Wild Bill Donovan's Office of Strategic Services.

From August of 1942 until May of 1945, the OSS had shaped them. After hypnosis and Freudian therapy, it was discovered they had no trouble killing even when it wasn't self-defense. And the kicker was, they were also patriots.

The OSS was disbanded in September '45, and its files and meticulous backgrounds on every agent were transferred to the Central Intelligence Group in Washington. A pitch had been made for them to remain in place while another spy ring was being organized but they didn't like the rumors. Headquarters for the new agency would be somewhere in and around Washington, a clear indication that a bloated, multi-tiered bureaucracy was being shaped.

Mr. Short and Mr. Tall learned of the offer while in Portofino taking a rare break from their deadly routine of the past three years. They gave hands-on instruction to underground resistance groups in the art of espionage, weaponry needed for sabotage, how to discover, capture and kill traitors in their midst, destroy railroads and bridges, and the art of the ambush. Both refused the Central Intelligence Group's entreaty.

They were deep into their second bottle of chianti with grappa chasers when Short said, "I can't get what we saw in that Milan square out of my mind. Benito Mussolini hanging by his heels beside his mistress."

"Yeah, that woman who pumped five bullets into his bead and screamed, 'For my five dead sons!'"

"And that goddamn black fascist flag. The closer we got to Austria, the more we saw," Tall said. "The war, where the hell was it? Everything so pristine and untouched, the two Il Dulce's flags flying over that winery near Aurozono explained why."

It was the incomprehensible brutish behavior they witnessed in Milan, the suffering endured by their Partisan comrades and the wineries and businesses that slavishly flew Il Duce's banner that prompted their enduring decision.

After turning down the CIG's offer, Short and Tall were honorably discharged from the Army's Counterintelligence Corps as captains the same month the OSS disappeared. After receiving their discharge papers and benefits package that included more than three years of back combat pay, they decided to remain in Europe.

And why not: For three years, they had perfected their language skills, hoarded their money, nurtured Wild Bill's contacts with aristocrats, active and displaced politicians, and military leaders. Furthermore, criminal gangs forced into hiding during the war, all of them screwed by the Nazis and now seeking revenge, proved to be valuable resources. They could not imagine a more fertile landscape to utilize their skills.

They finished their stretches and made sure their Daimler was secure in a district where auto theft was a cottage industry. They turned the corner onto Rue des

Martyrs, found Le Suprême de Chocolat in the middle of the block and being an hour early decided to relax with a kir in a café across the street. They were happy to find their crème de cassis was mixed with a rare Reuilly nearly impossible to find during the war.

"God damn good," Mr. Short said. "Tired of spoiling cassis with vinegar and water."

Before they got up from their café table, they agreed they would kill Paasche and not le Gang des Traction Avant. Lansky wanted positive proof that the man they killed was Paasche and they would never trust Buisson's specialist to take photos. Their Cine Kodak Eight, despite three years of heavy use, was tested and in perfect shape, loaded with an 8mm spool of Kodachrome film. Experts in photography they would supply Lansky with everything he needed including close-ups of passports and other credentials bearing Paasche's name.

They watched a steady line of customers enter the bistro, leaving with bags of pastry, boxes of chocolate mousse and crème brûlée. They walked over and joined the line with six legitimate customers giving them the time needed to size up whether the joint contained danger points. When their turn came, they each ordered a chocolate croissant and coffee and before they could pay, a guttural voice blasted from a dark corner, "Don't take their money. These men are my guests!"

The command made the pretty teenage brunette cashier noticeably twitch as she returned a twenty franc note to Mr. Tall. Another teenage girl placed the croissants and coffees on a tray and led them to the corner where Émile Buisson and four others were seated at a rough-hewed oak table. Each had demitasse cups with saucers and brandy digestif glasses in front of them and a large bottle of water and glasses were placed within easy reach. There would be no drunken profanity during this meeting, but the two killers knew their eardrums had to be calibrated to absorb the Parisian street slang.

Buisson, as Caïd and boss of the gang, got right to the point and introduced his second in command parrain, two spécialistes, men ever alert with wary eyes who did the gang's dirty work and seated at the end of the table a beautiful auburn-haired, green-eyed woman adorned in a lavish burgundy dress, a two-strand necklace they knew from experience to be real pearls, and a gold ring encrusted with an emerald to match her eyes. Her name was Hélène.

"Now tell us about Monsieur Johan Paasche," Buisson said. "Easy to see he's important to you. I also have to know how expensive he is, or why else are we sitting here."

Mr. Short reached inside his suit jacket and removed a thick business envelope. He pushed it toward Buisson who in turn flicked it unopened to his second in command. They all sat back and waited as the parrain methodically totaled the amount of Ben Franklins he had removed from the envelope. When he finished, he turned to his boss and said, "Ten thousand American dollars in one-hundred-dollar bills."

"Ten thousand dollars!" a barely self-controlled Buisson challenged. "After you called and asked once again for Gang des Traction Avant help, I had two of my best men tracking his blue Ford with Portuguese plates as he zig-zagged across France all the way to Luxembourg where he registered at the Grand Hotel Cravat. They turned him over to the concierge, who I pay very well for information. He removed three of his staff from other duties so by shifts, they had your man in sight around the clock. You see, we also have an investment, but Jesus Christ, tracking down a man and killing him for only ten thousand dollars…. Doctors at Loos Les Lille called me a criminal lunatic but your offer tells me you are the only two lunatics at this table."

"But you haven't killed Monsieur Paasche and we don't want you to," Mr. Short said. "All we want now is what you've given us, his location. How old is your information? Is he still at the Grand Hotel Cravat

"So, you're pulling a double-cross," Buisson snapped.

"What the fuck are you talking about," Mr. Short said. "We're the guys who pay you pretty goddamn well for the one and only job you did for us."

Before Buisson and the others could react, Mr. Tall reached across the table and deftly retrieved the envelope. "Here it is Émile, ten thousand American dollars, yours for the taking. Just tell us where Paasche was last seen and where he was headed."

He tapped the envelope knowing this was a dangerous moment. He was asking a criminal lunatic to eat crow witnessed by other members of Gang des Traction Avant. "We've proven we're as good as our word. We know you expected more but you're doing less. We'll do the killing.

More business like this," he again tapped the swollen envelope, "can be yours."

An unsmiling Buisson silently reached across the table, took the envelope, and turned to one of his spécialistes, "Fill them in." He wanted to kill them both, but already being sought since his escape from the Loos Les Lille loony bin, it would be best for now to lay low in the Pigalle.

He, his parrain and the two spécialistes rose without a word and left through a back door hidden by a seven-foot movable screen. A smiling Hélène arose and intercepted Mr. Short and Mr. Tall as they headed for the front door.

"So, all the way from Portugal." It was the first time they heard her speak and in perfect American English. "I just returned from Lisbon and points beyond myself. It was a very rewarding visit."

They were taken by her beauty and attire, which they surmised was her share of the booty stolen while a Gestapo collaborator. They didn't care, she was great to look at.

She leaned forward and with her index fingers, playfully flipped their ties, "You might not have known it but we've been kindred spirits." Before they could answer, she turned and disappeared behind the screen blocking the rear door.

"Kindred spirits?" Mr. Tall said. "I don't get it."

"It's a puzzle I'd like to unravel if we ever run into her again," Mr. Short said.

An easy puzzle to solve if they knew the headlines that transfixed Portugal for more than a week. The gutted body of Eric Svensson, third in line of command on the ocean liner S.S. Gripsholm, was discovered in his suite at Lawrence's Hotel. The Chief Investigator told reporters, "It was a professional job, only a small puncture wound in the belly and little blood, a serrated double-edged knife expertly reamed his lower lungs, diaphragm and stomach."

Two days later, the body of João Pereira, fourth generation scion of one of Portugal's most powerful families, was found on the patio of his cabin on the banks of the Mondego near Coimbra. He had been shot twice in the back of the head.

Meyer Lansky never forgot nor forgave.

Irony shaped much of the assassins' lives so it was only natural that they chose Hotel Le Pavillon, a former monastery with a good restaurant and beautiful women on call for their flop that night. The next morning, they made room and dinner reservations at Luxembourg's Grand Hotel Cravat planning to arrive in late afternoon.

Their contact was René Jaurez, the hotel's concierge, who kept Le Milice informed when travelers passing through Luxembourg were ripe for the picking, but only if the gangsters met his price. When he greeted the two killers in the hotel's lobby, he anticipated a windfall not knowing they had already paid handsomely for the information he would give them tonight.

At nine o'clock that evening, Juarez was ushered into the killers' suite, "Come on in, Monsieur Juarez. Make yourself comfortable."

Juarez accepted the cognac snifter offered by Mr. Short, took a deep sip and said, "Ah, yes, twenty-year Courvoisier.

Unmistakable." He eyed the two Americans, reassured that his early assessment was correct, big money.

"Okay, René, what do you have for us?" Mr. Tall said.

"Information? Am I to have information for you?"

The two killers had the same thought as they watched this pompous asshole sipping and smoking as he pushed comfortably into his overstuffed chair. Is he dumb enough to think that we're ripe for a skinning? Mr. Tall waited until his target had put out his cigarette and put aside his snifter, then leaped forward and punched him exactly where he wanted, mid-forehead just above the nose.

The concierge's head bounced from the back of the chair into Mr. Tall's waiting hands. The strong fingers around his throat stifled his scream, watered his eyes and forced a steady stream of mucus from his nose.

"Let up a little, he's about to turn blue," Mr. Short said, then waited until his partner loosened his grip reached over and mustering as much strength as he could from his awkward bending position slapped both cheeks. "Listen carefully, you slimy son of a bitch! You know what we want, Johan Paasche. When was he here? Has he changed from Portuguese to Luxembourg plates? In which direction did he head out? And did he make any cable calls on the hotel phone? If so, we want the numbers."

Juarez couldn't believe this was happening here at Grand Hotel Cravat, where he once laid out the red carpet for famous American General Omar Bradley and his entourage. Holy Mary, Mother of God, please spare me a big lump. He felt around with his tongue and discovered that the two monstrous slaps by Mr. Short had loosened three of his teeth.

"Yes, yes, I know now what you want."

"Give it to us, all of it," Mr. Tall had grabbed the Frenchman's hair and the harder he pulled the flow of the man's tears increased. It didn't take long before he was sobbing.

Before they left, the assassins learned Paasche's Ford now had Luxembourg plates. At a fork just outside the city, Paasche had taken the road to Alsace, a province of more than thirty-one-hundred square miles containing more than eight hundred villages.

"What do you think?" Mr. Tall asked, "Do we start with the small or the big? There's gotta be someone who remembers a shiny blue Ford with Luxembourg plates driven by a tall, blonde, blue-eyed German."

"Uh-huh. Just like we'd remember the car our first girlfriend's dad was driving."

52

New York County Homicide Chief Mike Shanahan hated when anyone got away with murder even second-degree. Johan Paasche had been in his jurisdiction for three months but he had let him slip away. Paasche had pulled off a disappearing act despite a nationwide alert.

In Manhattan, homicides came in bunches and his detectives had been bitching about their caseloads. The Commissioner had become a royal pain in the ass, but even with all this he couldn't get Paasche out of his mind. He pushed his intercom and had his secretary place a call to Nick Cisco.

"Mike, what's on your mind?" Nick said, and knowing the direction their call would take added, "I'm sorry we couldn't help you out with Paasche. Had a couple of my best men, both with great mob canaries, and all they got were shrugs and dumb looks."

"I'm having a hard time getting that son of a bitch out of my head, even wired Interpol. Again, nothing. The same on the disappearance of Rico Frenzelli's wife Guila, and his partner in that phony brokerage firm, Marcello Vitrioni. Any hint on anything at all on your end?"

"Everything's buttoned up, this almost never happens. Gangsters love to blow smoke up each other's butts and there's always a snitch," Nick said, "Just roll aside a rock and he'll pop up."

"Paasche dead or alive?"

"Know as much as you do that the Kraut has fucked over some big mafia bosses and right now, I'm thinking Meyer Lansky. If he hasn't been whacked, he will be and they'll take their time with the slicing and dicing."

Across the Atlantic, a phone call had just been completed. "What an extraordinary call," said Doctor Jonathan Cutter, renowned not only in England but throughout Europe for the magical results of his plastic surgery.

"Do you want to talk about it?" asked Suzana Winkle, his nurse of twenty years.

"The fellow's name is Johan Paasche. The operator told me I had a call waiting from a place I never heard of in Alsace, Hunspach, then routed through Colmar and across the channel. I wasn't aware our overworked cables were making room for plastic surgery calls."

"I can only imagine what the call cost Mr. Paasche. He could just as well have written."

"It seems he's in a rush and cost is no object. He's booked

a flight already and will take it from Paris to London if we agree to operate."

"Did you agree? Did he fix a price?"

"Unlimited. This man is cocksure of himself," the doctor said. "Right now, there are twenty-five thousand pounds deposited with Barclay's, a drawing account with no name as yet attached."

"So, if you don't take the job, there are others just next door who would?"

Doctor Cutter collected his thoughts and studied the features of the woman who had been his right hand for two decades. She wasn't one to pull her punches. "What he wants is a new, unrecognizable Mr. Paasche. Nothing wrong with that. It's been asked before. How many patients have we had over the years who could not recognize themselves after the healing was complete? With my ego, I'd say at least more than a few."

"That does not include the wonderful, even miraculous work during your three years in North Africa, Italy, the Azores, France and...I cannot even remember how many times we were stuffed into planes then pushed out in the middle of nowhere hoping the supplies for repairing bodies would be waiting. So, again, any problem with Mr. Paasche?"

"I believe he's on the run. From whom and for what, I have no idea. His urgency even over the phone was palpable. Is he a criminal about to flee the continent for England, then America? Could be. Taking it a step further, is he a killer on Interpol's most wanted list?"

"Doctor, please, forget the morbid and consider he might be in hiding from a husband of an adulterous wife he had been publicly bedding down. It could be his own wife wanting more and more since their divorce and had the attorneys to get it."

"We'll need some checking. My Scotland Yard, Interpol and Metro contacts will come through I'm sure," Doctor Cutter said. "It's in the States where some real digging is needed. Hopefully, Interpol and maybe Jimmy Southworth over at the Ministry can call in a due bill for us."

"He is a soft touch," Suzana said. "The last time, it was a five-course at The Ritz."

"You will recall that Jimmy's feast came only a few days after the five-digit miracle performed on Madame Prudhomme."

"So where do we go from here?" she asked. "You think as I do that he's on the lamb and not for anything good. Are you going to take the job?"

"Right now, I say yes, but let's wait until everything comes in. I'll cable him that I'll have a decision in no later than three days."

Across the channel, Mr. Paasche relaxed before the blazing living room fireplace of his mother's hunting lodge outside Hunspach convinced that Doctor Cutter was his man. This evening he would enjoy more than ever his favorite Alsace white, its beautiful nose, a hint of fresh berries and its remarkable oak essence. He drained his glass, rose, stoked the fire and walked to his cluttered desk to collect what he needed and discard the rest for burning.

He was about to sift through a small pile of passports and for a reason he couldn't quite understand stopped and pulled open the middle drawer of the desk. He removed the gold-framed, color photo of Deborah taken those many years ago in front of their honeymoon hotel on the Danube River. He sat down with the photo in his lap, closed his eyes and was amazed that something that rarely troubled him had emerged - remorse.

He placed the photo on the desk and reached into the bottom right-hand drawer to retrieve a portfolio that had remained untouched for years. He opened it and the first photo had his Uncle Gustav with his hands on Deborah's shoulders. Both were smiling broadly. She wore a designer dress carefully chosen for her first meeting with Johan's extended family. He had been standing nearby and could remember his Uncle's words as if spoken only the day before.

"So schön. Es ist so eine Freude, dass Sie jetzt Teil der Familie sind. Johan ist ein sehr glücklicher Mann."

Johan could not stop examining the photo. Yes, so beautiful and Onkle Gustav saw immediately that not only his nephew but the entire family were lucky and delighted to add her to the family.

The portfolio contained photos taken by both the Paasche and Hammerstein families. He browsed through them and stopped at a professionally taken group portrait that contained not only immediate family members but household staff as well. Standing in the back row to the far left were Eli and Sophie Green in their Sunday best with arms around each other's waist. Johan scanned the familiar faces and settled his gaze on Eli. He realized for the first time the magnitude of what he had done. He killed the man to whom Deborah entrusted her youth, the uncle she never had.

Five minutes were required for him to snap out of it. He felt a chill despite the blazing fire behind him. His open attaché case had passports, financial records and other important personal information, phone numbers, names, addresses, attorneys, bookkeepers and only those family members he could trust. Herr Johan Paasche was about to disappear.

He was ready to fasten the two brass hasps on the case when he heard footsteps in the mudroom that separated the back door from the lodge's sprawling great room. He opened the middle drawer of the desk to make sure his Mauser pistol was within easy reach and no longer on safety. The fireplace and his desk lamp supplied the only light. In near darkness, it was hard to discern the silhouette in the doorway. A sudden burst of flames from the fireplace was enough to see the pistol in the silhouette's hand.

"Come on now, there's no need for a gun. We can talk it out. Give me that much," he said while carefully reaching for his pistol.

The first pistol shot hit him in the forehead just above his nose. The second shot struck below the chin, crushing his trachea before splintering his cervical vertebra. He landed on his back.

The killer stood motionless waiting to hear any sound that betrayed a third person in the lodge and hearing only the crackling fire walked to the body, bent over and attended to business. It took just a little over a minute for the killer to complete what had to be done, shut the door on the bloody scene and return to the vehicle hidden in a stand of cottonwoods.

A bright uncompromising moon played a game of hide-and-seek with the puffy clouds overhead. A breeze-driven cloud transformed the driveway into total darkness just as the killer secured what had been taken from the lodge, the framed photo and the portfolio.

Before pulling on the leather glove removed to free up the trigger hand, the killer gave vent to a compulsive incontrollable habit. Her index finger softly brushed the long, thin scar on her right cheek. Certain that all the photos removed from Johan's desk were secure in the saddlebag of the BMW R62, she raised its kickstand, revved the machine she and Eli loved so well and sped into the shadows.

ABOUT THE AUTHOR

Steve Bassett was born and raised in Newark's crime-ridden Third Ward. He has been legally blind for more than two decades but hasn't slowed down. After college he joined the dwindling number of itinerant newsmen roaming the countryside in search of, well just about everything. Readers will share insights that earned him three Emmys for investigative documentaries and the California Bar Association's first Medallion Award for Distinguished Reporting on the Administration of Justice. His iconoclasm was a great asset during his thirty-five years as a journalist. He discovered that the largely ignored pre-war problems of racism, homelessness, corruption and police brutality are still with us today. Thus, the inspiration for his Passaic River Trilogy.

Printed in the USA
CPSIA information can be obtained
at www.ICGtesting.com
LVHW052052170724
785797LV00017B/55/J